QUORUM.

Only eight people attended the second meeting of the Ashworth Textile Pageant Committee. Seven of them were members and the eighth was a representative of local Youth Groups. The main item for discussion at this meeting was exactly where the pageant was to be held, and on the surface this seems to provide a very dull setting for a novel.

But the discussion brings to light the personalities of the people involved, and skilfully and methodically Miss Bentley takes her readers into the homes and minds of the members of her committee. This is a beautifully organized piece of writing, and even the committee minutes seem to reveal the excitement or anguish of the people who took part in the discussion they record.

QUORUM

Phyllis Bentley

CEDRIC CHIVERS LTD
PORTWAY
BATH

First published 1950
by
Victor Gollancz Ltd
This edition published
by
Cedric Chivers Ltd
by arrangement with the copyright holder
at the request of
The London & Home Counties Branch
of
The Library Association
1972

SBN 85594 643 1

Reproduced and Printed by
Redwood Press Limited, Trowbridge & London
Bound by Cedric Chivers Ltd, Bath

CONTENTS

Acknowledgements are due to Cecil Day Lewis and Messrs. Jonathan Cape Ltd. for permission to reprint the sonnet on p. 31 from the sequence "O Dreams, O Destinations" (*Word over All*).

Second Meeting
of the
Ashworth Textile Pageant Committee
Tuesday, 13th September, 1949

Thomas Armitage, J.P.
(*Chairman*)

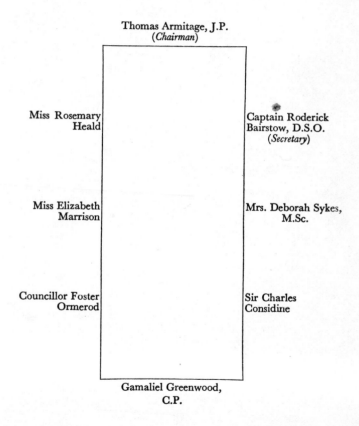

Miss Rosemary
Heald

Captain Roderick
Bairstow, D.S.O.
(*Secretary*)

Miss Elizabeth
Marrison

Mrs. Deborah Sykes,
M.Sc.

Councillor Foster
Ormerod

Sir Charles
Considine

Gamaliel Greenwood,
C.P.

Part One

A COMMITTEE MEETS

A COMMITTEE MEETS

THE CLOCK STRUCK SEVEN.

"We may as well begin, ladies and gentlemen," said the Chairman. "Stay a moment, though. Are we a quorum, Captain Bairstow?"

"I'm afraid I don't remember what our quorum is, sir," said the Secretary.

The Chairman glanced round the table. Besides himself and young Bairstow, there were present that bristling long-headed gingerish chap, Gamaliel Greenwood, the Committee's beauty, Miss Elizabeth Marrison—her customary air of fierce contempt hardening her dark aquiline face—and Sir Charles Considine.

"Look it up in the Minutes, will you, my boy?"

At this moment Councillor Foster Ormerod came in, round and pouting, followed by what was presumably, judging from her fresh complexion and lustrous curls, the newly appointed delegate of the Ashworth Youth Groups. She hung back diffidently, the colour deepening in her rosy cheek.

"The Youth representative?"

"Miss Heald from the Youth Groups," said Councillor Foster.

"Won't you sit here, by me?"

"Our quorum is five members, one of whom must be an official, Mr. Armitage."

"Ah. Then we're all right, we can begin."

"In any case we're all here now except Mrs. Sykes, who was late last time," said Sir Charles Considine quietly.

"We'll take the Minutes now, Captain Bairstow."

Roddie stood up and began to read.

"Minutes of the first meeting of the Ashworth Textile Pageant Committee held at 7 p.m. on Tuesday, 6th September, 1949, at the Mechanics' Institute, Ashworth. Present, Mr. Thomas Armitage, J.P., in the Chair. . . ."

Deborah Sykes, broad and fair, in a light blue suit, came in rather clumsily, knocking as she passed against the chair of Sir Charles, who straightened it with a frown. Her broad intelligent face remained calm, her large light blue eyes continued to beam. She gave the Chairman a smile of happy welcome and sat down.

"Terms of reference," droned Roddie.

He continued to read the Minutes in a clear and strong but somewhat monotonous tone.

From time to time the attention of the Committee members wandered to their own affairs, and before their mind's eye flickered a panorama of the events of the day just drawing to its close. . . .

Part Two

COMMITTEE MEMBERS

I

THOMAS ARMITAGE, ESQ., J.P.
(*Chairman*)

I

THE SIGNBOARD AT THE entrance to the mill yard announced in large white letters: *Women, Girls and Boys Wanted: Good Wages, Comfortable Conditions, Modern Canteen,* for it was 1949 and all the labour in the West Riding was needed to feed the textile export drive in order to earn dollars.

As the car turned in, bumping over some of the builders' débris, Thomas craned his neck, as he did every morning, that he might read the cheering words. They helped him to start his day. At least that is good, he thought, nodding his square grey head; I must try to like 1949, since that at least is good. For he remembered the bad days of the slump in the early 1930's, when a third of the total population of Ashworth was drawing unemployment insurance—Thomas, good Liberal that he was, never used that odious phrase *on the dole*—and the Highshaw Mills bore a notice: *No Hands Wanted.* In the midst of his own difficulties then, struggling along a razor edge to keep solvent without bankrupting his customers, losing some ill-spared thousands when his Ire Valley cousins crashed, his reserves draining away till he could hardly look his bank manager in the face—in the midst of all this he had been well aware of the Shaw Green workpeople's sufferings. Or at least, he had thought so then; certainly he had been active in all measures to relieve their economic distress. But lately he had begun to see that there had been a deeper wretchedness for them then than even the economic. Their work, their skill of hand or brain, had not been wanted; and to live in a world where one's best abilities were useless was, he was beginning to know, the most heartbreaking, the most discouraging, the most disintegrating experience a man could undergo.

This morning everything at Highshaw seemed as usual. The white steam curled off the green waters of the dam; the solid substantial hum of several thousand spindles—so much more satisfying, Thomas always thought, than the high peevish clack of looms—purred out from the old main buildings and the modern sheds. The view of the town of Ashworth far away down in the valley, with the West Riding hills rising and rolling away behind it into the distance, was as spacious, as characteristic and to Thomas as native, as of old. The small smoke-blackened stone houses below him climbed Shaw Bank in zigzag rows to suit the contours of the hill just as they had climbed in the 1880's when his father and his uncle rebuilt Highshaw Mills—the white roofs of the new prefabs could not be seen from here, they stood (or rather spawned, thought Thomas, for they looked to him like nothing so much as a bed of mushrooms) at the foot of the bank round a fold in the hills, with the new Palais de Danse just visible at the corner. As the car drew up by the office steps one of the numerous cat population of Shaw Green village leaped down from the containing wall, stood a moment at gaze with ginger paw uplifted, decided that Thomas was customary and slid elegantly into the boiler-house. Yes, all was as usual; all was as Thomas had seen it for many of his seventy-five years. Only the half-finished new shed was different—outwardly. But though outwardly Highshaw looked just the same as of old, beneath the surface all was different. It was so with the whole West Riding, thought Thomas ruefully. The elements in the chemical composition of the atmosphere had been rearranged, and he no longer felt at ease in the new climate; the West Riding had once been all his world, now he felt a stranger.

A staunch and bold progressive from his youth upwards, a man who carried his religious and political convictions into every department of his life, he had introduced good working conditions into Highshaw long before most of his contemporaries had even thought of them. He had been proud of his canteen, of his ventilation, of his profit-sharing, bonus, training, sick-club, welfare and pension schemes, for years. Now suddenly, since 1945, since the coming to power of

16

the Labour Government, all that seemed out-dated, old-fashioned, even a little laughable and foolish. Everything now was to be done by the State, by sticking on stamps, by regulation, by routine. His benevolence, his goodwill, his desire to serve his fellow-men, hitherto for seventy years the strongest motive of his life, had now no outlet; it simply was not wanted any more. All now was duty, nothing was love; in nothing at Highshaw could he express himself, in all he was directed to express the will of others. In addition, he was called vermin by a Cabinet Minister and told he did not matter a tinker's cuss. But no, no, Thomas admonished himself, descending rather stiffly from the car; that's not fair; it was the drones the man meant, and I've never been a drone. But of course he would think me a drone because I work with my head and not my hands, he reflected. And vermin! What a graceless expression! What a bitter thought! Such bitterness in politics is new in England. Is it, though? He asked himself, laying his hand on the rail—the lowest step of the flight was rather steep. One must be fair.

"Will you be wanting the car tonight, Mr. Armitage?" said the chauffeur.

"I don't think so."

"It's Tuesday, Mr. Armitage."

"Ah," said Thomas pausing. "A.T.P.C."

"That's right."

"Are you wanting the night off, Fred?"

"Nay, I'm not bothered—a couple of hours in Ashworth will do me nicely."

"Yes—well—I don't know whether I shall be up at Shaw for dinner or down at the Club. Remind me to tell you at lunch-time."

"Mr. Bernard wants you to lunch with him," said Fred.

"No doubt he'll speak of it to me himself," said Thomas stiffly, entering the mill.

Then he felt ashamed; it was terrible how the habit of snapping and snubbing was growing on him lately. He had the greatest difficulty nowadays in making himself be nice to people unless he liked them, and all the causes he had worked for all his life seemed suddenly so tedious, so exasperating that he didn't want to be nice to their supporters any more. All the same, as he walked along the panelled entrance hall, gleaming with polish—Bernard certainly saw to it that his old uncle's offices were nicely kept—and glanced up at the enlarged photograph of his father, Thomas reflected wryly on the difference in language and manner between his father's coachman and his own chauffeur. To his father, bearded, dominant, Victorian, Fred would not have been familiarly Fred but formally Boocock, and Boocock would certainly not have bandied about luncheon invitations between members of the Armitage family in Victorian times. All to the good, I suppose, reflected Thomas mournfully; or rather, much to the good but not really all. *I'm not bothered! Do me nicely! That's right!* So graceless! Well!

2

In the outer office the builders' foreman awaited him, a rueful look on his ruddy good-humoured face.

"What's wrong this time, Smithers?" said Thomas, passing in.

"It's awkward like," began Smithers. "Half a roof is no manner of use, I can't stretch it out to cover, no matter what Mr. Bernard says."

"Mr. Bernard asked me to let him know as soon as you came in, and Captain Bairstow is on the telephone, Mr. Armitage," interposed his secretary hastily, holding open the inner door and slightly rolling her intelligent eyes.

Thomas perceived that his nephew did not want him to talk to Smithers until he was present. Smiling in a temporising way at the foreman, he went into the inner office, hung up his hat and coat, sat down at his large neat desk and took up the 'phone.

"Good morning."

"Good morning, sir. It's just about the agenda for to-night."

"Is there anything special coming up?"

"Well, there's just that awkward matter about the field."

"Ah, yes," said Thomas thoughtfully. "Have you heard from Lord Intake?"

"Yes. Very favourably. But there's that other offer, you know."

"I gather you think that quite unsuitable."

"I do indeed. But it's awkward coming from a member of our own committee. I was just wondering whether you would like to take it as a separate item, or tuck it away in *any other business* at the end, where it wouldn't assume such importance, you know. And some of them might have left before we got to that point."

"We can't do that, my boy," said Thomas gravely: "Even if we wished. It will arise out of the Minutes of the previous meeting, you know."

"Oh, so it will."

Young Bairstow sounded rather dashed, which was just as well, thought Thomas. The war had shaken the morals of these young men, he reflected, shaking his head; they seemed to think that cheating—for which they had some new fancy name, he forgot what it was, not scrounging or wangling, those were out of date, he couldn't keep up with slang nowadays—cheating was clever.

"It's always best to keep to established procedure," he said in his kindest tone.

"Yes, of course. I was wondering—whether you would perhaps be a few minutes early at the Institute? You were last week, I remember. I should very much like a few words with you. Before the meeting."

The voice had an effect of urgency and distress.

"Couldn't we deal with the matter now?" suggested Thomas.

A sigh came over the telephone. "Well—no. No, I think not, sir. But if you could possibly——"

"I'll try," said Thomas. "Then, will you excuse me now— my nephew wants me on a business matter."

"Oh, of course. I'm sorry—I didn't mean to keep you. Goodbye," said young Bairstow in a flurry, and rang off.

Bernard came in with his quick light step, neat and dapper, admirably clothed in a black-and-white birdseye worsted coating, thought Thomas professionally, with a very clean white shirt, the platinum cuff-links Olive gave him as a wedding present and an expensively discreet dark green tie. His light frame and small sharp aquiline features and smooth dark hair were not at all like the Armitage side of his parentage, reflected Thomas; the Armitages were all tall strongly built men with square heads and a thick rough fairish thatch which early turned grey. Only in his fine dark grey eyes, very lustrous and piercing, did Bernard resemble his mother, Thomas's well-loved early-widowed sister, dead of influenza at the beginning of the war. A single deep narrow frown descended vertically the exact centre line of Bernard's forehead; from his teens he had shown this frown, but since his trouble with Olive it had deepened till it was quite a singular cleft. It lent manliness to his otherwise rather delicate features but gave him a somewhat angry and impatient air. This morning the frown seemed deeper than ever.

"The boy looks quite haggard," thought Thomas. "Worrying over Olive, I suppose."

He sighed. Bernard and his little daughter were the only kin left to Thomas in England, and even they, thought Thomas sadly, haven't the Armitage name. Thomas's daughter had married a Kenya coffee planter years ago and settled down out there and was a grandmother by now; his two sons he had lost, one in the air and one in the trenches, in the last year of the 1914-18 war. Their death had struck their mother to the heart; she seemed to shrink into herself, away from Thomas's touch and reach, once so beloved, and presently faded quietly away. At the last she had come back to him, looked at him with her former sweetness and love so that the parting had been a fierce hot agony—the Armitages were not patient men. Well! that was an old grief, why recur to it now; listen to what Bernard was saying, keep your mind on the present day. Smithers, he saw, had edged into the room again.

"Have you heard this nonsense about the roof, Uncle?" said Bernard sharply.

"The roof for the new shed?"

"No. To repair the shed by the boiler house. The permit's come from the Ministry of Works—for *half* the material only."

20

"Oh, nonsense."

"As I say, I can't stretch half a roof out to cover the whole, no matter what the Ministry says."

"Nobody expects you to, Smithers," said Bernard impatiently.

"But there must be some mistake," began Thomas.

"There's no mistake. Here are the papers. What I thought was this, Uncle," said Bernard in his quick sharp tones: "It's not one of your Bench days, is it. Suppose you drive over and see the regional representative or whatever they call him? The head man for this region, I mean. They'd take more notice of you, perhaps."

"Very well," agreed Thomas. "We'll telephone for an appointment."

"You start at once and I'll telephone," said Bernard. "Unless you go now he'll have gone out to lunch by the time you get there, and God knows what time he'll get back. You know what these Civil Servants are."

"You're a little unfair, Bernard," said Thomas mildly.

"Possibly. Will you go, Uncle Thos?"

The use of his nickname, by which he was known in textile circles throughout the Riding, pleased Thomas.

"Yes, of course. I'll lunch there afterwards."

"No—come home and lunch with me."

"No," said Thomas, not without a secret glee that Fred would find his lunch arrangements for his employer upset: "I'll lunch in the city—I remember now, I'm due at a prize-giving in those parts around three." He drew out his diary to confirm this conveniently remembered engagement. "Then I can dine early in Ashworth and go straight on to my A.T.P.C. meeting."

Bernard frowned and seemed to hesitate. "But in that case I shan't see you till tonight, Uncle. All right, Smithers. Look, Uncle Thos," he said when the foreman had left the room: "I've something important to tell you. I shouldn't like you to hear it from anyone but me."

"Tell me now, then." Bernard frowned and shook his head. "All this mystery," said Thomas testily, riffling the pages of his diary. "I don't suppose it's anything of the slightest importance." Bernard gave him an odd look. "Think of the waste of petrol—have some sense, Bernard."

"No, Uncle Thos. It's no use. I can't let you loose in Ashworth till you've heard. You'll have to come up to the Thorn for lunch. It's all arranged, and Audrey's excited about seeing you."

This was clever of Bernard, for Thomas was fond of all children and especially of this little great-niece.

"Very well, then. But I must leave early—I've to give these prizes and make a speech."

"Always the public man, Uncle," said Bernard, pretending to pretend a derision which in fact he really felt.

Thomas was aware of this shade of feeling and resented it; to avoid reply he raised to his already spectacled eyes the glass which hung by a black ribbon round his neck.

"I can't think why you don't use bi-focals, Uncle," said Bernard.

"You can't teach an old dog new tricks. Oh!" exclaimed Thomas, disconcerted. "I see the prize-giving is tomorrow after all."

Bernard slightly bowed his head and smiled. It was the polite restrained smile of a well-bred younger man showing proper respect to an elder making an ass of himself owing to his age. Thomas felt it to be so. Everything reminds me that I'm old and useless and out of tune with the times, he thought.

"Perhaps you'd rather see the Works man yourself, Bernard," he suggested drily.

His nephew's expression changed. "No, Uncle," he said decidedly. "You with your record will have more weight there than I. They'll believe what *you* say."

3

Accordingly Thomas felt reassured, indeed pleasantly bustling and *affairé*, as after signing a letter or two concerning the affairs of a very old bedridden aunt in a Cheltenham nursing home, he bowled away to the city behind Fred. When they were in a difficulty at Highshaw they had to call on the old man, after all. He hadn't the least doubt of his ability to put the case so that the regional authority would see the idiocy of granting half what was asked for, in the case of a roof. And as Bernard said, "they"—for so one always referred to officials nowadays, he found—would believe what he said and not suspect him of trying to obtain material beyond his proper need. The West Riding seemed to belong to him again, and the times were less out of joint than before.

A mirror in the entrance hall of the building which housed the West Riding branch of the Ministry confirmed his regained confidence. He was still tall and lean and strong-looking, his shoulders broad and solid even if a trifle bowed. He still had a good patch of colour on his cheekbones, and the rest of his square face, though lined and yellowish, was firm; his rough grey hair was abundant and his grey eyes behind the old-fashioned steel spectacles he affected were still large, well-set and except in the mornings, clear. His long arms and hands, though they had lost flesh lately and grown a little knobbly, were still muscular and competent. True, his clothes hung rather loosely on him, admitted Thomas with his usual blunt honesty, especially his pre-war suits, and he shambled a little sometimes, getting his feet mixed suddenly and interrupting his usual brisk swinging walk. But take him all round he looked strong and active and alert, young for his years and with plenty of life and usefulness in him yet. He strode cheerfully into the ante-room.

It was a mean-looking place, he thought, for a Government office; no carpet, shabby lino, light distemper walls very dirty, two doors much kicked at the bottom to the detriment of their pale dirty paint, one small table bearing a crumpled newspaper, one shabby metal chair occupied by a small man in hat and coat reading another crumpled newspaper. "Bernard can say what he likes," thought Thomas: "Mahogany and horsehair wore better." The wall facing the entrance had frosted glass all its length, and one pane was marked *Enquiries*. Thomas rapped on this briskly but pleasantly, leant on his stick and waited. Presently the man in the chair turned his newspaper, and in the process became aware of Thomas. He got up in a fluster.

"Why, Mr. Armitage," he said: "Good morning. I didn't see it was you. Have this chair."

"No, no," said Thomas, waving his stick affably to indicate that the man should re-seat himself. "I shan't be long—I have an appointment." He looked at the man shrewdly, trying to place him.

"You won't remember me," said the man, seeing this. "Shaw of Annotsfield."

"Are you one of our customers?" said Thomas pleasantly. "Nowadays my nephew——"

"Nay, Highshaw's too grand for me," said Shaw. "But everybody knows you, Mr. Armitage."

It was childish to be pleased, Thomas told himself, but yet he felt pleased and warmed. At this moment the glass window shot back and a pretty curly-haired girl said: "Yes?" enquiringly.

"Thomas Armitage of Highshaw Mills," said Thomas. "I have an appointment with your—er—principal."

"Will you wait a minute, please?" said the girl, and shot back the window.

The minute was a long one. Thomas leant on his stick, then against the wall; he began to feel that his legs were too long and would presently buckle. Mr. Shaw, apparently uncertain whether to offer his chair again would be good manners or no, shuffled his newspaper uncomfortably.

At length one of the doors opened, and a young man carrying a folder of papers entered and came towards Thomas. He was the kind of young man whom Thomas put down at once as immutably subordinate, irrevocably an underling; his timid eyes, his small features, his poor physique, his feeble attempt at bonhomous shagginess in dress and his general air of being unfinished, indicated in Thomas's opinion not only a lack of proper educational opportunity but a vague mind and a wavering will. Accordingly he felt sorry for the lad and smiled at him very kindly, and spared a moment to reflect that perhaps the new educational system would do something for such lads, he earnestly hoped so.

"Mr. Armitage?" said the young man, opening the folder. The papers at once splayed out on their cord, and Thomas saw several bearing the Highshaw Mills letterhead.

"Yes. I telephoned for an appointment."

"I'm afraid he's in conference," said the young man, his heightened colour proclaiming the lie.

"Ah. Well, it's true we gave him short notice. But the matter's urgent. This afternoon perhaps?"

"It's no use you seeing him really. Your application was dealt with in London, and if there's anything different wanted now it will have to be sent there again. We wrote to you," continued the boy on a note of reproach, turning over the paper: "Yesterday. Your application was partially granted. Probably the letter's on your desk waiting for you now."

"I've received the letter. If I can't see the head of this office, whom can I see?" demanded Thomas, his temper rising.

"Well, I've been forwarding the letters and so on."

"Look, my dear boy," said Thomas, controlling himself. "The preservation or otherwise of several thousand pounds' worth of valuable machinery, and the loss of an enormous number of man-hours, are in question. I must see someone in authority."

"I'm dealing with the case," said the lad. "I can take notes of any discussion." His voice rose to a squeak and his eyes seemed to flee from Thomas's in all directions. It was clear that he acted under instructions and was more afraid of disobeying them than of disobliging Thomas; to argue with him was useless.

"Very well, then," yielded Thomas angrily. "Let us go in and discuss it together." He pushed himself away from the wall, prepared to be led into a private room.

"I'm afraid it'll have to be here," said the lad.

Two strangers entered the ante-room at this point and were obliged to brush past Thomas to reach the enquiry window.

"Can we at least sit down somewhere?" demanded Thomas, trembling with fatigue and fury.

"Well——" said the boy. He looked round him helplessly and sent an enquiring gaze in Mr. Shaw's direction. Mr. Shaw, however, shaking out his newspaper, returned his gaze defiantly and made no offer. "There isn't a chair," said the boy weakly. "If you could explain your need for a fresh application I could note it down, but of course it'll have to go on a form eventually, and be sent to London."

"It's not a fresh application. Some weeks ago," began Thomas in a loud clear tone: "We had an explosion in our subsidiary engine-room. A piece of casting was blown up into the air and fell through the roof of a small neighbouring combing-shed. The damage was of course inspected by our architects, and the whole roof was condemned as unsafe. Tarpaulins have been drawn across the hole and temporary timbers placed as a precaution, but until the roof is mended, the combs are all in danger and no work can go on in the shed." (He's no idea what a comb is, reflected Thomas despairingly.) "We applied for certain materials for the roof. Your letter this morning grants us permission to purchase *half* of them."

"Yes, well, that's what London said."

"But don't you see, *half* is no *use*," shouted Thomas. "The *whole* roof is dangerous."

"Well, you'll have to apply again, I'm afraid."

"You should have applied for double what you wanted, then you'd be O.K.," put in Mr. Shaw suddenly, looking over his newspaper.

"Highshaw Mills don't indulge in that sort of chicanery," said Thomas stiffly.

"It's what most people do nowadays," said one of the two strangers, shaking his head.

"Aye, that's right," said the other. "It's the only way."

"You've said it," concurred a third who had just entered.

"Considine will do it," muttered Mr. Shaw, retiring behind his paper.

The young official glanced at each speaker in turn, and it was clear from his expression that to ask for double one's requirements was as normal as to be granted half, and that Thomas's application had been dealt with in this customary fashion.

"What do you suggest I should do now, then?" asked Thomas, his voice hoarse with rage.

"It's not for me to suggest. As far as we're concerned, your application has been dealt with."

"Shall I write to this office, or to London?"

"If you wish to make a further application, write to this office, and we'll forward it to London."

"Wouldn't it be more expeditious if I wrote to London direct?"

"Well, no. You see, they'd send it back here for us to attach the papers." Glancing timidly at Thomas's congested face, the young man took on an air of concern, and suddenly with an effect of gathering all his courage, he said: "It's not for me to make suggestions, of course, but——"

All those in the ante-room were very still and gazed at him with avid interest.

"——it's best to approach the matter through the proper channels."

A harsh laugh broke simultaneously from the lips of the five men present, and with this ringing in his ears Thomas burst from the room and hurried out of the building. Fred, who was lounging on the steps with a cigarette in the corner of his mouth, at sight of his employer's face actually threw the fag away and stepped forward smartly.

"Car's on the other side of the road, Mr. Armitage," he said. "It's No Parking this side today."

Thomas exclaimed and struck the kerb sharply with his stick. At this moment the petty regulation seemed more than he could bear. Fred shepherded him carefully across the road, put the rug over his knees with none of his usual slapdash, edged the car into the stream of traffic and drove on to the next traffic lights before asking in a very subdued tone: "Where to, Mr. Armitage?"

"What does it matter? The mill I suppose," exclaimed Thomas hoarsely. The Town Hall clock striking an hour above his head as he spoke, he recollected his arrangement with Bernard. "No—the Thorn," he said.

"Very good, Mr. Armitage," said Fred, respectfully conveying by his tone the suggestion that this was an entirely new destination to him.

For a few moments Thomas ranged with burning anger

over the scene of rebuff he had just experienced; the repeated recollection of the foolish untidy ignorant boy uttering imbecile official jargon which would ruin Thomas's fine Noble combs and keep some of his workpeople helplessly out of work for weeks, maddened him. Adrenalin poured into his old veins, and he made violent plans—he'd teach that little underling, he'd go off straight away to London, he'd catch the afternoon train, he'd telegraph, he'd see the Minister himself, if he couldn't get an interview he'd go to the House and Commons and secure the help of the Ashworth Member of Parliament. Suddenly he remembered that the Ashworth Member was now a Labour man. It would be useless to apply to him, reflected Thomas bitterly; however good the case about the roof, the man wouldn't dare to be seen helping a capitalist, an employer; it would put him in bad odour with his party, ruin him with his Trade Union. It was all hopeless, hopeless; this was a strange country, not his England any more, he didn't any longer know how to go about a perfectly legitimate and patriotic piece of business. He was useless, out of his element, behind the times, out of date; he'd better retire and leave Bernard to cope with this strange new England. England! A pang of despairing grief, of thwarted wistful love, stabbed his heart. When it had passed his heart seemed dead, he could feel no more. He shrank back into his corner, his head fell forward, his overcoat suddenly seemed too large for him.

4

The car mounted Shaw Bank, rolled past the Highshaw Mills entrance, and turned into the bumpy unpaved lane which led to Bernard's house.

Shaw Thorn was one of the many Jacobean clothiers' homesteads which nestle in the West Riding hills, with mullioned windows and beamed ceilings, agreeable to look at but rather cold and dark to live in, at least in Thomas's opinion. Still, Thomas approved of a modern spinner living in an old cloth manufacturer's homestead; to do so supported the continuity and dignity of the craft to which he was so proud to belong. The house was pleasantly set out with period furniture and softly coloured fabrics which Bernard had inherited from his mother—Olive had no taste for anything earlier than 1938 and her purchases struck an occasional garish note. Ah! Olive! Perhaps she was the subject of his nephew's promised announcement.

It struck Thomas that he ought to have given more thought to this business of Bernard's announcement. He roused himself dutifully and began to wonder what it could be. Money? A man with a separated wife always found things a bit tight, with two households to keep up, reflected Thomas, and now he came to think of it Bernard certainly had seemed rather careful in his expenditure lately. Well! If so, Thomas would soon put it right; sell a few of the Government stocks which owing to nationalisation all his investments seemed recently to have turned into, and give or lend his nephew the proceeds. The interest on them was so small, they seemed scarcely worth keeping. Some of his friends were already "living off the top," as they called it, living off their saved capital and watching it diminish every year. Thomas would never do that, he hoped; he had all the Victorian's prejudice against dipping into capital, into savings; still he cared so little for his future that he would gladly diminish his lien on it to help his sister's son. But Bernard was no fool, it was not like him to be in money troubles. If it was not money, what else could it be? Olive, of course, was a possibility. A memory, vague but alarming, rose up of something Bernard had said once when fulminating against the present Government. Something about no future. Thomas began to feel uneasy. Yes, decidedly I ought to have thought about this earlier, he reproached himself; there's scarcely time now.

The car drew up and he climbed out wearily. Bernard's man in a white coat came running out and helped him; it was obvious that he was thinking: the old man looks poorly to-day. On his side Thomas reflected that the problem of domestic help, which had caused a great many of the rows between Bernard and Olive because Olive liked to go out and was tied at home with the child, had been easily solved the moment Olive went away. Bernard had without difficulty secured a couple, a man and wife; the man was a former sea-steward and kept the house quite admirably, the wife was an adequate cook. Thomas had mentioned to Bernard the unfortunate timing of their arrival—they might have saved the marriage, he hinted, had they turned up in time. But Bernard said no; only a bachelor or widower could get domestic help nowadays; he said: nobody would go where there was a woman at the head of the household, because there they could not do as they liked. In any case, added Bernard savagely, since Olive was now rumoured to be partner in a teashop in Rye, it was presumably not just domestic work which had caused their separation.

Bernard came out now into the large square hall, with nine-year-old Audrey, very neat in grey wool, dancing ahead. The child was fair like her mother, with the wispy little plaits and wispy but hardy little body one so often saw in children nowadays. She danced up to Thomas and hugged him but turned her face aside quickly when he stooped for a kiss. Bernard shrugged his shoulders:

"No use coercing them nowadays," he said rather bitterly.

"Of course not," agreed Thomas, hurt all the same.

"Have a drink, Uncle?"

The enquiry was perfunctory, for Thomas thought it a barbarous custom to drink before meals. But today he said feebly:

"I believe I will, Bernard."

Bernard gave him a shrewd look but said nothing till the old man was seated and had sipped his sherry. Then he asked how things had gone at the Ministry of Works.

"We've to send in another application and they'll forward it again to London."

"That'll take another six weeks."

"We'll be lucky if it isn't six months."

"See anyone useful?"

"Only an underling. A clerk with a rabbity face. He can't help his face, of course," said Thomas.

Bernard gave a sharp sigh. "Well, if you're ready, Uncle. Run in, Audrey, and ring the bell, and then be off upstairs."

"Can I come in again afterwards when you're having coffee?"

"No, not today."

"Oh, *Daddy, please!*"

"No. I told you before, Audrey."

Thomas felt uneasy. These preparations for privacy presaged ill.

The two men went into the dining-room and ate an excellent lunch for 1949—soup, a joint of lamb, a fruit pie. The fruit was bottled, the soup from a tin, as things went nowadays, but the meat was real.

"You shouldn't have sacrificed your week's ration to me, my boy," said Thomas kindly.

Bernard coloured and said something about it's being a pleasure, and Thomas grew more and more uncomfortable. As Bernard ate little, and Thomas from rationing motives did the same, the meal was soon disposed of. Bernard led the way across the hall to the drawing-room, where most unusually a fire was burning. He settled his uncle in a large easy chair; coffee was brought, a cigar was offered. Then just as all preparations for the announcement seemed complete, the telephone rang in the hall, and Bernard rushed away. His voice after the preliminary greeting sank to a confidential murmur, so that Thomas felt embarrassed, and stretched out a hand towards the books below Olive's bureau in search of something to distract his attention. Among the brightly-coloured tattered paper backs of the detective stories and cheap romances which were Bernard's and Olive's usual reading, Thomas perceived a book of soberer hue. He drew it out. A bookplate of involved design concealed rather than revealed its owner's initials. Bernard's voice still rose and fell, so Thomas turned the pages. Poetry. *O Dreams, O Destinations*, he read:

> "*Older, we build a road where once our active*
> *Heat threw up mountains and the deep dales veined:*
> *We're glad to gain the limited objective,*
> *Knowing the war we fight in has no end.*
> *The road must needs follow each contour moulded*
> *By that fire in its losing fight with earth:*
> *We march over our past, we may behold it*
> *Dreaming a slave's dream on our bivouac hearth.*

> *Lost the archaic dawn wherein we started,*
> *The appetite for wholeness: now we prize*
> *Half-loaves, half-truths—enough for the half-hearted*
> *The gleam snatched from corruption satisfies.*
> *Dead youth, forgive us if, all but defeated,*
> *We raise a trophy where your honour lies."*

Thomas threw the book angrily aside. I don't know what it's all about but it's how I feel, he thought. Older! Once active heat! Lost the archaic dawn! Half-hearted! He felt as if the writer had laid a finger on a sore place in his heart and pressed relentlessly. The pain spread till his whole body seemed to throb.

Bernard returned; he looked flushed and excited, lighted a cigarette with jerky movements and gazed at the fire.

"Come, Bernard, out with it," urged Thomas. He spoke impatiently because he suffered. "You're making me nervous."

"I'm afraid it's going to be rather a shock to you, Uncle."

"It upsets me more, all this suspense."

"Well—there's no future any more in England."

"Nonsense!"

"Not under this Government. Not for private enterprise. I've made up my mind to go abroad."

"Well, I think you might have waited till I was dead," exclaimed Thomas passionately.

"I haven't the least desire for you to be dead, Uncle Thos!" cried Bernard angrily.

"But how can I possibly manage without you, Bernard? Do have some sense. Where are you going? You can't take your money with you, you know."

"Yes, I can. I'm going to South Africa."

"What are you going to do when you get there? Grow oranges?"

"Yes," said Bernard defiantly.

"What do you know about oranges? You'll be bankrupt in a couple of years."

"I'm sorry you've such a poor opinion of my business capacity, Uncle."

"I've a high opinion of your capacity in textiles. Why

exchange them for something you know nothing about at all?"

"I've told you," said Bernard crossly. "There's no future for private enterprise in England."

"You might give England a few more years before you leave her."

"I can't wait, Uncle. You mustn't ask me to wait."

"Is Olive going with you?"

"No."

Thomas was silent a moment. "It's another woman!" he exclaimed suddenly.

"Well, yes, it is. You can't blame me, Uncle. If you think of it, I haven't had much of a life. Married in 1938, the war in 1939, prisoner in 1940, and as soon as I get back, this trouble with Olive."

"I don't blame you, my boy," said Thomas quietly. "You'll get divorced, I suppose?"

Bernard nodded.

"Will Olive agree to bring a case?"

Bernard hesitated. "She has agreed," he said. "On certain conditions, of course."

"What's to happen to Audrey?"

"She'll go to her mother till she's educated, and then she can choose."

"And I suppose you'll want me to pay sums over to Olive for her education. There'll be Olive's alimony too. I don't know how I shall manage it all," said Thomas sadly.

An immense discouragement filled his heart, as he thought of the terrible complexities of business in the post-war world. How on earth was he to keep Highshaw Mills running? Bernard had organised it all on modern lines; standardised and numbered the qualities and shades; his desk was always full of typewritten reports—the daily top position, sales reports, weekly profits, average selling margins and heavens knows what besides; he ran the whole huge concern from his office. Not that Bernard knew as much about actual *spinning* as Thomas did, reflected Thomas; Bernard always admitted that himself, and when he made the rounds of the mill, as he did every two or three days, he always most carefully

33

invited his uncle to accompany him. He let the older man do the talking to foremen and operatives and listened carefully to his comments. Thomas attended the meetings of the Board of the Worsted Spinners' Federation; Thomas often diagnosed the cause of the defects of which customers complained, when Bernard was unable to do so. But it was Bernard who knew all the modern regulations, who did all the organisation, all the top-buying.

"But how on earth can I run the place by myself, Bernard? It can't be done. I can't do it alone. We shall have to advertise for a manager."

Bernard cleared his throat. "Well, Uncle, this is where I have another shock for you."

"But why should you go overseas, Bernard?" said Thomas, following his own line of thought. "It's quite unnecessary. Why not marry the girl and settle down here? In Ashworth? Or if you feel that's a little awkward—though people don't think much about divorces nowadays—why not move up into the Dales somewhere? You know you can have every latitude as regards attendance at Highshaw, Bernard; but don't leave me altogether. Is she an Ashworth girl, by the way? Not from Shaw Green, I hope. Not that it's my business."

"She lives in Ashworth. But, Uncle," said Bernard, clasping his hands tightly together: "The point is this. I shall have to settle a good deal of money on Olive."

"Why? She's only entitled to her proper alimony."

"She won't divorce me otherwise. She insists on being safely provided for."

"I never liked her. Well—I'll buy some of your Highshaw shares from you, Bernard, and you can put the money in Government stocks and settle it on her. It'll cut down your income, of course—but you'll get it all back after my death."

"Uncle," said Bernard in a desperate tone: "I've sold my Highshaw shares already."

"What do you mean?"

"I've sold them to Messrs. Burney Brothers. That is, I've arranged to sell them."

"Don't be absurd, Bernard!" shouted Thomas, crimsoning. "You haven't done anything so preposterous!"

34

"Yes, I have."

"But it's impossible! It's ridiculous! How dare you jest with me in this way! You're behaving abominably, Bernard!"

"Uncle, do calm yourself. It's no use becoming excited. I need money in trustee stocks to settle on Olive, because she won't consent to the divorce on any other terms."

"That damned solicitor her brother has advised her."

"I expect so. Anyway, I need the money."

"I'll buy the shares."

"How could you, Uncle? It would cripple you financially. You'd have to mortgage part of Highshaw to find the money. That would cripple Highshaw. No, I've looked at it all round and thought it all out, believe me, and I've decided that this is the best way for everybody."

"You can't do this, Bernard. Blood is thicker than water, and you can't do this to your mother's brother."

"Uncle, I *have done* it. That is, I haven't actually parted with the shares yet, because of course we shall have to call a Directors' meeting and you'll have to initial the transfer as Chairman of the Directors. But I've made the arrangements with Burney Brothers and I'm expecting to complete the transfer and receive the money by Saturday at latest. We must arrange a Directors' meeting for Friday."

"I shall never forgive you, Bernard," said Thomas.

"Well, I'm sorry. But I've a right to some life of my own, Uncle."

"Why didn't you tell me what you were contemplating? We might have found a way out together."

Bernard hesitated.

"You didn't tell me because you knew I should never agree," said Thomas bitterly. Bernard said nothing. His uncle was silent too for a moment, then cried out loudly: "Do you really intend that by Saturday morning *somebody else* shall own half Highshaw Mills? You can't mean that, Bernard?"

"Yes, I do. It's no use fighting against it, Uncle Thomas," said Bernard desperately. "The thing's done, or as good as. You'll have another partner instead of me, that's all. If you want to retire after a few years, I dare say Burney Brothers will buy you out."

"No Armitages at Highshaw," murmured Thomas.

Bernard moved his shoulders impatiently. "With all this nationalisation Armitages wouldn't be there long anyhow."

Thomas sat silent, his large bony hands spread out on his knees, to hide their trembling. This was the moment of defeat, this was the moment of realisation, this was the moment of anguish. He lived through it, conscious of nothing but searing pain. Then his mind slowly cleared. In imagination he heard men gossiping about the affair on the Bradford Wool Exchange. "His nephew sold out behind his back. It killed old Thos. He never got over it. Nephew sold out to Burney Brothers."

"Who are Burney Brothers nowadays?" he asked feebly. The question was a measure of his age, he thought with despair. Twenty years ago he knew the directors of every firm of importance in the textile West Riding.

"It's chiefly Considine," said Bernard, sighing with relief as he saw that the crisis was over. "Sir Charles, you know."

"I know Considine," said Thomas in the same weak voice. "He's our finance man on the A.T.P. Committee, you know."

"Is he," said Bernard, who clearly knew the fact already.

"I heard something about him this morning, too. I don't remember what it was, but I heard his name."

"Uncle—don't go back to the mill. Go home for a while and have a rest. This has been a shock to you."

Thomas turned his head slowly and fixed a long dark look on his nephew.

"I hope you're sure of your girl, Bernard. Your new one, I mean. You're paying a heavy price for her. Is it all settled between you, eh?"

"How can it be settled till I've got my divorce?"

"You're a fool, Bernard Clough."

"Well, at least this time I'll be a fool in my own way and not in Mother's."

"What's her name?" said Thomas, softened by this hint of a tragedy he had never suspected.

"Never mind. I want to keep her out of it till I can marry her."

"Do I know her?"

36

Bernard hesitated. "I believe you do. She lives in Ashworth."

"Is she a lady?"

"Of course, Uncle. Don't be so ridiculous. She's very beautiful."

"Olive was pretty too."

"Olive was an icicle."

Thomas got to his feet. "You've broken my heart, Bernard," he said: "Without cause or need. You want to hand a business that's been in the Armitage family for six generations over to strangers. I never want to see you again. But you're my only sister's son, and I suppose I shall——" His mind faltered and he could not remember what he intended to say. "I suppose I shall—I suppose I shall," he repeated vaguely.

"Go home, Uncle," said Bernard, laying his hand on his uncle's arm.

"Leave me alone!" shouted Thomas, jerking away his elbow. "Half Highshaw Mills is still mine and I won't be driven out of it."

"As Secretary of the Company I shall call a Directors' Meeting for Friday," said Bernard, hardening.

"I shall look up the articles of association of the company and if there's anything in them to stop you selling, I shall stop you."

"Of course there is and you can; I told you so," said Bernard impatiently. "Highshaw is a private limited company; you and I hold the shares between us except for those few which Grandfather gave to old Great-aunt Lou. You hold her proxy and can vote her shares, so you can stop me of course; you can vote me down. Legally. But you won't do it, Uncle Thos."

"That remains to be seen."

"It will be an act of tyranny if you stop me from selling, and I can't see you committing an act of tyranny."

"And what do you think your act of sale is?"

"I can't believe that you'll deliberately ruin my life by voting me down, Uncle."

"You've ruined it yourself already. Now you want to ruin mine."

"I've a good deal of my life left to live, Uncle," said Bernard softly.

The two men stared at each other.

"Well—goodbye, and thank you for a pleasant lunch," said Thomas at length sardonically.

Tripping over his feet, he stumbled out into the hall. Bernard's man was there, helped him into his coat and opened the door. It was clear from his expression and from that of Fred, who was leaning against the car just outside, that both of them knew pretty well what had been happening. Why, thought Thomas, remembering suddenly, even that horrid little Shaw of Annotsfield, in the Ministry's waiting-room that morning, had connected Considine with Thomas Armitage. Everybody knew. Sir Charles Considine. It was a name one had heard a lot of lately. Title gained during the war. I must try to find out about him, thought Thomas wearily. It's a coincidence that he's on the A.T.P.C. But of course in a small town like Ashworth, everyone's destiny is interlaced. If he's a decent chap, I'll sell out to him as soon as I can, thought Thomas. No Armitages at Highshaw. Well! What does it matter, after all?

"The mill, Fred," he said hoarsely.

"Yes, sir," said Fred in his gravest tones.

Oranges!

5

The afternoon passed strangely. He looked at the articles of association of Messrs. Armitage & Son, formed from the old family business into a private limited company in the 1900's; he looked at the power of attorney he held from his ancient bedridden aunt. He saw that his nephew was right: the shares could not be sold without a Directors' resolution, and holding his aunt's proxy he could easily vote Bernard down if he chose.

Returning the papers to the safe, he sat for a long time with his arms stretched out across his desk, trying to make clear to himself the moral dilemma into which Bernard had thrust him. He had only to harden his heart and lift his hand at the right moment, and Highshaw Mills would continue as before. He was quite capable of hardening his heart if he wished to and thought it right; he was no milksop, no peace-at-any-pricer, no sentimentalist. But could he feel it to be right? Could he reconcile it with his lifelong principles to ruin Bernard's happiness to save his own? However wild his nephew's folly appeared to him, Bernard was a grown man who certainly had a right, as he said, to be a fool in his own way. Could Thomas continue to respect himself if he imposed on Bernard a course of life he loathed? Thomas rather thought the answer was no. Suppose, on the other hand, he gave in and let Bernard have his way. In a few days' time this fellow Considine would be in effect his partner. Intolerable!

Of course Considine's quite a decent sort of chap, I believe, thought Thomas reluctantly; they don't give titles for nothing nowadays and he offered to come on the A.T.P.C. so he must believe in work for the community, must have some sort of social conscience. He must be pretty well lined, too; cost him a quarter of a million to buy Bernard out. No doubt it's just an investment with him; he will just draw the dividends which I shall have to make for him. But what are Burney Brothers anyway? My fires are certainly losing their fight with earth since I never thought of asking Bernard that.

He rang for his secretary and demanded the Bradford Area telephone directory; it was disconcerting to find it lay at his elbow on his desk. Burney Brothers were *Fine Worsted Mfrs*, said the directory, and their address was *Heygate Clough Mills*, which from the evidence of its name must lie in the valley on the northern side of Ashworth town. Well, if Considine makes fine worsteds, perhaps the partnership would work out not too badly after all, thought Thomas, trying to pluck up courage; Considine was probably sick of the uneven yarn and uncertain deliveries he got from the spinners he was dealing with, and wanted to make sure of better service by becoming associated with a spinning firm of his own. Natural enough. Thomas turned up the name of Considine in the directory. *Considine, Sir Charles*, he read, *High Hey, Ashworth*. And again: *Considine, C. & Co, Ltd., Worsted Spinners, Comer Mills, Bradford*. Good heavens, the man was a spinner too! Would that mean he would want to come in and have a say in the management of the business? At this thought Thomas's old heart leaped with pain. Surely it was impossible —it was too outrageous, too improbable, too absurd, to be true—that in a few days Considine would be strolling round Highshaw Mills as half-owner of the place? But if not, then he, Thomas Armitage, a man permeated with Liberal principles in every cranny of his soul, must force his nephew to surrender his hopes of a new and happier mode of life.

Thomas sprang up and began a tour of the sprawling buildings. If I've got to manage it by myself I'd better learn all the details I can, he told himself, and strove to prevent the completion of the sentence from echoing in his mind: *while it still belongs to me.* He walked through all the departments, standing to admire the lustrous white coils of the tops, their soft smoky hues when dyed, and following all the processes by which the soft broad slivers became strong fine slender yarn. Breadth to length, he thought, nodding his head, and then length to breadth again, by weaving; that's textiles. But this reminded him of Considine, who was engaged in both parts of the textile process; he frowned and walked on. The curly-headed girls in the colour-matching room astonished him by their youth; could such children really be trusted accurately to weigh drachms? Returning, he found himself suddenly by the door to the closed combing shed with the damaged roof. From this humiliating reminder he swerved away rather too noticeably, and found women's eyes resting on him as their owners looked up curiously from their machines. Pretending a keen interest in a nearby gill-box to cover his discomfiture, he saw a very rough piecening coming through. He stopped the machine, and gave the girl minding it a neat little demonstration of how to make a good piecening, burying the end of the wool in correct fashion, with a kindly harangue on the wickedness of rough joins, which would make a thickening in the yarn and show up as a lump in the finished cloth. The girl listened in apparently indifferent silence. Bernard said that operatives always displayed this apathy, this lack of interest nowadays, but Thomas had not met it in such a striking form before. Bernard! He moved on. He strove to walk briskly, to smile, to hold his head up, to look knowing and commanding and debonair, but the workers who saw his tottering gait, his white face and burning eyes, nodded to each other and when occasion offered made shrewd comments:

"It'll kill old Thos. Aye, he looks poorly. Still, you can't blame Mr. Bernard in a way. Who is she, then? Do you know? Eh, but it's a shame for the old gaffer. If textiles were nationalised as they should be, this sort o' nonsense wouldn't happen. Well, happen it won't be long."

When he got back to his office at last Thomas was tired out; he drank two cups of tea but couldn't manage his usual biscuit. An order lay on his desk for seventy thousand pounds of the finest Highshaw yarn (at 12s. 11d. a pound, shades to be specified later); the paper bore a pencilled note from Bernard: *Mr. Thomas will like to see this.* This morning he would have been pleased by the size of the order, which was considerable even for Highshaw, but now it simply made him wretched. Who was to look after it all, to see that the quality was kept up? He thought of the girl in the drawing shed with that horrid lump showing in her piecening, and fretted. The afternoon was dark, a shower was coming on. Thomas sighed deeply, his head fell forward and he slept. The mill buzzer sounded and the operatives poured out of the building; he stirred but settled back into sleep again.

His secretary, a most conscientious girl whom he shared with Bernard, startled him into wakefulness by bringing some letters and cheques for him to sign. He wrote his name carefully in his large angular writing, making a pretence of reading what he signed but not really taking in any of it— Bernard had dictated the letters, they would be all right, business-like and dignified. Bernard! Oranges! At the bottom of the pile lay the notice, signed by Bernard as the Company's Secretary, calling the Directors' meeting for Friday afternoon at three. He must take his decision before then, make up his mind how to vote.

"It's your A.T.P.C. meeting tonight at seven, Mr. Armitage," his secretary reminded him. "Fred's waiting."

He glanced at his watch and observed that the hour was late and he could not go up to Shaw Hall and eat a meal if he were to be in time for the meeting. This pleased him; of late his domestic arrangements had been uncomfortable, as most people's were, even the richest, in England nowadays; his housekeeper was a deafish cross old woman whom it was a pleasure not to have to face. He told the girl to telephone a message that he would dine in Ashworth; she made a slight *moue* indicating her knowledge of his housekeeper's probable reaction to this, but of course obeyed.

6

In the familiar Victoria Hotel grill-room the familiar grey-haired waitress, whom he had seen waiting at public and private functions in the town of Ashworth for the last forty years, bent over him to whisper in his ear that he could have a piece of real good steak tonight. Though he did not want anything to eat, out of courtesy he put on a show of pleasure.

"But you should keep it for somebody more active, who needs it more, my dear."

"Nobody deserves it more than you, Mr. Armitage, with all the public work you do," said the woman kindly.

Thomas sighed. It was true: in the past he had done a great deal of public work. He was on the local Bench and attended very regularly, he was President of this and Chairman of that, he was a Governor of several schools—by the way he must compose a speech for that prize-giving tomorrow. But should he bother to continue? Should he really go on trying to serve this strange new world? Was he any use to it? Today's events had taught him to think he wasn't. He'd give backword for the prize-giving; he really wasn't up to it. Rather short notice, perhaps. Inconvenient. Still, if he telephoned the headmaster tonight after the A.T.P.C.—good heavens, thought Thomas with a start: I promised to meet young Captain Bairstow at the Institute early, and it's a few minutes to seven already. What's happened to me today has driven it out of my head. He raised a finger to the waitress.

"I must be off. My bill."

"Another of your meetings, I suppose. Well, you look better now, Mr. Armitage—I was quite worried about you when you came in. You looked right upset." Thomas winced. "But your steak's done you good."

"I'm late, Fred," said Thomas, hurrying down the corridor —it was tiresome how often his feet tripped, today.

"Well, people are often late at meetings," observed Fred philosophically.

Still, he drove off quickly, and the Ashworth Town Hall clock still stood at a few minutes before the hour, when Thomas entered the Mechanics' Institute and hurried up the steps.

In the dingy little room on the right where the meetings were held Roddie Bairstow was talking to that designer woman, Elizabeth Marrison. Beautiful creature, thought Thomas as he greeted her politely, but unhappy and the cause of unhappiness in others, if his experience of life had taught him anything. Young Bairstow proffered him the agenda and they bent over it together.

"I'm sorry I was too late for a word alone with you," said Thomas in a low tone under cover of the entrance and mutual greetings of other members. "After the meeting instead, perhaps?"

"If it's not too inconvenient, sir," agreed Roddie.

His tone was markedly reluctant. He thinks it's not worth while bothering the old buffer after all, thought Thomas sadly. Yes, everything that's happened to me today says I'm useless. Well! Decidedly I shan't go to that prize-giving; I shan't go to any more meetings after tonight. I'll give in to Bernard and sell out the whole thing to Considine as soon as I can; I'll retire to Shaw Hall and moulder quietly and quickly into the grave. I'm useless.

7

The Town Hall clock struck seven.

"We may as well begin, ladies and gentlemen," said Thomas in the steady audible tones he used for public affairs. "How many meetings have I presided at, I wonder?" he asked himself. "Getting on for a thousand, I dare say. But this is the last one. Stay a moment though," he added aloud: "Are we a quorum, Captain Bairstow?"

He said *Captain* because to him Roddie Bairstow summed up in his handsome young person North Africa, the terrible days when Rommel was sweeping towards Cairo, General Montgomery, and a film Thomas had once seen with Olive of the night barrage before the first victorious advance. Yes, to Thomas the lad represented all the young men in the last two wars, both those who had not come back, like his own sons, and those who had come back to a difficult world. Thomas was grateful to these young men for saving England, and he took a pleasure in courteously expressing his gratitude by a respectful pronunciation of young Bairstow's rank.

"I'm afraid I don't know what our quorum is, sir."

Thomas glanced round the table. There were now present, he saw, besides himself, Bairstow and Miss Marrison, that bristling long-headed gingerish argumentative chap Gamaliel Greenwood and—Sir Charles Considine. Thomas's pulse leaped. Damn the fellow! Sitting there looking superior in his admirable dark blue suit, with a very clean white shirt, platinum cuff-links, a pair of expensive-looking hexagonal shell spectacles, and some sort of old school tie.

"Look it up in the Minutes, will you, my boy?" said Thomas to Roddie.

Somehow the mention of Minutes calmed him. It's not in accordance with the spirit of Committee work to judge a matter in advance, he thought. (Yes, a thousand meetings I've attended, I shouldn't wonder.) Considine looks calm and able. I mustn't be unfair, I mustn't judge him in advance.

At this moment Councillor Foster Ormerod—a good worthy honest man though limited, thought Thomas—came in, followed by what was presumably, judging from her fresh complexion and lustrous curls, the newly appointed representative of the Ashworth Youth Groups. She hung back diffidently, the colour deepening in her rosy cheek. Ah, youth, youth, thought Thomas; what a lovely time it is to look back upon, what an agonising time it is to live through. I remember

I used to feel as if I had toothache all over my body when I entered a meeting.

"The Youth Representative?"

"Yes. Miss Heald," bellowed Ormerod, who always spoke as if addressing a public meeting.

"Won't you sit here by me?" said Thomas gently, indicating a place to the right of the Chair.

"Our quorum is five members of whom one must be an official, Mr. Armitage."

"Ah. Then we're all right, we can begin."

"In any case we're all here now except Mrs. Sykes, who was late last time," said Considine quietly.

(What business is that of his?) "We'll take the Minutes now, Captain Bairstow."

The young man stood up and began to read.

"Minutes of the first meeting of the Ashworth Textile Pageant Committee held at 7 p.m. on Tuesday September 6th 1949 at the Mechanics' Institute, Ashworth. Present, Mr. Thomas Armitage in the Chair. . . ."

Deborah Sykes, broad and fair, in a bright blue suit of pleasant cheerful colour but rather poor quality cloth, came in rather clumsily, knocking, as she passed, against the chair of Considine, who straightened it with a frown. Her broad intelligent face remained calm, her large light blue eyes continued to beam. She gave Thomas a smile of happy welcome and sat down. Thomas returned her greeting with a little bow. Very high Science degree that woman has, he remembered. She looks it too. Fine face. Lots of character. Benevolent. Strong. Sad history, I believe. Jonathan Bamforth's great-granddaughter.

"Terms of reference were read," droned young Bairstow.

He continued to read the Minutes in a clear and strong but somewhat monotonous tone, while that unhappy Marrison girl fixed him with her undoubtedly beautiful but angry and tormented eyes.

Ah, women, women! reflected Thomas from the experience of a lifetime. Sex, sex! The source of so much ecstasy, so much anguish! Imagine Bernard ruining himself and High-shaw and his uncle for a woman's sake. . . .

II

MISS ELIZABETH MARRISON

I

"WHICH MAKE-UP SHALL I wear today, I wonder?"
thought Elizabeth Marrison, examining with pleasure the
reflection of her naked beauty in the long glass.

How people can live who are plain, like that Sykes woman
for instance, she thought, I really don't know; I don't know
how they can bear themselves. Her own face and figure
were as perfect as they well could be—in this imperfect world,
and considering she was thirty years old. Small women were
too often kittenish and dolly, she thought—she would have
been unendurable to herself if she had been kittenish or dolly.
But no; her slender gleaming honey-coloured body, though
small, was tense and taut; there was no sag, no slightest hint
of flop, about her pointed breasts; her waist and loins, her
slender arms, were muscular and firm; her long thick hair
was dark and smooth; her face was pale, aquiline and proud;
her violet eyes added a pleasingly sophisticated note of
colour.

"Altogether, I'm like a leopard," she thought, stretching
her arms above her head and admiring her profile from head
to heel. "A leopard in a very delicate range of shades. *Sister to
the bright quick spotted fiery leopard*—that's much more like me
than that boring Shirley."

She put on her black mules and a stiff silk housecoat
(*soie* or *soi-disant*, she thought, remembering an old joke
with the man who bought it for her) richly striped in purple
and gold, tied the girdle very tight with a feeling of satisfaction in the smallness of her waist, and sat down before her
cheap but elegant dressing-table to consider in detail the
question of what to wear for the day. It was important,
because what she wore, what matching face she chose,
would affect all her actions, even the designs she produced,
she knew, throughout the day; her colour scheme determined
which aspect of her character would be turned outward to
the world.

She sprang up and pushing the casement window further open, gazed upwards. (If somebody saw her in her dressing-gown, so much the worse for them—or the better, depending on their sex. Those Ashworth prudes would be shocked, no doubt, especially if her housecoat fell apart and revealed her breasts. She gave a tiny shrug to express: "Let them be shocked then!" which at the same time opened her coat a little more widely.) As far as one could judge from the small amount of sky visible between this block of flats and the as yet unconverted Victorian houses across the street, the day seemed cool for September. Fair probably but sunless. And of course a breeze. Always a breeze in this damned West Riding, thought Elizabeth angrily; always tugging at your hair and your hat and your skirts, never lets you be yourself for a moment, never leaves you alone. However, that wasn't the point at present; the point was to get a move on, get cracking as Roddie Bairstow would say, choose a scheme and get dressed and get down to the office, or she would be late. If she were late, as sure as fate one of the Directors would have phoned through, wanting to speak to her about some idiotic boring detail; that had happened when she was late last week. Well, which was it to be, then? Brown tweed and suntan complexion, or black suit, pale face and cyclamen lipstick to match the new jumper? She sat down again and began to brush her long hair consideringly, her bracelet tinkling pleasantly with each movement of her arm.

It was Tuesday. That tiresome A.T.P. Committee came tonight. What a bore. Old Thos Armitage would like the tweed best, she felt certain; but Roddie would be more impressed by the black. The others didn't count, and there was nobody at the office, nobody in the whole damned mill, she cared two hoots for. They were all as old as Methuselah, or else, my dear, violently—but violently—under-sexed. All things considered, perhaps better go for Thos and tweed. She opened a drawer to assemble the necessary accessories and was rummaging for lingerie when the letter-box flapped.

At once she was excited. Her hopes soared. There might be some letter, some wonderful letter, from somebody, which would liberate her from this boring job, this boring life in

Ashworth, these boring provincial men, and plant her down in the midst of the great world. She ran out of her tiny bedroom into the little sitting-room—but slowed down there to give an approving glance to its appearance; say what you like, she certainly had a gift for giving an air to even the smallest and least distinguished room. Of course the deep blue carpet, the blue net curtains, the white paint, the blue and white armchair, weren't all paid for yet—and that reminded her, she must go down and expend some charm on the manager of the furniture shop some day soon, that letter he'd sent her had quite a nasty tone. He ought to be glad to have his stuff shown off by a designer such as herself, with business connections all over the world. However, it was natural for him to want his money, she supposed; in the happy expectation of a wonderful letter Elizabeth was good-humoured and ready to forgive much all round. The charming blue glass horse on the mantelpiece was her own, given to her by a man she had been great friends with (was it in Bristol?); the same was true of the very dashing painting over the mantelpiece, the spoils of a friendship in her last London job. The colouring was delightfully lurid: sugar-pink, cobalt and violet, with sudden swirls of scarlet and lime; the composition somehow excited.

"It doesn't mean a thing, my dear," Elizabeth was fond of saying to her guests: "It's not representational. It's just colour and form. But I've no doubt sex is in it somewhere rearing its ugly head."

"More than its head, I think," Bernard had said drily.

Elizabeth laughed and gave him a quizzical look out of her beautiful eyes. The result had been very satisfactory—at the time, but nothing much had come of it since, unfortunately. Elizabeth liked her picture in her best moments almost as well as in her worst, and that was a great tribute to any picture. Oh, but the letter! She ran forward and stooped to pick it up from the floor.

At once her expression changed: eager expectancy gave way to a look of dark and angry reproach. She turned aside frowning and tore open the cheap envelope in vehement zigzags. Well, no, it's not exactly a *cheap* envelope, she corrected herself, but it's so boringly white and ordinary, and look at the address on the notepaper! Stamped on with one of those absurd little die-stamps. No taste, no style, no air; was it to be wondered at that she could not endure to live with such people? No, it was not to be wondered at, she told herself fiercely, not to be wondered at in the least; they had no right to be surprised, hurt, distressed, because she could not bear to live with such tasteless persons. That was the only reason she could not live with them, she told herself angrily, feeling her heart beat very fast and strong.

The letter was from her foster-mother—for so Elizabeth now chose to designate Mrs. Marrison. *My dearest Bessie*, it began, and at once Elizabeth quivered with rage and pain; powerful emotions of anguish, of resentment and of loss like wild horses tore her heart apart. The words *my little Bess, my dearest Bessie*, echoed agonisingly in her ears. Few people could labour under such an awful history as hers, thought Elizabeth, few people could have struggled against it, surmounted it as well as she. Look at her now, earning this good salary in this good job, sophisticated, distinguished, poised. Of course she owed much of it to the Marrisons, *of course* she did, she admitted it, she was grateful, she loved them, yes she loved them all especially Eda—or she *would* love them if only they would leave her alone. She threw the letter down and burst into passionate tears, sobbing wildly, storming in swift furious steps up and down the little room. Why did she have to remember all that now, when she was late already and had so much to do at the office? She wouldn't remember it; she would put it right out of her mind.

But in spite of herself she acted it all through again.

2

Elizabeth's earliest recollection was of sitting on a table swinging her legs in a large room where a great many small children were romping, toddling, crawling, all making a great deal of noise. This was part of some actors' benevolent association or other—she always tried not to remember its exact name. As far as she remembered her state of mind in the moment before the door opened to admit the Marrisons, she had not been actively unhappy; she had felt a little perplexed, bewildered even, but unintimidated and calm. She knew she was beautiful, even at three years old. Then the door opened and in came Mr. and Mrs. Marrison, followed by the head nurse. Mr. Marrison was thin and tall in his crumpled dog collar and his shabby ministerial clothes, his hair tumbled, his fine eyes beaming behind his crooked spectacles; Mrs. Marrison had that look of sad but gentle resignation which the deaf often acquire, on her sweet slightly faded face. They were in their middle thirties, Elizabeth knew later, and God had taken away—this was their version of the incident, not hers—God had taken away at birth the little girl on whom they had set such hopes. It was thought to be medically both improbable and undesirable that Mrs. Marrison should conceive again, so eventually, after much thought and prayer, they had decided to adopt a child, and had come to this orphanage to find a suitable one. ("A child we can love," said Mrs. Marrison.) Oddly enough, the moment Elizabeth set eyes on them she knew with a rush of tears how lost, homeless, loveless and altogether wretched she was become. With a loud cry she rolled off the table and rushed towards Mrs. Marrison with outstretched arms. Mrs. Marrison stooped and snatched her to her breast, and they both wept passionately together, cheek to cheek, while the nurse with her hands clasped in their proper official position smiled at them benevolently.

"What is her name, Matron?" wept Mrs. Marrison.

"Elizabeth." (Surnames of adoptable children were never revealed.)

"My little Bess!" exclaimed Mrs. Marrison, kissing her.

"She's a lovely little girl," said Mr. Marrison wistfully.

So it was all soon settled—if there was any hitch Elizabeth never knew it—and Elizabeth became Elizabeth Marrison and went to live with her new parents near Mr. Marrison's Baptist chapel in one of the suburbs of Birmingham.

The Marrisons never concealed from Elizabeth that she was not their natural child; on the contrary (after much prayer and thought) they taught her to take pride in it.

"We were looking for a little girl and out of all the hundreds we saw we chose you, Bessie," was the Marrisons' attitude. This was a shield and even a weapon to Elizabeth; when children taunted her at school with being an adopted child she replied with joyous confidence: "My parents *chose* me; they could have had lots of other little girls, but they chose *me*." At this her companions, whose birth they vaguely surmised had been conducted on different lines, retired discomfited.

So Elizabeth was a happy little girl and a good one, a God-given treasure to her father and the apple of her mother's eye. Her large violet eyes, fixed on them so trustingly, her beautiful little arms, her lovely face—they thanked God daily that the privilege of guarding such beauty had been permitted to them. Her mind too was quick and apt to learn; she read early and delighted in the occupation. She was honest and open, because the Marrisons had taught her not to fear them; she was obedient, she did not shirk or lie. If occasionally a violent paroxysm of temper convulsed her, the occasions were rare, the paroxysms short, the repentance hearty. The warm-hearted little girl could not bear to make her mother look sad; she rushed to throw her arms round Mrs. Marrison's neck and sob out her remorse for her transgression. Elizabeth could always make Mrs. Marrison hear her voice, and there were many little services of communication and interpretation which the child took pride in watchfully rendering to the increasingly deaf woman.

Then a miracle happened; Mrs. Marrison became pregnant. This was of course a danger-point for Elizabeth, and even now she could not but admire the way the Marrisons had handled it, though gnashing her (exquisite) teeth with fury at the remembrance of her own unconsciousness. The pregnancy was physically dangerous, and it was necessary for Mrs. Marrison to retain a horizontal position for several months if a miscarriage were to be avoided. Who then so helpful as little Bessie? Mrs. Marrison had explained to her that she was to have a little brother or sister, but this would only happen if she helped her mother to come safely through the ordeal. When malicious or tactless guests asked anxiously how Bessie felt about the coming baby (and even sometimes whether the Marrisons did not regret their over-hasty adoption) Mrs. Marrison with her sweet smile replied:

"But Bessie is *helping* me to have the baby."

And so indeed it proved; the child, a girl, was safely born, and, Mrs. Marrison's name being Edith, was named Eda. Led by her gentle foster-mother, Elizabeth took the greatest pride in little Eda. She learned with joy to bath and dress her, to brush her fair silky hair, to prepare her food. The Marrisons were scrupulous to make no shadow of difference between their daughters except that proper to the difference in age; Eda was confided to Bessie sometimes to guard and teach, and Bessie taking that little warm hand in her own and explaining the dangers or joys of fire and ice and dolls and kittens, felt a happy pride in her position of responsibility. As the children grew, Elizabeth took Eda to school, helped her with her lessons, defended her fiercely against anyone who ventured to state the truth that Eda was not as pretty as her elder sister.

Presently Mr. Marrison accepted a call to Yorkshire, and took up a pastorate in a busy West Riding town.

From the first things did not go as well there for Elizabeth. In their old home everyone knew about Elizabeth's adoption and respected the Marrisons for their honourable and skilful conduct to the child; here in Hudley chapel members commented with surprise on the difference between Bessie's dark beauty and Eda's fair gawkiness and had to be enlightened as to its cause. When they heard the story, they mostly shook their heads and looked commiserating, and if they were females kissed either Bessie or Eda (or sometimes, if they were particularly nice people, both) with special fervour.

Of course there was dynamite in the situation, reflected Elizabeth now impatiently, and probably it would have exploded in another way if not in the incident her fate selected. The match which lighted the fuse was ludicrously small: the mere matter of the initials on a handkerchief. A Marrison aunt sent as Christmas gifts a book for Bessie, a little handkerchief embroidered *E.M.* for Eda. The book was somewhat pious and decidedly beneath Elizabeth's capacity; without thinking—or did she think?—she assumed the handkerchief to be her own. She stretched out her hand to take it from the parcel, but Eda innocently forestalled her.

"That's mine, Eda," said Elizabeth a trifle sharply.

Eda stared. "They're my initials," she protested in her mild Midland tones.

Suddenly Elizabeth was in a rage, shouting and storming. Nowadays, the smattering of psychology which was the common property of her generation led her to question whether it was the initials alone which had "set her off," or whether it was also the chance which had brought Elizabeth to puberty that day. In any case, from the moment of this attack by Eda on her personality, her cherished identity (so dear to her because she had almost lost it in the anonymity of the orphanage) jealousy ravaged her heart. No doubt it had lain latent there since Eda's birth.

The Marrisons, perplexed and troubled, strove with all their might to assuage and allay this jealousy, but the unsophisticated methods which had answered before now proved useless; in no time at all, Elizabeth had become—or at least she felt it so—the wilful, turbulent, naughty daughter, and Eda the mousy little good one. In vain Mr. Marrison urged her to take her trouble to God in prayer; in vain Mrs. Marrison told her that she had everything in the world to make her happy.

This from the Marrisons' point of view was true, for in her teens Elizabeth's beauty unequivocally declared itself and her artistic bent appeared; her voice too became singularly smooth and charming, quite free of provincial vowels; so that in all the arts of music, singing, painting, dancing, acting, sewing, as practised in the local high school, she easily excelled. But these qualities did not make for peace of mind; as her taste developed, so did her revolt against the Marrisons' standards; the circumstances of her adoption strengthened her belief that she was a swan amidst ducklings —or was she a cuckoo in the nest? She did not know, and as she wished always to play a noble part, the question fretted her. Accordingly a mixture of jealousy (as she now supposed) with irritation at the Marrisons' lack of style, discontent in their narrow milieu, loving vexation over Eda's flat accent and undistinguished manners, helpless disappointment over her own ill conduct and resentment at any criticism thereof, continually surged in a dark hot corrosive flood through her heart. She was witty and fluent, read a great deal in a desultory but knowledgeable way and always knew the modern manner in social behaviour, so that she could easily defeat Eda and Mrs. Marrison in argument, and soon even Mr. Marrison himself could not stand against her. She could wound very neatly, with a light well-planted sneer, and the moment she had done so raged at herself for sneering and at the Marrisons for being hurt, for gaping so stupidly, for being so childishly unable to defend themselves. She felt so alien from the Marrisons now that she sometimes wondered about her real parentage and one day asked Mr. Marrison about it. He told her rather sadly that the records were deliberately destroyed, there was no way of finding out. She sighed. In the circumstances such a sigh was an insult. In a word, beneath a quiet, decorous, affectionate exterior, life in the Marrison household in the 1930's, when Elizabeth and Eda were in their teens, was simply hell.

Soon the seemly exterior cracked too. For Elizabeth, now eighteen and training as a dress designer at the local technical college, began to find herself admired by the opposite sex. Her sultry nature responded avidly, and she found compensation for her deep home unease in this male homage. It was a period when sophistication was the fashion; Elizabeth followed the fashion, smoked, drank, made extravagant demands for dress money and told bawdy stories. She declined to attend any place of worship, and was to be seen publicly doing all these things on Sunday mornings. This was horribly difficult for the Marrisons, whose official position, no less than their principles, required them to condemn such practices. Yet one of the main tenets of modern religious ministry, to which Mr. Marrison earnestly subscribed, was not to frighten away young people by intolerance of harmless pleasures. Greatly perplexed, they remonstrated with their elder daughter; at first mildly; presently, especially after Mr. Marrison returning late from a meeting had discovered

Elizabeth in a car at the front door embracing its owner with more warmth than decorum, with some severity. Elizabeth smiled, opened her beautiful eyes wide, and in her cool easy drawl informed them condescendingly that there was nothing wrong in what she did; what harm was there in driving about in a car with a young man and calling at a pub for a drink? Or in an innocent boy-and-girl kiss? To see anything wrong in that was ridiculously old-fashioned, hopelessly out-of-date, my dear, pre-Noah, before the flood. Prurient, too. Perplexed almost to distraction, the Marrisons veered between "trusting" her to behave well, and unhappy thunder when their consciences accused them of laxity towards their lifelong principles.

Presently, unknown to them, the fumbling embraces of these boys gave way to the more experienced intimacies of a married man, a schoolmate's uncle on a business trip from the East. It was he who gave Elizabeth the heavy silver bangle with the symbolic charms whose musical jingle and agreeable weight upon her wrist had become an integral part of her personality. He returned to India but she found others to take his place, whom she encouraged and frustrated with a pleasing sense of power. Now that there was more to conceal from her family she concealed it more carefully, and the Marrisons lived in uneasy doubt, unable to discover any actual sin but terrified whenever they saw a certain secret gloating in Elizabeth's preoccupied eyes.

In the intervals of these escapades Elizabeth, by way of proving how good and kind she was, how truly she loved her family, tried to smarten up Eda, subjecting the younger girl to a torrent of advice on her hair, dress, manners, general behaviour and speech. "You'll never get a boy-friend with hair like that, Eda," she joked. "Just because you're a minister's daughter you don't need to look like 1900, you know. . . . *Don't* say *nothink*, Eda, I implore you; you're not in Birmingham now." At the same time she took real pains to make for Eda agreeable frocks and to knit for her elegant jumpers and cardigans—it appeared she had rather a special knack for knitting.

One day after a tirade of this kind about Eda's hair the

younger girl unobtrusively left the room. A few minutes later Elizabeth, a half-made blouse in her hand ready for Eda to try, went after her. But on the lowest stair she halted. The Marrisons' house was small in size and undistinguished in arrangement; a loudish noise in any room could be heard from attic to cellar. Eda's wail to the deaf Mrs. Marrison came quite clearly to Elizabeth's ears:

"I can't bear it any longer, Mother!"

Had she, she the clever, beautiful, noble Elizabeth Marrison, really been making dear little Eda unhappy? Eda so sweet and gentle, so softly fair, so kind and mild and good? Had Elizabeth been behaving with gross ingratitude to the Marrisons? Was her whole course of life awry? She stood there and suffered; the pain was like a probe in the nerve of a tooth, burning, sickening, unendurable. Because it was unendurable Elizabeth winced away—it was she, after all, she told herself, she the orphan, the adopted child, the homeless one, who was the world's victim. That night she announced quietly to Mrs. Marrison that she wished to go to London for further training. The slight start of relief which Mrs. Marrison gave in spite of herself did not escape Elizabeth's observation.

"Do you think it would be wise, dear?" demanded Mrs. Marrison.

"Yes," drawled Elizabeth. "I think it would be the height of wisdom, Mother."

Her tone suggested that the Marrisons by their unkindness were driving her out, rendering her homeless.

Because the Marrisons in their heart of hearts longed for her to leave them and because they were good, religious and honourable people, for long months they put every obstacle they could contrive in the way of her departure. Then Elizabeth accused them of trying to spoil her life and break her heart by their lack of understanding.

"Of course I know I'm not really your daughter. I'm just a nobody—anonymous."

"My dear, we chose you," said poor Mrs. Marrison.

"I wish you'd left me for somebody else to choose," drawled Elizabeth.

At this Mr. Marrison stood up—his shabby coat sticking

out at ludicrous angles—and said sternly: "I think you had better go, Bessie. If that is what you really want. Is it? Are you sure?"

"Yes, I'm sure," lied Elizabeth passionately.

By considerable financial sacrifice the Marrisons arranged to pay her fees at a London dressmaker's and hostel. Hardly was it all arranged when Mr. Marrison received a call from Brighton and thankfully accepted. Elizabeth was furious. It was just like her luck that this should come too late—she felt she would have enjoyed Brighton. Her foster-parents went to Sussex to inspect the manse and returned enthusiastic.

"There's such a nice room for you, Elizabeth," said Mrs. Marrison.

"Wouldn't you like to give up your London plan—or at least defer it for a while?" said Mr. Marrison.

The speeches were obviously concerted. Elizabeth raised her eyebrows, opened her beautiful eyes wide and said in a tone of surprise:

"Why, no, Father!"

"Of course you'll be with us in the holidays," said Mrs. Marrison.

Elizabeth did not offer to help them through the removal, and they did not ask her. Possibly each was waiting on the other. Elizabeth resolved not to force herself on them if they didn't want her, as she phrased it, and she left Hudley a week before their leave-taking presentation ceremony.

She had never returned to their house again for longer than a few weeks. She had received all sorts of "trainings"— some of them rather costly—and held all sorts of jobs, none of them very lasting. She had also enjoyed several love-affairs, which had proved equally impermanent, but in wartime this had not seemed to matter. Since the departure of the Calcutta man she had not again actually "betrayed her early training," as she imagined Mrs. Marrison would describe coition unsanctified by matrimony, but had often gone far enough in intimacy to enjoy exciting foretastes of the pleasures of the flesh. Why she hadn't gone the whole way she really hardly knew; whether it was a reluctance to surrender, or a personal fastidiousness, or the imperfections of the men concerned, who always proved so weak, or just her general wilfulness and perversity—she certainly didn't attribute her recent continued chastity to any religious or moral scruple, or even to any unwillingness on her part to lose it; God knew (as she said bitterly to herself) she was willing enough. Perhaps it was just that at the crucial moments she had lost her job and had to move on elsewhere. She had held a job in London for flower-arranging, a couple of minor jobs with dress designers and a wartime job with the B.B.C. in Bristol; the job she had held longest was in the public relations department of a wartime ministry, where it was her work to help in the arrangement of exhibitions. There her real artistic talent was so useful that her superiors overlooked her "difficult" personality—which always caused trouble with her colleagues, the men running after her and the women resenting it—her lateness, her unreliability. She knew all this very well, but continued to believe that when she found a job she really liked, these faults would reduce themselves to a manageable minimum.

After the war, when the ministry job folded up under her, things had been so difficult that she had been obliged to ask the Marrisons for money. She was in debt a little and they made no end of a fuss about it and wrote pathetic letters and made her go down to Brighton and after saying: "We won't scold you, dear," proceeded to do it *ad lib* and *da capo*. By this time Eda, who had been in the A.T.S. during the war, had got demobilised and married a local man, a school teacher; one of the world's worst bores Elizabeth thought him, but Eda clearly liked him for she looked beaming and happy and actually pretty, and really rather smart with her quite charming chubby baby. Elizabeth knitted woollies for her nephew which were greatly admired, and Mrs. Marrison had an inspiration and wrote to a former chapel-member in Hudley and made him offer Elizabeth a job as a knitter in a firm spinning knitting-yarns. A knitter! But there was nothing else to do for she had no money and was indeed still in debt, not having owned up the whole amount she owed to the Marrisons, so she took the job and submitted to living with another chapel-member, a widow.

Her earnings were not large enough for much gaiety and beneath the widow's eye in any case her activities were deplorably restricted, so she devoted herself to knitting ambitions for a while and soon found herself helping the head designer in the preparation of the knitting leaflets. For it was not enough to produce knitting yarn, as her chief often said; one had to sell it, that is to stimulate women to knit garments and provide them with such clear instructions how to do it that the result was wearable. Presently he began to train her as a designer. The work really suited her, combining her taste in dress with her manual dexterity.

Then she had a stroke of luck. A smaller firm in Ashworth advertised for a designer, she applied and her beautiful looks and skilful smooth drawling sophisticated talk, together with half a dozen really admirable designs over which the kindly Hudley designer had cast a corrective eye, won the post for her. The Hudley firm wished her luck, gave her good advice and let her go—reluctantly as regarded her art, for her taste in colour was exquisite, but thankfully (she suspected) as regarded her personality, which once again was found to be "difficult." So she was able to wave goodbye to the widow and Hudley and come to Ashworth which at least wasn't Hudley even though still in the West Riding, and have a nice little flat of her own and meet several quite interesting men, including Bernard.

Of course she was aware—she prided herself on her honesty about her qualities—she was aware that she was not really quite equal to the job. Her technical knowledge was so clearly inferior to that of the Hudley designer that there was no soreness in admitting it. ("Of course I've not had your *training*," it was her habit to wail to him with a rueful smile. "If only my parents had given me more *training*.") She had not studied, as he had done, knitting in all the Scandinavian countries or taken degrees in embroidery in Vienna; she had not visited, as he had done, European capitals for years to study fashion trends. She knew little of the history of knitting through the ages, though she became quite interested in the subject while in Hudley, bought a book or two about it, and acquired a sufficient smattering to lecture successfully to the

Ashworth Textile Society, where she met Bernard Clough. She was too lazy, cynical and irreverent to go into the matter thoroughly—her former chief's enthusiasm seemed to her just a little childish; "It's a bit *much*," she said. Similarly, it was not her life's ambition to raise knitwear designing to the level of a profession, though she often quoted this remark of his in general conversation because it improved her own social status. Her knowledge of the technics of colour was sketchy compared with his, but her intuitions on the subject were remarkable; her designs, she knew, had style and were thoroughly feminine and full of sex appeal, and her invention when pressed was fertile. Altogether the job suited her and she wanted to keep it; it was well paid, she was her own boss and the sense of inadequacy acted as a spur—too often she had felt contemptuous of the work to which her hard fate, as she thought, compelled her. She organised her department on lines imitated from the great Hudley firm, and though occasionally her lazy inaccuracy caught her out, on the whole she had done good things for her Directors' sales, and they acknowledged it.

But all this depended upon her being left alone by her foster-parents, she thought angrily, snatching up Mrs. Marrison's letter from the corner where she had thrown it; how could she possibly work, create, if they continually tormented her with these reminders of the past? It's no light task creating three hundred designs a year, she thought, quivering with self-pity, the tears hot in her lovely eyes; my mind *won't* work if they keep sending me these worrying letters. *Eda is to have another baby in January*; well, good luck to her but why worry me about it? *She is so happy that our thoughts turn tenderly to you and we wish our elder daughter too could settle down.* (Daughter!) *We are troubled about you, dear Bessie.* (Bessie!) *Your work sounds very interesting, but you yourself don't sound very happy. You seem to live a rackety kind of life, always rushing round. Forgive me, dear Bessie, I don't want to intrude into your affairs, but are you wise to go about so much with a married man? Where are you heading for, dear? I sometimes have a feeling that you will involve yourself in some dreadful experience.* . . .

O God, O God! *O God, O Montreal!* Why, why, why was

60

she saddled with such antediluvian relatives? Who were not, of course, real relatives at all. Marrison was not her name. She was anonymous. She began again to live through those agonising early passages. Her earliest recollection was of sitting on a table swinging her legs in a large room. . . . But look at the *time*! My God!

She pressed those painful memories down into the recesses of her mind and closed the lid; then hurried into her clothes. It was the black suit she chose, of course, with rather heavier make-up than usual to conceal the traces of her tears. She twisted her black hair into its massive glossy knot, put on her silver earrings, snatched her bag and drew her cyclamen suede glove carefully through her fetish bracelet. Examining herself in the long mirror before going out—she always did this before entering the world's stage—she noted with pleasure that she looked calm, sophisticated, assured and even, because of her recent emotion, a little more animated and therefore attractive than was her wont.

3

Unluckily, just as she was about to enter the mill the Junior Director's car drove up to the door. She scorned to hurry to escape notice, and instead halted and turned towards him with her friendliest smile.

"Good morning," she drawled.

"Good morning, Miss Marrison. We're both a little late this morning."

"Yes. These beautiful clouds this morning," improvised Elizabeth, making an artistic shaping movement with her hands: "The two shades of grey against the cool blue, you know—they've given me an idea. I'm toying with the thought of a set of jumpers founded on the weather. A series is always rather popular." The implication, that she had set out in good time but delayed along the road to design from clouds, was skilful, and she decided not to over-emphasise by stating it. Amusingly enough, too, she reflected, it really was rather a good idea. Ah, she could always extricate herself; she was clever, she was quick-witted. The Junior Director seemed to think so, and was about to utter a cautious approval when Elizabeth forestalled him. "Of course the notion's the merest embryo as yet and I won't ask you to pronounce on it. So unfair to exact opinions on an unfledged scheme."

The Junior Director's approval deepened and his smile was friendly as he turned aside into his office; her unpunctuality, she felt sure, was condoned.

Elizabeth went upstairs in good spirits, pushed the heap of correspondence to one side of her desk and without pausing to take off her coat made a mass of rapid notes on the "Weather" idea. Her secretary was hovering about reproachfully with another heap of letters in her hand.

"Do sit down," said Elizabeth impatiently. "I can't work with you fluttering in the foreground."

"These are yesterday's letters, Miss Marrison."

"Well, I can't do them yet. The Junior Director's just approved a new idea."

The girl sat down respectfully and busied herself with fixing a tension square. Elizabeth having put down all the colour notes which occurred to her, rapidly sketched out a basic design for the new series. I'll do it first in black and white for *Rain*, she thought, and she drew out an elegant twinset: black jumper with graduated white horizontal stripes, plain black cardigan with white edge-band and cuffs. It amused her to reflect that if she hadn't received Mrs. Marrison's letter, if she hadn't worn her black suit, she would probably have designed it as a "sea" jumper, cheerful blue with wavy white bands for foam. But the black was better for winter, after all. Now she must put it on squared paper, calculate the stitches, dictate the instructions. But that was a boring job. She raised her head. Yes, it was time for a visit to the knitting-room. She rose with alacrity.

"Won't you do your letters now, Miss Marrison?"

"Don't bother me so about the letters, child. I'll do them when I've been to the knitting-room."

The secretary sighed, and Elizabeth felt a twinge of conscience. She knew she was apt to concentrate on the interesting parts of her work and leave the rest. But there was some excuse for this, after all, she told herself, since plenty of people could answer letters and dictate knitting instructions, but the designs could be invented only by Elizabeth. Still—she'd better do the letters after the knitting-room.

The knitting-room, where garments were knitted from the instructions, both to check these and to serve as models to be photographed for the leaflets, was a pleasant, bright, airy place and Elizabeth was always happy when she entered it. Partly it fed her sense of power to see the half-dozen women, each at her own well-arranged desk, knitting away with silent concentration from Elizabeth's instructions. Partly she took an honest pride in the charming garments which resulted. But partly, too, she liked the knitting-room because it contained one of Elizabeth's good deeds, an action of which she could be altogether proud.

She went over to this good deed now. It consisted in the presence of Leni Bruenner, a middle-European "displaced person." True, it was the Junior Director who had brought Leni to the mill in a menial capacity, but it was Elizabeth who had taken an interest in the girl, Anglicised her clothes, enquired into her knitting talent, trained her to knit in the style of the house and finally landed her in the knitting-room with a good solid salary. Poor Leni's dark rough hair and broad freckled face and foreign ways had not endeared her to the knitting-room at first, but now they all knew her warm heart and eager kindness, they all loved her. She had one of those terrible mid-European Jewish histories which made Elizabeth turn sick and cold and savage: the brother who was taken away by the Nazis and returned in a coffin which must not be opened; the father who was taken away and returned broken and beaten; the escape and wanderings of the seventeen-year-old Leni, cold, ragged, lonely, hungry; the parents who simply vanished and were no more heard of—presumably they had vanished into a gas chamber. (Where had Elizabeth's parents vanished, she wondered.) It was all quite commonplace, nothing unusual about it, many others had similar stories, but Elizabeth simply could not bear it when she looked at Leni. For Leni had the eyes of a persecuted race: great dark emotional eyes, imploring, liquid, terrified, the eyes of a hunted creature. These eyes gazed up now adoringly at Elizabeth; her adoration for Elizabeth was really most comforting and warming.

"Well, Leni, and how are things going today?"

"They go very well, thanks to you, Miss Marrison."

"Now, Leni, none of that."

"It is all due to you that I am here, Miss Marrison," said Leni, who certainly seemed particularly happy this morning.

"Well, don't let's make a song and dance about it. I see you're knitting the new ice-blue." She bent anxiously over Leni's knitting; the design was a complicated one, incorporating an openwork stem and flowers. "This is a difficult pattern, Leni."

"It is a beautiful pattern."

"Yes, but difficult. You must be careful."

"I am very careful, Miss Marrison," beamed Leni.

"You're all right so far," said Elizabeth with relief, raising her head. "It's coming out well, isn't it?" she said to the supervisor of the room, who approached and looked over her shoulder.

The supervisor agreed that the pattern was coming out well, and asked for Elizabeth's instructions about the buttons for a cardigan of an unusual (though elegant) shade of salmon. They conferred over the button cards for some minutes, and Elizabeth selected an opalescent button which suited the cardigan admirably. Then she went round to each knitter and checked their work, added an illuminating phrase to one of the instruction papers and looked at the making-up table. She sighed with relief; everything was going well, there were no errors. She knew in her heart that her instructions were apt to be a little sketchy, a little careless, and sometimes there occurred in this room a whole series of mistakes, of misunderstandings, which were more her fault than the knitters'. As she reached the door she turned for a last look at Leni, and met those richly emotional eyes, raised to hers in a look warmly loving. She smiled; she felt good and determined to clear off her arrears of correspondence.

Dealing with all the easy letters first, after an hour she found the pile of those laid aside on account of their difficulty mounting formidably. She ruffled them through; several were complaints that a certain line of wool had shrunk excessively in washing. In the great Hudley firm such complaints had been a matter for the research department, but here, though the Junior Director toyed sometimes with a little old-fashioned testing equipment, there was no real laboratory. She snatched up the house telephone and put the problem to the Junior Director.

"Surely that's a job for Landsberger?" he said impatiently.

"Who?"

"Moorhills. He's in charge of all that now."

"Oh, of course!" cried Elizabeth, completely bewildered. "How stupid of me! So sorry to have bothered you."

She rang off and demanded crossly of her secretary what all this was about a bundle of consonants being put in charge of something or other. It seemed that a Dr. Felix Landsberger, *anglice* Moorhills, had been engaged to work up a research laboratory. Born in Vienna, son of cotton cloth manufacturer, industrial chemist, left everything behind in 1938, enlisted in British Army in 1939, naturalised under name of Moorhills but people mostly called him Dr. Felix—the girl reeled off the details.

"Why didn't anyone tell me?" said Elizabeth crossly.

"There was a memorandum sent round, Miss Marrison. I put it on your desk."

That girl doesn't like me, thought Elizabeth, and she remarked with icy sweetness: "That was very helpful of you."

"You were supposed to go to tea to meet him," stabbed the girl.

What a fool the J.D. must think me, thought Elizabeth angrily.

"I'll go and meet him now," she drawled, forcing herself to sound easy and good-tempered. "You can get on with the letters I've already dictated."

She went down into the mill. She always disliked this;

she hated machinery which she could not understand, and rough working men who cared nothing for her and girls who stared at her from behind their bobbins with critical eyes; it irked her pride to be connected with such people. The great metal drums of colour might have seemed rather romantic if they had not been housed in a room commonly called "the stuff house," guarded by a man masked and clad in rubber, and if they had not given rise to such horrid pools of coloured water in the dyehouse next door—anything sordid or dirty she shrank from like a cat. She picked her way now fastidiously among the dyehouse pools and found the new chemist housed in a cubby-hole at the far end. His father had a cotton mill, he can't know anything much about wool, she reflected, picking a handy weapon with which to wound.

In a very new white coat Dr. Landsberger sat at a table below a window, examining a slide. His profile was towards her; he appeared good-looking in a sallow beaky way, with an abundant thatch of long smooth dark hair.

"Dr. Felix Landsberger?"

He turned. A cicatrice, white and puckered, ran from ear to jaw on the left side of his face. His eyes were like Leni's, large, dark, tragic, the eyes of a persecuted race; except that where Leni's eyes were terrified, his were contemptuous and defiant.

"Yes?"

His tone was as cool and hostile as Elizabeth's. Stimulated to combat, she advanced.

"I'm Elizabeth Marrison, the designer here. I thought we should become acquainted."

"I am already here three weeks."

"You won't believe me, but I didn't know until this morning." His face did not change. So that's not enough, decided Elizabeth; I must grovel lower. "I've been a fool over the whole affair," she drawled, looking into his eyes and smiling: "I must ask you to accept my apologies."

Now his face softened; he smiled and rose. At once Elizabeth felt the first delicious onset of the thrill of sex, for he was tall. She liked tall men. (Bernard alas was short.) Her body

66

warmed and flowered. Dr. Landsberger clicked his heels and bowed.

"Felix Landsberger. We forgive each other now, yes?"

"*I*'ve nothing to forgive," Elizabeth smiled up at him, widening her violet eyes.

"So. You do not resent my coming, my intrusion so to say upon your department?"

"Not in the least. I'm only too delighted to have someone to whom I can refer all these tiresome complaints." She rustled the papers in her hand.

"Let us look at them together."

"These are all about the same thing," said Elizabeth, mentioning the name and number of the wool concerned. "Apparently it felts when washed."

"Felts? What is that, felts?"

The words: "Ah, cotton doesn't felt, I suppose," rose towards Elizabeth's lips, but she decided not to speak them. "Shrinks and thickens," she said, pronouncing these technical terms with exaggerated care.

"Ah, now I understand. These English ladies, they use the wrong kind of soap."

"You use what you can get, nowadays."

"Still, there are soaps and methods. You should instruct them."

"Yes. A leaflet, perhaps."

"Or a sentence at the foot of each of your pattern leaflets."

"Oh, you've seen my leaflets?"

"Of course. The colours are delightful."

Elizabeth, who was no fool, as she often told herself, caught in his tone the hint of a disparagement of her technical capacity.

"I'm not such an expert on wool as you are, Dr. Landsberger," she said with her air of frankness. "I shall be *delighted* to have your knowledge to support my deficiencies. Meanwhile, could you just glance through these and pencil a word or two to guide my answers?"

"With pleasure. I will bring them up when they are done?"

"Oh, why not let us meet in the canteen at lunch-time?"

Landsberger hesitated. "Well, I have already half promised a meeting there," he began.

Fixed himself up with another woman already, thought Elizabeth with brutal candour. Well, he can unfix himself.

"A drink then? At the Packhorse across the way? Half past twelve?"

"Admirable," said Landsberger, bowing. (His hair was wonderfully thick and smooth.) "I shall be there. Shall? Will? Which?"

"Either so long as you're punctual," smiled Elizabeth.

As she crossed the dyeing shed, picking her way this time in a humorous and lively style, she saw the Junior Director gazing into a tank from which hissing scarlet snakes of yarn were just emerging. He gave her a perfunctory scowl.

"Just been in conference with Mr. Moorhills," Elizabeth shouted to him across the pools. "A real acquisition, isn't he?"

The J.D.'s brow lightened and he nodded.

Well, I've stopped *that* hole up, decided Elizabeth with sardonic satisfaction. What it is to have a Director who once holidayed in the Tyrol! Good thing I got on to Landsberger this morning.

She made another inspection of the knitting-room, dictated a couple more letters, and drew out the graph of the twinset car ligan—sexual excitement always stimulated her work, she reminded herself with frank amusement. She kept Landsberger waiting, she calculated, just the right number of minutes to put him on his toes, and was rewarded by his eager hurry towards her as she sailed into the bar of the old Packhorse. It was quite a low pub really and its counter was quite as sordidly stained with pools as the mill dyehouse, indeed if the Packhorse had been compulsory Elizabeth frankly admitted she would despise and detest and hate to enter it; but as it was looked at somewhat askance by the white-collar mill employees, with her customary perversity she delighted to frequent it. She explained all this to her new acquaintance now, as they leaned against the crowded bar, using her eyes and long dark eyelashes with an effect which Landsberger evidently thought charming.

"But will you not defeat your own ends?" said he, smiling down at her. "Will you not make this pub fashionable by your visits?"

"How right you are!" said Elizabeth, laughing to conceal her pleasure in the implied compliment. "I see you know *all* the answers."

"Not all, or even most, but some."

"Many."

"Very well: many."

"Well, here's our dope—it isn't strong enough to be called poison. What shall we drink to?"

"Our future friendship?"

"If you like," said Elizabeth, looking at him over the top of her glass.

"You know, I am very glad that we have become friendly like this."

"Are you, Felix? That's your name, I believe?"

"Yes indeed. I am honoured by your use of it."

"Oh, I always use people's first names. Free and easy, that's me. Unless I don't like them, of course."

"I hope you will continue to call me Felix."

"Neatly put."

"There is a table free just behind you. Shall we go?"

"Well, I suppose we must look at these complaint letters some time and a table is always useful. If we spread them out on the bar they might get stained with beer."

"That would never do."

"On second thoughts, I believe it's so weak nowadays it wouldn't leave a mark."

They edged their way through the milling crowd and sat down. Elizabeth gave a quick glance at her watch; it was already after one. Keep up the good work, she exhorted herself, and she entered with zest into Landsberger's comments on the letters.

"Well, that's splendid, I shall be able to choke them off nicely."

"Choke them?"

"With your help, I shall be able to show them that the defect they complain of is all their own fault."

69

"Forgive me if I say it is also a little because your design asks of the wool more than it reasonably can do."

"Oh, nonsense," said Elizabeth with a frown.

"Now you are angry with me again."

"No," said Elizabeth, turning and gazing deliberately into his eyes. "Definitely not."

Her tone was an invitation which her violet eyes strongly seconded; she meant it so and saw that he understood.

"I am very glad," said Landsberger warmly. He hesitated, then went on with less assurance than he had hitherto shown: "I am glad because, do you know—forgive me—previously I did you an injustice. I thought you held aloof from me because you disliked me."

"Why should you think that?" drawled Elizabeth, stubbing out her cigarette. It was a gesture she liked; it showed off her eyelashes, the curve of her cheek, her arm, her bracelet with the dangling charms.

"Well—because of—my race," said Landsberger.

Instantly the excitement of his presence died for Elizabeth. It was over, done, *fini*, extinct as the dodo; she'd had it. Not because he was a Jew—do me the credit to believe it isn't that, said Elizabeth to herself angrily, after all I knew that before when I was all het up about him. What was it then if not that? She asked herself the question with some honesty, and a revealing answer rose up in reply. It was because his reference to his race asked her sympathy, her pity. She couldn't bear men, she suddenly discovered, who asked her sympathy, her pity. (No doubt because she wanted all the pity in the world for herself.) She liked power in men; the power to stand alone, to disregard, to crush. The power to conquer. Felix Landsberger was now an agreeable colleague, kind, knowledgeable, reliable, useful, pleasant; but he had no longer the power to move her sexually.

"Yes, you did me an injustice," said Elizabeth shortly.

"We remain friends, then?"

"Of course. I hope we shall work in the closest co-operation."

"That will be my endeavour."

"You speak wonderful English," said Elizabeth. She sat back in her chair, and her tone similarly withdrew from intimacy.

"I have practised it much, in the Army."

"Yes, of course. I was saying to the J.D. that altogether you are a great acquisition."

"That was kind."

"By the way, do you prefer to be known as Landsberger or Moorhills?" said Elizabeth. She meant to wound, and probably succeeded, for a shadow passed over the Austrian's face.

"I am now naturalised and must accustom myself to my new name."

"Quite. Heavens, Felix, look at the time! I must get back to the canteen. The food is filthy here."

"I too," said Landsberger, glancing at his watch. He started uneasily. "Yes, indeed. I am very late."

"You must tell her I kept you," said Elizabeth, faintly sneering.

"You think that will soothe her? That I have been with you?"

"Why not?"

"Your eyes are the wrong colour, Miss Elizabeth Marrison."

"Neatly put. Well, I must be on my way."

She paid for her drinks and left the inn. After a struggle with the change from his note he hurried after her, and they crossed the road to the mill together. Oh this is a bore, this is a bore, this is one hell of a bore, fretted Elizabeth; I hope to God this woman (whoever she is) is still waiting for him and will take him off my hands. But the canteen was empty, except for the J.D. and some clients up at the far end. Landsberger looked round the stuffy deserted room with an air of quiet displeasure.

"She is gone," Elizabeth teased him.

"She? You assume much, Miss Marrison."

"Too much?"

"That I did not say."

"My name's Elizabeth in any case."

Landsberger bowed.

All this sparkling conversation over shepherd's pie, raged Elizabeth, hacking away with her fork at a parboiled potato till her bracelet jingled. How sordid this is, how tedious, what a hell of a bore; if I could catch the J.D.'s eye it might be more interesting with those customers. She caught his eye but only as he rose to leave, and his response was disappointing; he looked rather as though he thought the heads of his research and designing departments were overdoing their personal co-operation.

"I wish you'd explain again about the action of an alkali," said Elizabeth hastily.

"If you really wish to hear, of course," replied Landsberger.

"I'm such a moron I can't take it in at one hearing," drawled Elizabeth.

She listened with a well-arranged air of serious attention to a barrage of technical terms she did not understand, as the J.D. passed down the aisle behind her chair. His party left the canteen, he closed the door behind them. Landsberger stopped his narration in mid-sentence. Elizabeth raised her eyebrows.

"That wasn't the end, surely?" she said.

"It was enough for your purpose," replied Landsberger.

His tone was dry; he had doubtless uncovered her stratagem. Here's another who's turned against me, reflected Elizabeth; I've put him off, I've lost him; he knows my technical inadequacy, I shall have trouble with him. Well, what the hell.

"I must get back to work," she said, rising with a business-like air.

"I too," said Landsberger. He bowed her out of the canteen formally.

Quick work, thought Elizabeth, gracefully lounging away to her room; pick a man up at eleven and drop him at two. She forced a smile in pretended enjoyment of her own cynicism, but in reality she felt sulky and disappointed. Landsberger had seemed so promising, so *new*. To be made love to by a foreigner would have been so interesting. Now there wasn't a single man worth looking at on her whole horizon. On an impulse she rang Bernard Clough's home number. He was in and his eager tone was soothing from one so rich, so well-established in society. Pity he wasn't taller. Still, he was practically the only man in sight. Her voice became so smooth and caressing that her secretary positively blushed and held down her head. Bernard proposed they should meet for dinner on the following night; why not drive to Harrogate and dine there for a change?

"At an expensive hostelry? Bernard, how extravagant you are!" cooed Elizabeth, pleased. "But why not tonight?" she added, cheerfully throwing overboard the A.T.P.C.

"You can't—you've a meeting tonight."

"So I have. Thanks for reminding me."

"Be kind to old Thos. He's had some shocks today."

"I'm always kind to him. I love him, he's a perfect poppet," said Elizabeth.

"Ha!" said Bernard.

"What does that mean? I'm quite sincere, I love and respect your uncle, Bernard."

"Well, if it comes to that, so do I. Tomorrow night, then. I'll bring your book of verse with me if I can think on," said Bernard, using this Yorkshire locution in jest. "I'll call for you at your flat at seven."

"Seven," agreed Elizabeth.

She spoke the word softly, deliberately investing it with the romance she wished Bernard to feel; and for a moment she was herself excited by the excitement she meant to rouse, so that her eyes blazed and her pulse raced. But when she had replaced the receiver her face fell at once into sullen angry lines. Damn and blast Bernard Clough and Felix Landsberger, not to mention the A.T.P.C. Nothing of interest remained on the day's programme; the afternoon stretched away interminably, full of boring tasks, the evening stretched away interminably, a desert too. You couldn't count the members of the A.T.P.C. as men. Or could you? Well, that perhaps remained to be seen. Comforted a little by this thought, Elizabeth yawned and drew towards her the sheet of foolscap on which she was drafting instructions for the twinset. *Row 98*, she read; *knit . . . increase . . .* O God, O Montreal!

5

About three o'clock she broke off thankfully and went down the corridor for her afternoon's visit to the knitting-room.

As soon as she opened the door she felt that something

was wrong. Instead of the cheerful upward glance of the knitters and makers-up, who like herself welcomed a break in the monotony of the day's work, she saw rows of bent heads; all the women kept their eyes directed unswervingly on their needles. Such concentration was unnatural, and Elizabeth glanced keenly round to see if she could discern the cause—some quarrel perhaps, or rebuke from the supervisor—for she must immediately decide whether to take notice of the general gloom or no. The heads remained stubbornly bent and Elizabeth at a loss was moving towards the nearest knitter for her routine inspection when her eye was caught by a large black handbag standing on a neighbouring desk. There was a strict rule in the knitting-room that no impedimenta, personal or otherwise, should stand on the desks to bring a risk of dust or entanglement to the wool, and Elizabeth strode towards the offending bag and picked it up impatiently before she realised that the desk was Leni's.

"What are you hiding behind this for, Leni?" she said, hastily modulating her sharp rebuke into playful reproach. "You know you have a big drawer in your desk specially to keep your bag in."

"I wished to hide behind it, Miss Marrison," said Leni without looking up, in a lugubrious tone.

"Why? You need all the light you can get for that difficult pattern."

"I wished to hide."

"Let me look at your work," said Elizabeth, uncomfortably conscious that all the knitters were listening intently to the conversation.

She took the pale blue knitting from Leni's slack hands and opened it out flat on the desk. At once she exclaimed, aghast, for a leaf had suddenly appeared in the front of the garment, unattached to the rest of the pattern, ugly and meaningless.

"Good heavens, Leni! This is all wrong. This leaf shouldn't come here."

As she spoke Elizabeth felt sharply uneasy. Was the mistake really Leni's or was it her own? It would not be the first time since she came to Ashworth that her carelessness in drafting instructions had caused a disaster in the knitting-room. Her cheeks burned as she bent lower over the desk, and compared the rows in script and knitting. Perhaps the supervisor had already discovered the error? Perhaps the women had already commented on it? Perhaps they were waiting for her publicly to admit her inaccuracy so that they might gloat over her discomfiture? Her hands shook and she had difficulty in tracing the row where the blunder began; she heard herself uttering foolish inefficient little exclamations; she heard also the complete silence of Leni and the rest of the knitters.

The supervisor, a very sweet and kindly woman, now brought her a chair. Recovering some of her composure Elizabeth drew it up in a business-like way, sat down and began to check the knitting carefully. She received no help from Leni, who simply sat beside her with hunched shoulders and head turned away, silent and motionless. The hush in the room persisted.

"But it's here!" exclaimed Elizabeth with intense relief, laying her finger at last on the beginning of the error. "You haven't followed the instructions, Leni; you've mistaken the row, or something. You've repeated the end of the row in the middle. No, I don't know what you've done; you've just put a leaf in without rhyme or reason. The instructions are right; it's you who have gone wrong. What on earth were you thinking about? A good hour's work all wasted! It will all have to come out, my dear, as quickly as possible. Really, Leni, I don't know *what* you were thinking of!"

She was so eager to exonerate herself from blame that she repeated the gist of these remarks once or twice in rising tones before she realised what she was doing, and on her third "Really, Leni!" the girl burst into violent tears. She laid her rough black head on her arms on the desk and sobbed convulsively. Immediately Elizabeth was poignantly sorry for her.

"Never mind, my dear," she said, laying her hand kindly on the girl's jerking shoulder. "We all make mistakes sometimes. It *is* a very difficult pattern. Next time you must try something easier."

But Leni continued to sob in a loud unrestrained fashion which was quite alarming. She sounded really heartbroken. Elizabeth began to feel impatient.

"Now come, Leni," she said. "Pull yourself together. The world hasn't come to an end because you've made a mistake in knitting, you know."

"It is not that which trouble me, Miss Marrison," wailed Leni, half raising her face, which was tear-stained and contorted with what Elizabeth felt to be excessive agony.

"What is it them?"

"Something which cannot be helped. No, it cannot be helped, it is natural, it cannot be avoided."

"Has someone been unkind to you?"

"No, no!"

"Will you come along to my office with me and tell me what it is?"

"No! No!"

"Then you must pull yourself together and go on with your work, Leni."

"I cannot."

"Please stop making this scene, Leni," said Elizabeth sharply. "You're upsetting the whole room. If you can't accept the consequences of making a mistake better than this, you'll have to return to the packing room."

"I do not care."

"Now, Leni," urged Elizabeth, moved by the girl's desperation, in which she recognised something akin to her own nature: "Stop crying, my dear, and come along with me and have a cup of tea in my room." She pulled the girl back from the desk and tried to force her to rise. But Leni buried her face in her hands again and wept with passion. The eyes of all the women in the room were now fixed upon her.

"Very well!" cried Elizabeth, suddenly losing her patience and her temper: "If you can't behave yourself, you'd better go home!"

Leni sprang up, snatched her handbag and still in a storm of weeping fled from the room.

"Well!" said Elizabeth with an amused sigh, looking round. "Really! These Continentals!" She was playing for sympathy

76

and knew it, but she had no success; the women's eyes were once more all directed strictly upon their knitting. "Oh, dear, I *am* sorry!" she continued, forcing the note, like a comedian reformulating a joke which has failed to move the audience on its first impact, "Poor Leni! We must all be very kind to her tomorrow."

Still there was no response. I can't possibly go round and look at all their work, thought Elizabeth in a panic; what did I say, I must have been awful for them all to be so hard on me? A sudden notion brought her relief. "I'll put this right myself," she said in a warm kind tone, picking up poor Leni's ice-blue jumper. "Then she'll feel more cheerful tomorrow morning."

She glanced round again with a smile. But there was no response; nobody spoke, nobody smiled, nobody—not even the supervisor—looked at her. She collected the instructions and the knitting carefully and went out of the room without another word, holding her head high and walking rather slowly.

Well this has been a hell of a day, she thought; Mother's letter and the disappointment over Felix and Bernard so backward and not another man on the horizon, and now I've landed myself with this hateful knitting. She sighed impatiently. Just to make everything jollier, too, it now began to rain.

6

Accordingly it was a real pleasure when, after a sudden ring which caused her to drop a stitch and swear, her secretary announced that Sir Charles Considine was on the 'phone.

"Good afternoon, Sir Charles," drawled Elizabeth sweetly.

"I hope I'm not interrupting you at an awkward moment."

"On the contrary I'm *delighted* to be interrupted. I'm engaged in some most *tedious* work."

"I just wanted to have a word with you about this business of the field for the A.T.P."

"Yes?" cooed Elizabeth.

"Just a confidential word."

"Of course."

"I think we shall get off on the wrong foot, you know, if we accept Lord Intake's offer."

"Do you?" Elizabeth was amused by her own disappointment. Had she really been ingenuous enough to hope that the loan of a field might lead to her meeting an unmarried earl?

"Yes. There are many reasons why I think it unwise. We should alienate the Trade Unions for a start."

"Really? That plump speech-making man, Councillor something-or-other, didn't seem to think so."

"Ah but he isn't their delegate. I've been given to understand privately that it would be resented."

"If you say so at the meeting it would carry a great deal of weight, I'm sure."

"I'm not at liberty to reveal the source of my information, unfortunately."

"Oh, *dear*. That makes it awkward."

"So I just thought I would have a little chat with you and clarify the matter before the meeting. We shall be voting on it tonight, I expect."

"You needn't dot *all* your i's, my lad," thought Elizabeth: "I understand perfectly that you're soliciting my vote." The word *solicit*, with all its connotations, pleased her. Aloud she said: "Most kind and helpful, Sir Charles."

"Well, till tonight, Miss Marrison."

"Till tonight, Sir Charles."

"I do *love* a little intrigue, don't you," said Elizabeth sardonically as she put down the receiver. "I wonder why he *really* wants us to turn down Lord Intake's field."

Her secretary, shocked, suggested that possibly Sir Charles meant exactly what he said.

"Come, come, my dear!" Elizabeth exhorted her. "Do try to be your age!"

The dialogue had invigorated her, and she returned to Leni's knitting with renewed zest.

7

Oddly enough, this knitting of Leni's made Elizabeth early for the A.T.P.C. For her pride's sake the work must be done perfectly and must be completed before the morning, and since the pattern was genuinely difficult and she hadn't done much actual knitting lately, to complete it to perfection kept her so late at the office that she hadn't time to go home and get herself a meal. So she dropped into the Packhorse for a couple of drinks and a sandwich, instead. She half hoped that Landsberger might be there, for his rudeness in the canteen had been rather stimulating and it might be amusing to stage a reconciliation, but her luck was out and he wasn't, so she didn't stay long but strolled off pretty rapidly towards the Mechanics' Institute. It was a dreary building dating from antediluvian Victorian times, with lots of smoke-blackened gables and ugly deepset windows, quite revolting to Elizabeth's taste; it stood for all those stuffy, restrictive and boring aspects of life which she particularly loathed. To sit in such a hole and listen to a tedious committee meeting— what a way to spend a September evening! Not that the evening was particularly pleasant; though fine again after the shower it was cold and dull—Elizabeth was glad to be wearing her black suit. With an irritable sigh she lounged gracefully up the steps and turned towards the dingy little committee-room. It was open and lighted; that was one thing to be thankful for.

Roddie Bairstow was there alone, sitting at the long baize-covered table with a mass of papers around him. He started and looked up as she came in. His look was somehow rather odd, reflected Elizabeth; as though he were expecting somebody else and was both glad and sorry when not they but she had entered. Pity he was so much in love with his wife still, for he was really quite attractive. Masculine. A soldier.

"Evening, Roddie."

"Good evening, Miss Marrison."

"Why this formality?"

"Sorry. Elizabeth."

"How goes the day in your part of the battlefield?"

"Pretty foul, on the whole. I'm struggling with these ghastly Minutes," said Roddie, rearranging a few of the papers.

"*Poor* Roddie. May I look?"

"Of course."

Elizabeth lounged round to the far side of the table, rested a hand on the Secretary's shoulder and bent over the Minutes. As she did so she felt in her hand the sudden leap of the blood, the first slight but unmistakeable response of sex. She smiled and began to feel warm and happy.

"Of course all these resolutions and amendments and points of order and what not mean nothing to me," she murmured, stooping lower so that her hair brushed Roddie's ear. "Nothing," she repeated. She slightly shook her head in emphasis so that her earrings swung against his cheek.

"Nonsense. You've a clear head and you understand them perfectly."

"You flatter me, Mr. Bairstow," said Elizabeth, turning her head and rolling her violet eyes at him in comical exaggeration. Their lips were very near; she pouted hers slightly.

"It would be difficult to flatter you."

"How so?"

"To flatter one would have to paint the lily."

"Now is that meant to be complimentary or otherwise?"

"Take it as you choose. Good evening, sir," said Roddie, rising to greet old Thomas Armitage.

"Good evening, my boy. Ah! Miss Marrison," said Thomas, bowing politely.

His shrewd old eyes roved over her face, as he took the chair at the head of the table, and Elizabeth's cheek burned a little as she withdrew from Roddie. They had been very close together when he entered; old Thos might easily have imagined they'd been kissing. Well, if he did, he would never tell Bernard, and if he did tell Bernard and put him off she couldn't care less, so why worry? All the same she decided she would not sit next to Bairstow, it might appear a trifle marked. She slid round to the other side of the table and sat down in the middle seat so that she would have two neighbours, and waited hopefully.

It was always interesting to observe who sat next to whom, thought Elizabeth, even in a gathering as respectably boring as this one. Sir Charles Considine came in and without pausing went immediately to the chair next but one from Roddie, but Elizabeth saw that he had considered the matter really quite carefully, and wondered what made him decide not to sit next to the Secretary. That unpleasant belligerent Greenwood man with the bristling red hair planted himself defiantly in the chair at the foot of the table. It was clear to Elizabeth that Sir Charles hated him like hell and disliked his proximity and that the feeling was mutual, but they began a polite conversation about the weather, Considine very smooth and urbane, Greenwood firing off each brusque reply like a machine-gun bullet directed against the enemies of Soviet Russia. With her back to the door Elizabeth did not see the next entrants, till the Chairman spoke in greeting and she turned to examine the new member whom Councillor Foster Ormerod led into the room.

"The Youth Groups Representative? Miss Heald? Won't you sit here by me?"

This put plump old Foster where he certainly didn't want to be, next to Greenwood, reflected Elizabeth with gleeful malice, for nobody detested a Communist more than an old-fashioned Trade Unionist Labour man. But oh God, oh God, thought Elizabeth with a sudden deep pang of envy, how *young* this Heald child is! That wild rose complexion! That short upper lip and delicately tilted nose! Those beautiful clear grey eyes! Those thick fair springing curls! That's the sort of girl one ought to be! Innocent. Young. All life before her. Nothing gone wrong. I was like that once. No, I never was; things had gone wrong for me long before I was her age. That child hasn't a history like mine.

The clock struck seven; the meeting began and Roddie droned on through the Minutes; that fat old frau Mrs. Deborah Sykes came in, late like last week, and stumbled round to the vacant chair between Bairstow and Considine, wearing a blue suit so bright it made Elizabeth positively *blink*, my dear. Oh these people who wear clothes to match their eyes! Ingenuous creatures! If they only realised how they looked! At least I'm beautiful, reflected Elizabeth, I'm beautiful and I know how to choose and wear beautiful clothes. Not that it seems to do me much good in this company. Even Roddie Bairstow hasn't an eye for me. But then, he's in love with his wife. . . . Damn her! Damn all good virtuous comfortable wives—and damn their husbands too. . . .

III

CAPTAIN RODERICK BAIRSTOW, D.S.O.

I

"WE ARE—THE Eighth—Ar-ma-da,
The gallant—Eighth—Ar-mee,"

hummed Roddie Bairstow as he pulled back the bolts on the heavy front door.

No need to keep quiet about the house this morning; the children had been awake for hours already; Val and Di had had a row—he and Kate could hear them through the wall so they must have been making quite a noise—and Val had cried, as usual. *What* they were going to do with that child really Roddie didn't know; he was delicate, difficult, jealous, tetchy—just like his grandfather, why not face it. Diana now, though a little devil too in her way, was lively and high-spirited; quite a beauty too, with her chestnut mop and Kate's large eyes. Val and Di were always rowing, and this morning their noise had woken Baby Rex and he'd set up a howl. To save Kate, who oughtn't to be prowling about barefoot in her condition, Roddie had got up and fetched the little blighter into bed between them. Somehow then all Roddie's troubles had fallen away from him. The kid was such a brick, really; very like Kate, with her fine grey eyes and roseleaf skin, but with his own fair hair and strong physique; good-tempered and full of fun, gurgling and chatting in his own way and climbing all over them and pulling Roddie's moustache and then all of a sudden softly kissing Kate's cheek.

"He knows a good thing when he sees it," said Roddie at this, laughing; "I'm proud to follow my son's example."

Kate smiled and hugged them both, and really moments like that made up for everything. Rex was their post-war child, and it just showed what a difference a good settled home of its own made to a kid.

The bolts shot back and Roddie turned the handle and at once the door blew violently open, almost knocking him down and setting everything in the house into a clatter. There was always a wind blowing at Upper Head Cottage, for it stood on a farm near the brow of one of the massive interlocking hills which rose on every side of Ashworth. In the desert Roddie had thought of a West Riding wind on a West Riding hillside as a kind of paradise which he loved with all his heart, but now—let's face it—he was sick and tired of the wind and hardly had time to look at the admittedly fine view of the Pennines. The wind continually broke things—hinges and window-panes and jugs; it battered down Roddie's peas and Kate's flowers; it turned rain and snow into a series of piercing horizontal arrows, it tore the children's clothes. Of course the continual breeze was healthy, he supposed. Kate liked it, but found the hill and the wind together hard work now she was heavy again with child. For himself, Roddie felt that life at Upper Head was altogether too like an overlong seaside holiday, from which he would be glad to return home.

He went round the back of the house now and lifted the plank away from the bob-hole of the henhouse. After some squawking and scuffling within a brown comb was poked out, a Rhode Island Red bowed its head and emerged, and soon all the dozen were stalking disdainfully about the hillside. The wind blew up their feathers with an effect of indecency which made Roddie grin; for he disliked hens—their feet, their eyes, their voices, indeed everything about them but their eggs, they seemed to him to have such a petty, timid, niggling disposition—and he was not sorry to see them at a disadvantage, ruffled by a natural force beyond their narrow comprehension. However, he went into the house again, unlocked the back door, measured their grain carefully from the sack in the porch and took pains to scatter it equitably among them.

"Silly bastards," he said good-humouredly, watching the resulting scramble.

There was a night egg in one of the boxes, a nice brown one such as the children loved. He speculated with a touch of ribaldry on the identity of the hen who had laid thus untimely as he carried it into the house and put it in the egg bowl in the pantry.

Kate was getting the children up now; there was a good deal of noise overhead, taps gushing, small feet jumping. Val was crying as usual. Roddie filled the kettle and put it on the gas. The kitchen felt cold for September; what about a fire, he wondered. He went out to the front of the house again to look at the weather. The south-west hills where the weather usually came from lay across on the other side of Ashworth; Roddie gazed at the tumbled mass and then up at the driving grey clouds; it may rain in the afternoon, he thought, and it's certainly chilly. He shouted up the stairs to Kate about a fire but she advised against it. "But fetch the milk, please, Roddie," she called. All the same they'll need the fire in the afternoon, thought Roddie; he cocked an eye at the wood-box, and seeing that it was nearly empty fetched in a good armful of logs from the pile outside. Then he picked up the two big jugs from the pantry and walked along the rough muddy track to the farmhouse. I really must get some paving-stones down here before the winter, he thought; it can't be good for the children to live perpetually in gumboots.

"Where can I get some paving-stones for the path?" he called to the farmer as they passed in the yard; without pausing in his steady gait old Shackleton replied with a jerk of the thumb: "Help yourself. Plenty up yonder by the old quarry."

Mrs. Shackleton junior had evidently heard their voices, for when he reached the open dairy door she was already there waiting for him with a can beside her on the floor. Now *she* lives with her father-in-law and yet they all look happy enough, thought Roddie. A shadow crossed his face and he whistled moodily as he leaned against the jamb and watched the milk froth into the jugs.

84

"Good thing milk isn't intoxicating seeing how much we drink at the cottage," he said, trying to be cheerful.

"You need plenty with that young family, Mr. Bairstow," said Mrs. Shackleton junior soothingly.

By the time he got back to the cottage Kate had the children all sitting round the table in the front room with their feeders on. As he came in they all looked at him expectantly from their clear childish eyes: Rex's merry and roguish, Diana's blazing with life, Val's dreamy, melancholy.

"We're all waiting for the milk, Daddy," said Val reprovingly. Val always had his knife into his father, reflected Roddie, and it was no wonder, after all. He'd had his mother to himself for three years at the beginning of his life and naturally resented the intrusion of a great khaki soldier into the family. The child was jealous of his mother's affections. Roddie, a jealous man himself, understood his son's feeling very well and even sympathised with it. But what one did about it, heaven only knew.

"Yes—I'm afraid I'm a bit late," he said mildly now.

"Milk! Milk!" cried Rex, beating cheerfully on the table with his spoon.

"Don't make so much noise, Rex," said Val in a superior tone.

"Leave him alone, you," shouted Di, slapping her elder brother.

Where was Kate, to allow all this back-chat? Roddie looked round.

"Kate! What are you doing there?" he cried sharply.

Kate looked up, astonished, from his brief-case which lay on the sideboard. "I want the ration-books," she said. "Don't you remember, you took them yesterday to get the chocolates?"

"Yes, of course. I'll find them," said Roddie. His tone, he thought, sounded pretty normal, but the haste with which he snatched the case from Kate's hand was a mistake, and he almost pulled out the solicitor's letter with the ration-books from sheer anxiety not to do so. Not that it meant anything, of course, he thought uneasily; still, he didn't want Kate to see it. "Here you are."

"It's the new period this week, you see—I ought to go down to the village and do some shopping today."

"Be sure you take the bus, then."

"Well—I'll see."

Kate brought in the tea and breakfast began.

It was a curious thing, reflected Roddie with sardonic amusement, that children always seemed to eat either too little or too much. Diana gobbled everything in sight unless firmly checked; Val had to be urged to take each drink, to eat each spoonful—often he lay back in his chair with a fretful look and a trembling lip which threatened tears, and when persuaded, exhorted, commanded, to resume his meal, picked up his bread and butter again with weary reluctance. Rex put as much food on his person and the tablecloth as into his mouth; he seemed a centre of whirling arms, flying spoons, tossing curls and feeders but smiled so merrily all over his milk-stained face that everybody loved him. Kate looked tired and pale this morning so Roddie exerted himself to spare her; he leaned across the table, cut bread, poured milk, rescued overturning cups, scolded, exhorted, praised.

What a life, he thought, remembering Kate as she was when they married: her fresh rosy face, her cloud of dusky hair, her lovely soft curves, her high though gentle spirit. Their courtship under the shadow of war was delicious; a man of strongly protective nature, robust, debonair and virile (altogether too virile, thought Roddie with a rueful grin, surveying his progeny), he intensely enjoyed that form of sex-activity which consists in the man's slightly hectoring, slightly teasing, the woman in order by later caresses to console and reassure. Kate with her large startled eyes, her dreamy air, her social status inferior to his own, had been the ideal subject for this kind of love-making. But now he dared not venture on it, for Kate no longer spiritedly retorted, no longer gleefully contradicted, his simulated scoldings; she took it seriously and was apt to weep. (She had wept last night.) When one thought of all he was doing for Kate, it was a little hard. That letter in his brief-case threatening him with County Court proceedings would never have been sent if it hadn't been for Kate. Come to think of it, none of his present situation would have existed if it hadn't been for Kate.

2

The letter from the solicitors was in respect of arrears in the mortgage repayments on his house, which he was buying through the Ashworth Building Society, and he had fallen behind with his payments because of the heavy expense of maintaining his father in an Ashworth nursing home, and he had to maintain his father in an Ashworth nursing home because he could not ask Kate to receive him in her home. He could not ask Kate to give a home to his father because—well, that required his whole life's story to explain.

Valentine Bairstow, Roddie's father, was a solicitor, surviving member of a small but very respectable family firm in Ashworth. A small, precise and able man, his digestion or his temperament or both inclined him to be peevish and irascible when crossed, and at such times his whole person seemed to fly into battle, even the black ribbon by which his old fashioned pince-nez were dragged askew on his large nose. It was all right so long as Mrs. Bairstow, large and placid, was alive, but she died of influenza while Roddie was in his teens. After that the father and son had mutual explosions from time to time, for Roddie was vehement and spirited and of better physique than his father. Still, nothing really serious occurred; they both had characters worthy of respect and accordingly they respected and were fond of each other.

The Bairstows lived in a solid semi-detached Victorian-built house with a greenhouse, spacious back yard and neat front garden in a quiet road off Worth Lane, one of the long streets sloping up out of Ashworth which throughout Roddie's life were gradually becoming industrialised. The house had been inherited by Mr. Bairstow from his father, and his childhood memories were outraged by the sudden appearance, when Roddie was five or so, of a small grocer's shop on the opposite side of the street. Mrs. Bairstow found the shop convenient and the man who kept it had served in the same regiment and caught the same whiff of gas as Mr. Bairstow in the first World War, so surface relations were good, but

Mr. Bairstow never quite forgave the shop for its intrusion into his ancestral domain. As for Roddie, the name above the shop, Osword, was the first group of letters he successfully read, so naturally a place associated with this early triumph seemed agreeable to him. Mr. and Mrs. Osword had a little girl about the same age as Roddie, a shy little thing with big eyes and a light slim body who skipped about and tossed her head in a delightfully graceful manner. Roddie and the children next door and Kate from the shop naturally played about together, and in the melting of class distinctions which resulted from the 1914–18 war, Mrs. Bairstow made no great effort to stop it, though Mr. Bairstow, grumbling about Roddie's accent and manners from time to time in the way natural to fathers of lively romping boys, sometimes attributed his son's defects in these (quite unfairly) to Kate. Then the children reached the bicycle age; Kate who was the apple of her thriving father's eye had a bicycle quite as soon as Roddie, whose father had less indulgence and more commitments. Then Roddie went away to Sedbergh, whence it certainly never occurred to him to write to Kate; nor did the child expect it. So far, so good in Mr. Bairstow's view. But then Mrs. Bairstow died, and Roddie, now a big schoolboy and presently a tall strong lad found it comforting to spend a few minutes leaning over Mrs. Osword's counter (Mr. Osword had meanwhile died of delayed gas effects) talking to that motherly woman and looking at Kate, who stood quietly in the background with her great eyes shining. Mr. Bairstow chancing to drop in for a box of matches on one of these occasions, gave his son a sharp shrewd talk that evening on the inadvisability, considering the facts of life with which Roddie was doubtless well acquainted, of a lad in Roddie's walk of life hanging round a girl in Kate's. To Roddie's eternal shame, as he still felt—his face burned at the mere remembrance—he had taken his father's word on the matter and kept on the opposite side of the street from Osword's, passing the shop with a hangdog sheepish air. He would be off to Oxford in the autumn to study law, and no doubt Mr. Bairstow relied on absence and new companions to wean his thoughts away from Kate.

But instead of Oxford there was the war. Roddie enlisted immediately, in September 1939. His father was furious, and made Roddie really quite a scene, screaming at him epithets like *idiot* and *dolt*. Roddie was astonished but not particularly troubled; people disagreed, it was only natural, one just had to go ahead on one's own line without worrying overmuch. Mr. Bairstow glancing at his son's determined face told him he was an obstinate, stubborn, ignorant young mule. Roddie considered this and decided that on the whole it was probably true; he knew his own mind and liked his own way and wasn't prepared to give in to any man without due reason. The moment his father stopped talking he left the room, took up his new khaki cap and went across the street to say goodbye to Mrs. Osword and Kate—he felt it was the decent thing to do. It struck him then that Kate with her soft dark hair, lissom figure and shining eyes was a fine good girl and he would always be fond of her.

The next few years he went through the experiences common to young Englishmen at that time. He was in this camp and that camp; trained here and there; wore a peaked cap and then a forage cap, a hideous short jerkin and then a battle-dress; applied for a commission and got it easily; longed to be in France, fighting the Germans, and wondered what on earth the delay and the "phoney" war were all about. He was on board a transport ready to sail for France and the anchor was just coming up when the orders were counter-manded; thus by a mere matter of hours he missed being involved in the retreat of 1940 and the epic of Dunkirk—he regretted this all his life very bitterly. Presently he found himself sent off via South Africa to the Middle East for the defence of Egypt. Rommel had recently advanced to El Alamein, within sixty miles of Alexandria, and the British line there was beginning to develop an ominous bulge. Everything was rather muddled and miserable, and 2nd Lieut. Bairstow was sent up to the front without any real training. He went out on recce patrol the first night, lost his party in the dark, innocently climbed over the enemy wire, stepped on an anti-personnel mine, escaped death by an entirely accidental forward sprawl, lay out for twenty-four hours before he was found and was sent back to Cairo as a casualty with a label round his neck.

In Cairo he fretted so actively at being out of the fight when every man was needed that he retarded his own recovery. The heat and the glare and the dust, the sweat and the flies and the smell, the position at El Alamein, the disillusioning behaviour of the Cairo inhabitants under the menace of defeat, above all the fear that he would miss this show as he had missed France, really got him down. He made a perfect nuisance of himself to the hospital authorities with his continual appeals to be sent to the front; they all liked Roddie—such a strong handsome wilful lad—and wanted to do their best for him, but a wound on his shoulder would not quite clear up.

It was at this moment that he met Kate, who in the most natural way in the world for that period of history, had become a nurse and headed firmly out for that portion of the globe where she surmised Roddie was fighting. He met her in the street and they fell into one another's arms. Kate's eyes filled with tears, Roddie's sparkled with excitement. Someone from the West Riding! Someone from Ashworth! Someone with a Yorkshire accent! Over drinks together they talked of Ashworth as if it were Paradise: the steep streets, the mill chimneys, the hills, the heather, the wind, the rough humorous character—they both enthusiastically agreed that these things made Yorkshire superior to every other part of England, indeed of the world.

"What a marvellous coincidence, our meeting here! What a glorious chance!" exclaimed Roddie strongly.

Kate said nothing but her eyes shone with happiness. She was a lovely creature now, thought Roddie; with a delicious figure which her nurse's uniform suited, a fresh soft clear skin, long dark eyelashes and those beautiful eyes.

Ten days after they met Roddie was ordered to rejoin his regiment, and they married immediately in a most unauthorised way. Roddie made all the arrangements with the combination of obstinacy and charm which was beginning to be his personality; Kate was frightened but equally determined. They drove to the church together.

"Roddie, I ought to tell you," began Kate in her soft slow tones when they were nearly there: "It wasn't altogether a coincidence we met here in Cairo." She turned to him with a little perplexed frown on her smooth wide forehead, a look gently beseeching forgiveness in her wide eyes.

"How do you mean?" said Roddie.

"I volunteered for Egypt because I thought you were here."

At this such a gush of protective tenderness filled Roddie's heart that he could hardly speak; in that moment he grew from a boy into a man. He put his arm round Kate and hugged her warmly.

"How strong you are!" murmured the innocent Kate.

"My darling," he said: "Thank you for telling me, I hope you will never regret it—coming out here, I mean. It'll be my job and my—happiness to see you don't."

"I shan't regret it, Roddie," murmured Kate.

The next day Roddie went off to El Alamein. Montgomery had just taken over from Auchinleck and was beginning to shape the Eighth physically and spiritually to his own taste. Roddie threw himself into the new training with enthusiastic determination; it was deeply satisfying to him that the Eighth's emergence from its chrysalis should coincide thus with his own new manhood. Presently it was October, and Monty's attack began; the night came at last after the day of suspense, the terrific bombardment changed its range according to plan, Roddie rose up from the rocky desert and walked calmly towards the enemy lines. ("I couldn't have done this before I married Kate," he reflected as streams of tracer bullets whined diagonally across the front of the company.)

For the next eighty days it seemed to Roddie that he was never out of action. The Germans broke and, Rommel or no Rommel, the British chased them all the length of Cyrenaica, while Americans and British landed at Casablanca rolled them up from the other side. Day after day Roddie and his men tore across the desert in red-hot lorries with boiling radiators, flattening themselves in the sand when hostile aircraft flew over them. Night after night he was woken from an hour's snatched sleep, teeth chattering from the desert cold, to recce, or take his men to fill in road craters so that the armour could get ahead. There was a halt while Rommel stood at El Agheila, but Roddie was busier than ever then, going out ten consecutive nights on patrol. In the middle of all this he had another affair with anti-personnel mines. One night during the advance when after long circuitous marchings round the folds of wadis the men were at last ordered to dig in, a series of scattered explosions told Roddie that they had anchored, so to speak, in the middle of a minefield. One of the men, a young fellow, was badly wounded, and a corporal was blown to bits. Furious, Roddie led the men out to safety without any of them getting another scratch—how he did it he hadn't the faintest idea—and then went back and got the wounded lad over his shoulder and carried him out too. He was pleased about that. (The lad was still alive, too. He was a bus conductor in Bradford; Roddie sometimes saw him.)

This sort of thing—digging, patrolling, marching, fighting, digging—went on for three months, so that by the time the Eighth reached Tripoli, Lieut. Bairstow was a dirty, bearded, tough, experienced, resourceful soldier, highly valued by his superior officers. When they reached the mountains outside Tunis he was actually borrowed to give advice on battle procedure to a brigade of a new division which had just come out. By the time there were no Germans left in Africa save prisoners, and Roddie landed in Italy, Captain Bairstow was quite a legend, on whom young officers gazed with awe in mess. But it was those gruelling desert days, when he was in action day and night, which really earned him his decoration, Roddie always thought, and not that little affair on the road to Rome for which he actually received it, though of course his neat outflanking idea there had certainly turned out well.

He fought a third of the way up the sunny, rainy, muddy, smiling Italian peninsula. Although the dark Italian beauties were highly attractive to a man as fair as Roddie, he remained throughout meticulously faithful to Kate—though once, as he freely admitted, it was touch and go; Monty had announced his departure to England that day and Roddie was feeling thoroughly browned off.

Then he was back in England training troops for D-Day. With cheerful obstinacy he extracted Kate and Baby Val from Egypt, and wrote to his father to suggest that they should make their home with him.

To his astonishment he received a letter which was entirely incomprehensible, in reply. *Dear Roderick*, it ran, *Because you have behaved disgracefully, that is no reason why I should countenance your conduct. Your father, Valentine Bairstow.* Roddie turned this epistle over and over in his fingers, quite bewildered. What on earth was it about? A D.S.O., a wife and a son were not usually regarded as disgraceful to a man. He did not like to show the letter to Kate for it might—would—wound her. Instead he went to a house in the neighbourhood whose owners had befriended him, and telephoned his father.

"Roddie here. I don't understand your letter, Father. Will you have Kate and Val to live with you, or not?"

"That woman shall never enter my house!"

"Don't speak of my wife like that, Father," said Roddie sternly.

"Your wife?"

"Of course she's my wife. Didn't you get my cable from Cairo, telling you?"

"Certainly not."

"Well, you've had plenty of letters since then which made it clear. She's my wife and we have a fine son, and we're coming to Ashworth on leave, on Saturday."

"You will not come to my house!" shouted Mr. Bairstow.

"Now, Father, don't be ridiculous."

"Do not attempt to enter my house, for I shall not receive you."

"I shall come to see you on Saturday evening."

"No!" screamed Mr. Bairstow, and slammed down the receiver.

"What on earth's got into him?" wondered Roddie uneasily. As he walked back to the rooms where he had planted Kate, he decided to tell her only that his announcement of their marriage had gone astray and his father was cutting up rough about it.

On Saturday, after one of those wretchedly uncomfortable wartime journeys—Roddie stood in the crowded corridor all the way, and Kate who was pregnant had to hold Val throughout in her arms—they at last arrived in Ashworth in the late afternoon. There were no taxis at the station and Roddie had to leave Kate sitting on her suitcase while he went out into the town to find transport, so by the time they reached Mrs. Osword's they were both tired, and Val as white as a sheet was screaming his head off. Mrs. Osword, always a neat brisk body with plaits of dark hair twisted agreeably round her head, looked much the same, only a little plumper and greyer, but Kate told Roddie, as she put Val to bed after their first meal since breakfast, that her mother had confided to her while they were preparing tea that Mr. Bairstow was thought by the neighbourhood to be not very well.

"The war has got on his nerves," said Kate.

The little frown of perplexity was on her forehead, and she looked anxiously at her husband.

"I'd better go by myself first, then," said Roddie thoughtfully.

"Wait till tomorrow, Roddie."

Roddie scowled. "I told him I'd call tonight," he said.

Accordingly, having washed and shaved and put on his best uniform with the ribbons, he crossed the road to his old home. It was not yet black-out time and there was a light in the front room, but though Roddie rang and rang nobody came to the door.

"He needn't think he can keep one of *us* out," thought Roddie, meaning by "us" the men of the Eighth.

He went round to the back of the house, observed an open window upstairs, swarmed up a fall-pipe, climbed in without much difficulty, and was soon confronting his father in the dining-room. Mr. Bairstow in an arm-chair with a newspaper on his knee which he was not reading looked small and old, and wore an expression of acute anxiety on his pinched and faded face, in which his eyes appeared unusually bright.

"Roddie!" he exclaimed, starting violently. "How did you get in?"

94

"I told you I would call, Father. I want to bring Kate across to see you."

Mr. Bairstow tightened his lips. "I won't have her in the house."

"But why, Father? She's my wife. We're deeply happy together and we have a dear little boy, your grandson. We named him Valentine after you."

"You'd no call to do that," said Mr. Bairstow, scowling. "It won't bring you anything."

"We did it because we wanted to do it," said Roddie hotly: "Not for anything we could get."

"Why did you marry her, Roddie? You might have done so much better for yourself."

"I love Kate. Nobody could be better for me than Kate."

"That's child's talk."

"Now come, Father," said Roddie in a firm but kind tone: "I'm not a child, you know. I'm a man. I'm a soldier and an officer and used to responsibility——"

"And a D.S.O."

"Very well—and a D.S.O.——"

"You look very well, Roddie," said old Mr. Bairstow wistfully.

"I *am* well, and happy, and doing useful work. But I may have to go abroad again soon to do some more fighting, and I want my wife and my child to be where they ought to be, with my father."

"I won't have her."

"You've been too much alone, Father. It'll be good for you to have Kate and little Val here."

"I won't have her," repeated the old man obstinately.

But his tone was weakening, and all might yet have gone well if at that moment Kate had not tapped urgently at the uncurtained window. Her face expressed such alarm that Roddie ran to her and threw up the window.

"What's wrong?"

"It's Val—I think he's in a convulsion."

"Right—I'll come," said Roddie, and turning quickly, almost knocked down his father who had come up behind him.

"I won't have her in!" screamed Mr. Bairstow, and with a violent gesture he pulled the heavy black-lined curtain across the window in Kate's face.

After a doctor had been found and the child's state eased—it was not a convulsion, said the doctor, but simply a dangerous breath-catching after violent crying; some highly strung children were subject to it—Roddie returned to his father's house. But it was all locked up and heavily curtained, no windows open anywhere, and nobody answered though he both rang and knocked.

He made several other attempts, by letter, telephone and personal visit, to break down the barrier between himself and his father. But they were all unsuccessful; nothing but screams of rage and violent abuse resulted. Accordingly he left Kate and the child at her mother's. When next he came to Ashworth, Mrs. Osword told him bluntly that the gossip of the neighbourhood alleged his father was becoming "mental." He asked the doctor to call; when at length that overworked man did so, Mr. Bairstow would not receive him. Diana was born and Roddie put the announcement in the local paper, but no response came from his father.

Then it was D-Day and Roddie was caught up in the swirl of great events, and the next time he heard anything of his father he was in Germany. A letter reached him from the doctor saying that Mr. Bairstow was really in need of sustained nursing and skilled attention; a nursing home would probably be the best solution. Roddie managed presently to get leave for urgent private affairs, and rushed home to Ashworth. His father, pale and shrivelled, lay in bed unconscious. Roddie arranged for him to go into a nursing home and went down to the office to attend to his father's professional affairs. He found that there were none; no clerk was now employed, and from the dust and confusion of the papers it appeared to be years since a client had been on the premises. There was no goodwill, no practice, left to sell; all that could be done was to transfer such old clients as remained to another firm in the same building, which undertook to tidy things up without charge, from mere good-nature and old friendship to his father. Presently the old man recovered sufficiently to return home and creep quietly about the house. All excitement was forbidden, and a suitable nurse-companion was after protracted search eventually found for him.

The war ended and Roddie came home, eager for a steady settled life with his wife and family. Should he take a Government grant and resume his studies for the law? Now that his father's firm no longer existed, there seemed no point in it. Besides, he was twenty-six, and sick to death of training and billets and courses. As he had entered the Army at nineteen he had no expertise in any craft or profession. One of the members of the law firm which had befriended him before suggested that he should become an insurance agent, and offered to recommend him to a large and reputable company which needed a local representative. Roddie grasped eagerly at the chance; his energy, his appearance, his medal ribbons recommended him and he easily got the job. His gratuity was all spent on the down payment for Upper Head Cottage and the furniture, but at least, he reflected comfortably as he sat by his own fireside with his wife and his three children, at least he didn't owe anyone anything. He didn't dislike his job, either; he felt sympathetic towards people's needs, believed in insurance and was a good hand at explanations.

All would have been well, probably, had it not been for his father, whose health progressively deteriorated. It was impossible for him to keep a housekeeper-companion long; such persons were, in these days when the factories cried continually for well-paid labour, so scarce and their work in such demand that they would not stay where there were any tiresome duties. Old Mr. Bairstow needed to be nursed; in view of the feeling between him and Kate, a nursing home remained, as the doctor said, the best solution. The old Bairstow home was broken up and its furniture sold; the house it seemed was merely rented, did not belong to his father as Roddie had imagined. The nursing home, though not the most lavish of its kind, proved definitely expensive. Most of Mr. Bairstow's savings appeared to have vanished during his son's absence at the war—like many others, heavy taxation had driven him to live off his capital. The remainder soon took the same road. With his father, his wife and his children to keep, and handicapped by a lively open nature encouraged through seven Army years to be generous and carefree, Roddie soon found himself harassed financially. Of course the obvious course was to take old Mr. Bairstow out of the nursing-home and bring him to live at Upper Head, but the thought of what Kate's presence would do to Mr. Bairstow, and Mr. Bairstow's to Kate, prevented Roddie—always somewhat quixotic—from attempting the arrangement. Because of this he did not like to speak of his father to Kate, and a kind of barrier had grown up between them on this subject, which continually extended itself.

For instance: because it sprang out of his expenses for his father, Kate did not know that for the last few months Roddie had omitted to keep up with the payments on the house to the Building Society. He had had a polite letter from the Society saying that his payments were in arrears and it would be appreciated if he could remedy the matter; then he had had a couple of decreasingly polite letters, then a letter saying that if payment were not forthcoming the matter would be put in the hands of their solicitor. Then the solicitors wrote giving him a fixed date by which to pay; then yesterday a letter had come stating that the time had expired and proceedings would now be taken. What exactly this meant Roddie did not know; he intended to call in and see the solicitors, or perhaps the Building Society manager, about it that morning. It was this letter, lying in his brief-case, which he had feared that Kate, looking for the ration books, might see.

Yes, it was all highly disagreeable, and it all sprang from his meeting, that glaring morning in Cairo, with Kate. Did he regret that meeting? Well, yes and no; on the one hand, he thought he loved Kate and his children with all his heart, but on the other, there had been times lately when he wished life had offered him a spicier dish. He heard the guns thundering at El Alamein. . . . Those were the days! Wiping Rex's mouth on his feeder, he relived the incident in the wadi minefield.

3

Accordingly it was no surprise to Roddie, when having untied Rex's feeder and set him down he rose from the table, that his reflection in the mirror above Kate's head showed him clad in K.D. shorts and shirt, for they seemed a natural and familiar garb; what startled him was Kate's reminder that he must hurry to change or he would miss his bus. He glanced down and sighed—of course; the war was over; he was a married man with a load of debt and a subordinate job in an insurance company; he only wore his African uniform to feed hens and cope with children, to save his office clothes. He took the stairs in three strides and rapidly converted himself into a civilian. Kate was in the little hall waiting for him when he came down, with Rex in her arms and the other children hovering round her.

"Shall you be late, Roddie?"

"I'm afraid I shall—it's that A.T.P. Committee, you know."

Kate's face fell. "Shall you come home for tea, between?"

"No. I think I'd better take the opportunity of going to see Father."

Kate stepped back a little. "Of course, Roddie," she said. She hesitated, then added: "Give him my love—if you think he'd like to have it."

"I will. Bye-bye, dear."

He kissed her warmly. This was the signal for Diana to hurl herself upon him with face uplifted; he kissed her too, gave some butterfly salutes to the sticky mouth of Rex, who chortled gleefully, then with an ache of compassion in his heart stooped to Val, who hung back clinging to his mother's hand, and quietly and in the most fatherly manner he could command, kissed his eldest son's thin, pale, reluctant little cheek. "Goodbye!"

He seized his mackintosh from the peg, and after a sharp struggle with the wind got himself out of the cottage and closed the door behind him.

4

So now at last he was on his way to his office. Æons seemed already to have passed since he left bed that morning; he remembered with grim amusement—if he were a weaker man it would be nostalgia, he reflected—the days in his boyhood when all he had to do before leaving for morning school was wash, dress, and eat a substantial breakfast prepared and served by his mother's excellent maids. However, he was off at last; he had passed the farm and nobody had run after him with an urgent message; he sighed with relief, put on his urbane man-of-the-world countenance, gripped his brief-case firmly and strode down the steep lane towards the bus stop as briskly as the old cobble-stones allowed. The wind as usual buffeted him heartily, but its force decreased as he descended the hill.

At a turn in the lane he caught sight of the figure of a man in a bowler hat waiting at the foot where it debouched on the larger road. Who could it be, he wondered idly, running over in his mind the neighbours who like himself were new-comers, imposed on the old Ashley village, who worked in the town. This one had a car, that one took the earlier bus to get his child to school; the figure did not resemble another who habitually travelled by Roddie's bus. Come to think of it the figure did not resemble any Ashley villager he knew at all. And what was he doing waiting there anyway? The bus stop was a couple of hundred yards further along the road. Vaguely uneasy, Roddie craned his neck to get a look at the man again above the rough black wall. He was gone. But he was not visible along the stretch of road on either side. Astonished, Roddie continued to stare, and was rewarded by the sight of a slight black bulge above the wall—the top of a bowler hat. He's crouching—why? Shelter from the wind? No, it's blowing full against the wall that side. Hiding from me? Two can play at that game, thought Roddie grimly, and with the skill and suppleness proper to an Eighth Army man, he bent double, edged softly along in the shadow of the wall and came to within a few feet of the junction without Bowler Hat's being in the least aware of his presence. The hat moved; Roddie slipped through a broken gate into a field with practised ease. Bowler Hat now walked across the opening glancing expectantly up the lane. A respectable elderly type with a heavy tread, thought Roddie, viewing him through a convenient chink in the mortarless wall; retired bobby, I should say; he looks surprised by my disappearance, and no wonder. Indeed Bowler Hat's solid undistinguished features wore an air of real concern, and as Roddie watched, he slipped his hand inside his coat and seemed to finger something uneasily.

Roddie found himself rushing up the field as fast as he could go, for Bowler Hat had betrayed his vocation by his gesture; it was a summons which nestled in his breast-pocket, a summons from the Building Society to serve on Roddie. He carried ruin for R. V. Bairstow as surely as if the document were a hand-grenade.

Roddie's reaction to the danger was swift and capable. Throwing his mackintosh over his shoulder, he ran at speed up the steep uneven slope, vaulted over a wall and ran on. The process-server, sighting him as he jumped, shouted and began to pound up the lane towards Upper Head.

"You won't catch one of Monty's men," thought Roddie, wishing all the same he was still clad in his Army shorts.

Running steadily, he veered away from the house and continued to climb, intending to top the brow and gain the road on the other side of the hill. Unfortunately Bowler Hat did not persist up the lane to Upper Head, but rejoined the road and trudged along towards Ashworth. Roddie cursed as he looked back and saw this new manoeuvre, for the two roads joined half a mile further on, and the process-server with but one side of the triangle to traverse might well reach the junction in time to intercept the man he was seeking. Again, it was one thing for Roddie Bairstow to career up the green hillside in which his own holding was situated, another for an employee of the Insurance Company to be seen rushing along a public road. If only he had licensed his car! However, the only thing to do at the moment was to put as much distance as possible between himself and Bowler Hat, just as if he were one of Rommel's men. Hot, but not too dishevelled or breathless, and wearing a grin because in spite of everything he had enjoyed the chase, Roddie dropped over into the Mount Hey road and began to walk briskly towards Ashworth.

But when he had mounted the next rise in the road he halted. There below him lay the junction of the roads, and there just beyond the junction, dismounting from the bus Roddie should have caught, was Bowler Hat. I've only made matters worse by bolting, thought Roddie in dismay; at least the end of Upper Head Lane was private; to be served with a summons on the main road in full view of the bus stop will be a public proceeding, the story will be all over Ashworth by dinner time! He would lose his job for a certainty. Kate, oh poor Kate. And the children. What a fool he'd been. If only he could get out of this fix, just this once, he'd put things straight and keep them straight somehow. Served with a summons at a bus stop! There were houses and gardens ahead; in Italy one would just have made a détour round the village by edging through the back gardens, but to be caught climbing back-garden walls in Ashworth was almost worse for one's reputation than being served with a summons at a bus stop. Ah, what a fool! If he could only put it off for a day! Shame and contrition burned all over him.

"Do you want a lift, Mr. Bairstow?"

Roddie turned and saw Sir Charles Considine, a member of the newly formed A.T.P.C., leaning across from behind the wheel of his glossy black coupé to open the door invitingly. His white and well-shaped hand, resting on the cord of the door, emerged from snowy linen and dark blue cuff; his dark hair, thin but very smooth and well cut, was greying in a distinguished manner at the temples; his heavy-lidded eyes behind the tortoiseshell spectacles had a quizzical air, his rather pale thick lips smiled urbanely. "Get in," he said. "I'm driving past your office."

Thus snatched from hell to heaven, Roddie found himself quite unnerved and stupid. He stammered, coloured, laughed foolishly and had quite a difficulty in inserting himself and his brief-case into the coupé. When in, he felt large, clumsy and uncouth sitting beside Considine, who was always so smooth, well dressed and dapper. His shoes, damp and muddy, made marks on the grey carpet which he suspected (perhaps unjustly) that Sir Charles viewed with disfavour. The handsome heavy door of the coupé swung away in the wind and Roddie had difficulty in retrieving it. When he brought it to closing point the lock remained obdurate and Roddie who had read that expensive cars should not have their doors banged was at a loss how to cope with the situation.

"Pull the cord *down*," said Considine with a hint of impatience. Roddie pulled strongly; the fat twisted curly cord broke away at one end from its fastening.

"Awfully sorry," muttered Roddie, blushing.

"It's of no consequence at all," said Sir Charles icily.

The powerful car purred away down the hill; in a mere second it would reach the man in the bowler.

"This is not your usual route I think, Mr. Bairstow?"

"Er—no. No, I don't take it usually."

The car drew level with Bowler Hat, and for one sickening moment a knot of traffic ahead delayed its passage. The process-server saw Roddie, snatched the paper from his breast pocket and stepped purposefully off the pavement. But a lorry on the outer side of the road swept by, and Sir Charles with a skilful twist of his wrist sent the coupé out into the vacant space left by the lorry. It was a risk and a trespass, but it succeeded; the car leaped forward, swept past the bus, a car, and a stationary lorry and regained its proper line in the traffic. Bowler Hat sank back into the past, and Roddie, taking out his cigarette pack, found that his hands were not quite steady.

"Do smoke," urged Sir Charles in his silky tones.

"Thank you," said Roddie, abashed.

"That man—that fellow on the pavement—he seemed to know you?"

"Oh?"

"Yes. I believe he was a process-server."

"Really?"

"Come now, Mr. Bairstow, you know he was. You saw his papers. Were they divorce papers?"

"No, no! Good heavens, no!" exclaimed Roddie, thrown off his guard by the suggestion that Kate would ever leave him.

"A summons, then?" Sir Charles sounded amused. "You

young ex-officers! What's the sum?" Roddie hesitated. "Now don't lie to me, my dear fellow."

Vexed and confused, Roddie mumbled: "Forty pounds."

"Well, well. What is the debt for?"

"I'm a few months behind with the mortgage repayments on my house."

"You're in insurance, aren't you?"

"Yes."

"Your company won't like you to be hauled up before the County Court."

"No."

"Still, if insurance is nationalised, you'll be out of a job anyhow."

"I must contrive to pay the debt immediately," said poor Roddie.

"How do you mean to get hold of the money?"

"I've no idea, Sir Charles," said Roddie in a proud angry tone.

"It's against my principles to lend money, but I might be able to put you in the way of getting hold of some."

"That would be most awfully kind of you!" exclaimed Roddie, turning to him with eager gratitude and hope. "I haven't really done anything wrong, you know."

"No. Just a little carelessness."

"Well, hardly that, really," said Roddie. He hesitated, but could not bring himself to disclose his father's unreason and his own weakness. Sir Charles seemed to wait, so he added: "Of course with a wife and family, it's not easy nowadays to save anything."

"How many children have you?"

"Three. Well, nearly four," said Roddie honestly.

"My dear Bairstow, in this world one has to pay for one's pleasures."

Roddie was silent; he did not like this gross and sneering reference to his marital relations.

"Don't family allowances and all that sort of thing help you?" went on Considine. "And the National Health Service?"

"Yes, of course. I shall be quite all right if I can once get this debt off my shoulders," said Roddie sturdily.

"Well, we'll have a little talk about it after the A.T.P. meeting tonight, shall we?"

"Yes. Thank you very much indeed, Sir Charles," said Roddie, his hope subsiding. His disappointment was no doubt audible in his tone, for Considine at once proceeded: "Meanwhile, if you'll take an older man's advice, I suggest you ring up the Building Society and tell them you'll pay tomorrow. And keep out of Ashworth. Let me put you down at the station—I expect you have clients outside the town whom you can visit."

"Yes. I must ring Mr. Armitage about the agenda," reflected Roddie.

"There are kiosks everywhere," said Considine with cold impatience. "Here we are. Got any money for the day's expenses?"

"Oh yes, yes, plenty, thank you!" cried Roddie hotly. It was not quite true; he had his Insurance expense funds of course, but was otherwise shortish. But though he would gladly have accepted a hundred pounds from Considine, his pride boggled at a loan of a few shillings. "I'm afraid I've brought you out of your way, Sir Charles," he said, forgetfully banging the precious door and bending down to put his head through the window. "I'm *most* grateful for the lift and the advice and everything." Why was it, he asked himself with vexation, that he, an experienced soldier, a husband and father (which he believed Considine was not), felt and talked like a silly schoolboy in his presence? "I'll look forward to seeing you tonight, then?"

"Yes. Yes, tonight, most probably," said Considine, nodding and smiling without looking at Roddie. The car turned quietly in an easy sweep and purred away.

Damn it all, why does he blow hot and cold like that, thought Roddie irritably. Cat and mouse. After all I never asked him to lend me money; he offered to put me in the way of some and then withdrew, and then offered a small loan and backed away from the larger scheme. On an impulse— for I'm safe here surely, he thought; that summons man will look for me at my office—he rang up old Thos Armitage on the excuse of consulting him about tonight's agenda.

I'd rather borrow from him if I have to borrow at all, thought Roddie. But Thos was busy and couldn't see him before tonight. Oh well! He'd see Thos before the meeting, and then if nothing came of that he'd try Considine. Some people borrowed from banks, of course, but then banks, he understood, required security.

Emerging from the telephone-box with head down, full of these thoughts, he suddenly glimpsed at the end of the street a man with a bowler hat. In a panic he bolted across to the ticket office.

He booked to Hudley, one of the towns covered by his sub-branch office, and while the train wound along the valleys and through the tunnels of the West Riding hills, tried to decide whether or no to take Considine's advice and telephone the Building Society. It seemed to him of doubtful honesty to promise to pay the debt tomorrow when he had no genuine hope of doing so. Yet what harm could be done by such a promise? No harm, thought Roddie, and much good. He might conceivably be able to get a loan, from Considine say and pay the debt; in which case the Building Society would benefit and his own reputation would be saved. If he didn't get a loan, well then, the Building Society wouldn't get its money; but they wouldn't be any worse off on account of the promise. If a summons were served on him he was done for. A prominent business man like Considine wouldn't give him dishonest advice, surely. The promise was a risk, of course, a piece of daring; but then Roddie had taken a risk before and brought it off. He wished he could talk to Kate about it. How on earth was he to get back to Kate, anyway, with that process-server hanging around? The thought that he was cut off from Kate and the kids hurt him where he lived; that he should have exposed them to this peril was a blot on his manhood which he would never be able to wash out. He *must* get that process-man called off. A man like Sir Charles Considine, with a title and half a dozen businesses, would surely never give him off-colour advice. His only doubt, Roddie assured himself, was whether to ring up the solicitor or the Building Society. Since serving a summons was a legal process, it would probably be legal blokes who employed that retired bobby. The train drew up at Hudley; he climbed the steps of that hilly station, entered a telephone box and with his heart in his mouth put through a call to the number on the solicitor's letter.

It seemed an age before the 'phone was answered, another age before he was in touch with the principal of the firm.

"This is Roderick Bairstow here. Bairstow of Upper Head Cottage."

"Ah! Mr. Bairstow. We sent you a letter."

"Yes. I rang up to ask you to give me till tomorrow to pay."

"You didn't reply to our letter, Mr. Bairstow."

"No. I'm exceedingly sorry about the delay in the payments, but I've had special difficulties—illness and so on," said Roddie, hating himself for asking pity.

"It's only fair to tell you that a summons has been issued against you, Mr. Bairstow."

"If you serve a summons on me I shall lose my job and the Building Society won't get its money anyway."

"The Building Society will get the house, Mr. Bairstow."

"It's a shame to ruin me just for one day," cried Roddie.

"Our clients are not wishful to press you too hard, Mr. Bairstow."

"I appreciate that," lied Roddie, trying to sound placatory and reasonable.

"But have you any real hope of making the payments tomorrow?"

Roddie hesitated. But surely Sir Charles Considine——

"Yes!" he shouted. "I've fixed an appointment tonight to arrange—terms and things."

"It's a pity you didn't do that sooner, Mr. Bairstow."

"Everyone has his own difficulties."

"Quite. Well, I'm sure my clients will be pleased if the matter terminates happily."

"That's all very well," said Roddie: "But what about that fellow of yours—the man with the summons?"

"You avoided him at Upper Head this morning, I believe," said the lawyer with a certain acidity.

"Yes and I'm not in Ashworth now," said Roddie. "You must call him off till after tomorrow."

There was a pause. The telephone developed the stuffy deadness which is caused by a hand being placed over the mouthpiece. This was broken by the three-minutes' signal. The tinkling little pips maddened Roddie; another threepenny bit gone, he thought grimly. At the operator's request, he put in three more coppers.

"Oh, Mr. Bairstow," resumed the lawyer suddenly in a more genial tone: "As it chances, our process-server is in the office at the moment."

"Yes?" said Roddie. ("Surely they can't serve a summons by telephone?" he wondered wildly.)

"We will instruct him to desist from the service until noon tomorrow, if we have your assurance that you really mean to make the payment."

"You don't give me much time, do you?" said Roddie bitterly.

"Our clients feel that you've had a great deal of time already."

"Well—all right. Noon tomorrow. Shall I bring the money to you or to the Building Society?"

"You had perhaps better bring it to us, Mr. Bairstow."

"Very well. Goodbye. Thank you!" added Roddie hastily.

"Good morning, Mr. Bairstow."

Roddie came out of the box to find that sweat was rolling down his forehead. He was obliged to set down his brief-case, take off his hat and mop his head and neck with his handkerchief. Well, at least he'd gained himself a little time. But he'd have to find that money by noon tomorrow. If the worst came to the worst, he would have to try to raise something on his furniture. But the poor kids! Poor Kate! And it would take such a time in any case. Of course there were certain insurance moneys. . . .

"Nonsense!" said Roddie, horrified. "I'd better get to work," he told himself sternly: "I've got my living to earn, remember."

He threw his mackintosh over his shoulder and strode soberly up the hill towards the town of Hudley.

All through the day the thought of the debt weighed on his mind like a stone, though he worked hard and conscientiously and tried to forget it.

He began by calling on his agents in the town and explaining some new conditions which were about to operate in future annuity policies. One of the agents told him of a likely "prospect," a man who had just set up for himself in a joinery and cabinet-making business. Roddie called on him, and was able to fix him up with all the insurance he needed— fire, third party, workmen's compensation. It was a good piece of work, and Roddie came away whistling. On an ordinary day he would have considered his success entitled him to a drink and a good lunch, but he remembered the Building Society and instead ate what he thought a horrid little meal in a repulsive vegetarian restaurant. He called on another agent, was told of a "prospect" who had just bought a house and finding the place with some difficulty in a heavy shower, spent an hour with her, only to discover that she meant to insure with a rival company for whom her nephew was agent. Then he called on an old lady—flustered, pathetic, trying hard not to be tearful—who had recently lost her husband, and explained to her very simply and clearly the advantages of exchanging all the old overlapping policies, taken out at intervals years ago by her husband, for a comprehensive new one. Roddie's company had just paid the widow her husband's life insurance, so she had great faith in Roddie and made him a cup of tea with her own trembling and rheumaticky hands. Roddie liked old ladies and was kind and filial to this one; it was a good piece of tidying-up work, too, such as he enjoyed and the Company appreciated. On the whole, therefore, a good average day's work was done by our representative Mr. R. V. Bairstow. But the debt and the summons seemed to be suspended inside him like a stone from some vital organ.

He took a bus back to Ashworth and toiled wearily up to the nursing home. The sun was making one of its fitful appearances just then and his heavy mackintosh was a nuisance. Of course under the new Health Service his father could go into one of the public hospitals for nothing, but Roddie had lacked the heart to do that to the poor old chap. Now he was afraid there was no help for it. Oh well. He wouldn't broach the subject today at any rate.

It was a small room, just a back bedroom very sparsely furnished, and this fact always hurt Roddie. He felt that he had failed in his duty as a son, to let his father be so poorly accommodated. Today was one of old Mr. Bairstow's good days, clearly; he was raised high on his pillows and looked, though depressed and sad, in full possession of his senses. Roddie bent over and kissed him; his father said nothing aloud, words shaped themselves on his trembling lips only to be rejected.

"How are you today, Father?"

"Pretty fair."

"Has the new nurse answered your bell more promptly?" said Roddie, remembering a long complaint voiced by the old man on his previous visit.

"Eh?"

"The new nurse. Is she quicker now in answering your bell?"

"They're always having new nurses here," said the old man wearily. "Nothing but new faces."

Roddie sighed. "But you're pretty comfortable here, taking it by and large, aren't you, Father?"

"Pretty fair."

"Is there anything you want that I could get for you?"

The old man moved his head restlessly as if this questioning vexed him. "No. No. All I want is to be finished with everything."

"Don't talk like that, Father," said Roddie insincerely.

Mr. Bairstow sighed and closed his eyes.

Roddie sat at the bedside for several minutes, unable to think of anything to say to him. The subjects which filled his thoughts, the debt, the summons, Kate, the children, were all unsuitable for mention to his father. He glanced furtively at his watch. His father opened his eyes at this moment and saw him.

"Time to go?" said Mr. Bairstow, faintly sardonic.

"Yes, I'm afraid so. I have a committee meeting to attend at seven," said Roddie.

Mr. Bairstow gave the faintest possible sound of understanding and closed his eyes again. Roddie stood up, wondered whether to give him Kate's message, decided against it, and left him thankfully.

6

It was quite a stretch down the hill again, and when he reached Ashworth there was no time left for a meal. He went into the Crown instead and had a couple of drinks to get up his courage. He was tired, and it was not going to be easy tackling old Thos. Come to think of it, would he really have the face to tackle him? After all, he hadn't the slightest claim on the old man. It was begging in public, really. How should he begin? He had another drink while he meditated his opening sentence. Suddenly the clock said a quarter to seven and he left in a rush. As he strode along the street the mere fact of his haste gave him the illusion of doing something, but when he had reached the Institute this all fell away. The lights were on in the dreary little room, the chairs were arranged, the table spread with a green baize cloth; the caretaker looked in to see if all was as the committee desired and at Roddie's request opened a window; Roddie took out the A.T.P.C.'s Minute Book and papers from his brief-case and arranged them on the table. There was nothing else to do. He waited. The caretaker's footsteps died away in the distance.

He waited. Mr. Armitage did not come. There was complete silence. The dust disturbed by Roddie's advent settled again slowly and remorselessly. Yes, I must say, mused Roddie, I should prefer a spicier dish.

Footsteps sounded in the hall. "My God, it's Thos!" thought Roddie. "This is zero hour. What on earth shall I find to say to him?"

He half rose in agitation, but sat down again as not Mr. Armitage but Elizabeth Marrison came in.

"Damn her! Now I've no chance for a word with Thos.

Painted little bitch," thought Roddie savagely: "I shan't let Diana use cosmetics when she's grown up, I promise you."

As usual the Marrison woman drifted round to him and began to drawl the flirtatious badinage which was her speciality. "She thinks she's Lili Marlene," thought Roddie sardonically, remembering a Two Types cartoon in Italy long ago. He kept his side of the talk going, lest worse should befall; he could roll out that kind of light sexy back-chat in his sleep.

Here came Thos now, when it was too late. Damn the Marrison; but it was something of a relief all the same. Only putting off the evil moment, though.

"Good evening, sir."

"Good evening, my boy. I'm sorry I was too late for a word. After the meeting instead, perhaps?"

"If it's not too inconvenient for you, sir," said Roddie. It was awkward; if he stayed for a talk with Mr. Armitage he might lose Considine. Damn that Marrison woman!

7

The Town Hall clock struck seven.

"We may as well begin, ladies and gentlemen," said Mr. Armitage. "Stay a moment, though. Are we a quorum, Captain Bairstow?"

Roddie flushed with pleasure. It was the first time that day anybody had called him *Captain*. Old Thos probably didn't mean anything by it, still it was a pleasure to feel that somebody thought of him as an officer and a gentleman. He apologised for not remembering what the quorum was, and turning to look it up in the Minute Book, received a shock. Considine had come in and seated himself further down the table. He was smiling his fixed inscrutable smile and not looking at anybody, as usual. One thing was certain: Considine wouldn't hang around after the meeting waiting for Roddie to finish talking to Mr. Armitage. He'd have to choose between them.

Sufficient members for the quorum were present, and Mr.

Armitage called the meeting to order and asked for the Minutes. Roddie stood up and began to read, but in spite of himself his thoughts wandered: which should it be, old Thos Armitage or Sir Charles Considine?

IV

SIR CHARLES CONSIDINE

I

"THESE YOUNG ——s," thought Considine as with a turn of his supple wrist he guided his coupé away from young Bairstow into the main stream of traffic: "These damned young ——s, strutting about in their silly uniforms, paid for doing damn all and want you not to forget it. Forty pounds!"

His customary half-smile and downcast eyelids accentuated into a sneer. What a ridiculous sum to be in trouble for! He would rather lend a man four hundred than forty, and rather four thousand than four hundred—more chance of being repaid. Could Bairstow be useful in any way in the present emergency? That twenty-five thousand had to be found somewhere, and found tomorrow, or better still today. He's in insurance, there might be some way, mused Considine, smiling, but I don't just see it yet. Still, he might lend Bairstow the necessary forty, merely to put him under an obligation.

He turned into the yard of Heygate Clough Mills, and frowned at a barrel which had been left by the gate. When would they learn he would not endure untidiness of that kind? He must speak about it again, this time very sharply. He drew up his coupé exactly in the centre of the private garage he had cut off from the old spacious stables. A man came out at once to take his instructions about the car—he'd taught them that at any rate.

"Please mend the left door-cord and then turn her," he said in his quiet, precise rather mincing tones.

Nobody was better able than he to back the car out of the narrow yard and turn it gracefully, but he thought backing cars undignified for Sir Charles Considine. He walked quickly, with a light easy step, towards the main entrance. The worn old plate, put up way back in the 1870's by some old Burney, gleamed in the sunlight. Its gleam was the product of much brass polish and elbow grease, and Considine, who had had to speak about its condition last week to the morning charwoman, nodded slightly in satisfaction with its improvement.

The offices of Messrs. Burney Brothers, though scrupulously neat, clean and in good condition, were dark and old-fashioned, in appearance and equipment fifty years behind his chromium and plastic rooms at Comer Mills. It amused him to think that once, as a boy, he had been awestruck by the massive mahogany furniture and red-leathered swivel chairs. In this very room thirty years ago, Mr. Bob Burney, high-coloured, genial, prosperous, tilting his chair back at a carefree angle and swinging himself slowly from side to side with one foot, had engaged the hobbledehoy Charley as a general office runabout. It was a good day for Bob Burney, thought Sir Charles, smiling his half smile as he gave his hat to his secretary, who placed it carefully in a wardrobe he had provided for the purpose, a lucky day for Bob Burney when he took Charles Considine into the firm. Or was it? Some people might choose to think otherwise. He frowned. As though she had known this turn of thought, his Heygate secretary, a subdued elderly efficient woman not in his confidence, said diffidently:

"Lady Considine was just on the 'phone, sir."

"Ah. Ring back to her at once, will you?" said Considine smoothly, putting on an air of suitable concern. One should always be the devoted husband in public, he told himself with his ironical smile. By the time he had washed and touched his hair and glasses, Eileen was on the line.

"And what can I do for you, my dear?" said Considine in his politest tone.

2

All their history was in that sentence, which was intended, and accepted, as an insult.

When Charley Considine, that clever ambitious lad from one of the slums of Ashworth (cleared now and rebuilt with those neat prefabs), was a young and utterly unimportant clerk in Bob Burney's office, he fell madly in love with Mr. Burney's daughter, Eileen. She was very fair, pretty in a dolly way, and very smart according to the West Riding standards of the 1920's. (Now, of course, those old drab gaberdine costumes and cloche hats and long-waisted dresses he adored seemed simply ludicrous, and their wedding-group looked too absurd for words, as he often mildly pointed out to Eileen when there was company present.) Eileen did not love him, but she was flattered by his earnest unwavering devotion; it was agreeable to find burning eyes fixed on her whenever she went to the mill on an errand to her widowed father, to see how the poor lad blushed and stammered; a conquest to boast of to her friends was a useful acquisition and, lacking as she did a mother's eye on her doings, she found herself going down to Heygate Clough rather often. Then Charles Considine grew into a polite and personable young man and somehow managed to invade her social group; though it was useful, of course, to have such a faithful partner she did not care for him much and was apt to be pettish with him; but her father always spoke well of Charles; he was *most* useful at the office (such a head for figures and a smooth way with customers) and Mr. Burney really thought of giving him a junior directorship. Presently he did so, and Considine, now twenty-five, asked Eileen to marry him. In a fright she declined, and her fright made her unintentionally cruel: "Oh no, I couldn't, Charley. I'm sorry, I'm very sorry, but I really couldn't."

"I shall always love you, Eileen," said Considine quietly.

He was most dignified about it all, behaved very well indeed, but Eileen, who was fairly shrewd when she gave her mind to it, felt uneasily that he was sore all over from her refusal. She tried to avoid him, but he said in his quiet way: "Surely you won't forbid me to be your friend, Eileen?" and continued to dog her path. Other men did not like to thwart such a well-known devotion—it was not as though Eileen Burney had anything special, she was just an ordinary girl, dozens like her grew in every West Riding town. Her friends married, and Eileen began to take the line that she couldn't possibly leave her dear old Daddy, she was very very happy at home. Charles Considine now left Burney Brothers and took a mill in Bradford and began to prosper rapidly, and the impression gained ground in Eileen's circle that she had made a mistake in turning him down, let a good thing slip by. To an Ashworth girl Bradford was quite an exciting city, with far more opportunities for enjoying oneself than in dull old Ashworth—besides, Considine now began to take frequent trips to London and even abroad. As he was now in spinning, Mr. Burney dealt with him largely for yarn—he had been his first customer for kindness and old times' sake, and remained a customer because Considine was prompt in delivery, accurate and business-like in all his dealings. So he often spoke of Charley to Eileen, sometimes in a rather reproachful tone. Considine did not attend Ashworth social functions as often as he used; on his rare appearances he seemed more sophisticated than of old, and told Eileen he had no time for such youthful activities nowadays.

"I'm sorry, Charley."

"If my presence would give you pleasure, Eileen, I would come," said Considine, his eyes wide open for once and gleaming behind his newly acquired tortoise-shell spectacles.

But even now, though Eileen felt it was foolish of her, she could not bring herself to speak the words which would encourage another proposal.

Meanwhile the years of slump had been accumulating, and the awful spring of 1931 approached. Textile firms fell like ninepins, bowled out by economic factors over which they had no control. Mr. Burney became very snappy and cut down Eileen's housekeeping money drastically; then he became harassed and pathetic and cut it down much more. He stayed out and began to drink a good deal; then he stayed in and began to drink, alone, a good deal more. They dismissed their maids and ceased to entertain. Mr. Burney paced the dining-room of a night with his hands clasped behind him, occasionally flicking his cheek with a perplexed finger. He slept and ate ill; his cheerful red face sagged. After the manner of most women of the period, Eileen knew absolutely nothing of her father's business, but by persistent and genuinely loving enquiry she discovered that he must pay large sums to the spinners from whom he bought yarn, on the twenty-fifth of every month. The twenty-fifth passed and Mr. Burney became jovial; it approached again and something like terror appeared in his round brown eyes.

One night he went up to have a bath, he said, while Eileen sat mending an old blouse below. It struck her suddenly that he had been a long time absent and that no cheerful sounds of splashing could be heard. Uneasy, she ran quietly upstairs and listened at the bathroom door. No sound from within reached her straining ears. In a panic she banged on the door: "Daddy! Daddy! Are you all right?"

After a long pause a voice replied feebly: "Yes, of course. I'll be out in a minute," went on Mr. Burney in a stronger and more irritable tone.

When he came out he was as white as a sheet, with a strange look of resignation in his eyes. Eileen flung her arms round him and wept.

"Now, now," said Mr. Burney mildly, patting her shingled head. "I'm not so well tonight; I'll go off to bed."

He did not attempt to deny, in speech or manner, that "something awful" (which was as near as Eileen dared go to it) had almost happened, and as soon as he was tucked up between the sheets with a glass of whisky and hot water in his hand, she shut herself into the downstairs cloakroom with the telephone, and rang up Considine. He was difficult to find—she tracked him down at last at a somewhat exclusive Bradford club—and this difficulty made her all the more urgent and determined. As soon as his voice sounded, quiet, light, slightly impatient though urbane, Eileen said breathlessly:

"It's Eileen, Charles. Charles, I'm so worried about Father."

Her use of the word *Charles* marked her first acknowledgement of his power. She had always called him *Charley* before, not troubling to think whether he liked it; she knew now, suddenly, that he did not and that it would be wise to use the more formal address.

"Ah," said Considine thoughtfully.

"Naturally I turned to you for help," said Eileen, breathless.

"Naturally." (Was there a hint of irony in his tone?)

"Charles, are you very busy?"

"Well, I'm engaged in a business conversation."

"Oh, dear. I wanted you to—I did so hope you'd—could you possibly come out here tonight?"

"To Hey House?"

"Yes."

"I'll come at once, my dear," said Considine.

By the time he arrived, between worry for Mr. Burney—who had dropped into a nap and looked very old and tired—and a deep unconscious worry about Considine, Eileen was in a state of high nervous tension, and no sooner had she admitted him to the house than she burst into anguished tears.

"My dear Eileen!" said Considine soothingly. He drew her down to a settee, sat down beside her and in the most natural way in the world put his arm comfortingly about her. "What can be the matter?"

"It's Father, Charles. I believe he tried to—to drown himself tonight."

"Drown himself?"

"In his bath. He's so terribly worried about Heygate Clough."

"Everyone in business is worried just now," said Considine soberly.

"Yes, but Charles, to drown himself! I'm sure he meant to."

"I can't believe he would be so cowardly. What would become of you if he were gone?"

"Oh, Charles!"

"Where is he now?"

"I put him to bed. He's in a doze."

"Shall I go up and talk to him? Perhaps it would ease his mind to speak of his troubles to someone he can trust."

"Oh, Charles!"

"And don't worry, my dear," said Considine, squeezing her shoulders gently: "We shall find a way out, never fear."

The upshot of all this was that Messrs. Burney Brothers weathered the storm, Considine became co-director with half the shares, and Eileen became Mrs. Charles Considine. It was an old familiar story, but none the less true on that account.

When the first natural excitement of matrimony had subsided, Eileen found herself bored and unhappy. She did not love her husband, nor even like him very much, in spite of all her efforts; outside the bedroom she found him cold and supercilious, inside savagely exacting. They had no children, and this was a great disappointment to both. Deep in her heart Eileen resented her marriage; not on account of its Burney Brothers' circumstances, of Considine's contrivance in which she had no suspicion, but because she had never been allowed to feel love, to enjoy romance, to partake of the common woman's destiny. Without consciously meaning to do so, in an unconscious expression of this resentment, she always took a high tone with her husband, as though she had indeed done him a favour in marrying him. He appeared perfectly subservient to her wishes, taking very great trouble to secure for her the material things she wanted. He built a fine new house over the hill from Heygate Clough, which rather to her annoyance he called High Hey; he supplied her plentifully with money, urged her to expensive tastes in dress—his taste was quieter than hers, which sometimes irked her—and put a neat car and an elderly chauffeur at her disposal. They took expensive holidays, often visited the theatre and never entered any hotel or restaurant which was not the best in its locality. He also bought her jewels, plentifully and in excellent taste. He did not drink—her father alas continued to drink rather heavily—and was decorous, reliable and polite towards his wife always, in public. Eileen accepted all this as her right but still felt bored and unhappy, and this went on for ten years, while her fair face took on peevish lines and her figure decayed. During the war it seemed natural that he should be much away from her, especially when he was put on some Government regional committee or other; she did not much mind his absences and as they resulted in a title she had no cause to complain. It came therefore as an overwhelming shock to her when, owing to an indiscretion of her father's, she came upon irrefutable evidence that her husband was unfaithful to her. She waited up for his return that night, and in angry astonishment blurted out all the muddled tiresome details of telephone calls and lies and times and places which formed the evidence. Sir Charles received this in perfect calm, smiling his fixed half smile, his thick white eyelids down. When she had finished her spluttered accusations he continued to smile and smoke his (specially manufactured) cigarette in silence.

"But, Charles!" expostulated Eileen uneasily. "Aren't you going to say anything?"

"What is there to say? Your deductions are quite correct. The woman you mention was my mistress for a time."

"Charles!" exclaimed Eileen, her bourgeois ears horrified by this word—she read it in library books with an agreeable titillation, but to hear it spoken in her own drawing-room by her own husband made her blush. "It's over now, then?" she said timidly.

"Yes."

"And you won't do anything of that sort again?"

"Probably I shall," said Considine smoothly.

"Charles! Don't you love me any more, Charles?" cried the dumbfounded Eileen, weeping loudly.

"It's years since I felt anything like that for you."

Eileen gaped at him.

"You loved me when we married—you were always saying how much you loved me," she wailed.

"You wore that out long ago."

"Wore it out?"

"Yes. You never cared for me. You never tried. You only married me for what you could get out of me."

"It's not true! I married you because you badgered me into it," wailed the hapless Eileen.

Considine's forehead contracted. "It seems to have been a mistake on both sides," he said coldly.

"Do you want to end it—end our marriage?"

"No, of course not. Don't be silly. What would be the point of that? We shall continue as before. There's nothing to get excited about. Why not go up to bed? You'll feel better in the morning," said Considine with his air of slight impatience, as though what he said was so obvious that even the mean intellect of his present hearer should grasp it at once.

"I simply don't know what to say," moaned Eileen.

"Say nothing and go to bed."

Considine spoke affably, but rose with decision to terminate the interview; his wife, though hesitating and fumbling with her bag, had no alternative but to follow his recommendation.

Since then, pondering in the light of this interview over all his actions and speeches during the years of their marriage, Eileen perceived the ironic intent of many of them, and fancied she perceived it of even more. Indeed one of the most painful items of her present wretched humiliation was that she could not exactly discern when her husband's affection had been lost to her. She probed continually into the past in an attempt to remember, to discover; Considine observed her probing and smiled ironically.

To ask her what he could do for her was therefore a reminder of the ambiguous foundation and hideous superstructure of their marriage. Not a clever woman, she had yet been taught his meaning by his brutal candour on the occasion, never repeated though often deserved, of her marital reproaches; she faltered at the wound but could find no effective reply.

3

"What can I do for you, my dear?"

"I'm so troubled about Father."

"I seem to have heard that before," said Considine, stabbing again—in a pleasantly rueful tone in case his secretary should overhear.

"Charles, he isn't at Hey House and he isn't with you at the mill, unless he's come in since I telephoned before."

"No, he's not here. He's probably on his way between the two."

"No. . . . His housekeeper rang up to tell me he never came home last night."

"Oh! Well, that certainly is more serious. Don't worry, my dear, I'll attend to the matter."

"Will you—will you let me know when you've found him?"

"Certainly. As soon as I can. Don't worry—I have an idea where he may be."

Stupid old fool, thought Considine, ringing off; he's drunk himself silly, I suppose, and not been able to get home. I hope the police haven't picked him up. He sent his secretary on an errand, then put through a few calls; Mr. Burney was not at either of his clubs, and the billiards saloon he occasionally frequented hadn't seen him for a week. With a grimace of distaste, Considine dialled the number of the Hey Dean Inn. A woman's voice answered.

"Sir Charles Considine here."

"Oh," said the voice with an effect of irony. "Well, you're right. He's here. Been here all night."

"Isn't he able to leave yet?"

"It's not what you think," said the voice. "At least, not altogether. He had a kind of heart attack and had to go to bed."

"Did you send for a doctor?" said Considine coldly.

"No. . . . He wouldn't let me. He's better this morning but still in bed. I don't really think he's fit to get up yet."

"Keep him in bed. I'll come," said Considine.

He rang off just as his secretary came into the room.

"I'm afraid poor Mr. Burney has been taken ill," he told her smoothly. "I must go at once and see him. Please ring for the car."

He knew, of course, that Mr. Burney's habits were a familiar subject of comment in Heygate Clough Mills and had no particular desire that it should be otherwise, but appearances must be kept up; he could see his secretary admiring him for keeping them up so nicely.

4

It was tiresome in a way to be called off his work to attend to the old man, but he was not sorry to have time for thought—

that ass young Bairstow had interrupted him on his way from home. Now on his way up to Mount Hey and down again to the valley he thought hard about his problem for the day, which was quite simply how to find another twenty-five thousand pounds from somewhere to complete the purchase price for Bernard Clough's Highshaw shares. It would be disagreeable to have to "hock" his car and house, and not enough in any case. Well, he must be resourceful.

It wouldn't be the first time in his career he had been resourceful, reflected Considine, smiling. He remembered an occasion in his early days at Comer Mills when he had got himself out of a financial hole by a simple but ingenious arrangement. By a traditional and immutable though in Considine's opinion idiotic law of the textile trade, spinners have to pay for their tops, their raw material, twice a month, on the seventh and the twenty-first, whereas manufacturers pay spinners only once a month, on the twenty-fifth. For spinners there is therefore an uncomfortable gap between the twenty-first and the twenty-fifth when they have paid for two lots of tops and a month's wages since they have received anything from their customers. During this period the spinners' resources are at their lowest. On the occasion Considine remembered, his payments on the seventh, coupled with his wages bill, had left him without the means to pay his account on the twenty-first. His credit at the bank was already stretched as far as it would go; if he couldn't find the money somehow, another promising young firm would go down. Accordingly he made out the cheque for his top-maker and posted it late in the evening of the twenty-first. But he "forgot" to sign it. His top-maker received it on the twenty-second and of course returned it with a note (not as polite as could be wished, but after all that didn't matter) pointing out the omission. The date was now the twenty-third. Considine signed the cheque and posted it, with profuse apologies, late on the twenty-fourth; on the following morning it reached the top-maker, who, not too trusting of Considine whom he didn't like anyway, very promptly banked it. But meanwhile Considine had banked with even greater promptitude the cheques from his customers which he had received that morning, rushing down with them the very instant the post brought them in. His bank balance shot up and his cheque was duly honoured. It was a neat device; yes, neat, simple and not illegal—or any at rate not provably illegal. Just resourceful. That, coupled with an occasional overstating of the quality of his yarn—mixing more of an inferior quality into the blend than its description warranted—had seen him through.

Nowadays, of course, he did not indulge in such capers as milking his blend; he was too well known, his actions were of too much public interest, subject to too wide a public scrutiny. Besides, such forms of chicanery required a good deal of technical textile skill, and Considine's technical skill was not—he admitted it openly with cheerful frankness, secretly with icy rage—not really very great. In finance, now, nobody in the West Riding could touch him, he had a quite superb mastery of figures; and who would toil over making threepence in the pound by a manipulation of greasy wool, with the danger of a foreman getting hold of the trick, when by a neat little juggling, a skilful manipulation, of different companies' assets, figures on paper, thousands could be gracefully slid into the quarter which most needed them?

At the moment, however, all his manipulations had left him twenty-five thousand short. He was playing with large sums, he realised, perhaps rather too large for comfort, for after all he had nothing but what he had made himself in the last twenty years, he was not one of those old West Riding family firms which had the savings of a century to draw upon. But he was determined to get hold of some such concern, really large and old-established and prestige-conferring. He wanted it for itself; also he wanted it as a springboard in case the disaster of nationalisation should befall the textile trade, for he intended to be chosen as a member of any national textile board or commission which might be appointed. Bernard Clough's idiotic South African notion gave him just the opportunity he required. No doubt Clough's decision to leave England had something to do with his silly wife, who, Considine understood, had left him; there was certainly another woman in the case, reflected Considine, but who she was he did not know. (N.B. Find out; the knowledge might be useful.) Imagine a sensible man caring more about a woman than his business! Women were two a penny, but a firm like Highshaw Mills took work and time. Yes, he was determined to get into Highshaw Mills whatever it cost; for once he was inside them, he would have old Armitage with his horse face and his out-of-date welfare ideas outside in a couple of shakes.

He would begin smoothly with the old fool, of course—he had already begun smoothly, by getting himself put on the Ashworth Textile Pageant Committee. At the public meeting to consider the project, the moment the Mayor in the chair announced that the employers' representative on the Committee would be Mr. Thomas Armitage, Considine had risen and quietly offered his services in any capacity. "If there are any financial aspects to be considered or Government departments to be approached," he said in his precise affable tones, smiling his fixed half-smile at the meeting: "Possibly someone with a little experience might be useful." The meeting chuckled with enjoyment, as he had meant it to do, at this under-statement of his capacities, and promptly put him on the Committee. At first he was vexed because the Committee did not elect him Chairman but chose old Armitage instead, but afterwards that became just one more argument for the securing of Highshaw Mills, for he supposed that in spite of his title, his textile concerns weren't imposing enough yet to win him the chairmanship of voluntary Ashworth committees. However, he would show the A.T.P.C. a thing or two before he'd finished with it. By the way, why not press that matter of the field, tonight? Young Bairstow, hoping for the forty pounds, would of course vote with him. He must remember to get a special forty of consecutive fives from the bank for Mr. Bairstow; he'd take care to hint to the bank teller that he wanted it for a protégé of his, for one might as well get as much credit for one's good deeds as possible.

Well, this hadn't taken him much nearer to the solution of his problem; he still hadn't found the way to another twenty-five thousand pounds. He had a feeling the way would be connected with young Bairstow, somehow, but didn't see it clearly as yet. Young Bairstow and old Burney. Insurance. If the old man were to be heavily insured in his son-in-law's favour, now, and then conveniently die. But he wouldn't die, not for another seven years or so. Or if he were already conveniently dead, and the policy could be antedated? But no; insurance policies necessitated medical examination. No, he didn't just see how Bairstow and Burney could be combined to get him Highshaw Mills. What he needed, of course, was Burney's half of Messrs. Burney Bros., to offer the bank as collateral security; but even his father-in-law was not quite such a fool as that. Oh well, he'd think of a scheme somehow.

He turned the coupé, with an elegant flick of the wrist, into the steep, rough, winding lane which led down to the old Hey water-mill, now called Hey Dean Inn.

5

The old mill had been an inn for almost a century now but still bore traces of its original function; one side overhung the Hey Beck, and a rusty iron shaft projecting from this wing and odd protuberances and depressions in the ground nearby revealed the former positions of wheel, dam and leat. In the 1930's it had become a kind of roadhouse much visited by the youth of Ashworth and Hudley in search of sophistication; after languishing through the war and the period of no basic petrol it had recently regained a similar clientèle. Young people told each other knowingly that the food was first-rate though probably black market, and the licensee, Mrs. Lily Binns, a real good sport. The outside of the old building had recently been smartened up by a coat of whitewash and some tasteful blue paint, chosen and paid for by Considine, and baskets of pink geraniums similarly purchased were suspended in mid-air in appropriate places; within, the place had been thoroughly cleaned out and redecorated and its old furnishings furbished into "ye olde." Considine had enjoyed doing this at the time, but now he disliked the place and could not imagine why he had lowered himself to its level. It seemed to him now ramshackle, musty, unpleasantly smothered in heavy decaying foliage, and because of its site on the small trickle of compensation water which was all the Hey Dean Mills higher up the valley allowed to escape down the bed of the stream, odorous and fly-haunted. The jocular notices directing patrons to outside lavatories, at which he had once smiled, struck him this morning as not only obscene but adolescent. The door stood open. He gave a sharp rap with the imitation brass knocker and walked in.

No doubt the sound of his car had already advertised his approach, for black patent-leather high-heeled shoes with ankle-straps clasped tight round very thin ankles were already visible descending the turn of the stairs, and soon the whole of Mrs. Binns appeared in the hall beside him.

"Oh, it's you," she said on an ironical note.

"Yes, Lily," said Considine. "How is your patient?"

He spoke with his usual slightly impatient, slightly condescending and precise affability and smiled his usual stiff half-smile, but inwardly he felt revolted. How could he ever have touched the woman? He knew the answer to that question, however; there were times when, stifled by the arid respectability of his life with Eileen, a sudden overwhelming *nostalgie de la boue* (a phrase he had picked up from a foreign customer of Burney Brothers) swept him into some savage secret excess. But that sharp foxy little face which aped youth by thick cosmetics, that bang of red hair over the narrow forehead, those two "curls" (save the mark!) of red hair tied on the shoulders with bows of green satin ribbon, those thin predatory hands with their orange talons—how could he have endured their proximity? With a shudder of repulsion he noticed that on either side of the parting between front hair and back the colour had reverted from red to its natural dusty brown.

"Well, he had a bad turn, you know," said Lily.

"You shouldn't let him drink so much."

"It's not my job to wet-nurse Bob Burney."

"Not even to please me?" said Considine smoothly.

Mrs. Binns slightly blenched. "You know I do my best," he whined. "Are you coming upstairs?"

127

Considine replied with a gesture inviting her to lead the way.

He gave her credit for having as she said done her best when she ushered him into the best front bedroom, where Mr. Burney lay beneath a pale green satin eiderdown. Unshaved and wearing his yesterday's shirt, his high-coloured face mottled, his grey hair tousled, Mr. Burney was a dreary object, and the perplexed resigned look in his small brown eyes was dreary too.

"Well, Charles. Good of you to waste your petrol on me," he greeted his son-in-law. "But I forgot—you always have plenty of petrol, don't you."

Considine let this pass.

"Eileen was worried about you," he said.

"Ah! Eileen," said Mr. Burney. Staring away from his son-in-law, he slightly raised one gnarled hand and let it drop on the eiderdown. Really Considine felt quite sorry for the old fellow.

"Would you like a doctor?" he said.

"No. I'll go home this afternoon. You might send a taxi for me, say about four."

"Very well. Do you feel well enough to sign a few papers?" asked Considine, bringing forward his brief-case.

"No, no! God, no! I never want to sign any business papers again. I never want to do any business again. I never want to go into Heygate Mills again. I'm sick of everything. And I'm especially sick of you."

Considine in a flash perceived how he might combine Burney and Bairstow to get him twenty-five thousand pounds.

"Why not sell out, then, and go and live in the South? Eileen can come and stay with you."

Mr. Burney turned his head to gaze in surprise at his son-in-law.

"Sell out to whom?"

"Me, of course."

"And what would you buy me out with? You're having enough of a job to find the money for that Highshaw Mills affair. A piece of pretentious nonsense, that's what your buying out Bernard Clough is."

"I'll buy you an annuity with one of the big insurance companies tomorrow, if you say the word."

"Do you mean it?" said the old man, astonished.

"I never say what I don't mean."

"Oh yes, Charles, you do."

"Not in business," countered Considine. He slightly coughed, and gave Mrs. Binns, who stood at the foot of the bed, a quick glance.

"Take the offer while it stands, dearie," she urged hastily. "That's my advice."

"I should want the income from thirty thousand pounds," said Mr. Burney doubtfully.

"Well, that's not an unreasonable figure. Of course I shall have to make enquiries about the purchase price of annuities from various companies," said Considine with a thoughtful air.

"What are you up to, Charles?" exclaimed his father-in-law. "You're up to some trick or other."

"I simply wish to have Heygate entirely under my own management," replied Considine with truth.

"Well, as far as I'm concerned you can have it, if you'll pay me thirty thousand pounds."

"I'll buy you an annuity which will represent the interest on that sum."

"What's the point of an annuity? It'll die with me; Eileen won't get any of it."

"I can provide for Eileen."

"I'd rather have it in Government securities."

"Why?"

"Because you want me to have an annuity," said Mr. Burney with a hoarse guffaw. His colour was now better and his eye brighter; the discussion had revived him. "Speaking seriously, I don't see the point of an annuity, Charles."

"It won't cost me thirty thousand pounds to buy you an annuity which will represent the interest on that sum. Not at your age."

"But it's throwing money away—it'll die with me; Eileen won't touch a penny of it."

"You've said that before," said Considine coldly, rising.

"We needn't go over it all again. Think it over. I'd like your decision not later than next week. Indeed this week would be preferable. But I don't want to hurry you."

"Charles," said Mr. Burney, sitting upright: "You needn't try to cheat me over this, because I'm not having any. I won't sign a single paper of any kind until I hold the annuity policy in my hand with the company's seal and signature on it."

"You shall have it," said Considine with his mild condescension. "Now don't excite yourself. I'll send a taxi for you at four. Would you like to come to us for a few days, till you're better?"

"No!"

"Just as you like," said Considine, shrugging. He looked at Lily, who after straightening Mr. Burney's pillows with a great air of virtue, followed him downstairs.

"Try to persuade him," said Considine to her in a very low tone.

She looked at him for a moment in silence.

"Didn't you get your money?" murmured Considine, looking away.

"Yes. Oh, yes."

"He'll get his, I promise you."

He wasn't even lying, reflected Considine sardonically, for though the annuity bond would be a fake arranged on one of his company's forms by young Bairstow, he himself would pay the old chap the agreed annuity every year. It would be a good bargain all round. Drinking as he did, Bob Burney couldn't last more than ten years at the outside and he would be comfortable, safe and at ease for the rest of his days, while his son-in-law would only have a few years' income to pay him in return for his half of Burney Brothers. Considine would get the money he needed for Highshaw—or as near as made no matter—on loan from the bank now he could offer them his father-in-law's shares as security. Of course banks didn't like making loans on private company's shares, but they knew him, they had faith in him, he'd borrowed and paid them back before, they'd do it for him. Highshaw was in the bag.

"He'll get his money every year all right, I promise you."
Lily lowered her heavily blacked eyelashes.

"Should I have the yard asphalted?" she murmured.

"Certainly not," said Considine emphatically. "You can't afford it."

Mrs. Binns, oddly enough, appeared relieved to find her attempted blackmail a failure. "Well, all right; if there's no hanky-panky about it I'll see what I can do with him," she said.

Highshaw was in the bag, thought Considine, making the coupé shoot up the steep tree-clad curves of the lane exultantly.

6

The rest of the day was mostly a restless passing of the time until he could get hold of young Bairstow at the A.T.P.C. meeting.

He called in at High Hey, relieved his wife's mind about her father (keeping her in ignorance of the inn where he lay so that she should not visit it) and scolded the gardener about the unsatisfactory appearance of the sloping shrubbery at the side of the house, which from the road somehow looked stiff and unnatural, as though the bushes were planted mechanically in rows. The gardener remarked in a surly tone that he had simply followed Sir Charles's instructions last year about the shrubbery, whereupon Considine said sharply that he had given instructions to be carried out by a skilled gardener, not by a labourer's boy.

"Well, it'll have to wait a few m nths now," said the gardener.

"Surely not?" said Considine smoothly.

It was then too near lunch time to begin an important interview with his bank, so he drove over to Bradford and put in an hour's work at Comer Mills. Although admirably organised and equipped, this firm did not produce quite as good work as Considine wished; it maddened him to see the products of men of ability greatly inferior, as he thought, to his own, enjoying a reputation for quality which neither Comer nor Heygate seemed able to achieve. He lunched at the Midland alone, abstemiously—he could not eat when excited by the chase—then drove back to Ashworth and had a highly satisfactory talk with the manager of his bank. It was agreed that the money he needed would be forthcoming as soon as Mr. Burney's shares were deposited as security. All he had to do now was corral young Bairstow. As he went out he obtained eight nice clean five-pound notes from one of the cashiers; in his experience actual money was a more effective temptation than a cheque. He then drove back through a shower to Heygate Clough, sat down and worked out a really admirable scheme for financing the Textile Pageant—it gave him real pleasure to see the thing so well laid out. He wished he could rise into the realms of pure finance, where commodities such as textiles became mere figures in a total. Well, perhaps soon he would achieve this long-desired elevation; Highshaw would be a big step up. Should he show any awareness, at the meeting tonight, of his forthcoming partnership with Thomas Armitage? Not unless the old man himself spoke of it, he thought. Armitage belonged to a generation and a class which had a delicacy about that sort of thing—believed in keeping private affairs out of public life, and so forth.

Thinking of the meeting reminded him of the matter of the field. At the last meeting it had been decided to approach Lord Intake, on whose land a good deal of Ashworth (though not as much as formerly) still stood, with an enquiry as to whether he would be willing to lend a large unkempt stretch of grass, the remains of the grounds of an ancestor's house of which most had long been sold for housing, for the purposes of the pageant. In Ashworth, fields flat enough for pageantry were rare. Considine himself however possessed, across the road from his gardens, a sloping field which terminated at the foot in a flattish ledge. The ledge could form the stage, the slope would become a grandstand for spectators, and to loan his land without charge for a pageant which would be visited by the whole West Riding would gain for Considine a most desirable access of prestige. Also, he could put a veto on pretty well anything concerning the pageant which he didn't like, if it was to be held on his field. Power over the whole thing would fall into his hands. He had put forward the suggestion in an undertone to Thomas Armitage at the meeting, but it had been tepidly received, so on the following day he had written an official letter to young Bairstow, making a formal proffer of the land. The matter would be bound to come up for discussion tonight. Could he do a little canvassing beforehand? Young Bairstow of course would vote on his side, with an eye on favours to come. The T.U. delegate and the Labour Councillor were employees, without telephones of their own; better leave them alone and play them off against each other at the meeting. The schoolmarm, Mrs. Sykes? Too dangerous; she might blow the gaff. That left the Marrison woman—oh and the representative of the Youth Groups whom they'd decided to ask for, last time. He managed to get hold of Elizabeth Marrison on the 'phone and had a few minutes' useful talk with her; in a few well-chosen sentences he briefed her pretty cleverly. Meanwhile he put his secretary on to track the Youth representative down, but she wasn't successful; the Youth Organiser was out and nobody else at the Education Office seemed to know anything about a Youth representative for the A.T.P.C., but they would give her the message when she came in. "The inefficiency of some people, really!" thought Considine, shrugging his shoulders in disgust.

By this time the mill buzzer—only it was not an old-fashioned buzzer but an agreeable musical horn of his own installation—was sounding; when the workpeople had left, Considine drove home for a light meal. (Some people, it seemed, had difficulties with their domestics nowadays and had to take care about the times and composition of their meals. The more fools they. Considine had none. One had only to bribe and browbeat in suitable proportions.) The road between Heygate Clough and High Hey always gave him a moment of pleasure, because to the right, halfway up the slope, stood Hey House, his father-in-law's house, which had once seemed so lofty and unattainable a residence. But before the war the rising tide of small houses and shops had almost engulfed the neighbourhood, and the house now looked dank and dark and ill-cared for, the lower windows darkened by haggard old rhododendrons which never flowered and the rims of the paving-stones of the entrance choked with sparse sickly grass. Eileen indeed had once or twice commented sadly on its appearance recently and suggested that now the war was over, surely it could be improved. Considine affably encouraged her.

"I agree—it's an unpleasing spectacle. Why not speak to your father about it, my dear?"

"I thought I'd like to have the garden done up, and fresh curtains for the house, perhaps, as a birthday present for Father."

"Do," said Considine—"if you feel you can spare the money from your dress allowance, my dear."

Hey House remained unfurbished, and the contrast between its decaying Victorian gloom and the bright aspect of High Hey, standing on the open sunny hillside, with its fresh yellowish stone and orderly lay-out, was pleasing to Considine. He put his car carefully into the garage—he did not like to see a car standing untidily about in the front drive, dishevelling the gravel, even for an hour—and went to look at the sloping shrubbery about which he had scolded the gardener. The man had broken its too obvious symmetries by a few small laurel bushes. They had a rather wilted look but the afternoon's showers would no doubt settle them in. On the whole they were an improvement, thought Considine, and he nodded his head, satisfied.

At last it was time to set off to the A.T.P.C. It was useless to arrive too early; he had told young Bairstow he would see him after the meeting, not before, and it was necessary to keep to this schedule in order by delay to "soften up" the young man, to subject him to an immersion in suspense sufficiently protracted to dissolve his moral resistance in anguish. He can't have had a very comfortable day, thought Considine, toying for a moment with the idea of putting him out of his misery before the meeting. Just then he passed one of the new housing estates, a rash of prefabs on an area made available by slum clearance. His smile stiffened; his boyhood had been spent in that slum and he resented it tidying-up for the present generation. Why should they hav an easier time than he? Let Bairstow wait. Another couple of hours would make him easier. Better still, perhaps: give him the money after the meeting and arrange an appointment, allegedly about Heygate Clough insurance, for noon tomorrow. Bairstow would have paid over the money to the Building Society by that time and be unable to return it; he would be committed. Considine could put on the screw—of course the annuity scheme would be presented merely as a kind lie, a benevolent deception of poor worried old Mr. Burney; agree to it or return my money. Still, he'd like it settled tonight. Well, as to that wait and see; be guided by events; meanwhile be coolish, though friendly, to young Bairstow. He parked his car, backing it into a space only just large enough with easy skill, and entered the Mechanics' Institute.

7

His decision to leave young Bairstow till after the meeting turned out well, as his decisions usually did, for old Thomas Armitage was already in the room, talking to young Bairstow, and Considine certainly did not wish his future partner in Highshaw to gain any inkling of his annuity transaction. Accordingly he sat down, bowed and smiled at Chairman and Secretary jointly, and looked with apparent interest at the other members. He saw he had seated himself next to that Communist fellow Greenwood, and for a moment all his body was filled with hate. Greenwood obviously returned his hate. They greeted each other.

"Cold for the time of the year?" said Considine to Greenwood smoothly.

"I don't go in for weather averages."

"Still, I see you've brought your raincoat."

From the other side of the table Miss Elizabeth Marrison, that silly woman who spent her life drawing pictures of clothes for other silly women to knit, smiled into his eyes at this neat retort. "A bitch if ever there was one," thought Considine with the secret coarseness he enjoyed, "and not often out of heat. Handsome enough, however, and knows how to use her eyes." Mentally, he stripped her and found the picture agreeable. That ass Councillor Ormerod now came in, with a pretty silly fair child, rather like Eileen used to be when young, and probably just as foolish. Considine folded his arms and gave her a look which he hoped she would find contemptuous and intimidating. The clock struck seven; time to begin, but young Bairstow and old Armitage were engaged in a discussion about the committee's quorum—so futile and unnecessary, when all the members were already here save one. Considine said so with his usual smooth slightly condescending competence, and the meeting began.

Young Bairstow—who had tried several times to catch his eye but Considine coolly evaded him—was just beginning the Minutes when the missing member, Deborah Sykes, came in. Wearing a silly smile all over her florid face as usual, she pushed round to the vacant chair between Considine and Bairstow, knocking his chair clumsily as she passed. "School-marm! Cow!" thought Considine furiously. "These damn women are always late." Because of his early humiliations with Eileen, it was agreeable to Considine to feel himself superior to all women, to despise their minds and to deride even while enjoying the attractions of their bodies. His line was that a woman's body was the only useful thing about her—if she lacked a body agreeable to his eye she was mere rubbish—and even the most charming body was not much. A woman whose mind was able and whose body did not appeal to him was therefore doubly displeasing, and he detested Mrs. Sykes on both these counts. Not that her mind was really able, of course, thought Considine contemptuously; it only appeared so by contrast with the nitwits of other women. . . .

V

MRS. DEBORAH SYKES, M.Sc.

I

> "*Thou, whose Almighty word*
> *Chaos and darkness heard,*
> *And took their flight;*
> *Hear us, we humbly pray,*
> *And where the Gospel-day*
> *Sheds not its glorious ray,*
> *Let there be light.*"

So sang the three hundred pupils and forty staff of the Ashworth Girls' High School, with the exception of the science mistress, Deborah Sykes. She too sang with vigour and enthusiasm enough, her broad fair face smiling, her large blue eyes beaming with light, but it was Truth, not Jehovah, she addressed, and knowing the hymn from childhood training, she had long since composed a version which suited her own convictions.

> "*Hear us, we humbly pray,*
> *And where Truth's piercing ray*
> *Sheds not its glorious day,*
> *Let there be light.*"

The children beside her, hearing these words which she made no attempt to conceal, gave her a questioning look while continuing to sing; she smiled serenely back at them and they returned to their hymn-books reassured, their short hair falling about their young ears, as Deborah thought, very agreeably.

It was just another of Deb's odd ways, thought the children comfortably, and there were plenty of those, heaven knew. Her untidiness of person was a byword in the school; her great fair plaits were always tumbling from their pins, her blouses though clean were habitually creased, even her stockings were sometimes wrinkled. She liked bright colours, blue and pink and gold, and sometimes came out in the most extraordinary patterns.

137

"*Have* you seen Deb's blouse today? My dear, it's like a cushion cover, honestly! Well, that's not inappropriate, after all," the older girls jested.

But their jests did not exceed kindness nor preclude respect, for Deb was not one to be derided. Her person might be untidy but her mind was not; in conversation she might stumble and laugh a trifle foolishly; but before a class her exposition, though mild and apparently casual, never faltered—without any fuss, somehow at the end of the lesson you found you had learned something interesting. Her handwriting was strong and handsome, whether on paper or blackboard, and her fair smooth hands manipulated scientific apparatus with such skill and ease that one longed to try the experiment for oneself.

Of course even in science and maths she had odd quirks. She always illustrated one's first lesson in algebraic equations by beans and a pair of swinging scales—it made equations wonderfully clear, of course, but the beans had been in existence since the year dot and were definitely shop-soiled. Again, unlike all other mistresses she positively encouraged girls to cluster round her in an untidy way while she was doing experiments (actually allowing them to sit on the top of the front row of desks and swing their feet) and she never scolded if someone broke a test tube, but if you left a blue flame in a Bunsen burner or tried to jump a stage in an experiment, above all if you pretended your experiment had come out right when it hadn't, she came down on you like a ton of bricks. Yes, you might think her soft but you came up against a rock in her sometimes, there was a wonderful calm friendliness about her always but she wasn't sentimental. She would kill a fly firmly and without hesitation, because she said that what with its eggs and its descendants' eggs, one fly if left alive would be responsible for producing thirteen million flies in a season, and against such a menace humanity was justified in defending itself. But she didn't despise the fly or avoid responsibility for its death by pretending that the fly felt very little and wouldn't mind being murdered; its life, such as it is, is all the fly has, she said, so *of course* it hates to surrender it. Flies, spiders, worms, mould human fæces, she did not despise anything however revolting to normal taste but saw them all as part of the wonderful fabric of life, and far from being upset, as some of the elder girls were when they first came in contact with these theories, by the suggestions of modern psychology as to the low physical origins of art and love, she took the line that to have constructed art and love from such small sordid origins was a most marvellous achievement on the part of man—the more lowly the origin, the more marvellous the achievement. To Deb, nothing was ugly save falsification, nothing was vile save pretence.

She was very strong about this, and at the beginning of every year gave each class a short harangue on these lines about the Purpose of Science. It was always the same harangue, expressed in such simple language that it served pretty well all down the school, and it was known as Deb's Daniel, because it was founded on a saying of Daniel Defoe as he rode over the Pennine hills from Lancashire into Yorkshire during his tour of England. "Then it was," said Defoe, after he had been looking carefully for some time at the hills and streams and scattered houses and cloth-çovered tenters of the Yorkshire Pennines and asking his riding companions questions about them—"Then it was I began to perceive the reason and nature of the thing." The thing in that case was the domestic system of cloth manufacture, but that was irrelevant; whatever the object of investigation was, the purpose and mode of the investigation should be the same. To perceive the reason and nature of the thing so as to be able to act justly with regard to it—that in Deborah's view was the purpose of science, as to inculcate the desire and practice of acting justly was in her view the purpose of morals. Yes, Deb was odd and somehow naïve and at times even silly, but all the same there was nothing petty or mean about her, in her presence one felt calm, refreshed, at ease; in spite of being silly in the worldly sense, in a universal sense she was wise.

The next two verses of Hymn 360, provided one mentally substituted the thought of Truth for that of a jealous Jehovah— though indeed Truth is a jealous enough god, visiting sins against itself upon the children of the sinners to the third and fourth generation, reflected Deborah soberly—but if one thought of Truth as one's addressee, the lines were well enough:

> *"Thou, who didst come to bring*
> *On thy redeeming wing*
> > *Healing and sight,*
> *Health to the sick in mind,*
> *Sight to the inly blind,*
> *Oh! now to all mankind,*
> > *Let there be light.*
>
> *Spirit of truth and love——"*

"That's science," thought Deborah, singing heartily—

> *"Spirit of truth and love,*
> *Life-giving, holy dove,*
> > *Speed forth thy flight:*
> *Move on the waters' face,*
> *Bearing the lamp of grace,*
> *And in earth's darkest place,*
> > *Let there be light."*

The last verse, however, Deborah did not care for; the thought of anything whatever, even Truth or Science, *rolling in fullest pride*, made her shake her head. Pride was an abomination, the ever-flowing source of cruelty; one could not pursue Truth, one could not perceive the reason and nature of the thing, if pride blinded the eyes.

> *"Holy and Blessed Three,*
> *Glorious Trinity,*
> > *Wisdom, Love, Might."*

So far, so good; Wisdom, that is to perceive the reason and nature of the thing, so as to be able to act justly with regard to it; Love, that is to wish to act justly by everything; Might, that is the will and the power to make that wish effective. But for the next lines Deborah had a version of her own:

> *"Let me thy servant be,*
> *Show truth to humanity,*
> *Though it bring grief to me,*
> *Let me give light!"*

2

The second line didn't quite fit the pattern of the verse and Deborah's voice sounded across the children's; the headmistress, up on the platform in gown and hood, smiled a little and sighed a little, and recalled—somewhat imperfectly, since her own faculty was English—the tale of how Deborah won her scholarship, which had become legendary in her college by the time, seven years later, the headmistress arrived there.

In Deborah's young days, just before the first World War, there was little provision for the teaching of science in Ashworth, and the notion of an attempt by a girl to win a science scholarship to London University was quite revolutionary. Deborah, firmly supported by her family, who belonged to that Nonconformist Liberal tradition which believed in culture for the Lord's sake, studied by herself at the High School, with occasional mild coaching at the Ashworth Technical College. Accordingly her opportunities for practical biology were scanty, and when she was confronted at the scholarship examination with the instruction to make a permanent preparation of specimen A and identify it as nearly as possible, she found to her grief and alarm that she could not classify the organism from which A came more closely than by its genus. She cut sections and stained them and mounted them on slides and was satisfied with the neatness and accuracy of her work; clearly the tiny little object was one of the head appendages (maxillules) of some crustacean. But turn the slide as she would beneath the microscope, which crustacean it was she could not tell. It might have been a lobster, she guessed that it was, but scientific certainty was lacking. With a deep sigh and a conviction that she was depriving herself of the scholarship, she gave its family name alone. At lunch with her fellow-candidates, it was said, her depression deepened, for all had boldly dubbed the crustacean a Norway lobster save herself. In the oral examination which followed later, the examiners tormented her with questions about this unlucky (as she thought) specimen, pressing upon her the enquiry: why had she not attempted to identify its species?

"I *did* attempt it," repeated Deborah in her rather slow and lumbering speech, "but——"

"You didn't describe it as a lobster."

"No——"

"Why not?"

At this point Deborah, hot, flushed, anxious, cried out the answer which became a classic: "I went to the limit of the evidence at my disposal!" Seeing the three examiners all apparently dumbfounded, she added in a quieter but no less determined tone: "Anything further would have been mere unscientific guesswork."

The joke was that the scientific attitude of mind which had prevented glib identification was fully justified, for the head appendages of *all* crustaceans have the same structure, so that any conclusion as to species drawn from one of these tiny waving feelers alone was quite unwarranted. The shellfish in question was, in fact, a Norway lobster, but from the only piece of it available to the examinees they were not entitled to say so. The other candidates had thus fallen headlong into an unintentional trap, for their identification was revealed, without any mitigating possibility, as a barefaced guess.

Deborah was awarded the scholarship, and her subsequent university career fully justified the examiners' encomiums, for she proved to be one of the most able students ever to pass the portals of the college. She was also, legend said, one of the best liked; sturdy and genial, with a hearty ringing laugh and a gleeful sparkle in her fine blue eyes, she was kind with an unstudied ease, never snubbing yet never putting a fellow-student under the burden of an obligation. The year when she was Senior Resident was referred to with awe by subsequent student-generations as a kind of Golden Age, when the College worked immensely hard but sensibly, in a cheerful sunny candid vigorous mood, with no failures and no nervous breakdowns. Sykes—it was a "modern" novelty in those days in women's colleges to speak of fellow-students by their surnames alone—Sykes (D) graduated with exceptional brilliance; rumours indeed went round that three—even one would have been striking enough, but three!—of her Final papers were awarded full marks, one hundred per cent. She seemed all set for a brilliant career. But then——

"*Aaa-men*," sang the children.

The headmistress stepped across to the lectern and began to read an undramatic but salutary passage from the New Testament.

"Two tragedies in a lifetime. And now teaching in a small provincial school. I don't know how she sustains that mild serenity, that placid smile. She's not maimed at all. Of course she could never have been a headmistress," thought the headmistress, reading *Judge not, that ye be not judged* and reflecting: Alas as a head it's my duty to judge, but this means not judging uncharitably. "She is not, no definitely *not*, suited to administrative work. She's the most exasperating member of my staff. Unconventional. Unpunctual. Untidy. Naïve. Frightens parents out of their wits by speaking the literal truth to them. Then her agnosticism, which she reveals as artlessly as a child, is so awkward. (Though it's *not everyone that saith unto me, Lord, Lord, shall enter into the kingdom of heaven, but he that doeth the will of my Father which is in Heaven,* I know.) She's not very good at getting examination results, either. But she *grounds* the younger children so well; they always know what the subject's really about. And of course with the older girls she's wonderful—gives them a truly spacious vision of the universe. They all believe in her and rely on her. Why? I think it's because she has that *dévou absolu* to her pupils which Charlotte's M. Heger postulated as the first requirement in a teacher—complete laying aside of self as far as they are concerned, complete devotion to their interests. In fact, in spite of her maddening unworldliness I have for her the greatest possible affection, admiration and respect," concluded the headmistress emphatically, beginning to intone the Lord's Prayer: "*Thy Kingdom come*—and I must maintain that attitude. One mustn't allow oneself to slip into Mammon-worship as one approaches middle age."

3

A very touching sight, all those young heads, thought Deborah Sykes. Brown hair, fair hair, black hair, red hair; hair tied in bows or woven into plaits; hair short and curly, hair thick and long. Wonderfully fresh rosy faces, clear large shining eyes, neatly convoluted ears—their ears were revealed as they all now respectfully gazed upwards, watching Henty reading Matthew VII. The fact that Dan's left ear had come from her womb slightly distorted, requiring to be kneaded into shape, did not mean she was to shirk the subject of ears or withhold her admiration from perfect specimens. However, she must not dwell on Dan, but sublimate her grief, as always, into a strong helpfulness for these young things whose view of the phenomena of the Universe was confided to her charge. They were lucky in Henty, who not only read Prayers and did all the social tricks admirably but administered the school admirably as well. Henty was indeed a graduate in whom College might take legitimate pride. She had done all the proper things, was a thoroughly useful member of the teaching profession and had never caused the authorities a moment's anxiety.

Deborah gave a slight chuckle as she remembered how much anxiety she herself had caused the authorities. After her degree, which came off well—the questions were singularly easy in Deborah's opinion—several admirable teaching posts immediately offered themselves, for it was wartime and women teachers were in immense demand. She could still see the old Principal's look of angry alarm when she declined them all and said she was going in for research, and recall her letter of remonstrance, in that tiny scholarly hand, when her best student, as she was pleased to call Deborah, accepted an ill-paid and unimportant laboratory position in a northern university, though far better openings of a similar kind were proffered in the south. Even her friends objected to this, but she smiled at them calmly: "I have a reason for wanting to be near home at present," she said: "I shan't stay long."

The reason was her cousin Daniel; in peacetime a promising young mathematician—the West Riding ran rather to mathematics—who had just become a schoolmaster; in wartime a pilot in the R.F.C. They had been brought up together, roamed the Pennine hills and dales, attended concerts far and near, revolted against the narrow parental creed and developed their views of politics, culture and religion by endless discussions, together; why should she dissimulate her expectation of marriage with Daniel? She surmised he was waiting until she should have taken her degree to mention the matter to her, and she wanted to be on hand in Ashworth for his next long leave, whenever that should occur.

The long leave came and the proposal of marriage with it, and soon they married and spent a blissful week's honeymoon walking in the Yorkshire dales. The trumpets sounded, the blood stirred, the hills were bathed in golden light and the streams sang with ecstasy. Daniel was tall and lean and agreeably ugly; warm-hearted and capable, he was rather vehement in speech but kindness itself in action; his laugh was hearty and he had a merry look in his keen brown eyes. (That boy Roddie Bairstow, the Secretary of the A.T.P.C., rather reminded Deborah of Daniel.) Daniel's brain was not of quite the same high quality as Deborah's; she knew it, he knew it and each knew the other knew it; it was just a fact of nature and caused them no concern.

At the end of the week they went to London so as to have as long a time as possible together. Their embraces on their last night were so gloriously prolonged that they both over-slept in the morning; they dressed in a scamper, laughing heartily at their lateness and its cause, and Daniel had to leave for France before Deborah was sufficiently clothed to accompany him through the streets. A strong warm kiss and he was gone. But Deborah did not, fortunately, sit down and cry; she threw on a long all-covering coat and galloped after him. She rushed about the streets—it was pouring with rain—crying out for a taxi to take her to Victoria, and after a series of rapid intrusions upon other people's taxis by each of which she drew nearer to the station, she at last arrived there just before Daniel's troop train went out. Clambering over various barriers and other impedimenta, and disregarding guards, with so hearty a cheerfulness that official remonstrances died away in smiles, Deborah actually succeeded in seeing Daniel depart, from the top of a porter's laden barrow on another platform. She shouted and waved; he saw her and laughed; they blew each other a kiss.

It was the last time he saw her. He crashed the following week and was dragged out of a burning plane with an arm withered and his eyesight gone.

After a period of training at St. Dunstan's he settled down to life in Ashworth with Deborah and their child, little Dan. He had a pension, of course, and Deborah made it her work to look after him, aided by his recently widowed mother, her aunt. Presently, as an airman's pension would not go far in providing the kind of education they both wanted for Dan, she began to teach in the Ashworth Technical College.

But why dwell on all that wretched time, thought Deborah, shaking her head. It was wretched, because the once strong, kind, protective Daniel gradually became a selfish, peevish, fretful invalid. (At that time Deborah sometimes caught herself longing to tell Daniel, the young cousin she had loved so long, all her trouble over this peevish ailing man, her husband.) Of course it was not his fault; Deborah understood the physical causes of the change well enough and made all allowances. His damaged hand made Braille reading difficult and he never achieved real fluency; she fully realised what a terrible frustration this must be. The one point she found it difficult to condone was his resentment over the child's slight malformation. Even that she understood; no doubt to his acutely sensitive touch the ear seemed more disfigured than it appeared to the mere eye. Still, his endless harpings on the matter wore on her nerves, and to contrive that in spite of it Dan should grow up a healthy normal child was not easy. Her own parents, too, grew old, and Daniel's mother, broken by the disaster to her son, began to need attention, so that whether Deborah ought to go on with her teaching or not was a continual worry to her conscience.

After ten years of this the question was solved by the death of Daniel. Deborah would not pretend it was other than a relief, for the husband she loved had died ten years ago in the blazing plane. But Daniel's mother now failed altogether in health and had to be nursed, and then her own parents did the same; to keep the households going, Deborah's earnings were now a necessity. The whole situation was a protracted ordeal; but Deborah enjoyed her life because of her happiness in little Dan. The malformed ear had no counterpart in his brain; he was strong and clever; tall like his father, fair like Deborah; lively and merry and vehement, a favourite with everyone, kind and candid and devoted to his mother.

The elder Sykes generation died at last, affectionately and faithfully nursed to the last by Deborah. Then she had three happy, happy years with Dan. Though they used no endearments to each other, rarely touched hands and never kissed, they were the deepest, the closest, the dearest of friends. In the holidays they travelled all over Europe together, walking whole countries with rucksacks on their backs, admiring with intelligent zeal the great buildings and fine works of art they had crossed mountains and rivers and plains to see. At home they dressed shabbily in order to be able to attend plays and concerts—Dan was a good amateur violinist and took a keen pleasure, when no other form of musical activity was available, in the silent reading of scores. They read much music in this way, they read also much poetry and history, economics and politics, and discussed what they read with keen enjoyment. They had large vocabularies and enjoyed keeping them in practice. Dan's mind was finer and stronger than his mother's—she knew it and rejoiced—and everyone predicted a superb future for the exceptionally promising lad.

He was at Cambridge with a scholarship when the second war came. Deborah could not help rejoicing then in his poor little ear, which she thought would prevent his acceptance by any of the services; surely she would not be called on to lose son as well as husband; surely she would be allowed to keep young Dan safe. The services refused him as she hoped, and since he was taking Science his call-up was deferred; he took his degree and was directed into one of the hush-hush wartime research departments, did excellent work there and was killed in a bus by a V-one bomb while on an official journey to London in the summer of 1944.

But why think of Dan, why think of Dan now; she must strive once again to sublimate her grief into a strong helpfulness for these young things with their fresh faces and curly hair and neatly convoluted ears. (In the old days the Board of Education would not employ married teachers, but that prejudice had been smashed by the war, thank goodness, there was a shortage of women science teachers and Henty had almost begged her to come to the Ashworth High School.) Indeed to feel love and strong helpfulness towards her pupils was not difficult, for it was now the great desire of her heart (as truth was of her mind) that young people should be happy while there was still time. Just a week's happiness Daniel and Deborah had before fate struck them; just three years' happiness Deborah and Dan had before fate struck again. While there was still *time*, young people should be *happy*. Of course she must not allow this feeling to become an obsession with her; she must watch carefully lest it deflect her service from truth. Still——

"If there be any evil here, O Life," prayed Deborah as all the heads bent again for the Lord's Prayer: "If there be any evil, O spare these young happy creatures, let it descend instead on me."

4

Tuesday was a very busy day, thought Deborah, threading the polished corridors to her laboratory after Prayers, but a happy one, though it was perhaps just a little unfortunate that the A.T.P.C. had chosen to meet on that night. Or perhaps it was a little unfortunate that she had been chosen to represent on that Committee the teachers of the town. A music mistress or an arts mistress would have been more use. Still, she saw their point; most of the other mistresses were not of local birth; she, Deborah, having been born and bred in Ashworth of a textile family, knew the textile trade pretty well and could add a smattering of the arts as well as a knowledge of the children's capacities and time-tables. After all, Elizabeth Marrison had the art side of the Pageant in hand. Yes, no doubt her nomination as delegate to the A.T.P.C. was reasonable, and not just a mere dumping of an unwanted extra chore on her shoulders—though doubtless there was a little of that in it as well, she thought with a smile. And why not, after all? Teachers nowadays had so many administrative tasks, so many forms to fill, so many responsibilities for the physical and economic welfare of their pupils, that they had hardly time to teach, much less to live any private and personal lives. To fall in love successfully took time, which young teachers ought to have allowed to them. She had no objection to taking this A.T.P.C. work off younger shoulders. Presently, if the Pageant scheme materialised, they would have enough to do.

Meanwhile one must forget the end of the day and concentrate on the present, thought Deborah, rapidly assembling test tubes and racks and holders and a jar of copper sulphate—she did not believe in waiting on her pupils usually, but her first class this morning consisted of eleven-year-olds, the year's new intake into the school; this was only the second science lesson of their lives and their entry into the world of chemistry needed a little easing if they were not to be afraid. Few things, in fact, gave Deborah more pleasure nowadays than precisely this process of guiding eager ignorant young feet over the threshold and through the great portals of Science.

Here they came now, thirty of them, tumbling in, their blue "science overalls" very bright and clean and new. (Deborah's new autumn suit was just the colour of these overalls; she had partly chosen it for this reason, and it gave her real satisfaction now. The girls too, had already noticed it, she thought, with pleasure.) Their notebooks, their pens and pencils and rulers, their indiarubbers and their minds, were all equally clean and new, thought Deborah, but alas not equally bright—one could see already, by the very differences in the bows of their overalls tied at the back, differences in their mental capacities. It was her part to lead each one as far as the child's abilities allowed.

The children were rather quiet at first this morning, overawed by this new world of backless stools and spatulas and Bunsen burners, but soon in the continual *va-et-vient* of a junior science class they lost their shyness and came alive. Drawing it all out of them by carefully thought-out questions, Deborah revised their first lesson last week, when they had made a solution of salt and water. Owing to her preliminary harangue about Defoe the lesson had remained unfinished; the children had written down the *Object* of the experiment, *to find out what happens when salt is put into water*, and the *Method*, but the *Result* remained as yet unrecorded. Guiding them gently towards that impersonality of statement which is Science's pride, Deborah wrote on the blackboard at their dictation: *At first the salt dissolved in the water. Then no more salt would dissolve. The salt dissolved in the water is called——*

"Now we've got to have some scientific terms," announced Deborah, beaming, as though to achieve the use of scientific terms was to scale a peak in Darien—as indeed it was. Stimulating answers from the cleverer children and explaining them to the less quick, she wrote again at their dictation: *The salt dissolved in the water is called a salt solution. The water is called the solvent, and the salt, the solute. A solution which will not hold any more of the solute is said to be saturated.*

"Now copy all that down neatly into your notebooks."

There was the usual rush for inkpots, and Deborah, smiling, gave the usual caution about not using these as reservoirs for fountain pens. Silence fell upon the room as the children wrote laboriously, with tense fingers and bent heads.

"Watch the spelling carefully; there's no excuse for copying things wrongly from the blackboard. Besides, all these new words have to be learned for homework."

Not too soon and not too late—there was a skill in hitting the right moment for an inspection—Deborah came down from her platform and went along between the benches, overlooking the notebooks.

"I see some very nice tidy writing; that's good. I also see

some people sitting up very nicely. Now there are more people sitting up nicely," said Deborah in her cheerful tone. "Read it through carefully. Watch the spellings. See the full stops are where they ought to be. I want to be able to mark each exercise with a tick, with no corrections in the margin. That's very nice. Yes, you've done that very nicely. Now does anyone know any other solvents? For dirt on your hands? For grease? For paint? Come along now! Of course you know! Quite right, but put it in the new words you've learned today. Yes, very well, girls, now we'll go on to a fresh experiment. Object: *to find out what happens when a saturated solution is warmed and then cooled*. This time we're going to make our solution with copper sulphate. Yes, it *is* a pretty blue. First of all there is something important we have to learn about Bunsen burners. . . . Go two at a time to the burners on the bench by the window. . . . Now close the little hole. What happens to the flame? What colour is it? Now open the little hole. What colour is the flame? Yes, and this scarcely visible blue flame is very much hotter. . . . So you see the danger. . . . If anyone ever leaves a Bunsen burner without turning it back to the yellow flame, they are exposing other people to the danger of burns. . . . Yes, I should be very angry, certainly, my dear; but the point is that your neglect might harm your classmates. . . ."

A saturated solution of copper sulphate was duly made and warmed and observed, and left in labelled saucers to cool on the long broad window-sill, the bell rang and the first two periods of morning school were over. Deborah went upstairs to the staff-room for the mid-morning cup of tea. and sat down beside her young second in command, the junior science mistress, who was arguing, not very seriously, with a contemporary, the respective merits of Science and History as a career.

"*You* sit comfortably at a desk all day and harangue the children. The Science teacher is always on her feet. Isn't that so, Mrs. Sykes?"

"Well—yes—that is, not always. My next period—besides, there are advantages——"

But the discussion had long since passed ahead.

The bell rang and Deborah descended to a small group of older girls. Neat and well-groomed in their white blouses and matching cardigans and skirts, they showed in the arrangement of their carefully cut hair, in their budding bodies and more restrained gestures, in the fact that they wore stockings (the younger forms sported bare legs and socks) that they were approaching the threshold of the grown-up world outside school. Indeed they were taking a nursing examination in a fortnight. They appeared somewhat overweighted by the knowledge of this coming ordeal, and Deborah entered into their earnest mood. Their homework had been written answers of some length to hygiene examination questions of previous years; she discussed each girl's efforts separately in a low tone, guiding them by questions to perceive their errors; they listened with an air of serious concern.

"I wish we hadn't to do all this *written* work," protested a big red-haired girl, tossing her head impatiently.

"But don't you want to be a nurse?"

"Yes, of course. But——"

"It's useless to wish for incompatibles, Norma," said Deborah in her frank good-humoured tones. "It leads only to frustration. You must choose. If you don't know anatomy you may easily with the best of intentions break your patient's leg."

The girls giggled, though not unkindly, and Norma laughed and said: "Oh well! I suppose I choose to be a nurse."

"Good," said Deborah.

But you won't be a professional nurse, she thought, smiling at the gloriously healthy young creature, or at any rate not for long; you'll marry and have children of your own to nurse; and I hope you are luckier than I have been.

"Joan, you make it sound as if the capillaries took the blood by the hand and led it to the heart. Your expression is inexact. . . . The biggest fault of all of you is not expressing what you mean. Use words of one syllable and sentences that are simple and short."

"But, Mrs. *Sykes*, there's so *much* to *say* about the circulation."

"Pick out the salient facts and make them fit into a half-hour's answer. Now what questions shall we choose for next time? What about the composition of air and systems of ventilation?"

"We've done that before, Mrs. Sykes."

"I know, but it was early last term. Would it be valuable to do it again, for revision?"

"I think it would."

"I don't, I know it quite well."

"Perhaps we needn't all do the same questions."

"I quite agree with you, Julia. It will be good experience for you to choose which questions you think most useful. I'll pick out three or four from these, and each of you do two. By the way, there's something rather good about circulation in the last Penguin *Science News*. You might take it, Joan, and see that it gets passed round."

The bell rang, and Deborah enjoyed a forty minutes' free period. She spent it in correcting exercise books and preparing apparatus for the afternoon, then went out into the garden and collected a few "fruits" for a botany lesson, in case the girls had not responded sufficiently to her invitation to bring specimens. The bell rang again and it was the dinner-hour, and alternate Tuesdays were Deborah's days on duty with the children. She did not enjoy this very much, for one of her functions was to ring a large hand-bell when the noise became too great. Silence then supervened and lasted until the bell was rung again. The silence was irksome to the girls, the noise to the mistresses; to decide the exact moment when justice would be done to both by clanging the bell was an anxiety to Deborah. She was apt to let the noise grow too great, when she received reproachful glances from her colleagues at the staff table by the door.

This happened today. Sitting on her solitary chair, bell in lap, she was off in a dream, listening to Tchaikowsky's Fifth with Dan, when suddenly the Junior Science mistress, her young face flushed with embarrassment, appeared at her elbow and began to speak. The surrounding din was so great that she was quite inaudible. Shocked by her obvious distress, Deborah raised the bell and clanged it so vigorously that the peals, as she afterwards discovered from the chance remark of a non-dining pupil, were heard in the road. An awestruck silence fell.

"Now, what is it, my dear?" said Deborah, leaning towards her junior with a smile.

"Only the noise, Mrs. Sykes."

"Oh!" said Deborah, discomfited. "Well—I see—please make my apologies to the other mistresses."

Blushing more deeply than before, the young woman withdrew.

Would it be well to keep the children silent for a long period, wondered Deborah, to repay them for that abominable noise? But that was her fault, after all. Why should she punish them for her mistake?

Quite soon, beaming benevolently upon them, she rang the releasing bell. At first the talk was decorous and subdued, but soon the young voice rose again. . . . Well, that was only natural; young memories were short.

After the children were gone and she had eaten her meal alone she went out into the grounds—ample though terraced out of one of Ashworth's surrounding hills, Worth Bank—and strolled about, keeping an eye on the children, who were playing scratch games of hockey and baseball or sewing, reading and talking. The September day was pleasant but rather chill. Deborah looked carefully to see that no child was lying on the dampish grass without a protective coat, and picked a few more lupin pods, antirrhinum capsules and dandelion clocks for the afternoon class. Some fine hawthorn berries proving somewhat beyond her reach, she borrowed one of the younger children's hockey sticks to draw the branch downwards. This excited the players' interest and they clustered round her.

"Didn't we make a noise at dinner, Mrs. Sykes?"

"You did indeed."

"Why didn't you ring the bell sooner?"

"I'm afraid I was thinking of something else."

"How do you decide when to ring the bell, Mrs. Sykes?"

"In the absence of an instrument for measuring decibels, Hilary, I just have to guess."

They all laughed heartily and jumped about, tossing their heads so that their plaits leaped and their curls shook, revealing their youthful ears.

"What are decibels, Mrs. Sykes?"

"Units of noise, Wendy. You're creating several now."

"Oh, Mrs. Sykes!"

Presently the bell rang, afternoon school began and some three dozen second-year children poured into the laboratory. Deborah knew them well and hoped good things of them, for they had done well for her in the previous year. Their science overalls were a little faded and showed a tendency to be too short and tight—children grow so rapidly at twelve, thought Deborah smiling. They were thoroughly familiar with *Object, Method* and *Result* and wrote their homework corrections rapidly so as to be able soon to cluster about her at her desk. Practical work began, and four out of five substances were burned in oxygen successfully. The fifth, however, misbehaved; instead of bursting into purple flame as it should, it smouldered and fizzled sulkily. A cry broke from the children of genuine disappointment and commiseration.

"Oh, Mrs. Sykes! What a shame! It isn't burning!"

"Never mind. What do we do when an experiment doesn't turn out as we expect?"

Hands shot up from all quarters, for last year this had been the subject of frequent exhortations.

"Well, Hilary?"

"We do it again to see if it really is so or if we have made a mistake in doing it."

"Right," said Deborah emphatically. "Right and very good. All great discoveries begin in that way." Here the bell rang. "We'll do it again next week and see what happens."

The next class, the last of the day, was peaceful but somewhat boring. Deborah always found botany just a little boring; always had, since those happy days at College when she had actually had the temerity to ask the Principal, in the middle of her second year, to allow her to change her subject from botany. The Principal's refusal had been firm and horrified, and no doubt it was just as well as things had turned out, reflected Deborah, drawing follicles and legumes on the blackboard handsomely. The girls, who were fifteen or so in age and had public examinations looming ahead of them, took these fruits seriously but were a trifle bored too, she suspected; however they had brought quite a number of specimens to class and drew and labelled them accurately. She passed among them, commenting on their work; when she was at the back where the front rows could not see her, the front rows began to chatter. For some time Deborah could not find it in her heart to scold them for this familiar phenomenon, considering the boredom of botany, but at last she was obliged to do so.

"You're talking rather louder than I like. If you must talk—and I agree it's necessary in some cases—talk in a whisper. And don't talk at all when I'm speaking," concluded Deborah sharply.

She mitigated this rebuke, however, by gently straightening the strap of a handbag slung over the offender's shoulder—she had often noticed how attached this form was to shoulder handbags: these appurtenances evidently marked a stage of development which one reached at a certain year of age. They were good girls, but a little tired and sleepy from the mental efforts of the day; come to that, she was a little tired herself and would be glad when the bell rang.

It sounded at last and the teaching day was over.

Deborah went down to her class-room and supervised the class's departure, then attended an extra rehearsal of the School choir for a looming speech-day. She played the piano while the music mistress conducted. This was a great refreshment and Deborah enjoyed it, though sad thoughts stole through her mind inevitably, for she had heard this familiar Bach chorale many times, both with Daniel and with Dan. The rehearsal over, the children left, their clear young voices gradually fading as they walked down the drive, and Deborah went to her lab to prepare apparatus for the morrow's lessons.

5

This took some time and when at last Deborah finished her tasks and glanced at her watch she found it was already

156

almost the hour for her weekly conversation class with the E.V.W.'s at the Ashworth Technical College.

She took her blue hat from its peg in the staff cloakroom and pulled it on her head and stuffed her plaits inside, smiling at her reflection in the glass between affection and amusement for the large plain features and fresh-coloured cheek she saw there. Then snatching up her brief-case she made her way out of the echoing building, empty now save for the caretaker sweeping the entrance hall, and hurried down the road and through the Ashworth Public Park in her rather lumbering but powerful and space-covering stride.

Thinking of the E.V.W.'s already waiting for her in the class-room—their situation made them touchy and they would take her unpunctuality as another item in their long persecution—she did not look about her as she went. But presently she became conscious of a noise as of young boys in the distance—"You did!" "I didn't!" "Yes, he did!" "I saw him!"—and as she emerged from the Park found herself cannoned into and by-passed by some half-dozen dirty, untidy, rather ragged little boys who were chasing with angry shouts another boy, smaller, dirtier and if anything more ragged than the rest. They were no doubt inhabitants of the grimy and ill-built streets, products of the early years of the Industrial Revolution, which lay between the Park and the station side of the town.

A few yards up the road the pursuers caught the pursued, who stood with his back to the wall surrounded by the jeering crowd of his contemporaries. Such a situation was an intolerable spectacle to Deborah; she sprang forward and thrusting her way through the circle, seized the frightened child's hand protectively. Small and thin and fair, with a look of under-nourishment, he trembled perceptibly and his pale blue eyes seemed to bulge out of his head like a hare's, with terror. He did not strike her as a very pleasant child as he looked up at her; his nose was running, and his face bore a somewhat mean and furtive air.

"Why are you frightening this little boy?" demanded Deborah.

"What's it got to do with you?" said the largest boy rudely. He had a sturdy frame and red cheeks, and tiresomely enough, as Deborah reflected, looked a nicer child altogether than his victim.

"It makes me feel sick to see six boys setting on one," replied Deborah truthfully.

"Well, he stole some flowers."

"I didn't! I didn't! Them flowers was given me."

Howls of derision greeted this defence.

"Even if he stole them, you shouldn't bully him. But how do you know he stole them? Where are the flowers?"

"I dropped 'em while I were running."

"He was afraid to be seen with them! He stole them!"

"Well, now," said Deborah mildly: "Let's go into the Park and sit down on a seat and examine the evidence."

"How do you mean?" enquired the largest boy, hesitating.

"Let's try to find out what really happened. Come along."

She led the hare-eyed child by the hand towards one of the iron seats. Astonished and silent, but in spite of themselves intrigued, his persecutors followed.

"I live across there," said the hare-eyed child wistfully, pointing.

"I'll take you home afterwards. Now who gave you the flowers?" said Deborah, seating herself.

"A gardener with an apron," wailed the child. "They was lying on the ground. He'd cut 'em off. They were old ones. I looked at them and then I picked some up and he said, he said, you can take 'em if you've a mind, he said. They was given me, was them flowers."

"Which gardener was it?" enquired Deborah, for several stooping figures were to be seen on distant terraces.

"He were right over by t'other gate, by some pink flowers," wailed the child.

"There aren't any pink flowers over there," cried a boy.

"Yes, there are," cried another.

The others took sides over this and shouted their opinions violently. A definition of the colour pink, thought Deborah, would be useful at this point. Always define your terms.

"Yes, there are some pinky-mauve dahlias over by the

158

gate," she said, recalling them. "There was a gardener too. We'll go and ask him if he gave the flowers, shall we?"

"Happen he won't remember," wailed the victim. His protest did not, however, reveal the keen distress of a guilty conscience but only the natural reluctance of any child to approach an official "park-keeper." The other boys seemed to perceive this, for they fell silent and their faces took on looks of disappointment and disgust.

"You needn't all come," said Deborah. "But I think *you* ought to," she said to the largest boy.

"I'm not bothered," said he, swinging disdainfully on his heel.

The Ashworth-born Deborah fully understood the significance of this local idiom.

"Then you must admit you were wrong," she said sharply. "All that about the flowers was just an excuse to be cruel."

For a moment they all stood there silent and sullen, staring at the ground. Then: "Come on!" shouted the largest boy, and rushed away towards the gate. The others flew with him, and suddenly the hare-eyed child snatched his hand from Deborah's and ran after them as fast as his spindly legs would go. As the boys gained the safety of the road they looked back over their shoulders and shouted something rude at Deborah. The hare-eyed child's insult was particularly shrill.

"Silly old nosey!" he screamed.

Deborah, getting up, laughed and waved to them cheerfully, but as she turned towards the road her face clouded with thought and she began to analyse the incident. She had prevented a miscarriage of justice and assisted a triumph of truth. Yes; but had she really done the hare-eyed boy any good? Or had she merely deepened the gulf between him and his companions? His insult to her had been sycophantic, uttered to curry favour with his erstwhile friends, of whom he was perhaps now even more afraid than before. Perhaps she had done harm; perhaps her interference was essentially selfish and satisfied only her own need. Between the exercise of a principle and the welfare of a person, how was one to judge aright? One met the problem at every turn of the day: in the dinner hour with the silence bell, in lessons over discipline and the imposition of a fixed syllabus, here in the park with the slum-children. Useless, though true, to say that past and present economic conditions over which she had no control had malformed their minds; what one wanted to know was how best to act now for their welfare.

Had she done more harm than good? She went on her way pondering this question and not finding a certain answer.

6

As she climbed the steps of the Ashworth Technical College Deborah became conscious of a reproachful face flattened against a nearby window. It belonged to one of the European Voluntary Workers; Stephanie was the English version of her name. Because of her greater ease in the English tongue, acquired in contact with American occupying forces during some part of her complicated tragic "displaced person" story which Deborah had never yet managed completely to unravel, Stephanie had constituted herself the leader of the Ashworth E.V.W.'s in all linguistic matters, and it was largely owing to her that this conversation class had continued so long.

The class had arisen a couple of years ago in a natural way, when the man who was teaching the E.V.W.'s, not being of West Riding birth himself, had asked Deborah to help him with the textile terms which some of the E.V.W.'s who were mill-workers continually encountered in their daily round. The experiment was a success, and E.V.W.'s engaged in other work—engineering, domestic, chemical—begged eagerly that Mrs. Sykes would perform the same service for them. Scientific terms and domestic terms were familiar to Deborah; the language of other local industries she took some pains to acquire; the habit grew, at first of half an hour's conversation after, and later of an hour's conversation before, the official class in English. The affair was purely voluntary on either side and formed no part of the official syllabus. From time to time official eyes frowned on this use of a College room for an unofficial purpose at an

160

unofficial hour, but a torrent of Stephanie's East European eloquence from without, and a natural compassion from within, the official breast caused the eye to be discreetly turned in the other direction, and Mrs. Sykes's conversation classes continued and flourished. There were usually between twenty or thirty persons present; Deborah arriving at the class-room door after a hurried trot down the long echoing corridors saw that the larger number was correct today. Stephanie was standing in the doorway to greet her.

"You are very late, Mrs. Sykes."

"Yes. I'm sorry."

She went in, laid down her brief-case, took off her hat, pushed in a hairpin which was escaping from her plaits, and ran her eyes over the class. There was the usual mixture of Austrians, Poles, Lithuanians, Ukrainians and Czechs; there was the spruce prosperous talkative engineer, the pretty little housemaid, the two gloomy Russian lads, the mass of Austrian mill-girls all with bright jerseys, slacks and fair hair arranged in high pompadours; there was Stephanie in her pink dress with her severe sallow face and straight dark rat-tails; there was fat Maria who always joked; there was neat middle-aged housekeeper Anna who would never, but never, know more than three words of any language but her own; there were several respectable elderly men with the dirt-engrained hands of the lifelong manual worker; there was that dark-eyed freckled Leni who was doing so well in the knitting-yarn mill; there were three girls beside her in the back row who were clearly newcomers to the country, for they still wore relics of their former clothes and looked bewildered and lost.

"Good afternoon."

"Good afternoon, Mrs. Sykes."

"It is almost good evening, however," said the engineer in smiling reproach.

"Yes, indeed," said Stephanie severely.

"We have three new members with us today, I see."

"They are Austrian. They work in the same mill with Leni and me," announced Stephanie.

"I see. So they live in the same hostel as you?"

"Yes. But they cannot say its name."

"What is its name?"

"Fairfax House, thirteen Fairfax Place," said Stephanie, enunciating with great correctness.

"Well, it is rather difficult," said Deborah soothingly. She went down between the desks and stood in front of the newcomers. The others turned to watch her. "What is the first thing we teach to new members? Anna, you tell me."

Anna sighed and shook her head.

"Who they are, what they are, where they live," said the engineer.

Deborah began to elucidate these essential items for the newcomers—it helped the official teachers to take this off their shoulders.

"Here you are no longer Displaced Persons," she said to them in English and German: "Here you have a home and a place to work, here you are European Voluntary Workers."

They gazed up at her sadly. She wondered whether to ask them the names of their native towns or not; sometimes to do so cheered them, sometimes it brought a burst of tears. Still it was better for the rest of the class to know their origin, so that persons from the same home district could group themselves together. She continued her enquiries, wrote a few simple phrases on the board for them to copy, and turned her attention to the others, who were becoming restive.

"You, Ivan; tell us what you have done today."

"Oh! Impossible!" said Ivan with a despairing gesture.

"Yes, come along. The rest of us will help you."

Ivan began solemnly to describe his day in the colour-matching department of a local firm of textile manufacturers. When he came to words he did not know, he sometimes drew the object in question on the board and once produced it (a small weight) from his pocket. The class offered suggestions and comments, laughed and grew merry.

"Now you, Leni," said Deborah. The girl seemed quiet this evening, she thought, so she said this to draw her into participation. "Tell us what you have done since morning."

Leni's freckled face contorted into a mask of agony; she

burst into loud tears and leaping from her chair ran out of the room.

"Oh, what have I said?" cried Deborah wretchedly, starting after her. She felt quite sick to think she had inadvertently wounded a young creature, a harmless stranger. "What is wrong? Poor Leni!"

"It is useless to go after her," said Stephanie reprovingly, rising to bar the way.

"Someone must go after her."

"No—it is useless. She is better alone. I explain at the end of the class."

"Are you sure?" said the troubled Deborah, glancing round and trying to remember which other members of the class lived in Leni's hostel.

"Yes—it is better to leave her alone," chorussed several.

"Did I speak too peremptorily? *Sprach ich allzu kurz?*"

"No, no."

"That you can never do," added the engineer courteously.

"It is an affair of the heart," said Stephanie in a sepulchral tone.

This is another case like the boys in the Park, thought Deborah, uneasy. Ought I to interfere or not? The hare-eyed child's *silly old nosey* rang in her ears.

"Oh, well! In that case perhaps you are right," she said aloud unhappily.

"Let us continue the class, if you please," said the engineer.

Deborah sighed and turned to Maria. But her whole body felt full of pain. How could she have been so inconsiderate, so tactless? She had hurt a vulnerable fellow-human, she had filled a moment of youth, which should be so sweet, with pain. Her thoughts wandered to Daniel and Dan. The class became dull and stiff and dismissed itself when the clock struck, promptly.

"Now, Stephanie!" called Deborah, and this time her tone was certainly peremptory. "Come here and tell me about Leni."

"She is sad. She come home early from her work and weep and then go for a walk lonely."

"Alone. But why is she sad?"

"She is very passionate."

"Emotional."

"Yes, emotional. Recently she had been very happy, because at our mill where we work there comes a doctor from her district of Vienna, and she think he likes her."

"Oh, that would be splendid!" said Deborah, beaming.

"Yes. But today I think something goes wrong. He does not keep his appointment."

"Oh dear. Poor Leni. Perhaps it's only a temporary misunderstanding."

Stephanie shrugged. "She is not very beautiful, Leni," she said.

"And I asked her to describe her day," said Deborah sorrowfully. "Please give her my love, Stephanie, and tell her how sorry I am to have been so tactless."

"It is not easy to give such messages to Leni," demurred Stephanie. "She is emotional."

"Please do as I say," said Deborah sharply.

Stephanie grimaced and shrugged her shoulders.

7

All this, again, had taken time, and the clock was already striking seven as Deborah crossed Cloth Hall Street towards the Mechanics' Institute. She sighed a little as she surveyed this building, and smiled a little too.

The sigh was for its architecture: a horrid mingling of the over-decorated and the nakedly utilitarian, highly characteristic of its Victorian period. Its many-faced stone lozenges and chubby pillars, its carved mouldings and projecting brackets (all now black with Ashworth smoke) ceased abruptly, as though shaved off with a knife, above the second storey, where the windows decreased in size. The lower portion held public rooms, in the upper, once devoted to classes, clerks to various firms now worked in the dreary light afforded by the disproportionately small windows.

The smile was for the nobility of the Institute's purpose when it was founded: to give Facility to the Working Class, as the printed notice said, towards the Attainment of Knowledge Useful to their Several Callings. That knowledge

164

brought power in its train had perhaps been forgotten, would perhaps have disconcerted some of the founders of the Institute, reflected Deborah, but not her great-grandfather, who she was proud to remember had been one of its prime movers. He had presided at a Conference of Mechanics' Institutes held in this building some time in the 1890's, just before his death, and had uttered a characteristic remark to a too enthusiastically organising member about disliking the element of compulsion which appeared in his proposition. His portrait—bright-eyed, whiskered, fierce, with a flat collar and a crooked bow—hung in the Committee Room behind the Chairman's carved chair. Deborah looked up at it now as she entered and gave Great-grandfather a mental tribute while outwardly smiling her apologies for being late to Mr. Armitage—who, she thought, gets to look very old and worn. Thus looking up, thus smiling, she did not see the foot of Sir Charles Considine's chair, and slightly tripped over it; he drew it in impatiently.

"I'm sorry the only empty place is next to Sir Charles," thought Deborah, seating herself and looking round: "For though I know nothing to his disadvantage, I don't much care for him. All that suavity rings false—a kind of chilly purr."

Beyond Sir Charles sat tense, bristling, bolt upright, the Communist young man whose name she never could remember. Probably, in spite of his pride in his C.P. card and Party number, he would be vexed to know that, thought Deborah smiling; we ourselves are always individuals, it is the others who form the collective mass. It was clear that the bristling young man and Sir Charles detested each other icily, but in truth they differed less from each other than both differed from dear old Thomas Armitage. Captain Bairstow on her other side was a nice young fellow, though over-vehement and with parts of his nature forced into too lush growth by war; he had married a nice girl whom his father disapproved, Deborah understood, which was splendid; they had lots of children and she hoped they were burningly happy.

But what a charming creature was sitting at Mr. Armitage's

right hand! Joy filled Deborah's heart at the sight of that lovely young face—though at present, she thought shrewdly, it has a sulky air. She smiled at the child; she's the Youth Groups representative, I suppose; how delightful to have her here. Pity she's placed next to that beautiful bitter Marrison woman; poor Miss Marrison, thought Deborah commiseratingly, she's a nympho I'm afraid, glands and something wrong in her childhood. She won't enjoy sitting between that fresh young charmer and Councillor Foster, who'll have no eyes for her. Plump, short, black-eyed, with the large lips of the orator and a deep cleft in his forehead drawn by a perpetual cocking of one eyebrow to herald the prepared joke, Councillor Foster Ormerod was often called Councillor Foster to distinguish him from the innumerable other Ashworth Ormerods—they were no relation, it was just the Ashworth name, as Greenwood and Shackleton were the names in other West Riding towns—and the familiarity was encouraged by him, for it was a real asset, Deborah guessed shrewdly, to his political career. He was the staunch Trade Unionist, the Labour politician, the man who could speak for an hour at a moment's notice without a pause—no grammar and endless repetition, but jest and earnest skilfully juxtaposed. Dan had yawned his head off through many a Foster speech and mimicked him admirably.

Deborah caught the Councillor's eye now and he gave her a jerky little nod—the nod was not on her own account, she knew, but on that of her great-grandfather, between whom and Councillor Foster had occurred, many years ago, a famous Ashworth incident. The whole industrial history of the West Riding, thought Deborah, could be seen in that nod to Jonathan Bamforth's great-granddaughter in the Mechanics' Institute, Cloth Hall Street, Ashworth, from Councillor Foster Ormerod. . . .

VI

COUNCILLOR FOSTER ORMEROD

I

"Go steady, love, chance you fall!" called Councillor Foster Ormerod (Bolland Ward) to his youngest grandchild, who was skipping precariously along the top of a heap of flat rockery-stones which lay by the back door awaiting his attention.

"I *am* going steady, Grandpa!" shrilled Hilary, tossing her fair head and trying the next stone with the toe of her neat strapped shoe. The stone wobbled; Hilary's expression changed from defiance to alarm and her outstretched arms flapped, but by an agile convulsion of her plump little stomach she managed to retrieve her balance. "I am going steady," she repeated with less conviction.

Councillor Foster looked around. "You, Leslie," he called to the boy who was throwing a ball up against the back of the house: "Look after 'Ilary on them stones."

Leslie gave a somewhat petulant sniff and jerked his head protestingly, but he pocketed the ball and crossed to his sister.

"Now then! What are you up to, you silly kid?" he cried. "Come down!"

He put his arms round her waist and tried to lift her to the ground. Hilary gave a hearty scream and dug her toes in, and a few minutes of friendly horseplay followed, the light high voices of the children tinkling like bells on the evening air. Leslie's light brown eyes sparkled, and his cheeks were red as apples with laughter; he hugged his sister's middle and playfully bit her ear, which was temptingly near his mouth, for he was tall.

It was pleasant in the little garden tonight. After a showery afternoon the evening had turned fair. There was a brisk autumn tang in the air, the sun was going down in a red ball behind Highshaw Bank, the light was falling, dusk would soon be here. In front of number thirty-five the ground fell away abruptly, so that the roofs of the other brick houses on

167

the Bolland Clough Lane housing estate—the last built in Ashworth before the war—did not hide the sky or the view of Ashworth and its surrounding hills, which was extensive. In the gloaming the distant slopes, bristling with mill chimneys and furred with rows of small houses, took on a picturesque misty bloom—"but you needn't try to come it over me that mills are picturesque," thought Councillor Foster grimly: "I've worked too long in 'em." Wonderful to escape from the smoky, grimy streets below each night and come up here into the fresh air, he thought; wonderful to live, not in a "single room and chamber" cottage in a lousy row with neither light nor water, but in a neat, commodious, clean brick house, with indoor sanitation and electric light. (The payments to the Building Society were almost ended.) He gazed with pride, too, at his trellised ramblers, his half-made rockery. 'Tisn't every chap could put in a full day at the warehouse, he thought, and keep his garden like I do and attend all my committees as well. But then I'm as strong as a bull—always was. And a good thing too. I should never have come through if I wasn't. He walked over for a fresh stone and slapped his deep chest complacently.

The children's mother came to the back door to shake out the tablecloth from tea. She gave it a quick expert flap and the crumbs flew off in all directions.

"If you two knock one of those stones down and break it," she said warningly to Leslie and Hilary: "Your grandpa will be cross."

The children laughed shrilly, and tossing their heads each explained volubly that it was the other's fault.

"Aye, and so shall I be cross," came in a deeper tone from within the kitchen.

This was their grandmother's voice; the children at once sobered and Hilary allowed herself to be lifted to the ground.

"Are they off the stones?" enquired Mrs. Ormerod.

"Yes," said her daughter-in-law, closing the door.

"Leslie, let me walk just once along," urged Hilary. "Give me your hand—let me walk just once along."

"Well—just once," conceded Leslie in an elder-brotherly tone.

Hilary gleefully climbed the pile, and giving her hand to Leslie with a queenly air, trod carefully along the low uneven wall.

"It's your bedtime, Hilary," said their mother, opening the door again.

Hilary was too deeply absorbed in maintaining her balance to reply, but Leslie said mildly:

"She's just walking once along the stones."

At this Mrs. Ormerod's large bulk and cheerful red face appeared beside her daughter-in-law, Councillor Foster raised himself from his stooping position and all the Ormerods stood in affectionate silence to watch Hilary's progress.

The brother and sister made a pretty picture, Councillor Foster thought. Look at Hilary's well-brushed hair with its neat blue bow, her short blue frock, her rounded sunburned arms and legs, her little white socks and smart brown shoes—who would ever have thought he would have had such a dainty little grandchild? And Leslie beside her in his grey flannel shorts and grey shirt and tie and grey flannel coat with the new school badge on it, he was a fine upstanding lad. Wick as an emmet. Councillor Foster gave a moment's sorrow to the cause of the difference in age between them, Hilary just rising to five and Leslie just past ten. The war had made the gap and Hilary never saw the strong young man who had fathered her on embarkation leave, for on D-3 Day, taking up beach mines in France, he was shattered by wounds. Invalided out of the Army, Arthur returned a wreck and died when the child was a few months old. Pity, pity. Waste of a good life. In 1938 Arthur was the youngest full-time Trade Union organiser in the district. Still, the lad had left children; be thankful for that. His mother'd taken his loss hard, but she'd brightened up since Mary and the children came to live with them. Yes, Hilary was five, and Leslie ten. Seeing Leslie like that, a laughing carefree child in his smart grey suit, straight as a dart, with nothing to do but school and play, Councillor Foster suddenly felt his eyes sting, and knew that his life had been worth while. For Leslie was ten. Ten.

It was a wintry morning in the 1890's, the day after Foster
Ormerod's tenth birthday. Foster, a strong bright-cheeked
lad, the eldest of the large family of Ormerods crammed
into the centre cottage in the row halfway up Bolland Clough
Lane, jumped eagerly out of the bed he shared with his
brother. At ten years of age in the 1890's you became a half-
timer, and Foster was to begin work in the Bolland worsted
spinning mills today.

When you were a half-timer in the 1890's you divided your
day between work and school; one week you went to school
in the morning, mill in the afternoon, and the next week the
other way round. Foster had to put in the morning hours
at school today. But school was a nuisance, a hindrance, an
exasperation this morning; he lolled on his bench and could
scarcely be bothered to listen to the teacher, for whom in
any case he now felt contempt—he was a man, a worker
now, earning one and six a week, he had no longer any use
for teachers. At last the clock said the wished-for hour of
noon; Foster pulled his cap from his pocket and rushed
from the room. He ran all the way home, lifted the sneck
on the door with a vigorous hand and burst into the house
crying loudly for his dinner.

"Tha'll non be so up on going to work tomorrow," said
his mother sardonically.

However with hand and voice she quelled the younger
children shouting and tumbling on the hearthrug, made
him a mug of tea and cut him a piece off Sunday's joint and
two thick slices of bread-and-butter. He gulped it down,
sluiced his hands and face from the bucket at the sink,
changed into his new "workclothes"—a pair of his father's
trousers cut short and his old jacket—and set off running,
for he had two miles to go. Looking back at the turn in the
lane he saw his mother standing at the door, shading her
eyes with her hand, gazing after him. He wondered if something was wrong perhaps and she needed him, and slackened
his pace to see if she beckoned, but after a moment she
went in and closed the door, and Foster turned into the

path which was the short cut through the woods and ran on.

He ran down the hill—beneath the leafless trees the air was still and cold, the path was frosty—crossed the plank bridge which was frosted too, mounted the bank the other side, turned to the right at a fork in the path, hurried by the old ruined cottage and came over the flank of Bolland Brow into the main road between Ashworth and Annotsfield. There down in the fields beside the river stood the big Bolland Foot mill, its tall six-sided chimney shooting thick black smoke straight up into the pale cold sky. He ran eagerly towards the mill door—not the smart office door with the polished brass plate, but a worn door at the side where some men and women in working clothes stood lounging. But as he entered the shadow of the mill his footsteps slowed, his clogs ceased to rattle a lively tune on the cobblestones. He felt as though the shadow had fallen not only across his body but inside him, across his heart. Active and sturdy as he was, not afraid of the rough and tumble of school life, able and ready always to defend himself with word or blow, he felt for the first time in his life daunted—this was something bigger than he could master. The men spoke to him with rough kindliness, and directed him to the foreman within.

The foreman, a big man with a beard, standing amid the silent spinning frames, explained to him that he was to be a bobbin fetcher, keeping these frames here supplied with bobbins fetched from the winding-room. A few lads of his own age, half-timers like himself, who were sitting on the floor nearby with their backs against the wall eating their midday teacakes, looked up at him and sniggered, digging each other in the ribs with their elbows, but he didn't need this to know that the frames he served were the furthest from the winding-room, being the newest he was given the worst place. Well, that was natural and he didn't care; he'd soon get on terms with the other lads, he'd show them the sort of chap he was. He was moving towards them to begin when the buzzer sounded; it was half-past one. At once the machinery began, and Foster Ormerod's working life began with it and did not cease.

The afternoon seemed to go on for ever. Of course Foster

had often been in a mill before, taking dinner to his father or aunt who worked down in Ashworth, or a bite of supper if they were on overtime. He was familiar with the noise of machines, the hot air, the smell of oil, the odd prickle in nose and throat caused by breathing in floating particles of wool. But being in a mill for a few minutes was very different from being in a mill four and a half hours. The noise of the wheels, the buzz of the spindles, the clatter of the bobbins, went on and on and on till his head rang and he grew quite confused; the smell of oil and wool sickened, the hot air stifled, him; sweat gathered in pools under his arms. The fast whirling tubes hurt his unaccustomed fingers as he stopped them; after an hour his clogs felt heavy as lead, he could hardly lift his feet as he ran backwards and forwards down the narrow alleys between the frames. Worst of all, try as he would he could not keep up with the pace of the machines; there were no spare bobbins and the frames he served often had to stand for lack of them; men shouted and women screamed at him, the foreman bellowed: "Now then! Look sharp!" and gave him a shove which sent him down on hands and knees, and a personage with a watch-chain—one of the bosses, he supposed—whom he ran into head-on at the doorway gazed at him with fastidious distaste and pushed him off as though he were an animal.

Now it was dusk and the gas-lights came on; the heat in the long unventilated shed became unbearable. Somebody opened the door, a terrible blast of icy wind swept in and curled round every frame, the workers shouted indignantly and the door was closed. But it was still not time to go home; it was not yet five o'clock, never name six. Foster continued his work as bobbin fetcher.

And now the last hour of the working day had come. The flaring gas-jets, the sickening smell, the incessant twirling of the revolving bobbins, the long long alleyway, the weight of the basket on his arm, all mingled into a lurid nightmare in the tired child's mind. For he was a child now; not a carefree schoolboy, not a bold grown-up worker, but just a tired, haggard, dirty, weeping child. He bit his lips to keep back the tears, and brushed his dirty cuff across his eyes, behind the winding-room door so that no-one should see. He felt he should never see home, never see his mother, never see daylight again. All of a sudden he could bear it no more, he broke down and sobbed aloud, his face crimson, contorted with grief, his black eyes pouring tears. Luckily the machinery made so much noise that no-one seemed to hear, or perhaps they kindly pretended not to notice him.

The buzzer sounded. The machinery slowed and stopped. The workers poured rapidly from the mill. Pulling his cap from his pocket, holding his head down in shame, sniffing quietly and keeping back so as not to show his tear-stained face, Foster followed them outside.

The December cold struck like ice on his sweat-drenched skin; he shivered and began to run across field and road. After the gas-lit mill the night seemed very dark, but here at last was the foot of the path; he climbed as fast as he could go, fatigue forgotten in the longing for home and mother. Now he was over the brow and in the Bolland Clough again; he looked back—the lights of Ashworth had dropped out of sight. The wind sweeping down the gulley moaned round the rocks and whispered through the bare trees. It was very dark. He was afraid. He stumbled over the stony uneven path. His breath came in such loud gasps that he could hear it, and this increased his fear. Rounding a fold of the hill, he found the distant sky a little brighter—perhaps the moon was rising behind the cloud. For a moment the child's heart was cheered. But only for a moment; for against this dim diffused greyness the ruined cottage loomed. Its broken roof, its gaping windows, its empty doorway, the pile of stones which had been its stairs, appeared to Foster terribly sinister. It was a dead cottage and it hated life; it stood in the path of all things living and jeered hatefully. Foster began to tread very lightly and carefully along the path, as if the cottage might hear and resent his approach. At the corner of what had been its croft, its little field won from bracken and moor, he stopped. To pluck up his courage. His breath rasped. Then—for he was after all a bold and sturdy child—he forced himself to advance, step by step, beside the wall. There was rough grass beneath his feet here.

That was good, for he could tread silently. The cottage looked out at him from its gaping eyes malevolently; it made no move but looked crouched to spring.

His foot turned on a stone beneath the grass and he fell headlong. With a scream of terror he scrambled up and ran at full tilt past the cottage; the stones flew from his feet, he cried aloud and the sound of his passage echoed up the gulley, but he did not care.

At last he recovered from his fright. Ashamed of his recent cowardice he knuckled his eyes, shoved his hands in his pockets, and settled to a walk. Then he began to look about him uneasily. Could he possibly be on the wrong path? He did not remember that fallen branch, that thorn bush by the square rock, that runnel (half-frozen) trickling sluggishly across the stones. Moreover, the stream seemed still to sound from his left, whereas surely by now he had crossed the bridge, it should be on his right. Had he crossed the bridge at all? He racked his memory. In his panic flight he thought he had crossed the stream, but he could not remember descending the shallow earthen steps which led to it. Perhaps he had not yet reached those steps? Well—he must go on; perhaps soon some familiar landmark would appear. Deep in his heart he guessed that he had taken the wrong turning at the fork, but he would not admit it. He could not face the need of returning to within sight of the ruined cottage.

He walked on, and on, and on. The path continued level through the woods and he saw nothing that he felt sure he knew. But who could feel sure of knowing all Bolland Wood? The rough grass, the rocks and stones, the stunted oak trees, the slopes, the little streams—there were dozens, hundreds, thousands perhaps of these. How could he tell whether these were the ones on his side of the clough, or others like them?

At last the path turned upwards. Foster's heart bounded up in sympathy. Now he would reach a road! He might possibly—he admitted it to himself now a road seemed near—he might possibly not be on the path he knew, but this other path would bring him out higher up Bolland Clough Lane, he felt sure. He could run down the lane, the row of cottages would come in sight, he would lift the sneck and rush in and there would be a bright hot fire, and his mother opening the oven, his father perhaps back from work sitting in his chair smoking his pipe, and the children tumbling all over the hearthrug round his feet. The moon came out from behind a cloud, white and cold and clear, and in her light Foster saw, quite distinctly, a wall, a stile, a road. He cried out happily and scrambled forward, his clogs slipping on the icebound stones. He reached the wall and pushed through the stile; there was a gas lamp opposite, yes, it was a real big road.

But it was not a road he knew. In the white moonlight the contours of the hills showed very plain, and here—oh horrible!—the country sloped the wrong way. Instead of Bolland Bank there was a valley, instead of Bolland Clough there was a hill. It was so horrible, so devilish, this reversed landscape, that Foster threw himself to the ground and screamed with fear.

"What's the matter, my boy?"

Still sobbing wildly, Foster sat back on his heels and looked up at the speaker. He saw a very old man, very thin and frail, with thin grey hair and very bright dark eyes. He wore a frock coat which dangled loosely from his body because he stooped so much, and a watch-chain with medals dangling, and a top hat; he leaned on an ebony stick. A boss, thought Foster.

"Tell me what's wrong, my boy," said this old man in a kind soft voice. "I won't hurt you. I'll help you if I can."

If his voice was the kindest Foster had ever heard, his eyes were the kindest Foster had ever seen. Altogether he inspired the completest confidence. One need not be afraid with him.

"I'm lost," said Foster, and began to cry again at the dreadful word.

"Well, never mind. I'll take you home. Where do you live?"

"I'm a half-timer," wept Foster, getting out the essential fact of his universe first. "I began work in t'mill this afternoon and now I'm lost."

"How long, O Lord, how long!" exclaimed the old man

passionately, striking the ground heavily with his stick. "When will the cry of these little ones reach Thine ears?"

Foster, astonished, gaped at him with his mouth open.

"I live in Bolland Clough Lane," he said in a subdued voice.

"My poor child, you're right out of your way," said the old man compassionately. "You're almost in Annotsfield."

"If I go back along this path and turn right at t'fork and down across bridge and up t'other side, I sall get to t'Lane," offered Foster. "I took wrong turning at fork, I can see that now."

"Yes?"

"But I'm feared to go alone. It's that dark. And there's a house in t'delph wi'out any windows."

"We'll go together, shall we?"

So Foster scrambled up and rubbed his knees and his eyes and the old man led the way through the stile and they went off down the path together. The old man limped, which it seemed was why he carried a stick, but he got along pretty quickly. At first, that is; but when the path turned downwards he found the declivity difficult—that's what he said, declivity, and then explained the word to Foster. Presently he began to stumble so often that Foster was really troubled for him, and presently Foster ventured to take his arm and guide his steps. All the time he talked; he told Foster that he himself had worked in the mill, more than seventy years ago.

"That's a long time," said Foster, quite dumbfounded.

"Yes, a long time. A long long time," said the old man in a remembering way. "I'm eighty-four now. It must be seventy-six years ago—more than three quarters of a century."

In those days, it seemed, there was no half-time rule about children; they went to the mill as soon as they could walk, and worked twelve, thirteen, sixteen hours a day. Foster shook his head very soberly when he heard this; four and a half hours in the mill that afternoon had been enough for him. A great man named Oastler had risen up and tried to make Parliament pass a law for a ten-hour day; the old man had marched to a great meeting at York; it was exciting, with songs and speeches and banners.

"Were you a piecener then in t'mill?"

"No. By that time my circumstances had improved."

"Why did you go then?"

"To help my fellow-men," said the old man sharply striking his stick on the ground. "I had no wish to escape from wretchedness and leave others there."

By this time Foster and the old man had reached the ruined cottage; there was nothing frightening about it now at all, it looked quite friendly, half asleep and enjoying the moonlight. The old man stopped to look at it and said it was a very old house, not a cottage at all but a hall; from the way its windows were made you could tell the date when it was built. He pointed his stick at the windows, and explained about mullions or some such word. Foster pretended to understand though he didn't, because he was anxious to get the old man moving again.

At last they started off down the slope. The old man was breathing heavily now and seemed very tired. When they reached the earthen steps Foster had to put his arm round the old man's waist and take his hand; the hand shook and jumped in his grasp so that Foster felt really quite frightened. I shall never get him over the bridge, he thought; and he wished very much now that he was on familiar ground the old man would turn round and go away. There would be such a fuss and ado if he came right up to the Ormerod home.

They reached the bridge and stood looking at it. The old man was panting.

"I shall be all right now," ventured Foster. "I'm less nor five minutes from home."

The old man looked at him. His dark eyes seemed to pierce right to Foster's heart and read what was being felt there.

"Very well, Foster," he said. "I'll go back now. You run on, and call out to me when you reach the road."

Foster hesitated, ashamed.

"Would you rather come up wi' me? And—have a cup o' tea?"

"No, thank you," said the old man gravely. "I must hurry off, or I shall be late for the Town Council."

Foster's clogs thundered on the bridge. He rushed up the

177

hill and paused by the wall. How awful if, when he went through the opening, the road proved not to be his own familiar Lane, but some strange nightmare road, as it had done before! He gulped and went out into the road. Oh, joy! It was his own Bolland Clough Lane! The paving-stones on the road, the gas-lamp, the higher wall on the other side with the grass tussocks behind—they were all his own. He cried out joyously:

"I'm all right! Goodnight!"

A faint cry: "Goodnight, Foster!" came up to him from the delph.

He ran up the Lane and in a few minutes all was just as he had hoped.

In fact it was even better, for as he lifted the sneck and ran in the whole family seemed to rush forward in welcome. Far from being scolded, he was hugged; his mother wept over him, held his head against her breast and rubbed his cold hands between her own; the children clung to his knees; even his father took his pipe out of his mouth and exclaimed: "By gow! I'm reet glad to see thee, Foster!" It seemed there was a girl a' little further up the Lane who worked where he did, and as she was passing their row she told one of the Ormerods, who was out visiting the privy, she'd seen their Foster rushing away on the wrong path. At first they thought it was just Foster's usual devilment and his father made great play about the leathering he would get when he came home. But presently they grew anxious, set the door open and gazed down the Lane, sent their Herbert down to the path top to call out for his brother. Herbert reported that the wood was very dark and quiet. At this Mrs. Ormerod wanted to rush out at once to look for Foster, but her husband forbade it.

"Tha cannot keep lad tied to thi apron strings," he said. "Foster's got plenty o' sense. He'll come home when he's a mind. And Ah sall ha' summat waiting for him 'e won't like when 'e does, Ah can promise thee."

With every quarter hour that passed without bringing Foster, however, these threats diminished, and now all his father said was:

"What happened thee, lad?"

"I was lost," said Foster. "And an owd man brought me home."

But this mildness could not, in the nature of things, endure. When, washed and warmed and seated on a three-legged stool in front of the fire between his parents, with a mug of tea and a piece of teacake in his hand, Foster remarked casually in his usual loud cheerful tones: "I don't like mill, Father," he was conscious at once that the period of parental humouring was past.

"There's mony another 'at thinks t'same," said his father on a sardonic note, without removing his pipe.

"I don't want to go to mill any more," pursued the obstinate Foster.

"Tha'll go whether tha wants or not!" shouted his father, banging his fist on the wooden arm of his chair.

"But——"

His father leaned forward and clouted him on the side of the head, not heavily, but enough to make his head ring; the tea slopped over and scalded his knee.

"That's last Ah want to hear o' such tomfoolery."

"Tha can go and come wi' Lizzie o' Tom's, tha knows," put in his mother soothingly.

"I don't need no lass to show me t'road," said Foster stoutly. "I just don't want to go, that's all."

"Happen tha doesn't want to eat, either?" suggested his father.

"Th'owd man thinks it's wrong for childer to work in mills."

"That's last Ah want to hear o' thi owd man, too. So now I'm telling thee. I'm t'master here, bear in mind."

To the menace implied in this phrase, there could be no reply.

3

On the next afternoon, after the gruelling hours' labour which had now not even the attraction of novelty, Foster trailed drearily out of the mill to find that a thin snow had fallen and was resting in the hollows of the iron ground.

Hitherto snow had been a pleasure and a joke to Foster; but now its icy breath struck like a whip on his overheated frame. He began to run fast to keep warm, then suddenly halted and crouched by the engine-room wall. Beneath the gas-lamp by the yard entrance he saw Lizzie o' Tom's, obviously waiting for her young neighbour. She was taller than he and perhaps a few months older; a gradely lass enough with red cheeks, standing very steady on her feet. Some of the men threw out jests at her as they passed; without being over-forward, she gave as good as she got, and Foster could not but approve. In this painful cold he envied the thick grey fringed shawl which after the custom of the mill-girl of the day she wore so as to cover her person from the crown of her head to her hips in its woollen folds. The line of hair which showed on her forehead below the shawl was dark and curly. Foster lingered in the shadow of the engine-room until, tired no doubt of waiting, she moved off; her clogs rang briskly on the paved road.

Foster now followed, trying to tread softly; he was not going to be taken home by any girl, not he. At a distance he followed her; up the yard, along the Miryroyd field, across the road, into the Bolland Clough path. The lights of Ashworth sank away; but from behind heavy clouds the moon shed its dim greyness. His plan was to keep the little shawled figure ahead in sight, without himself being seen; thus he would have the advantages of her company without any cowardly implications. Once or twice on looking up he found her nearer than he expected, as though she were waiting for him; he dallied obstinately behind. The wind rose and moaned down the clough; the snow began to fall again, thin, whispering, eerie. There was a mile of this dreary landscape yet to traverse. Almost—but not quite—he permitted himself to quicken his step.

The path wound in and out of folds of the hills. He turned a rocky corner and leaped back in panic, crying out at the figure which confronted him.

"Lizzie o' Tom's!" he exclaimed then in angry disgust, recognising her.

"Aye. I saw thee following. I kept waiting for thee, Foster."

"You'd no call."

"Nay, I'd promised thi mother."

"*She'd* no call," said Foster resentfully.

"Well, I should be glad o' thi company through t'delph, choose how."

This of course put a different complexion on the matter. To seek his protection thus brought courage flowing back to his childish heart.

"Why, art afeeard?" cried Foster manfully, strutting forward.

"I'm non feared," said Lizzie quietly. "But I'd be glad o' thi company, Foster."

Oddly enough, he believed both parts of this statement.

"Well, come on then."

The two children stumbled on through the grey darkness, side by side. The snow thickened, and as they climbed and lost the shelter of the brow, a blast of wind drove it stinging into Foster's face. He sniffed and shivered.

"Art starved, Foster lad?"

"Well, I'm cold," admitted Foster cautiously.

With a gesture as wide as love, she threw open her shawl. "Come close," she said.

He crept in beneath her arm and she folded the shawl over his head and shoulders. He slipped his arm round her waist. How soft and warm!

Thus wrapped together, they ran on through the snow-lashed woods.

4

When at last they thankfully reached the Lane, Lizzie withdrew the shawl. It was a delicacy Foster appreciated, for he certainly did not wish to appear before the keen eyes of his brothers and sisters sheltering beneath a girl's shawl. The sound of the wind, previously hushed by the sheltering wool, now burst with renewed vigour on his ears, and when the blast died another sound came to startle him. It was of excited human voices. As they rounded the bend they saw a group of shawls and caps clustered round the Ormerod's door.

"What's up?" exclaimed Foster anxiously, quickening his step.

"Nay, I don't know," said Lizzie in the same tone. "Mi mother's there."

They ran together.

"Well, Foster!" exclaimed Lizzie's mother in shrill excitement: "You're all in t'paper, lad."

It was true. For Foster's old man was, it seemed, Mr. Jonathan Bamforth, a Councillor on the Annotsfield Town Council, Chairman of the School Board, the Mechanic's Institute, and heaven knows what besides; a noted teetotaller, a Liberal, nay a Radical, a man loved and hated throughout the West Riding by the forces of progress and reaction respectively. In his youth, in the early days of the Industrial Revolution, he had worked as a piecener in one of the first mills in the district to be driven by steam; his uncle had been hanged as a Luddite (whatever that was) for resisting the introduction of machinery. Councillor Bamforth had visited Bolland that afternoon to see one of his sons, a minister in the Ashworth Wesleyan circuit, and was walking back to the Annotsfield horse-tram when Foster met him. He had to make a speech in the Annotsfield Town Council that night, proposing an amendment to a proposition about the old Annotsfield Piece Hall. The Council wanted to pull it down and sell the land for building shops, but Councillor Bamforth wanted to turn it into a Public Library. He entered the Council Chamber late, and it was noticed that he seemed breathless when apologising to the Mayor, and limped more than usual on his lame foot when taking his seat; clearly he had hurried more than a man of eighty-four was wise to do in order to reach the meeting. Almost at once the Minutes of the General Purposes Committee came up for approval, and he rose with a proposition to refer back the Piece Hall item. He began his speech by describing his meeting with Foster—"This little boy whose education has ceased at ten years old so that he may make money for some heartless manufacturer"—and pleading for a library where such boys could continue their education in after years. There came shouted interruptions; the half-timer's education was not

182

ended, only halved, the manufacturer was not necessarily heartless, our manufactures were the wealth of England, and so on. Councillor Bamforth drew himself up to his full height, his eyes blazed, the vein in his forehead throbbed, his voice rang like a trumpet call. "Gentlemen," he cried: "In the name of this innocent and ignorant child——" His voice died suddenly to a strangled moan, he put his hand to his head and fell forward heavily. When the horrified Councillors nearby managed to raise him and set him back on the velvet-covered bench, he was found to be dead. The double walk through Bolland Wood, the excitement of his speech, had fatally overtaxed his dauntless old heart.

All this was reported at length in the *Ashworth Times*, in the small print and pompous phraseology of the day. Councillor Bamforth, concluded the *Times* sententiously, had done his last good deed, fought his last good fight, in the cause for which he had battled all his life, then passed to his well-deserved rest.

Foster stood sober and silent while this story was conveyed to him, partly read out by the neighbour who had brought home the newspaper, partly told by those who had already heard it, in repetitious snatches.

"Well, I'm reet sorry," he said at length.

" T'weren't your fault, Foster," his mother defended him.

"No—don't fret thysen, lad; it's nowt to do wi' thee," said his father.

"I'm not fretted," said Foster stoutly. "I'm sorry, that's all."

And indeed his reaction to the incident was not quite what his parents imagined, and certainly not what sentimental middle-class people made of it sometimes, later. That old chap's been struggling to get children out of the mill for nigh on three-quarters of a century, thought Foster, and he's died without succeeding. Childer are still there. *I'm* still there. We shall ha' to try summat different, or we shall never get out, thought Foster. We mun fight for wer rights wersen. Mester Bamforth were a grand old chap in his way, but his day's over. He were too soft for this world. "I had no wish to escape from wretchedness and leave others there." Well, that's reet enough. But them others has got to take their share. We mun fight for wer rights wersen, without expecting help from any boss.

5

Whether Foster Ormerod thought all this at the time, or whether he merely received then a strong but obscure impression which grew clearer as he grew to manhood, he could not at this distance of time be sure. But whichever it was, the incidents of those two days settled the lines of his life, for he married Lizzie and became an active Trade Union man.

"And when I say active, I mean active," thundered Foster in his later years. "Not like you young chaps that think you've done summat wonderful when you've paid your Union dues."

He had indeed in his youth visited every house in Ashworth where he had reason to believe there was a textile worker living, and canvassed him to join the Union. He became first Secretary, then President of the local branch; the membership trebled itself during his long period of office. Elected to the national executive, he held the office of President twice, and of course represented his Union at the Trades Union Congress. This however was the limit of his range, as he himself knew and frankly admitted; he was not the type to sit on the Trades Union Council or be appointed to National Boards. But as a practical man, with a knowledge of working conditions gained in over fifty years of life in the mill, he was a thoroughly valuable member of his Union and of the Labour Party. Nationalisation of industry was his creed; the national ownership of the means of production, so that the workers might have decent living conditions and the power to impose them, was the cause to which, it might fairly be claimed, he had devoted his whole life.

He had had his temptations, from time to time. As a young man, football threatened to lure him from Union work to the playing-field too frequently, so he gave it up completely—a great sacrifice to a hearty, robust, active lad like himself. Women, too, were a temptation to him in those days, and he admitted frankly that it was the Union rather than Lizzie, though he loved her dearly enough, which had kept him straight. But Lizzie was a good helpmeet to him always; a keen Labour party worker, though not a speaker, always being in the background with cups of tea, and full of sound advice and common-sense.

Foster went through the first World War in the infantry, and was in the thick of all those maddening experiences of mud, blood and waste which characterised that conflict and by disgusting the combatants with the social system which produced them accelerated so markedly the pace of social change. He came out a sergeant, and though not exactly a pacifist, very much a hater of war.

In the course of his canvassing he had discovered that he could speak with fluency and vigour, and had a strong full resonant voice; now he carried these capacities into another sphere; after three stubborn fights which ended in defeat but sent his poll up every time, he at length got elected to the Ashworth Town Council for Bolland Ward. "Be true to your class and vote Labour!" was the habitual climax to his speeches. He was not one of those speakers—"and I'm glad of it," growled Councillor Foster with a grin—who drew a sheaf of notes out of his pocket and carefully and relentlessly worked through them to the very end, in long words and a quiet voice, with frequent pauses while he found his place. No! He stood up before his audience and beginning with a few local references, a bit of pathos about the children's lack of playgrounds—they hadn't an inch in the ward, in spite of all that wood down the hill—and a joke about the new trams (which found the Bolland gradient intimidating), soon found himself launched in a vigorous unceasing flow of denunciation of the capitalist system. Phrases like minimum wage, guaranteed week, payment by results, holidays with pay, evil legacy of private enterprise, payment for overtime, nationalisation of the means of production, the five-day week, poured from his lips with the fervour of a lifetime's belief, the sincerity of a lifetime's resentful experience. If he thought his fellow-townsmen's behaviour absurd or their propositions a waste of time, he never hesitated to say so bluntly, and if

185

his grammar grew mixed, his dialect broad, what in heck did that matter, thought Councillor Foster contemptuously. If his lapses raised a titter, he made capital out of them by referring to his half-time days—"you don't get much schooling, friends, when you're in t'mill half every school day"—and went on to tell the story of his meeting in Bolland Wood with old Jonathan Bamforth. He often told this story, used it for pathos or—sometimes—to gain a laugh. "The questioner asks me if I'm not afraid what would happen to textiles if they were nationalised. No; I'm not afraid—I did all t'fearing I mean to do, i' Bolland Wood when I were ten."

Tough in fibre, stout in self-assurance, not especially sensitive to the more delicate feelings, which he characterised as "silly work," Foster yet had a warm heart for material sufferings which he could understand. In the slump which culminated in 1931 he fretted himself sick over the "on the dole" queues at the Employment Exchange, and the Means Test drove him frantic—he turned crimson and shouted whenever it was mentioned. When the unemployed rioted round the private house of the manager of the Ashworth Employment Exchange, Foster's eldest son, Tom, working in the bus depot opposite, saw the beginning of the affair and had the sense to telephone to Bolland Mill to tell Foster. The boss's son came down to the warehouse to give him the message. With an angry roar Foster tore off his overall and ran out of the mill into the yard. "Get in," said Mr. Richard, opening the door of his two-seater, and they drove off hell for leather to the house. Foster shoved through the crowd, climbed the steps and got up on to a silly sort of middle-class ornament, a kind of plaster flower-pot, which stood at the side. He waved his arms and shouted:

"You know me, lads!"

And it was true; they knew him; they'd known him twenty years. They said so in a confused growl.

"Then what do you want to do a daft thing like this for?" shouted Foster angrily. "Aren't you in trouble enough? D'you want some more? D'you want to give *them* a chance to shove you a bit further into t'mire?" Suddenly his voice broke, his big mouth trembled, his square face turned crimson and tears suffused his eyes. He was so sorry for them, and so furious with the capitalist system which caused their suffering and with that traitor Ramsay MacDonald who'd sold them to the Tories, that he felt choked, his grief and resentment seemed all "balled up" in his throat. But come; he wasn't a softy; he was a man, wasn't he? He was a Union man, wasn't he?

"I've been in t'textile trade, man and boy, for thirty four year," shouted Foster. "I've been in t'mill sin' I were ten year old. I mind that day i' Bolland Wood as if it were yesterday . . ."

He didn't know what he said, but somehow he and the crowd all wept together and promised never to lose heart, and presently he was marching back to the centre of Ashworth at the head of an orderly procession, the police who'd come out to quell a riot riding alongside in a friendly way. Mr. Richard followed the procession in his car for some time, but then had the sense to make himself scarce down a side street, speeding up and giving a wave of his hand to Foster as he did so.

Foster himself escaped unemployment during this terrible time. He wasn't a first-class craftsman, but he was a steady, honest, reliable chap, and shrewd; he was in the warehouse by now and knew his job, though he never expected to rise any higher. But in any case, thought Foster angrily, they'd think twice before they sacked a Town Councillor, and if they did, by gum he'd raise such a howl about victimisation of a Trade Union official that they'd be sorry. No; they didn't sack him, but at one time the whole mill nearly closed down. Mr. Richard sent for the foremen and warned them, and the news went round from mouth to mouth. It was a shock. Of course plenty of other West Riding textile firms went smash during the depression, but somehow Foster had never thought Bolland Mill would go off too—though it was true you'd only to look at Mr. Richard's face lately to see the way things were going. Foster felt sorry for a moment, and sick; vistas of life on the dole for him and his four children still of school age stretched before him, and he felt he understood fully, for the first time perhaps, why his own father had sent him into the mill at ten years old. But then he rallied.

"What d'ye expect?" he said in a tone of angry disgust. "These old family businesses, father and son and grandson, there's too many living out of them, they draw all the money out and never put it back into t'business, then when trouble comes they've no reserve. If they were nationalised, as they ought to be, we should have none o' this silly work."

His hearers listened, impressed, and Foster felt cheered. But in the event Bolland Mill managed to squeeze through the depression without closing down. Heavily in debt to the bank, and with reserves all gone, the firm lost its former glory but staggered on. Gradually, with the pound leaving gold, it recovered, and got firmly on to its feet spinning yarn for cloth for the forces, during the recent war, so Foster had never had a day's unemployment in his life.

"All t'same, I'd rather mill'd closed and we'd kept our Arthur," thought Foster with a pang. "That damned Hitler!"

He thought of his son's funeral service with mingled grief and pride. Grief, for Arthur had been a son after his own heart, destined, Foster had felt sure, to carry his father's work on and up to greater heights. Pride, for as he entered Bolland Road Wesleyan behind the coffin with his weeping daughter-in-law on his arm, he had been struck by the appearance of the rows of Ormerods sitting there. His brothers and sisters and their offspring and his own sons and daughters and their offspring amounted to more than forty persons, and when you added Lizzie's relations and Mary's relations, sitting on the other aisle, there couldn't be far short of seventy or even seventy-five. There'd been a mass of Bolland neighbours and Ashworth citizens behind them, too, for of course the Council and Union wished to show respect for Foster, and Arthur had plenty of committees and connections of his own; he was such a promising lad. But that wasn't the point; what had struck Foster that day was the sight of his own respectable working-class family, all so neatly attired in good black which in spite of coupons they'd managed to rout out from somewhere; the children's fair heads and clean collars, the neat decent hats of their mothers, the well-brushed

hair and broad strong shoulders of their fathers, the grand-
fathers somewhat bowed but still at work. The women all
kept their gloves on, knowing their hands to be rough from
housework; the men's hands, large, red, rough, capable, lay
in unaccustomed ease on their solid thighs. What a mass of
work those Ormerod hands had performed for England!
That was the kind of family record to be proud of; every one
of those Ormerods *worked*, worked every weekday of their
lives for fifty years. That was the sort of family entitled to
respect, not lords' sons la-di-da-ing about in night-clubs, or
middle-class manufacturers playing golf. The Ormerods were
the backbone of the country, it was their lot that ought to
govern, ought to have the power. One of these days, they
should have it, or he'd see!

And then, by gum! in 1945 they got it! What a glorious
triumph! The sweeping victory of the election, the swift
putting into operation of the Socialist Welfare State! The
National Health Service! The forty-hour week! The Nationalisation of the Railways and the Mines! The Labour Party
were in real power at last, and had got those damned bosses,
those damned Tories, down. "Our heels on their neck,"
shouted Foster, crimson with joy, as the results came rolling
in: "We'll see who's master now. Let *them* try a bit of Bolland
Wood, for a change, and see how they like it!"

All this was summed up for him, beautifully and endearingly
expressed, in the sight of his grandchildren, Leslie and Hilary
Ormerod, nourished on green-ration-book orange juice and
cod-liver oil, playing with their fine straight backs in the
garden of his good brick house, in their clean, new, pretty
clothes. Leslie was ten. . . .

6

His new rockery was looking champion; pity he had to
leave it, but it was nigh on time for him to be off to that
A.T.P.C. He represented the Council on that committee,
so he mustn't be late; he took all public work with stubborn
seriousness. He tidied away his tools and went indoors.
Leslie was reading a book from the Ashworth Free Library.

Lizzie and Mary were sitting knitting with the wireless on. He grimaced a little, for he thought his wife too plump, his daughter-in-law too thin, to wear home-knitted jumpers with advantage; but what could you do with womenfolk? If something was the fashion, they'd have it choose how it suited them. He cocked his eyebrows and gave them his well-known grin, then went upstairs, washed in his neat bathroom and changed into his good suit. When he came down again they could hardly throw him a glance and Leslie scowled at him, for that Dick Barton serial was just beginning. Foster did not approve of Dick Barton. All that gun-play and such; he made nowt of it. Like religion, it was dope to keep the workers quiet; lads ought to have something better to think about; there was no Dick Barton, but the hard realities of the mill, when he was ten. Still better that nor Bolland Wood. . . . By the way, if Dick Barton was on he was a bit late; he must hurry if he was to catch the ten to seven bus at the turn of the lane.

Bustling out of his front gate in the twilight he fell in with one of Lizzie's brothers, going down like Foster to the bus. He was a quiet little man, grey-haired, bow-legged, not a leader but a staunch right-thinking Labour man and given like Lizzie to occasional remarks of salty shrewdness. They greeted each other with a nod and a word.

"Nathan."

"Foster."

"We're a bit late for bus."

"Aye."

"Going to your Lodge?"

"Aye."

"I'm for this A.T.P.C."

"How's it coming on, like?"

"Not so bad. There's too many middle-class on it, though."

"Ah!" said Nathan, shaking his head.

"Nye's been giving it 'em lately," he added with a chuckle. They laughed together, recalling and savouring the Minister of Health's mordant phrases.

"What do you think of this Steel Bill, though, Foster?" enquired his brother-in-law with a hesitant air.

"Think of it? I believe in the nationalisation of the means of production."

"There's many don't want steel nationalised, though," said Nathan in a tone of doubt.

"We shall do it whether they want it or not!" cried Foster belligerently.

They joined the bus queue and were soon borne away down the hill.

The fish and chip shops were just opening and made cheerful spots of light and animation, the friers in white coats busy within, the jostling queues joking pleasantly outside.

"There won't be much left of your Bolland Wood soon, Foster," said Nathan, jerking his head towards the new housing estate which was rising there.

"Well, I shan't cry."

"You won't be able to tell your Bolland Wood story much longer, however," said Nathan slyly.

"Aye—well," said Foster, a trifle disconcerted: "I'm on th'Housing committee, tha knows. The old order has to go, the people's welfare can't be stayed for a few personal hardships," he added in his platform manner, with a grin.

The bus drew up at the Ashworth terminus. They nodded farewell, edged down the crowded bus and parted. Nathan ambled off towards his Oddfellows, Foster walked briskly towards the Mechanics' Institute.

7

In the entrance, below the steps, stood a young girl, smartly turned out, with good tan leather shoes, a good grey coat, one of those square silk scarves the women set such store on. A nice-looking lass, too; Foster could remember the day when his heart would have quickened its beat at sight of her. She was a shorthand typist, he judged shrewdly, or worked in a shop. She hung back in the shadows and looked diffident.

"Can I 'elp, my dear? I'm Councillor Foster Ormerod."

"Is this where the Ashworth Textile Pageant Committee

is holding its meeting?" whispered the girl, holding down her head.

"That's right. You're the Youth Groups representative, happen?"

"Yes."

"The youth of the world is our greatest asset. We must do all we can for our youth," said Foster. He spoke very sincerely, for he was thinking of Bolland Wood, and of Lizzie when she was this girl's age, going to work in shawl and clogs. "I've done my bit, like, to turn clogs into them smart shoes," he thought and his whole body glowed with pride and satisfaction.

It was all the more hurting, all the more of a shock, therefore, like ice on a warm skin, when the first person he set eyes on as he entered the Committee room was that confounded Communist, Gamaliel Greenwood. Just when everything was going so well, those confounded fellows had to come along and spoil it all! In Foster's young days Communists were a joke. Now they were a menace. All over the Trade Unions, like a clutching trailing weed. To think that Gamaliel was representing the respectable Trade Union to which he belonged, a textile Union, not Foster's but allied, made Foster feel sore all over. Of course this A.T.P. committee was not very important politically, it wasn't indeed a political affair at all. But why send a Communist to represent you on any Committee? It was all wrong, it was the thin edge of the wedge. Give those fellows an inch and they'd take a mile. The new campaign against Communist infiltration in the Unions had not come a moment too soon, thought Foster, reassuring himself; we shall take care not to let them get too strong a hold. But looking at Gamaliel Greenwood sitting there, erect and smug, so sure that he was right, so sure that he was the new, the coming, order, Foster suddenly remembered his brother-in-law's joking taunts: "You won't be able to tell your Bolland Wood story any more." A profound uneasiness rolled in his stomach like a dark, heavy, burning ball. Could it possibly be that he and his party were outdated by Gamaliel and his lot? That Gamaliel looked on Councillor Foster Ormerod as Foster looked on old Jonathan

Bamforth? Well, if he does he's wrong, thought Foster stoutly.

He greeted his fellow-members. Old Thos Armitage in the chair. One of the few good employers, one of the few you could really trust. Young Bernard was nothing like so sound. Yes, Thos had been a good man in his day for helping the workers, but of course the workers didn't want to be helped nowadays, they just wanted their just and proper rights. Young Roddie Bairstow, the Secretary. He'll find himself working for the State soon, will that one, thought Foster with a grim chuckle, if indeed he doesn't find himself altogether out of a job. Extravagant and not much of a worker. He fought well, though. But he was an officer. Sir Charles Considine. Ah, now there you had a nasty bit of work. While such as my lad were fighting and getting wounds which killed 'em, Sir Charles was sitting on his backside in a well-warmed office chair wangling himself a title. He's up to tricks, too, with his labour force; insincere welfare, and bribing chaps to get hold of weavers for him; he needn't think we don't know. I make nowt of this Marrison female beside me; decay of the middle class, that's what she is. Handsome piece, though. Mrs. Sykes is not here yet; late like last time, but I reckon it's because, like old Jonathan Bamforth, she's got too much to do. Kill herself with it one of these days like her great-grandfather, I shouldn't wonder. Her father was a lad playing in the minister's house that afternoon when I met the old chap in Bolland Wood; or happen a young chap just married.

Thinking of Bolland Wood cheered Foster, and he sat down defiantly next to Gamaliel. He needn't think I'm afraid of him, thought Foster. He fixed the young man with his eye, and said coldly:

"Good evening."

"Good evening, Councillor," replied Gamaliel with contempt.

VII

GAMALIEL GREENWOOD, C.P.

I

WHEN GAMALIEL GREENWOOD was a boy his mother called herself Mrs. Greenwood and wore a plain gold ring on the third finger of her left hand, though everyone in the village of Ashley Foot knew that she had no right to either ring or prefix. Everyone, that is, except Gamaliel. Born towards the end of the 1914–18 war, as the village thought the offspring of some over-excited soldier on leave, he assumed in his childhood that his father had been killed in the war like so many other children's fathers. As for his mother's name being the same as that of his grandmother, with whom they lived, he never gave it a thought—there were so many thousands of Greenwoods in the West Riding, hundreds in Ashley Foot alone, that for a Greenwood to marry a quite unrelated Greenwood, as he imagined her to have done, was a commonplace.

Gamaliel did not resemble his mother physically. Avice Greenwood was a plump but sallow woman, with soft dark eyebrows, sleek dark hair and a very smooth olive skin; everything about her was smooth, curved and fleshy. She was silent and reserved; though she smiled often it was at her own private jokes, her large dark bronze-green eyes had a secret look and her mother in moments of anger was wont to call her sly. These moments occurred rather frequently in Gamaliel's early days; in recollection, his childhood seemed to consist entirely of lying drowsily in the big bed at the back of the living-room, his eyes closed against the Friday evening gaslight, listening to his grandmother "badgering" his mother on some mysterious subject.

"Don't badger me, Mother," said his mother from time to time in her slow smooth drawl.

At this his grandmother's voice rose and went on and on, scolding, reproaching; his mother made no other reply.

From these rounds of argument old Mrs. Greenwood—short, massive, rheumatic, very clean-looking, with a knob of scanty ginger hair—turned with a sigh to her grandson. "Well, lad isn't sly, that's one comfort. He takes after his grandfather, does your Gamaliel."

Gamaliel could not see much likeness between himself and the moustached young man whose tinted photograph, together with that of a rejuvenated but recognisable Grandma, hung on the wall in a red plush frame, but possibly if more of Grandpa had been visible the likeness would have been more visible too. Gamaliel was tall and lean, with long bony arms and a long wedge-shaped head, on which sandy wiry hair stood up like a brush; his hazel eyes were well-opened, his face long but square-chinned; his nose was large and fleshy, his cheek fresh though pale. Gamaliel did not at first mind being compared to his grandfather, whose first name he bore, because old Mr. Greenwood had been coachman and later chauffeur up at Ashbank, and to a small boy this seemed an agreeable and admirable occupation. His grandmother had been cook at Ashbank, even his mother had been maid there at one time. Ashbank was a place with agreeable associations. The solid two-roomed cottage in the neat gabled row in which they lived belonged to Ashbank; Christmas presents of attractive food and toys came from there, and sometimes clothes. Both Mr. and Miss Crabtree were very fond of Grandma; Mr. Crabtree because she belonged to his childhood days, his daughter for his sake and from a general kindly feeling and proper respect for worth. Miss Crabtree was very active in all good works in the villages which spread along the side of the Aske River towards Ashworth. Old Mrs. Greenwood had a pension from Ashbank, and Avice worked in the big Ashroyd mills by the river which belonged to Ashbank, so the Greenwoods did not live too badly.

But one day, at school, when he was rising eight years old, Gamaliel's whole life changed. At school he was not especially popular, being reserved by nature and not often merry, but he was not disliked either; he was staunch in trouble and though not aggressive or over-quick with blows, knew how to make himself respected. It was after a row with a biggish boy over (save the mark! as Gamaliel often thought afterwards with sardonic fury) the alleged substitution of a flawed glassy marble in his opponent's set that as they rolled on the ground in battle the lad, who was getting the worst of it, called out:

"Bastard! You're nobbut a bastard!"

Gamaliel was so astonished by the application to him of this word, which he knew as a vile insult to one's parentage without exactly understanding, that he stopped fighting.

"Mi mother says so," added the lad. "Your mother 'ad to leave Ashbank because of it, so there."

They rolled over, sat up and glared at each other, then scrambled to their feet. An awed silence had fallen on the other boys who stood around. Gamaliel glanced at them. Some faces wore a look of expectant glee and others of embarrassed pity.

"You don't know who your father is," taunted the boy.

Gamaliel was silent.

"Nobody knows," concluded the boy.

Gamaliel stepped up to him and clenching his fist struck him hard on the side of the head. The boy fell to the ground, and angry shouts arose from his companions. They made as if to attack Gamaliel, who leaped on the low decaying wall which bordered the piece of spare ground where they played, and ran away. The group trailed after him down the street, shouting.

"Aw, let him be!" shouted the boy he had struck, rising and bending himself about to knock the mud from his clothes.

They hesitated; Gamaliel outdistanced them and with an insulting gesture vanished from their sight round the corner of the street.

He ran home as fast as his long legs would carry him, rushed up the two neat yellow-stoned steps, raised the sneck and threw open the door. His mother, home from the mill, sat on a low chair by the fire. At the noise of his entrance she turned her secret eyes towards him. At once Gamaliel knew that what he had heard was true, and that he could never speak to her about it. Assuming a jaunty air, he slammed the door shut with his foot and called out a raucous demand for his tea.

196

From that day forward he despised his mother and, though still retaining some respect for his grandmother, hated all the circumstances of his home life. Ashbank and all its inhabitants he loathed; he always disparaged the gifts which came from there, and broke and tore them quickly so as to insinuate that they were of poor quality, worthless. At eleven, he won a place in the Ashworth Secondary School. The daily tram fares to Ashworth which would be necessary were a difficulty to the Greenwoods' small budget; it seemed that Ashbank help might be invoked, but Gamaliel, with gleaming eyes, announced that he would walk. He did this every weekday for three years, nor did he ever, though he was not greatly interested in school, plead the bitterest Yorkshire weather as an excuse for not making the journey.

At school he was something of a problem to his teachers. He realised this himself and was scornfully amused. Clearly he was intelligent, he wrote good if slow English and could argue his way accurately through an arithmetic problem, and he gave an impression of strength of character; but he showed none of the aptitudes which decide the career of the ordinary promising boy. On the one side, he was not particularly clever with his hands, did not make models at home and showed only a moderate attention to the weekly lessons in carpentry. On the other, though he read a good many books from the school library, they did not seem to excite him very much, and when invited to express his opinion he spoke of the classics of English literature with cold contempt. He had the ordinary boy's interest in machinery, but no more. Music meant nothing to him. He played games in a sensible competent fashion, because they were part of the curriculum and had to be gone through, but displayed neither talent nor interest in their pursuit. Altogether, although it was generally agreed, when he left at fourteen, that he was "too good to go into the mill," it was difficult to discover what else he was good for.

"Perhaps you'll find your right path later," said the headmaster to him uneasily.

Gamaliel said nothing but looked stubborn.

"Are you content to go into the mill?" exclaimed the master.

Gamaliel said nothing, but his eyes gleamed. Content! No, he was content with nothing, nothing! Everything was wrong! But what was the use of saying so? Certainly he did not want to be a chap in a white collar and a shiny suit, writing nonsense in a ledger all day and afraid for his life of losing his job. He did not want that, and he did not want to go to work in the large handsome Ashroyd Mills, because they belonged to the Ashbank folk. It was necessary that he should go to work at once, because for the past year it had been a time of slump in the West Riding, his mother was working only half a week and food was not as plentiful at home as could be wished.

By a stroke of good fortune, as he thought, he got taken on by a small firm of dyers, whose ramshackle old works were tucked in on the river bank between railway sidings and an old bridge. The building being old was intensely inconvenient; ill-ventilated, ill-heated, bitterly cold in winter, when the low rays of the sun, cut off by the hills, touched the roof for only a few moments a day, hot in summer from the coloured steam. A single sordid lavatory, so filthy that fungus grew in its bowl, served all the workpeople; the machinery and apparatus were ancient, precautions ill-observed. In such a small firm, too, there was little scope for advancement. But Gamaliel was not looking for advancement. What was he looking for? He did not yet know. Cool, reserved, remote, he went about his business, not in a dream—he despised dreamers—but as one watching an action in which he is not yet concerned, for his cue has not yet sounded; in these years, while his resentments grew to burning indignation, Gamaliel awaited the beat of some different, some yet unknown drum.

2

When he had been at work for a year or so it became clear to Gamaliel that his mother was about to marry. The man was an overlooker in one department of the Ashroyd mills recently widowed, with grown sons and daughters, the last of whom was just marrying, he still retained some good looks, being tall and limber and of florid complexion. He came to the Greenwoods' house a few times and his intentions were unconcealed, as was the joy of Avice. Her eyes glowed, her olive cheek took a brighter tint. Gamaliel watched the courtship without much interest, for he did not feel near to his mother in any way, and when after much circumlocution and mystery his grandmother broke the news of the coming marriage to him, he remarked coldly:

"Aye—I thought so."

"Is that all you have to say?" demanded his grandmother, vexed.

"Well—I hope they'll be happy," Gamaliel forced out the conventional words.

"You don't care about leaving me?" barked his grandmother, tears suffusing her old but still alert greenish eyes.

Gamaliel considered the matter. He found himself so indifferent either way that he could not frame an answer.

His mother was married at the Registrar's office in Ashworth on the Saturday before Ashworth Wakes, and went to Blackpool for Wakes Week, for her honeymoon. On the following Saturday evening, when thin plumes of smoke rising from the Ashley Foot chimneys showed that fires were being lighted again on household hearths and in mill boilers, Avice, looking very smart and smiling, appeared in her mother's house.

"I've come to take Gamaliel along home with me," she said in a rather hesitant tone.

Old Mrs. Greenwood broke into tears.

"Let him stay wi' me," she wailed.

Gamaliel, who was descending the stairs with his packed bag in his hand, paused, and sat down on a step to listen. He was tired of living with his grandmother, but did not much fancy the prospect of a stepfather. Still, a man in the house would be a change.

"He'll be miserable with you," continued old Mrs. Greenwood.

"Why should he?"

"That man o' yours'll always hate him."

Avice was silent.

"I suppose," said old Mrs. Greenwood, as if suddenly struck: "I suppose he knows truth about lad? Eh?"

Her daughter said softly, but on a note of triumph: "Who better?"

There was a moment's pause, then old Mrs. Greenwood exclaimed, spluttering:

"What? What? D'you mean he—and you never told me, all these years! You're a sly one, Avice!"

An icy rage filled Gamaliel from top to toe. So he was that man's son! White as a sheet and trembling, he stumbled down the stairs.

"I'll stay with mi grandma, Mother," he said in a harsh uneven tone.

Avice glanced from grandmother to grandson.

"*He*'ll happen be vexed if I don't take him," she said, alluding to her husband.

"Not he," said Mrs. Greenwood staunchly.

"I'll come to tea tomorrow," proffered Gamaliel. He felt ashamed of this childish suggestion even as he made it, but the discovery of his parentage had shaken him.

"*He*'s never done owt for him all these years," muttered old Mrs. Greenwood sideways to her daughter.

"How could he?"

"He can't care much for t'lad, or he'd have found a way."

Avice hesitated.

"Well, stay for a week then, love, till we're right settled in," she conceded.

In the event, Gamaliel continued to live with his grandmother. He visited often with his father and mother, however, and behaved politely to them. Nor was he unkind, either in word or deed, to the new young family which shortly grew about his parents. Sometimes he even took them for walks on Sunday afternoons. But he never touched their hands. He was not concerned with them.

3

At the dyeworks, though the workers there were not of high mental calibre, he naturally heard political and economic

200

talk. One year during his late teens a County Council Election was held in the district covering the Aske Valley. A Labour candidate was nominated and seemed likely of success, when suddenly Miss Crabtree of Ashbank was put forward as an Independent. Her connections and family influence would secure the votes of one section of the valley; other sections which would not have voted for a Conservative were glad to be able to record their appreciation of her past public service and their trust in her future usefulness, since she did not wear a party label. In the Labour camp the anger was naturally deep.

"She's no more Independent than I am."

"An out-and-out Tory, that's what she is."

"Aye, but it'll lose us the election."

"Then why don't you *do* something about it?" said Gamaliel impatiently.

"What can us do?"

"Expose her somehow."

"What, in the Press?"

"Yes. And on the platform."

"Well, we can try."

"Trouble is, she *thinks* she's Independent."

"Aye—she's only a Tory when she's asleep."

The laughter which greeted this mild sally infuriated Gamaliel by its futility.

His way home led past a Woolworth store. On an impulse he went inside and visited the paint counter. It was Friday; his week's wages were in his pocket; he came out with a bottle of turpentine, a flashlight torch and a brush in his pockets, and a tin of red paint beneath his coat.

His grandmother slept lightly during the early part of the night, but more soundly when the dawn drew near. It was easy to slip out of the house and up the lane, to switch on the torch and prop it between two stones, to paint in good bold letters TORY TORY TORY along the wall by the Crabtrees' front gate. He slipped back into the house as the first streak of gold came into the sky, slipped into bed and presently rose and went to work as usual.

He heard of the "outrage" which had occurred, at his

work, and his lip arched scornfully at the disapproving comments with which it was received. At noon when he reached home, his week's work done, he found a twittering group of village women round his grandmother's door. Had the author of the "crime" been discovered? Well, he did not care. But no; the group had met with another aim; they set off up the lane presently with buckets and scrubbing-brushes, and from sheer idiotic, slave-like devotion to the Crabtrees (as Gamaliel thought) scrubbed the front wall clean. Well, so much the more fun for him. It was not as easy as he had thought to go against his grandmother's feelings, but he steeled himself against any sentimental nonsense of that kind, and wrote next night: ADMIT YOU ARE A TORY. Each day for a week the women in indignation scrubbed the wall; each night, his skill and ease growing with practice, he wrote a longer, more insulting slogan. The secrecy of the proceeding satisfied some deep need in his heart.

It was next Friday evening when old Mrs. Greenwood, returning unexpectedly early from shopping, caught him mixing turpentine into the lessening paint. She stood by the door and stared at him; Gamaliel, in his hand the stick he used for mixing, stared back defiantly. For a long moment neither of them spoke. Then suddenly:

"You fool!" exclaimed the old woman in disgust. "D'you think I didn't smell it?"

She swooped upon the tin of paint, snatched it from his hand, poured the contents down the sink, then turned to him.

"We'll have no more of this, Gamaliel," she said grimly.

They never exchanged another friendly word. (Incidentally, Miss Crabtree was elected.) Next Friday noon when as usual he offered his grandmother the agreed proportion of his wages, she said angrily: "I don't want it." He raised his eyebrows, said nothing, did not touch the little pile of silver on the table. When he came in at teatime it was gone. Gamalie smiled contemptuously, and as soon as he could he found himself a job in Ashworth and went to live there. When (being still a minor) he informed his mother of his intende departure she invited him to live with his parents. But the invitation was half-hearted and she sighed with relief when he refused. Gamaliel smiled and withdrew. From Ashworth he sent his grandmother a postal order for the amount he had formerly paid her, every week until she died ten years later; but he never saw her again in life.

4

His lodgings were very mean but the mill where he worked was larger and better equipped and his new workmates more politically conscious than had been his lot in Ashley Foot. Now that he had his leisure to himself and not much money to spend on it, he read a good deal; he had been taught at school to use the Public Library. The Ashworth Library was large and modern, and his reading, influenced by what he heard at the mill, took a political turn. Of course he was now a member in good standing of the appropriate textile Union, and attended all the meetings punctually. But he was looking for something to counteract the burning draughts of futility and injustice he gulped down daily, and to his thinking Trade Unionism and the Labour Party did not offer antidotes sufficiently strong to that bitter and heady brew. They seemed to him insipid, ineffective, altogether contemptible and negligible, mere soothing syrup. (His father was quite a keen Labour man.) He read one or two works, among the rest, on Communist theory and the Russian Revolution, and grew interested—or rather, as Gamaliel told himself, he would have been interested if he could have believed in the sincerity of what was written. But for his part he found it difficult to believe in the truth of any public professions; there was always some dirty under-side. Still, he liked well the idea of the complete break-up of the present form of society which Communism seemed to postulate. Destroy it all, root and branch, this robber state of Capitalism which so humiliated him. The words *class struggle* and *dictatorship of the proletariat*, though he did not understand their full significance, raised a bitter glee in his breast, while the story of the early revolutionary movements of Russia, their daring secret activity, the printing and smuggling of newspapers under the very eyes of the police, the escapes across breaking ice and smoking peat, gave him the keen pleasure of an exciting adventure story to a boy. The *Capital* of Marx, on the other hand, he found too difficult for his understanding; he restored the fat close-printed volume resentfully to the shelf.

One Saturday afternoon in the autumn of 1936, as leaning against the stack of shelves devoted to Political Economy in the Ashworth Library he turned the leaves of a new work on Communism and savoured a phrase about "rending of the veils of cant and hypocrisy from the face of society by rough working-class hands," he felt someone's attention resting upon him, and looking up saw standing on the other side of the alley a girl, a clerk from the Welfare Department of the mill, Vera Illingworth was her name. Not pretty, though tallish and rather graceful in her gait and always very neat, she was earnest and sincere and the workers mostly liked her. She had a bush of dark hair, a pale cheek and rather prominent grey eyes which were now fixed upon Gamaliel. He gave her a grave nod of acknowledgement, but did not smile— he was not interested in women—and returned his glance to Milnes' book again. The analysis of the aims and development of the class struggle seemed rather good, and he decided to take the book home for a closer reading.

Accordingly he was carrying it beneath his arm when he left the Library. Beneath the gas-lamp outside the entrance he was somewhat irritated to see the Illingworth girl. He frowned as he again gave her the nod convention required.

"I was waiting for you, Mr. Greenwood," said she.

Vexed and astonished, Gamaliel said nothing but moved away down the street. The girl walked at his side for a few yards, then began:

"I saw you reading Comrade Milnes' book in the Library."

"Do you belong to the Party?" said Gamaliel, astounded.

"Yes. I thought you might like to come and hear Comrade Milnes tomorrow night. It's at Number 39, Heygate."

"What, in Ashworth? Is he coming to Ashworth?"

"Yes. He's a West Riding man, didn't you know? From Hudley."

"No. I didn't know," replied Gamaliel. His heart began to beat fast; the thought that a Communist distinguished enough to write a book sprang from Hudley and was visiting Ashworth seemed to open up worlds of possibility, to bring action, noble action, within his own reach and sphere.

Vera went on talking about Comrade Milnes. It seemed he sprang from a comfortable middle-class home.

"Oh!" said Gamaliel with derision.

He had taken high degrees at a University, and wrote for the papers in London.

"What does he know about working-class life, then?"

"He's been trained in Moscow," said Vera reproachfully. "He spent three years at the Marx and Engels Institute."

Gamaliel was silent from interest and surprise.

"The meeting tomorrow is open to all. Come if you like. He's to speak on *Two Worlds at War*, with special reference to Spain."

"To call for recruits for the International Brigade, I suppose," said Gamaliel bitterly.

"Why not? The battle between Communism and Fascism is being fought out there."

"Let him go himself then."

"As far as I know, he's going as soon as he can get away. He's come to Yorkshire to say goodbye to his family."

"In the true Communist State family ties will wither away."

"Well, come to the meeting if you like. It's in a room on the second floor."

The following evening Gamaliel found himself sheltering from a cold drizzle in a Heygate doorway, gazing across the dark street at the lighted windows of an upper room. He crossed the street once and made to go in, but swerved away as he met the interested glances of an entering couple. Presently the slight hum of talk subsided, and one resonant voice rose and continued. If only he could hear without being seen! The ground at the back of the building rose abruptly, in the customary Ashworth way; could he not perhaps hear and see from the yard at the back? He walked up the side street and looking round to see that nobody observed him, slipped into the yard. The lighted windows were still well above his head. The ground was uneven, muddy, and full of puddles; in the black shadow he stumbled, a disturbed cat fled with a shrill complaining mew.

"This is ridiculous," Gamaliel rebuked himself sternly.

He walked with a firm step and a composed face out of the yard, down the street, into the dimly lighted doorway, up the brown-linoleumed stairs; steeling himself as he had done (he remembered) over painting the Crabtrees' wall, he turned the handle of the door and went in.

To his distress—though his face was calm and his step steady—the audience were seated on benches facing the door, so that all their glances fell on him, especially as he entered almost directly behind the speaker. On the front row Vera quietly made room beside herself; he crossed the intervening space which seemed wide as the steppes, and sat down.

A slight young man in a rumpled grey suit, with tumbled fair hair, a fine head, aquiline features and blazing grey eyes, was speaking in a clear strong voice, using slender hands in occasional gestures. He paused to give Gamaliel a friendly nod and continued his exposition.

He was reminding the comrades, his hearers, of the Marxist basis of Communism. He explained how the workers, who produce goods greater in value than the wages they are paid, create thus a "surplus value" on which the capitalist lives. Capitalism was thus a social method of production, of which part of every product was appropriated to private profit. It created two classes: the wage-earners whose labour was partially exploited, the owners who lived on the exploitation. (Between these classes, the working-class and the bourgeoisie, hovered uneasily the petty bourgeois, wavering from one to the other according as his advantage served.) The central contradiction in capitalism between the mode of production and the allotment of the product rendered any kind of reform quite useless; the whole system was founded on falsehood; capitalism with all its long tapering roots must be wrenched out of the organism of society, like cancer from a body, before the organism could be healthy, before the social relation between man and man could be established on a basis of truth. The working class could only resolve the contradictions

206

of capitalism by revolution, by establishing themselves as the ruling class to carry through the transition from capitalism to socialist classless society. In the U.S.S.R. this had been done; in Spain the process, just begun, had been interrupted by a Fascist rebellion against the legally constituted working-class Government. It was essential to defend the working-class revolution wherever it appeared, by military means if necessary—for a horror of war was merely naïve sentiment when the revolution was at stake—and to press it forward all over the world, by heroism if that were demanded, by sacrifices of time and money and above all by work, which was unremittingly required from every Party member.

The audience, of whom there were some fifty or sixty, mostly men, stamped their feet and applauded at appropriate moments, and Gamaliel found himself warmly interested. The young man certainly spoke well; he used no highfalutin middle-class terms, but simple clear words which all could understand. Although he thus rejected all tricks of oratory, however, his ardent enthusiasm warmed and coloured everything he said. At the close of the address he invited questions, and answered them in a friendly tone, and with an abundance of knowledgeable detail, which Gamaliel could not but admire.

Before the proceedings closed a collection was taken in aid of the equipment of the International Brigade, composed of workers from all lands now fighting in Spain with the Government forces. Gamaliel mentally grimaced as he dropped his contribution into the basin; it always comes down to a demand for your cash, he thought.

But though he told himself this cynically, declined Vera's whispered suggestion that he should be introduced to Comrade Milnes, and slipped away before she could draw him to any other worker's attention, he was decidedly impressed, and from then on began to read Communist literature seriously. Now that he had the clue he found that he could read Marx, though somewhat laboriously. If he could really believe in all this, it seemed very much what he wanted; the thorough destruction of the existing form of society was what he needed to satisfy him.

From time to time during this period he saw Vera Illingworth, greeting her in the Library, gravitating to her side at meetings or entertainment committees in the works; but he never sought her company outside the mill, though he knew she lived in a terrace not very far away. (A terrace, not a street or a row, because Vera, alas, was one of the petty bourgeoisie, belonging by birth to the lower middle-class.) To seek her would commit him politically, and he was not ready to be committed yet. This state of uncertainty continued until one winter evening early in the following year, when as he was clumping briskly down the hill Vera suddenly sprang out at him from a side street. There were tears in her eyes. Gamaliel recoiled, frowning, from this inexplicable emotion.

"Have you heard the news about Comrade Milnes?"

"No. What news?"

She thrust an opened newspaper at him. He took it soberly from her hands, turned it to catch the light from the street-lamp and read: *MR. GERALD MILNES KILLED IN ACTION. A telegram from Madrid today confirmed the news that Mr. Gerald Milnes was killed in action in Spain last Monday, while fighting with the International Brigade in support of the Spanish Government against General Franco. Mr. Milnes, who was thirty-seven years of age, was the son of . . .*

"By God," thought Gamaliel: "He meant it, every word!"

A burning rage rushed through his body at the thought of that bright face, that well-shaped head, that mobile generous mouth, turned into a clammy lump of flesh by a Fascist bullet, that clear friendly voice speaking ardent truths stilled forever. (His grandmother had recently died and in accordance with custom he had been obliged to view her in her coffin, so he was very fully aware of the difference between death and life.) He thrust the paper back at Comrade Vera.

"Thanks very much for showing me," he said hoarsely.

He tried to keep his gait steady as he walked off down the street, but his emotion was too strong; suddenly he broke into a headlong run.

That evening, as soon as he thought the man would be back from work, without changing from his working clothes he went to the Secretary of the local branch and asked to be made a member of the Party.

5

The authorities now applied such clamps to the means of exit for volunteers to the International Brigade that it proved impossible for Gamaliel to join. But in spite of this disappointment, from the moment he took out his Party card he became a happy man.

His life now had an aim, a focus, many duties; it was lived by a strict code, an austere, disciplined, continually party-active life. He found his fellow-workers easier to bear with now that he saw them as the "grey anonymous masses," the "exploited majority," who needed "strong collective leadership" from active Party members, and his Trade Union membership now had point; he became active in his Union, as a means, as Comrade Pollitt said, of developing and deepening the political consciousness of his fellow-members and drawing them into the Party. This took much time. Indeed, although Gamaliel would not presume to claim that he, like the great Ilyich, was busy for twenty-four hours of every day with thoughts of the working-class revolution, there really were not many waking hours when he was not so occupied. By day his work in the mill was the mere tending of a machine, which he could accomplish (to his own satisfaction if not always to his foreman's) with less than his full attention; the remainder he devoted to the Party. In the evening, he read, spoke, attended classes or meetings.

It was about this time, too, that the Ashworth police were troubled by an outbreak of wall-defacement. Slogans relating to the Spanish war appeared in huge red letters wherever there was a suitable stretch of wall: DOWN WITH FRANCO, DEATH TO THE FASCISTS, NON-INTERFERENCE IS HELPING FASCISM, splashed the dingy smoke-blackened walls all over the town. A strict watch was enjoined on constables on the beat, but the perpetrators were not discovered. The coming of the lighter mornings of summer made the painting operations more difficult to carry out undiscovered, by confining them to a shorter period; Gamaliel found it better to paint

in the earlier but darker hours, and one night between twelve
and one as he was finishing the M OF FASCISM on a lonely but
visible field wall high above the town towards the summit
of Hey Hill, a policeman turned the corner of the street.
Gamaliel dropped his tools and ran, but footsteps echoed
after him, and he had an uncomfortable feeling, even when
he reached the lower streets near the mill where a few people
were still walking home from late entertainments or meetings,
that he was still being followed. Suddenly a policeman
crossed the bottom of the hill, a hundred yards away, which
he must pass to reach his lodgings. In this awkward predica-
ment, as he turned somewhat breathlessly into a side street
to give himself time to think, he ran into Vera. Without a
word she seized his arm.

"I'll go with you past the policeman," she whispered.
"Clasp my hand."

Their arms locked, her strong warm fingers interlaced
with his, her head near his shoulder, they gave a convincing
impression of lovers trailing dreamily home. As they drew
near the policeman, who was now walking up the hill, Vera
began to chatter in a low caressing voice, and Gamaliel
leaned over her to listen.

They passed the constable, who looked at them with a
cynical but benevolent eye, and walked in their lover-like
embrace over the bridge. When they had turned the corner
into the shadows of Heygate, and were concealed from the
policeman's gaze even if he turned to look after them, Vera
stood upright and made to withdraw her hand. But Gamaliel
retained it in his clasp.

"Let us marry, Comrade Vera," he said.

"Yes, let us do that," returned Vera simply.

It was a particular pleasure to him that her name was
Vera—a Russian name, which one often met in Communist
books.

6

So here they were now, he and Vera and the child, in
one of the new little pre-fabs at the bottom of the town.

It had not been easy. Vera's parents—the most hopeless

reactionary type of petty bourgeois, in Gamaliel's view—had disliked the match and thrown every possible obstacle in its way, even falling ill at appropriate moments. Even when they began to yield, they did their best to hinder and delay. They wished, for example, that the marriage ceremony should be performed in chapel. Gamaliel of course refused, whereupon they wore down Vera by petty nagging to such a point that at last even she came to him in tears and begged for some concession. In Hudley, she said, there was some sort of Free Christian Church which was not bound to any specific dogma but only to general principles of brotherly love, would Gamaliel not consent to be married there? Although by this time Gamaliel had come to depend a great deal on Vera's companionship and wished strongly to take her to wife, he sternly refused; for what would the Party, when triumphant at last in England, think of a member who had taken part in a disgusting religious ceremony. Vera's grief at this decision was so despairing that her parents gave way, and the pair were married in the office of the Ashworth Registrar. This too was an ordeal for Gamaliel, since his parents had belatedly legalised their union there; however he steeled himself and carried the affair through.

Hardly were they married, however, than the War fell upon them. Regarding it as merely a capitalist-imperialist war for spheres of investment, raw material and cheap labour-power, Gamaliel was prepared to resist his call-up and go to prison; but to his chagrin, though in public the party line was to denounce the war, his private instructions were to enter the army and try to convert it into a revolutionary working-class force. It was not easy to accept this tame surrender to capitalist authority after the prospect of revolutionary martyrdom; but he steeled himself to follow the party line, and of course was delighted, when Germany attacked Russia in the summer of 1941, to be in a position to render the cradle of Marxist revolution active assistance.

It was not his fault that he had a fairly quiet war; he fretted over his protracted stay in England and longed to be fighting, to be drawing some of the German divisions away from Russia. (While on leave in 1943 he managed to paint OPEN

A SECOND FRONT NOW in really large letters along the side of the mill where it could be seen across the valley—Vera conceived their son on the same night.) He eventually found himself guarding occupied Germany, but alas not in Berlin, so he never saw a Russian soldier. It was a keen disappointment, but of course such small individual preferences were of no importance in the great forward movement of the proletariat. He came back safe, though late; got his old job back, lived in great mental discomfort with Vera's parents for a couple of years—though he took his share of the domestic tasks with a stern politeness which quite cowed them—and at last as an ex-serving man with a young child was allotted one of these new pre-fabs near the mill.

The site of the pre-fab estate, which had been made available by slum clearance, was not particularly salubrious, lying as it did at the foot of a couple of Ashworth's many hills. Across the main road, beneath a sharp dip in the ground, the River Aske wound its slow way; in this reach of its course it was filthy, stained by dye effluent, sluggish with refuse, bedded in a stone drain and overhung by mills. Indeed nineteen mill chimneys could be seen close at hand, without turning the head, from the Greenwoods' front window. But Gamaliel, though he resented on behalf of his class the situation which was thought good enough for them, was glad in the present state of the revolution to be living in Ashworth's industrial heart, in the centre of the oppressed masses.

He approved the structure of the pre-fabs too: a sitting room, two bedrooms, a proper lavatory, a rectangular kitchen with refrigerator and cooker run by electricity. Of course compared with the mansions of the capitalist bourgeoisie his house was a wretched affair, but he did not wish for better treatment than the rest of his proletarian comrades and it was possible to live there in decent cleanliness. The doors and window-frames of all the whitish pre-fabs were painted light blue, and this was part of a uniform scheme which tenants could not alter, but the Greenwoods had scarlet curtains at which Gamaliel gazed with proud political consciousness whenever he climbed up the path to his home. The Greenwoods' bungalow was most admirably kept; they were indeed model tenants. It was not so with all the other pre-fab dwellers, for many of them were careless, rowdy and dirty. But they offered great scope for serious mass work, and Gamaliel of course began this work without delay and very earnestly. He had already formed his co-dwellers into a Tenants' Association which continually pricked the Ashworth Town Council Housing Committee about the bungalows' defects—their coldness in winter, their inadequate chimneys, the sinking of the stone pathways into the mud, and so on—and he hoped that when he had gained their confidence in this way he would be able to give them some political guidance. Indeed this was his firm intention; to make dozens of fresh contacts, secure their confidence, teach them and draw them in was an essential part of the programme of struggle for the creation of a victorious revolutionary party laid down by Lenin.

Gamaliel sat at the table in his pre-fab now, carefully reading the *Ashworth Times*, the local evening paper. Vera had cleared the tea-things away, and they had washed them up together; now she was putting the child to bed. A long, thin, dreamy boy, sallow but strong, young J. V. Greenwood had just begun to go to school and was now babbling happily about his day's experiences to his mother. It seemed as if he were proving a clever child, and Gamaliel sometimes indulged fond dreams that when the Party triumphed in England, John would be some great and trusted Commissar. This was only a dream, and must not be indulged too far; still Lenin himself had said that such dreams, pictures of the completion of the work in which a man is already seriously engaged, are a stimulus to his action. Gamaliel found them so; and after all, he was not desiring personal success for John, but only that he might greatly serve the revolution. The boy had been named *John* because it was a good plain proletarian name which had never been held, as far as Gamaliel and Vera knew, by any members of their families, and *Vladimir* after Lenin; they wished to bind their child to the future, not to the past. Sometimes when they were feeling especially tender to the lad they called him Volodya. . . . But they did not, of course, allow themselves this indulgence often; they must not permit themselves to become sentimental, even about their child.

Was there any item in the paper tonight which offered an opening for useful Party activity? Gamaliel rather thought there was. A column headed: CONFERENCE WITH CONTINENTAL WORKERS URGED reported that in a neighbouring West Riding town a proposal had been brought forward to the Trades and Industrial Council that a special meeting should be called of British and Continental workers in the town, with a view to winning over some of the European Voluntary Workers to take a real part in the British Trade Union movement. This proposal had been brought forward by a Communist member, who added that he would like a complete picture of the background of many of these E.V.W.'s. *We shall be able to approach the question of E.V.W.'s better when we know something of their environment*, he said. It struck Gamaliel at once that a similar meeting ought to be arranged in Ashworth. These Continental workers, with their history of Fascist persecution, ought certainly to be drawn into the Party. Some of them might of course think themselves the victims, not of Fascist but of Communist pressure, reflected Gamaliel, and in that case there was all the more reason for discovering their origins and taking the necessary precautions. Possibly, even, something might be done with their relatives back there. . . . At any rate, he remembered with sudden joy that one of the members of the A.T.P. committee which he was supposed to be attending that night on behalf of his Union, Mrs. Deborah Sykes, taught classes of the Ashworth E.V.W.'s. He must talk to her about them; to contact them through her would probably be a far more effective way to their confidence than a political approach. And on the way, so to speak, he might be able to do some useful propaganda with Mrs. Sykes herself. She could be such a useful member of the Party if she chose—she was quite a revolutionary type, unconventional, unafraid, of strong intelligence and will, but spoiled by counter-revolutionary elements, reactionary idealism, inculcated during her bourgeois upbringing. Gamaliel feared she was irretrievably a middle-class intellectual. Still, it was worth trying; an approach through her to the E.V.W.'s might well bring down two birds with one stone. Gamaliel decided to cut the meeting of a small Party group where he was due to discuss arrangements for the winter's campaign, and attend the A.T.P.C.

7

Although he had been obliged to call at the house of a comrade to notify him of his absence from the group and its cause, Gamaliel was of course in ample time for the A.T.P. Committee. He could not endure any kind of sloppiness and inefficiency in Party work such as unpunctuality. He had had to walk briskly through the streets to reach the Mechanics' Institute in time, but he liked to walk briskly; his long legs swung rapidly over the ground, he carried his head well up and his shoulders back—very different, he thought contemptuously, from these bowed and slouching wage-slaves whom he passed. Bowed by their economic troubles. If only they would look up, look up and *see* that the only way to the classless state was through the dictatorship of the proletariat. He himself had no troubles; his line was clear, he knew just what he had to do.

He frowned as he crossed the road towards the Mechanics' Institute. What a misnomer. This monument of an attempt at bribery and corruption, at dividing the working-class by elevating the educational status and earning capacity of selected groups, had certainly never belonged to any mechanics. Now in the U.S.S.R. a Mechanics' Institute would be the headquarters of an engineering Soviet. . . .

Just as he reached the pavement a car drew up and old Thomas Armitage climbed out and stumbled towards the steps. Thomas Armitage is getting to look very old, thought Gamaliel, stepping into the shadow till the Chairman should be out of sight; he's not long for this world—and a good thing too. A reactionary idealist if ever there was one. Of course, to do him justice, in the first stage of the revolution, the stage when the "critically thinking person," the Liberal, perceives the injustice of the capitalist régime and acts as a ferment, a leaven in society, Thomas Armitage would play a noble part. One could imagine, for instance, that Lenin's parents, who, as we are told, reflected Gamaliel, were representative of what was good in the Russian middle class of the 1860's, might well resemble Thomas Armitage. But that day is over, dead and done for, long since past! The car drove off; Gamaliel stepped out of the shadow and at a discreet distance followed Thomas Armitage into the Committee room.

The first thing he saw as he took off his coat was the back view of Elizabeth Marrison, a typical example of the decadence of the middle class. A brothel was her natural home—or rather, not "natural," for if she had been a member from birth of a classless working society, subject to strong collective leadership, her character would no doubt have developed on healthier lines. But as it was, she was rotten all through and the only place for her outside a capitalist brothel was a correction camp. To Gamaliel she seemed positively to exude an odour of decay; he was so sensible of it that he did not wish to sit near her, and seeing the chair at the far end of the table free, he took it. (Besides, it was a position of dignity, suitable amid these specimens of decaying bourgeoisie to a member, however humble, of the Party.)

Thomas Armitage, who was bending over some papers with the Secretary, Roderick Bairstow, looked up and greeted him; Bairstow did the same. It's a pity Bairstow is so hopelessly counter-revolutionary, thought Gamaliel with regret, because one can see he's a good soldier, original in his tactics, daring, determined and bold. Perhaps under strict supervision from a friendly political Commissar. . . . For a moment he imagined himself in this capacity, in a friendly tactful way keeping Bairstow steady on the Party line. But no! He dismissed the picture as an idle dream as he gave Chairman and Secretary his grave derisive nod. Bairstow was too hopelessly reactionary, too perversely individual; he wouldn't last, in any Communist army, more than a couple of days.

Sir Charles Considine now came in and planted himself at Gamaliel's right. Now there's a man it would give me very great pleasure to eliminate, thought Gamaliel. A firing-squad's the only cure for him. He'd betray his own child, his dearest cause, for money.

"Good evening, Mr. Greenwood." (What a despicable decadent voice he had! Its smoothness oozed corruption.)

"Good evening."

"Cold for the time of year?"

"I don't go in for weather averages."

"Still, I see you've brought your raincoat."

"Have I?" said Gamaliel indifferently, glancing up at the pegs behind the door. His raincoat, a somewhat shabby garment though well-mended, hung there. "I suppose I have," he agreed, smiling with cold uninterest.

But the smile and the coldness were struck from his face by the next member who entered the room, for it was Councillor Foster Ormerod. Gamaliel's eyes sparkled, his colour rose, with rage. That traitor to the revolution! That reformist! That cowardly opportunist (in the Marxian sense)! A man who believed in the peaceful democratic transition from Capitalism to Socialism, not perceiving that such a phrase was a contradiction in terms! That splitter of the working-class! That collaborator in the class war! That supporter of American Imperialism! Traitor! Betrayer of his class! He actually had the nerve, the impudence, to seat himself next to Gamaliel, a tried and trusted member of the Party, and say good evening to him!

"Good evening, Councillor," replied Gamaliel with open contempt.

"May I introduce to you all Miss Rosemary Heald, the delegate from the Youth Groups?" old Armitage was saying in his thin polite middle-class intellectual tones.

"I'm not really the delegate, I'm just taking his place."

Now who was this? A young girl; a girl of unformed, still flexible mind; somebody who might be won over to the joyous and confident philosophy of Marx, the clear straightforward outlook of the revolutionary! Of course one could see from her dress, her hair, her gait, one could hear it in her speech, that she belonged to the petty bourgeoisie, that servile and treacherous class, the breeding-ground of Fascism. But she was young; and had not Lenin himself thundered against the craven fear of youth, urged in lightning phrases that youth, youth was the hope of the revolution! "Go to

the youth, gentlemen! That's your sole, all-saving means."
What a good thing he had come to this meeting tonight,
thought Gamaliel joyously! Even if Mrs. Sykes did not come—
she wasn't here yet, but then come to think of it she had been
late last week; if she came, there was herself to be angled
for and the European Voluntary Workers through her—but
even if she didn't come, there was this young girl, this
Rosemary Heald. As her glance rested on him in a tour of
the committee table, he gave her his most compelling
revolutionary stare. How different she would look if instead
of a Youth Group she belonged to a Comsomol! If I could
only draw her into the class struggle! . . .

VIII

MISS ROSEMARY HEALD

I

IT WAS LOVELY WALKING down to the Speedway in
the twilight. At first you were just mixed up with ordinary
boring Ashworth people, people going in different directions
on different errands. But gradually the people going your
way grew more and more and the people going the other
way grew less and less, and soon you were in a thick wide
stream of people all going to the Speedway, and in the
distance along the road you could see another thick stream
of people pouring in at the other entrance; everyone was
going to the Speedway and it felt exciting. That distant
entrance was the cheap entrance. Rosemary and Lilian always
paid two and three—Lilian only paid one-and-nine really, of
course, because she was a "supporter" and belonged to the
club—but they went in at the expensive entrance and it
made Rosemary feel nice. The music was already playing
from the loudspeakers and some of the lights were on; it
was exciting.

You bought a programme just inside the gate, and then

you walked down the shallow earthy steps as quick as you could and hurried along the side of the track to the paddock. However early you were there always seemed to be some girls there before you, tossing back their long hair (which would be all the better for a shampoo and set, thought Rosemary scornfully), pressing themselves up against the pointed palings and calling out: "Ken!" and "Ron!" and "Tony!" and waving autograph books or postcard photographs to be signed by the riders. One of the track attendants in white coats sometimes took a pile of these into the pavilion and brought them back signed. If you were wearing a supporter's badge and if it was a postcard, he seemed to catch your eye more readily somehow.

Now the mechanics in their white suits came in and out, and some of the machines were started up and began to roar, it was lovely to hear them. Soon some of the riders came out to their machines and looked them over, very seriously. Tony came out like this; he was in his leather suit and big boots, with his scarf already tied at the back of his neck, but without his helmet; his long fair hair fell over his forehead and he kept shaking it back; the girls all cooed at him as he did this, admiringly. He squatted down by his machine and said something Rosemary didn't hear, to his mechanic, and then there was a hissing sound—it seemed as if they were letting out a little air from the back tyre, or something.

On the other side of the enclosure, away from the track, stood the machines of the Southern Club which was riding the match against Ashworth this Tuesday: their colours were red and gold—just a number, not a lovely pattern, like the Boars—and the riders came out wearing them. Rosemary and Lilian did not think much of these Southern riders. Some of them looked quite old! As old as thirty! One of them even wore spectacles! But now three girls came out of the pavilion wearing huge red and gold striped scarves—"I suppose they're married to those Southern riders or perhaps just engaged to them," said Lilian wistfully. What would it feel like to be married to a Speedway rider? Tony, say? One's heart would be in one's mouth every match evening. Would it be better to travel around with him, or stay at home waiting? Tony looked up and his big brown eyes seemed to stare straight into Rosemary's; of course it was difficult to tell, those big arc lights cast such deep shadows, but it really looked as though he saw her. He raised one hand in a sort of salute. "Well, you're the lucky one!" said Lilian crossly, and all the girls looked enviously at Rosemary—it was quite embarrassing.

Now the announcer in his kind friendly voice was appealing for rakers. "We want four rakers . . . over eighteen . . . if any of you chaps feel you'd like to see things from inside, and earn a little pocket-money and do a spot of raking. . . ."

"I don't see why they don't have girl rakers," said Lilian.

"Oh, Lilian!" said Rosemary, shrinking.

"Well they don't so you needn't get hot and bothered," said Lilian. She still spoke rather crossly, she was jealous still because Tony—the great captain, the hero, Tony—had looked at Rosemary and waved to her. Well, not quite *waved*. Still . . . He'd moved his hand as though he recognised her, anyway.

The grand stand and the slopes around the track were all pretty full, now. It looked lovely, really; not like Ashworth at all; it was almost dusk, and the lights on Shaw Bank, on the other side of the field, looked really lovely, stretching up into the darkening sky. ("You've had it, rakers! We've got our four.") The air began to feel fresh, not cold really but just nice and fresh; Rosemary drew her silk head handkerchief up over her curls. (It was a very expensive silky handkerchief, patterned in lovely colours, fuchsia and pale blue and dusty pink and brown, a present from Dorothy last birthday. Dorothy *was* generous, she really was, although so strict and tiresome sometimes.)

"If you want a place by the barrier, you'd better come," said Lilian.

They moved aside and were lucky in getting a place not too far from the starting line. The machines were all roaring now; it seemed deafening, though it was nothing to what was to come, and the smell of hot oil began to fill the air.

"What about giving our boys a little encouragement with

our war-cry?" demanded the announcer. "Come along now: BOARS!"

"B-O-A-R-S," chanted the crowd obediently.

"Very nice, very nice. Hope the boys ride as well as you shout," said the announcer in his benevolent tones.

And now—hurrah—the music died, the buzzer sounded, the lights all came on blazing over the track so that it was as light as day. The music turned into a march, and the starting-line marshal and all the other men in white coats and overalls, and the rakers in blue overalls, marched out of the paddock in a procession, so nice and dignified, to the starting-line, and then the rakers spread out all round on the oval grass field inside the track. The announcer read out the names of those riding in the first heat—there was no change from the programme—and their machines were wheeled out of the paddock, and Tony and Ron mounted and were pushed off by the white men, and they and the two Southern-ers rode—so easily and gracefully—round the track. The starting-line marshal stood across the track with his arms stretched out wide, and the four riders—Tony was nearest the inside; his face was covered with goggles and scarf, but you knew him by the black helmet—besides you would know him anywhere, really. He had such a way of sitting on his machine: so graceful and light.

The marshal stepped back; there was a pause; then the three white ribbons flew up and with a deafening noise the riders tore along the course. Tony shot ahead of them all—his machine seemed really to fly through the air. Round and round they went; on the narrow curves of the oval sparks flew from their boots as they used their left heels to keep them from falling. One of the Southern men was trying to cut in between Tony and the inside of the track. Surely he would not . . . but he was gaining. . . . As they came down the long side towards Rosemary they were almost side by side; it was a pity you could never see Tony actually pass, but you were obliged to duck down behind the barrier to avoid the dust which came pelting over as the machines rushed by. Oh! There was a sudden delighted roar of laughter from the crowd as Tony seemed to lift his front wheels from the ground and bounce ahead. He gained and gained; now there were ten yards between him and that horrid Southern man, now there were twenty; now the course marshal waved the chequered flag to show it was the last lap; Tony flashed past far ahead and the heat was won for the Boars. He slowed at the turn and rode sweetly and softly along the far side of the track, pulling down his scarf and pushing up his goggles so that his face, flushed and happy, could be seen. The crowd applauded their favourite warmly, and when the track lights went out and the stand lights up, and the announcer read the scores and Tony's track time, there was another burst of applause.

"Only seventy-two and one-fifth seconds!" murmured Lilian ecstatically.

She took her programme out from her bag and wrote it all down carefully in her clumsy scrawl, moistening her blunt stub of a pencil between her ruby-painted lips: the name of the winner and the points won by Ashworth, and Tony's track time. Rosemary hadn't bought a programme, just as she hadn't bought a Boars' badge or a postcard photograph of Tony; it was a way of saying that she hadn't really decided yet to be a Speedway fan, a real supporter. At home they disapproved of the Speedway, Father and Mother and Dorothy. That made her more inclined to it, of course. But when she got away from them and was listening to Lilian, she wasn't so sure herself about the Speedway. But it was so *exciting*. . . .

At least, to be quite honest, at *first* it had been terribly exciting. Fear for the riders as they hurtled round the track was a sensation so powerful that it filled your whole body, seemed to run along every nerve or muscle or whatever it was to the very tips of your fingers and toes. But after you had been to the Speedway a few times, the sensation grew dull, and you began to long for close finishes and daring cut-ins—sometimes, Rosemary was ashamed to say, you almost began to long for an accident. Not that she really wanted one, of course, she told herself hastily; but it was strange how, when two machines were close and the slightest waver by one of the riders would crash them, the crowd roared and one felt that painful but delicious tingle of excitement course instantly through one's body. Tonight was not one of the most exciting nights, because the Boars were so much swifter than their opponents, they won all the heats and often had the second place as well. But next Tuesday, said the announcer, there was to be a wonderful match, with a team which was practically in the First Division! When Tony spoke over the loud-speaker, too, in the interval, he talked about this almost-First-Division team, and you could tell he was excited about it, he meant what he said, he spoke really seriously. He had a lovely voice, had Tony: kind of proud, not sucking up to the spectators, but warm and friendly too. What would he be like to talk to privately, Rosemary wondered. He certainly had looked straight at her and kind of saluted her. Perhaps next Tuesday he would stroll across to her and speak. Lilian thought he might.

"I shouldn't know what to say, I'm sure," said Rosemary, blushing.

"He'd do all the talking, my dear," said Lilian in her sophisticated way.

Perhaps next Tuesday. . . .

And now it was Tuesday, hurrah, hurrah, thought Rosemary. Tonight she would go to the Speedway with Lilian, and have all that lovely sophisticated excitement again. If only it were tonight now! If only there wasn't the long dreary day to get through before the Speedway!

She finished sweeping out the last cubicle, took off her coloured overall and put on her white one. Lilian did not bother about her overall and would often sweep out in her clean white one, but in spite of it being Dorothy's rule about changing the overalls and Rosemary liking *not* to keep Dorothy's rules, she always changed quite carefully. She loved her beautiful white overall to be very clean, it was like the clean white coats worn by the men at the Speedway. Her arms looked very round and slender, coming out of the short white sleeves—even Dorothy thought she had nice arms and hands. She pulled the belt of the overall a long way through the buckle and tucked the end well in so that the belt clasped her waist firmly and made thick beautiful folds in the starchy white below. Yes, she was looking well this morning, she thought, glancing in the mirror and making just the slightest adjusting touch to her pale thick fair hair. Her hair curled naturally and was quite pretty really, thought Rosemary wistfully, but of course she wasn't a real chromium blonde like Lilian. Lilian's hair was so smooth and sleek and sophisticated. . . . Still, she was looking well this morning; her face looked slender, not plump, and rather pale, serious somehow and grown-up, just as she liked it to be.

If only something would happen this morning! Something exciting, something romantic! If somebody would come in to have a shampoo and set who would change all Rosemary's life! Somebody with a brother, perhaps. Somebody with a brother who came to fetch her in a car. Not *too* beautiful a car, just a nice neat little car that he and Rosemary could run about in it. The brother was—he was—well at any rate he was very tall and dark and romantic. Or perhaps he was fair, with his hair falling over one eye, like Tony? Perhaps he *was* Tony? Anyway the brother was romantic somehow, so that you had that lovely feeling which all the girls in the films seemed to get but which never seemed to come your way in real life. If only something exciting would happen! Still tonight there would be the Speedway.

2

The telephone bell rang. Suppose it was a kind of answer to her prayer, suppose it was something really exciting!

"Dorothy Heald, hairdresser."

"Hullo, Rosemary."

Oh dear! It was only Harry. Not that Harry wasn't a pleasant nice-looking boy enough. Well, he was more a man really; he'd done his conscription and was over twenty-one. He was tall and what she thought film magazines mean by "rangy," with narrow hips and broad shoulders, a rather long narrow head and features quite "well chiselled," really not at all coarse and blunt as some men's features were. His hair was an ordinary brownish shade, but not unpleasing his hands were rather too large for the rest of him, somehow

224

but definitely strong. She didn't know what colour his eyes were really, reflected Rosemary; a sort of hazel, she rather thought; but they certainly had a kind of sparkle, a kind of twinkle in them; he was a good one for a joke. Not *silly* jokes, I don't mean, thought Rosemary swiftly; to do him justice, Harry's got plenty of sense. But girls don't like jokes much, I think. Jokes make girls feel young and foolish when they want to feel sophisticated and grown-up. Still, Harry didn't look bad even in his dirty blue engineering overalls, and at the Youth Club where he was secretary for the under-sixteens and played Badminton and sang in the Concert Party with the older members, in his white sweater and shorts he looked ever so nice, especially at the beginning when his hair was well brushed back and looked dark and smooth. Mr. Lister, the Worth Lane Youth Club Warden, thought a great deal of Harry. Rosemary went to the Youth Club to please Dorothy though she thought it rather too childish for her, really, but after all she'd met Harry there, and playing Badminton and table-tennis and dancing was quite fun. Mr. Lister wanted her to join a Drama class or a discussion group, but Rosemary hung back—she'd left school, she didn't want any more teaching, thank you. Harry always walked home with her, so she was sure to see him, and of course it was nice to feel you had a boy of your own when other girls were talking about theirs, even though there wasn't anything serious between her and Harry really. But the Speedway was so much more exciting than Harry.

"Harry, you shouldn't ring up in business hours. You know Dorothy doesn't like it."

"Is Dorothy there?" whispered Harry cautiously.

"Well, no. Not yet."

"That's all right, then," boomed Harry in his natural tones. "Look, Rosemary. I've got to go to the Tech tonight."

"That's nothing new. You're always there for classes in the winter."

"Yes, but look. I shan't be able to see you tonight."

"No," said Rosemary coldly. (I shall be at the Speedway, she thought.)

"Come out in the dinner hour for a few minutes?"

"Oh, I don't know, Harry," said Rosemary pettishly.

"Yes, come on. Do. I've something to tell you. The usual place in the Park. By the Girl?"

"You and your Girl."

"Quarter to one?"

"No. We've a lot of appointments, we shall be late finishing and Mother doesn't like me to go out till I've had my dinner."

"I shall be there at a quarter to one and wait for you."

"Oh, Harry, I don't know—here's Dorothy," said Rosemary with a quick change of tone.

"Twelve-forty-five by the Girl," said Harry, ringing off.

3

Dorothy came into the shop from the house.

"Your belt's too tight," she said.

Rosemary made no reply. Why did older people always criticise, always find something horrid to say? Just because their own waists were larger!

"Where's Lilian?" went on Dorothy sharply.

It was so obvious that Lilian was not in the tiny shop that Rosemary again made no reply. She had drawn back the curtains of all three cubicles so as to sweep them; surely Dorothy could see for herself that Lilian wasn't there?

"I often wish I hadn't engaged that girl," said Dorothy ominously. "For more reasons than one."

Poor Dorothy! She was so large and bulgy, her face so sallow, her dark hair so dull and heavy, it was not surprising she was still unmarried at twenty-five. Sometimes there was a kind of hint in the air that Mr. Lister admired her, but surely that couldn't be true. Nobody could admire Dorothy— not in *that* way. Of course as a person, as a daughter and an elder sister and all that kind of thing, she was perfectly splendid—one knew that really, at the bottom of one's heart although one rebelled against her one really respected her— but the thought of anyone making love to Dorothy, marrying her, was simply ludicrous. Anyway Mr. Lister was ever so old. Thirty-five at least. So why trouble to think about it? Rosemary told herself impatiently; there was no romance

nothing lovely or exciting, about Dorothy and Mr. Lister.
Sometimes indeed Rosemary wondered wistfully if there was
any romance anywhere nowadays outside the films. Of course,
there was the Speedway.

Just then the door-bell yapped and Lilian blew in, her
chromium hair gleaming, her nails and lips thickly red. In
a tone which hardly expected to be believed she announced
that her bus had been late. Dorothy glanced balefully at the
nails, but before she could say anything the bell yapped
again and the first appointment came in. Dorothy put on
her customers' smile, and ushered her into the largest cubicle
and left her to take off her coat. Before Lilian had finished
combing her hair in the mirror over the hearth, her appointment came in.

"This way, please," said Lilian. As she passed Rosemary
she whispered: "They won at Plymouth last night."

"Really?"

"Yes. Tony had a maximum."

"Shampoo, please, Rosemary," said Dorothy sternly.

It was a boring morning. Rosemary shampooed Dorothy's
customers, handed pins for Lilian, swept the cubicles after
hair had been cut, answered the telephone, wrote appointments in the big diary, let Tinker in and out when he mewed,
and made the mid-morning cup of tea. It was not disagreeable, it was even interesting in a way, but it was not romantic.
The little shop grew hot, the windows steamed; Rosemary
made the excuse of fetching clean towels from the house, to
get away for a moment. It was while she was upstairs, getting
the towels from the cylinder cupboard, that she heard her
sister calling her urgently. She ran downstairs, and found
Dorothy at the telephone with her hand over the mouthpiece
looking frowning and worried.

"There's a Miss Barraclough on the 'phone," said Dorothy
in a low voice. "A new customer. She wants a perm in a
hurry, must be this afternoon, she has to go away for an
important engagement unexpectedly tomorrow."

This was awkward, because both Dorothy and Lilian were
going out that afternoon to a bride-of-tomorrow's home, to
"do" the bride and a couple of bridesmaids.

"Do you think *you* could manage it, Rosemary?"

Rosemary nodded vigorously. It would be only the second perm she had given in her life, of course, and really you could hardly count the first one. Mother had volunteered to be the guinea-pig, and she had kept jerking her head about and giving advice, and Dorothy had been in and out all the time, superintending everything. Rosemary's arms got so tired, so heavy she could hardly hold them up; she could have cried from weariness! Especially when she was doing the pieces in front—they were so awkward, somehow, to reach, and Mother's hair was like Dorothy's, heavy and thick— really you wouldn't think an old person like Mother would have such a lot of hair, and so very little grey. All of a sudden, just when Rosemary felt she simply couldn't roll another curler, Mother kind-of beckoned her, and when Rosemary bent down, she whispered in her ear: "Sit in my lap, love." That was the funny part of parents and elder sisters and grown-ups generally; they were maddening, so strict and severe and unsympathetic, and then all of a sudden when you felt you couldn't bear them another minute, they turned round and were lovely. So Rosemary sat on her mother's knee to finish the front pieces, and of course Dorothy came in and caught them. Rosemary felt terrible, but she couldn't move because she was just moistening a strand of hair with the lotion, and if she'd moved some drops might have flown into her mother's eyes. So she just blushed and went on with the job. Dorothy gave a kind of snort, but she only said, "Well, well, well!" and luckily the dryer was going in the next cubicle, so Lilian did not hear. Afterwards, when the shop was closed and they were all at tea in the house, Father, looking at Mother's hair—which was, Rosemary admitted, too stiff at the back, as though cut out of corrugated tin, and too soft at the front—asked how the perm had gone on.

Father was always just a little sarcastic about perming and setting and tinting, he wasn't in favour of Dorothy starting the hairdressing business really, he kept on saying it was "silly work."

"It's no sillier than adding up figures in a textile mill office all day," Dorothy had said sharply.

"Yes, it is. It's nothing but pandering to womenfolk's vanity," said Father.

"Well, so is making dress-weight cloth," said Dorothy.

"Aye; in a sense you're right," said Father—he was always just and kind, if a little slow: "But there's reason in all things, Dot."

"I don't say you're not right, Father," said Dorothy in a mollified tone: "But hairdressing's so lucrative, d'you see. And Rosemary can learn it too, without having to go somewhere else to work."

Her father turned his long serious face and large brown eyes towards Rosemary, and without speaking winked at her. Rosemary smiled with delight; she took the wink to mean that Rosemary was fitted for more romantic, more exciting things than hairdressing, that she would soon marry, that Dorothy was inclined to be a bossy bore—oh, that wink meant all kinds of jolly things!

Father didn't oppose Dorothy about the hairdressing very long, he gave way and helped her to buy the little hairdressing business in New Park Street with ANNE above the shop-window, and change the name to DOROTHY HEALD, and he was quite nice about the removal—after all, this little street halfway down Worth Lane, that wide road of roaring traffic, one of the main entrances to Ashworth, was quite convenient for his cashier's work down at Worth Mills in town. He'd made himself very useful, too, with screw-driver and hammer and paint-brush—heaven knew when the re-decoration of the place would have been finished without him—and of course he did the accounts every week. But he was always just a little sarcastic about the hairdressing, and so, that day of Rosemary's first perm, you could tell from his voice that he wouldn't have minded a bit really if she had made a mess of it. So of course Dorothy out of perversity had passed it off without saying much; she just said that on the whole and. for the first time Rosemary had done quite well, and dropped the subject. She'd never mentioned it again, since, and never given Rosemary another perm to do, either. In her heart of hearts Rosemary was rather disappointed—not that she really cared about hairdressing, of course. Still . . .

At any rate, now there was a chance, she nodded her head vigorously.

"You'll be all alone," said Dorothy, doubtful. "You'll have it all to do yourself."

"I can manage," said Rosemary, impatient.

"You won't get too tired?"

Really it was *mean*, it was *insulting*, to say that now! Especially as there was no dryer going, and Lilian and both customers could hear quite plainly. Rosemary coloured and shook her head.

"You got too tired before," said Dorothy.

"That was *long* ago, when I was *new*," cried Rosemary angrily. (And indeed it was quite six weeks.)

"Would you like to try it, then?"

"Of course!"

Dorothy uncovered the telephone and in her customers' voice made the appointment.

Wouldn't it be lovely if Miss Barraclough turned out to be a girl just her own age, with whom she could be terrific friends? (Lilian, after all, was older.) Or suppose Miss Barraclough wanted somebody to go away with her—to London perhaps—tomorrow, and took a fancy to Rosemary and invited her to go? (But Dorothy probably wouldn't allow it.) Or of course Miss Barraclough might have a brother. She might have a brother who was a Speedway rider. In London. Rosemary smiled to herself, and felt happy and excited.

4

As she rounded the bushes and came out at the foot of the broad shallow steps, Rosemary slowed to a walk, for she saw Harry lounging as usual in the corner of the ironwork seat by the statue of the Dancing Girl at the end of the terrace. The legs of the seat were made with knobs and joints, to look like wood, but they were iron really, you soon found out when you kicked them.

It was nice in the Park even in September, with quite a lot of flowers still in bloom. There were big white stone urns with nasturtiums spilling out all over them, and long beds laid out in patterns with fuchsias and pink geraniums and mauvy-pink dahlias and a green plant in the middle, Rosemary didn't know its name, very fluffy and pretty. A lot of statues stood at intervals along the terrace with their backs to the seats—they had been rewhitened since the war and really looked quite nice against the green. Some of them had no clothes on, or next to none—she wouldn't like to have sat by one of those with Harry, it wouldn't have been nice. But this Dancing Girl that he fancied was all right; she had a short full dress tied round at the waist, and stood on one toe and held two of those plate things dance bands have, to clash, in her hands; her head was turned sideways a little and her hair was done in some old historical way, with curls and a knot, rather stylish really.

Harry stood up as Rosemary climbed the steps—he had quite nice manners, nothing out of the ordinary, but still quite nice. He was certainly tall, and his overalls suited him; the day being Tuesday, they weren't very dirty yet. He had a sparkle in his eye and a grin on his face, and altogether looked rather pleased with himself. Rosemary at once felt nervous and contrary, and her heart seemed to flutter as if she were in a net and trying to get out. Why should he look so pleased with himself just because she'd consented to come out for a breath of fresh air? It didn't mean anything, he needn't think it did. She'd soon show him.

"Hullo, Rosemary."

"Hullo."

"Sit down a bit."

"Is it warm enough to sit?"

"Yes, of course it is. Look at the sun." (A gleam of sunshine was indeed playing over the Girl's raised arms.) "Besides you've got your coat."

"Is the seat clean?" said Rosemary pettishly, rubbing one finger along the iron bars and looking at it disdainfully.

"Of course it is. Aw, Rosemary! Come on and sit down."

Rosemary, gathering her coat tightly round her, sat down in what she hoped appeared a temporary attitude, her feet very close together and her back erect. She was some distance away from Harry, who at once edged up.

231

"Well? What did you want to tell me?" said Rosemary in a sharp tone, edging away. "Something about the Youth Club?"

"No. It's about the Tech."

"I suppose you're going to take another Course and stop coming to the Youth Club," said Rosemary crossly.

"No. That is, yes."

"Make up your mind," said Rosemary, very pert. But she felt rather sorry and cross, really; that finishes the Youth Club for me, she thought.

"Well, I shall have to give up one night at the Youth Club, because the engineering classes at the Tech are so full this year—they've had so many enrolments—that they need another assistant demonstrator; and I'M GOING TO BE IT!" shouted Harry suddenly, bouncing on the seat in exultation.

His voice was so loud that a gardener away in the distance, bent over a bed, actually straightened himself up and looked round. But Rosemary forgave him, for the news was certainly important. She forgot to sit straight up and turned to Harry smiling warmly.

"Well, I congratulate you, Harry. I do really. I'm very glad," she said. "Your father and mother will be pleased, I'm sure."

"Oh yes, they're pleased," said Harry, lolling back. "But are *you* pleased, Rosemary?"

Rosemary's heart fluttered again. "I just *told* you I was pleased, Harry," she said coldly, edging away from him.

To her horror she found that his arm, which she now remembered to have seen lying along the back of the seat, had slipped down and coiled itself round her waist.

"Harry Hanson!" she exclaimed in a fury. "Let me go at once!"

"No—I don't want to."

Rosemary plucked angrily at his hand. "Let me *go*!"

"Rosemary—why don't you and me get engaged?"

"Let me *go*!" panted Rosemary.

"Well, I will if you'll give me a civil answer to a civil question."

"I didn't hear you ask any question, not to mention a civil one."

"Will you be engaged to me? With my wage at the works and now this Demonstration fee, I can start saving to get married. Will you, Rosemary?"

"No!" exploded Rosemary. "I'm too young to get engaged," she added hastily—somehow she did not want either to take him or refuse him.

"Aw!" exclaimed Harry on a long-drawn-out note of fond reproach: "Come on, Rosemary! Have some sense!"

"No!" cried Rosemary in a panic.

"Now look, Rosemary," began Harry, turning earnestly to her.

But the movement relaxed the pressure of his arm, and Rosemary shot away to the far end of the seat.

"Oh well, of course, if you're going to be nasty," said Harry in a huffy tone.

"I can't say yes or no now, Harry," said Rosemary, trembling. Her throat felt tight and tears smarted in her eyes. Harry glanced at her.

"Well, what about Christmas?" he suggested.

"I can't say, Harry," repeated Rosemary, sniffing so as not to weep.

"Aw!" said Harry as before: "Are we walking out or aren't we?"

"I wouldn't know," snapped Rosemary, borrowing a phrase (not without some pride) from the films.

"Now, Rosemary," began Harry.

But just then came an interruption. An old, old man, with a bowler hat and an old torn coat and a thick grey muffler round his neck, came doddering slowly up the steps, leaning on a stick, and tottered towards the seat. And believe it or not, he sat down in the middle of the seat, between them! Rosemary simply couldn't help laughing, though she looked away politely, of course, so that the old man shouldn't see her. After a moment she turned and leaned forward a little so that she could see Harry round the old man, and of course Harry's face was a picture! He really looked comical, between trying not to laugh and rolling his eyebrows about, trying to signal to Rosemary. He jerked his head back as a sign to her to get up and walk off with him, and Rosemary was just considering this and wondering whether to go along the terrace with him as he seemed to wish or down the steps towards home, when the old man heaved a deep sigh and planted his stick firmly in front of him and began to try to rise. Harry sprang up at once—Harry was always kind— and helped him to his feet.

"Too cold to sit," said the old man in a thin high voice, and doddered away.

Harry and Rosemary looked at each other and giggled. In order to giggle quietly, so that the old man shouldn't hear, they edged together again in the middle of the seat.

"Fancy him sitting down between us!"

"Well, you were that far away."

"But why ever did he come to *our* seat, Harry? There are dozens of others for him to choose."

"Well, there's twelve. Perhaps he likes this seat."

"Perhaps he thinks it's sheltered by those shrubs."

"Perhaps he just likes it, like me."

"Why do you like it, Harry?" said Rosemary casually.

To her astonishment Harry turned bright red.

"You know why, Rosemary."

"No I don't."

"I think that Dancing Girl's like you," mumbled Harry looking at his shoes.

Dumbfounded, Rosemary shook back her curls and gazed up at the statue. The Dancing Girl had a sweet, pure, delicate face. Pretty arms. Graceful body. A lovely gentle smile. Yes, she was sweet and lovely, as that old tune said. . . . I was really very sweet of Harry. . . . Just for a moment— moment only—Rosemary had that lovely feeling which girl seemed to have on the films. It might be sweet to love Harry to marry him, to be true to him till death, to go through a the trials and joys of life at his side. But no, no! revolted th other side of Rosemary strongly; marry a Worth Lane ma and live in Ashworth! Oh no! I don't want to do anythin dull and sensible like that; I want something beautiful an romantic and sort-of poetical, I want soft lights and swee music and rich colours, I want excitement, I want the Speedway! She sprang up.

"What's the matter?" muttered Harry, still looking down.

"I must get back," panted Rosemary. "It's late."

"Aw—don't go, Rosemary."

A raucous sound hurtled like a blunt spear through the air.

"My God, the buzzer!" shouted Harry. " 'Bye, Rosemary! Remember—Christmas!"

He leaped down the steps and disappeared from view behind the pond.

A feeling of danger escaped lightened Rosemary's step as she sped across the park back to New Park Street. For a moment she had feared something serious was about to happen, something which would commit her, tie her down to earth, to Ashworth. The fear had been a burning hollow ball inside her stomach, a nauseous taste in her mouth. But the danger had passed and nothing had changed. There was still the Speedway, still Miss Barraclough. It had been so nice, just for a moment, to hear Harry admiring her, that Rosemary couldn't help wanting to hear somebody really exciting admiring her in the same way. Tony of the Speedway, perhaps, or perhaps—Rosemary giggled at her own foolishness but couldn't help hoping all the same—perhaps Miss Barraclough's brother.

5

By the time she reached the shop she was a few minutes late for her appointment, and the taxi from the Worth Lane end of the street was already standing at the door. But luckily the taxi-driver, who had often taken Dorothy and Lilian out on similar errands before, entered the shop from the street just as Rosemary came in from the house, and he made such a bustle and noise, crying: "Which dryer do you want, love? Will you take the hand one as well? Are these the towels?" and so on, that Dorothy's attention was distracted, and before she had time to scold her sister, Rosemary was standing in the large cubicle, neat in her white coat, making the necessary preparations for Miss Barraclough's perm.

"Sure you'll be all right, Rosemary? Your belt's too tight. The telephone number's on the pad—if anything goes wrong ring me up," cried Dorothy over her shoulder, going out.

The bell yapped sharply as she pulled the door shut behind her; then they were gone, and all was quiet.

Rosemary got out the perm box, looked at the rubber rings, the hook, the curlers, the clips (like butterflies on a merry-go-round, she thought, perched on their vertical rods) and was filling up the bottle with shampoo mixture when the bell yapped again and Miss Barraclough came in.

Oh dear! Miss Barraclough was not at all romantic. She was quite elderly, in a dull brown coat and boring squashy hat, with stooped shoulders and grey hair hanging all wispy round her face. Rosemary greeted her very politely—for I *have* nice manners whatever Dorothy says—and hung her coat carefully on a hanger, and settled her nicely in the chair with the footstool just right.

"I'll just pop a cushion on the chair. Would you like the radiator on, Miss Barraclough? It's rather chilly this afternoon?"

"If it's not too much trouble, I think I would."

A nice, timid old thing. Fifty at least. Rosemary swathed her carefully in nice warm towels.

"Oh! Is your pussy safe?" exclaimed Miss Barraclough suddenly, glancing upwards with a look of fear.

("Pussy!") Tinker was lolling along the top of the cubicle partition, as he often did, gazing down at Miss Barraclough from green eyes as bright as the signal lamps at the Speedway. His black velvety tail hung over the partition in a graceful curve. Tinker was not a special favourite with Rosemary—he thought too much of himself—but in that attitude he looked ever so nice, he really did.

"He often sits there, Miss Barraclough. He's quite safe, he won't fall. Shoo! Go away, Tinker."

"No, don't send him away," said Miss Barraclough bravely. "He's a handsome cat. Have you had him from a kitten?"

"Yes. He's my sister's cat really," said Rosemary.

She gave Miss Barraclough's hair a very thorough shampoo, rubbing each part of her head three times, just as Dorothy said. After all, she was quite grown-up and responsible now, and knew how to do things properly—she'd really received what you might call a proposal today from Harry, which after all was more than Dorothy had ever had. Oh, poor Dorothy! thought Rosemary, with a warm gush of love and pity; it was horrid of me to think like that, I'll do this perm very well, really I will. She combed Miss Barraclough's hair very carefully, being kind about the tangles and trying not to pull, and arranged her under the dryer, then went to the table to fetch her some magazines to read. Oh dear, what should she give her? Film magazines wouldn't be any good, she felt sure, and magazines about home and children obviously would be useless too. Poor old Miss B. She chose a few tattered copies of *Picture Post* and *Illustrated* and roughly sorted them into appropriate covers and laid them beside her client. However, she needn't have bothered, for Miss Barraclough had brought a book of her own. Rosemary read a sentence or two over her shoulder; it was a love story. Fancy! The noise of the dryer prevented conversation and that was a blessing, for the subject of Tinker seemed exhausted, and Rosemary simply didn't know what to say to people as old as Miss Barraclough. How did they live, she wondered? What did they do at night? I might ask her if she ever goes to the Speedway, thought Rosemary as she set the clips on the perming machine and plugged it in to get hot. She giggled a little to herself at the thought—Miss Barraclough would probably have a fit.

Now at last Miss Barraclough's hair was dry enough for the perming process to proceed. Her hair looked quite a bush, dried all fuzzy without any set, and Rosemary thought Miss Barraclough looked at it in the mirror rather fondly.

"Your hair is nice and thick," said Rosemary in a flattering tone.

Miss Barraclough smiled.

"Do you ever go to the Speedway, Miss Barraclough?" said Rosemary politely, dividing Miss Barraclough's hair into strands.

Miss Barraclough looked astonished and discomposed, just as Rosemary expected.

"No," she said. "I never thought of it." She seemed to consider for a while, then added: "I hear the noise of course. Do you go?"

"Yes, often," said Rosemary, nodding. (Her fair hair flashed in the mirror; really it was quite pretty in spite of not being chromium.) "It's ever so exciting."

Miss Barraclough smiled vaguely but said nothing.

"Do you like Ivor Novello's plays, Miss Barraclough?"

"I've never seen one, love."

"They're lovely, really."

"I'm not one for the theatre," said Miss Barraclough comfortably, opening her book.

Well, she certainly doesn't need much talking to, at any rate, thought Rosemary thankfully.

The long, long process of dividing the hair, drawing a strand through the rubber ring with a hook, applying the solution with the little brush, rolling the hair up on the curler and applying the hot clip, went slowly on. When the clips were first put on the solution hissed and went up in steam, and a curious acrid smell began to fill the little cubicle. Who would have imagined Miss Barraclough had so much hair? After all this time only about a third of her hair was in the clips.

Mrs. Heald put her head in at the door between house and shop.

"Are you ready for your cup of tea yet, Rosemary?" she called.

"Not quite, Mother," called Rosemary cheerfully.

"Come here a minute, dear," said Mrs. Heald.

"Excuse me, please," said Rosemary, and ran out crossly. "What is it, Mother?"

"How are you getting on, love?" said Mrs. Heald in a loud whisper.

"Very nicely, thank you," said Rosemary in a cool professional tone. "We'll have tea in about half an hour, please."

When she returned to Miss Barraclough she was alarmed to see that an uneasy look was shading that lady's face.

Rosemary's heart sank.

"Are you quite comfortable, Miss Barraclough?" she asked timidly.

"Yes. It's just that these clips weigh so heavy. I feel I can hardly hold up my head."

"I'll be as quick as *ever* I can," breathed Rosemary, tremendously relieved.

She put up another set of clips, then took a hand dryer and fanned the first set till they were cool. At least, they were barely cool when she laid the dryer down, she scorched her fingers a little in her eagerness to get the clips off. She pulled out the curlers and pulled off the rubber pads; oh joy, oh joy! The strands of hair were all neat little spirals, really and actually and most professionally and evenly permed.

"It's taken beautifully!" cried Rosemary in a joyous tone.

Miss Barraclough smiled, relieved.

"Now we shan't be long," said Rosemary, setting to work on the front hair with zest.

"You mustn't think I was grumbling, love, when I mentioned the clips were heavy," said Miss Barraclough mildly.

"Oh, no! I'm sure *you* aren't a grumbler, Miss Barraclough," said Rosemary.

"No. I'm not, really. It's only that I get neuritis in the back of my neck sometimes."

"We shan't be long now," said Rosemary comfortingly. "And as soon as ever I get these up you shall have a cup of tea."

She put up the last set and called to her mother, fanned the second set and held a clip near to her cheek to see if the clip (and therefore the curler) was cool enough to handle.

"Oh! Don't do that, love!" exclaimed Miss Barraclough.

Alarmed, Rosemary paused, clip in air.

"I mean, don't put that hot thing near your cheek. You might burn it."

"Oh, I shan't!" said Rosemary confidently. "But it's nice of you to care, all the same."

Mrs. Heald brought the tea. Fortunately Rosemary heard her in time to meet her outside the cubicle. If she had come in, and started making remarks about Miss Barraclough's hair, it would have been just dreadful.

Now all the hair was permed, dozens of tight little yellowish-grey spirals shaking and bobbing wirily as Miss Barraclough stretched and turned her neuritic neck. The second shampoo was begun—and finished; the hair, now crisp and curly, was combed and parted neatly and accurately along the side of Miss Barraclough's head.

By this time Rosemary felt as if she and Miss Barraclough had been living together for centuries, as if life contained nothing but Miss Barraclough's head. It seemed as if Miss Barraclough felt the same; she smiled at Rosemary in the mirror as if they were old friends.

"Now we shan't be long," she said, imitating Rosemary.

It was a pity that the part of all this perm affair which showed the most had to be done last, when one was tired, thought Rosemary. However beautiful the perm, if the set were not nice the hair would look ill groomed. Carefully and methodically she set to work, dividing the hair and steeping the back in setting lotion with the comb.

"How many waves do you like at the back, Miss Barraclough?"

"I'll leave it all to you, love," said Miss Barraclough comfortably. "I've never had a perm before."

Imagine! Her first perm! With grey hair! Poor old thing! For a moment Rosemary had a touch of that strange sweet feeling she had experienced in the park with Harry, looking at the Dancing Girl. Poor Miss Barraclough! She *must* have a good set, thought Rosemary protectively. She *shall* have a good set. Put on her mettle—though why, she didn't know—Rosemary looked hard at Miss Barraclough's head, considered its shape, thought the matter over carefully, then made three large waves at the back slightly crosswise. She resisted the temptation to be lazy and roll the long hair up into big curlers, and instead set every small strand in flat pin curls, with two pins each.

"Now this," said Rosemary aloud, with a smile meant to be reassuring, "is the important part."

She set some really beautiful waves in front, curving up from Miss Barraclough's parting, then put her a net on, and cotton wool over her ears, and brought the dryer down over her head once again.

While the hair was drying Rosemary called Tinker down

and let him out, and tidied away all the perming apparatus and washed the brush and comb, and let Tinker in again, and felt Miss Barraclough's hair and adjusted her net, and answered the telephone twice and folded the damp towels, and then, leaning against the wall of the empty cubicle, she began to read every word of Lilian's last Speedway programme, which had dropped on the floor out of her coat pocket as she left.

Suddenly she heard Miss Barraclough's voice gently calling: "Miss! Miss!" Good heavens! It was half-past five! In a panic Rosemary flew to the next cubicle.

"I think it's dry now," said Miss Barraclough timidly. Her face was very red and the cubicle felt like an oven.

Rosemary turned the dryer off, removed the net, combed out the little curls and turned them over her finger into a neat, flat roll. She applied a touch of brilliantine and stood back to judge her handiwork.

Well! It was lovely! Really lovely! The waves in front were really beautiful! Miss Barraclough looked quite distinguished! Quite alert and young! Even her dull brown wool dress looked quite different, more expensive somehow. Rosemary fetched the mirror from the mantelpiece and, smiling happily, held it at suitable angles so that her client could see the back and side views of her head. Miss Barraclough exclaimed with pleasure.

"It's really ever so nice," she said, turning her head slowly, with a preening action. "I shall go to my interview with much more confidence now."

And as luck would have it, just at that moment in burst Dorothy and Lilian and the taxi-man from the street, and hearing the noise Mother came in from the house.

"I've just finished, Dorothy," said Rosemary quietly, drawing back the cubicle curtain.

Dorothy gave her a sharp look and stepped inside. Miss Barraclough was still in the chair, fumbling in her bag for notes and silver; on her bent head her neat, well-groomed, slightly wavy, silvery hair made quite a picture—almost like a good advertisement. Rosemary, watching her sister's face, saw her expression change, and knew that her perm and set were really good. Her mother, too, peeping in at the door, was smiling proudly. Wouldn't it be wonderful if Rosemary were to turn out really a marvellous hairdresser! Really a wonderful one, winning prizes and inventing styles.

Miss Barraclough, dressed again in her dull brown coat, with her dull brown pull-on hat covering her lovely hair stepped out of the cubicle and paid for the perm.

"For you, love," she said, colouring all over her withered cheek—and pressed a two-shilling piece into Rosemary's hand.

It would almost pay for the Speedway tonight!

"Oh, thank you ever so much. I hope you'll let me set your hair again, Miss Barraclough," said Rosemary politely, opening the door for her first perm client.

"Well—you see I'm hoping to get this housekeeper's post in Leeds tomorrow," said Miss Barraclough doubtfully. She stepped out of the shop, jerking her head in token of farewell.

"I'll call for you at quarter to seven, Rosemary!" cried Lilian, dropping a pile of towels and rushing off to catch her bus.

"Well, I congratulate you, Rosemary," said Dorothy in a kind voice. "You've done a good job of work this afternoon."

Would it be romantic to be a really wonderful hairdresser, entering competitions and winning silver cups? She could go to London, have a shop in Bond Street with purple carpets and chromium fittings, dress in slinky black and fox fur capes, and dine out in wonderful restaurants with dark romantic men. Her clients would be glamorous film beauties— not like poor old Miss Barraclough. You couldn't help smiling at someone who'd never had a perm before. Still, Rosemary was glad the perm had turned out so well. She wouldn't like poor old Miss B. to have spent her money on a mess.

Good thing it was the Speedway that night—after so much excitement she could never have settled down at home. She would see Tony. After that do with Harry in the Park, she was somehow very curious to see Tony.

She was just arranging her silk handkerchief round her shoulders and shaking out her curls when the telephone rang downstairs. "I hope it's Mr. Lister for Dorothy," thought Rosemary kindly, and she made no move to answer it, so that soon she heard Dorothy go along the passage into the shop.

"It's for you, Rosemary," called Dorothy up the stairs. "It's Harry."

"Oh bother!" exclaimed Rosemary crossly, running down. "What is it, Harry? I'm just going out."

"I'm glad I caught you."

His voice sounded so serious that Rosemary said quickly: "Is anything wrong?"

"No. That is, yes."

"Make up your mind."

"There's nothing wrong with me, but the Youth Groups are in a hole."

What has that to do with me, thought Rosemary, looking up at the clock. Lilian would be here in a minute. "Do be quick, Harry."

"The Ashworth Textile Pageant Committee asked the Youth Council to send a delegate to the Committee from the Youth Groups."

"If I didn't know that I should be deaf," said Rosemary sarcastically: "Considering they've talked of nothing else the whole week."

"Well, it's the meeting tonight and the delegate the Clubs elected can't go."

"Why not? Never mind, don't tell me," said Rosemary hastily: "I haven't time to listen."

"We have to find another delegate to attend the meeting at seven and I want you to go."

"Oh, don't be silly," said Rosemary uneasily.

"What is there silly about it?"

"I'm not suitable. I'm not a real Youth Group person."

"Well, in a way, that's true," admitted Harry soberly. "You're what the Organiser calls an in-between."

"What do you mean?" snapped Rosemary, insulted.

"You're neither a real Speedway-and-Cinema fan nor a real Youth Group-er."

That's all you know, thought Rosemary, furious.

"Why ask me, then? Get a real Grouper."

"But you see it's so difficult to get hold of anybody at the last minute, Rosemary. Youth Club members aren't often on the telephone. I've tried, but I haven't any more time to go looking for anybody—I'm at the Tech now."

"Let the Youth Organiser find somebody herself."

"She's tried. But you see the delegate's a Worth Lane lad, and so Worth Lane ought to find somebody else as a substitute. We mustn't let the Groups down. Just to attend this meeting and report."

"Well I think it's absurd!" cried Rosemary in a shrill tone, not far from tears.

"What's the matter, love?" said her mother, suddenly poking her head out of the sitting-room into the hall.

"Harry wants me to go to a Committee meeting to represent the Youth Clubs," wailed Rosemary. "It's that Textile Pageant business."

"But that's a great honour, Rosemary," said Mrs. Heald. "Why there was a big public meeting about it, don't you remember?"

"Yes, it's a great honour," chimed in Dorothy, appearing behind her mother. "The newspapers were full of it a week or two ago—A.T.P.C. the Committee's called."

"Let her decide for herself," called Mr. Heald from his armchair by the fire.

Oh dear! If only Harry hadn't compared her to the Dancing Girl, if only she hadn't given Miss Barraclough such a good perm, Rosemary would never have agreed! But somehow she felt grown-up and responsible today; much as she hated the idea she couldn't let Harry, she couldn't let Worth Lane, down.

"Where is it?" she cried crossly down the 'phone.

"Mechanics' Institute. Room 10. Seven o'clock. Rosemary, I am *grateful*," said Harry in a tone of respect. "I do truly thank you."

"You needn't," snapped Rosemary. "I shall probably do something awful and disgrace Worth Lane."

"No, you won't. You've just to listen to what goes on and report to us. Goodbye. I must go to my lab now."

"Oh dear, I don't want to go!" wailed Rosemary, slamming down the 'phone and stalking into the sitting-room. "It's too bad! I don't *want* to go! I want to go to the Speedway!"

"You've promised Harry now," said Dorothy irritatingly.

"I know. I hate Harry for letting me in for this!" cried Rosemary. Catching sight of herself in the mirror above the hearth, she was quite astonished—but not dissatisfied—by the angry sparkle in her eyes, the contortion of her face, the frown on her smooth brow. "Well! I must go I suppose. You'll have to make my excuses to Lilian."

Dorothy looked as though this would be an agreeable task, which made Rosemary angrier than ever. Her heart full to bursting with mingled disappointment, resentment, vexation, pride and alarm, she flung out of the house.

7

Rosemary ran in long easy strides from the town terminus of the Worth Lane bus to the Mechanics' Institute—although she didn't want to go to the meeting, she didn't want to be late. Besides, she enjoyed leaping swiftly along the streets. But when she reached the great doors, and saw the stone steps rising away into the unknown, a feeling of fear overcame her, like when she was with Harry in the Park. How could she possibly go in, walk into a Committee meeting of old people and announce her name? She entered the lower foyer, looked at the steps, dallied a moment and came out again, feeling hollow and weak and burning inside. Nobody was going into the Institute. Perhaps this wasn't the place where the meeting was being held? Could she just slip away and tell Harry afterwards that she couldn't find it? It would be cowardly, of course, but what a relief! Only what would Dorothy say? If only someone would come! Oh dear, now somebody was coming; how dreadful! She shrank back into the shadows, pressing herself against the wall. But the light in the hall above shone on her face, and the large round man stopped and spoke. Oh *dear*!

"Can I 'elp you, my dear?"

"Is this where the Textile Pageant Committee is held?" muttered Rosemary, hanging her head.

"Yes, it is. You're the Youth delegate, I suppose?"

"Yes. That is, I'm representing him."

"A very fine movement, these Youth Clubs. We must look to our Youth, the greatest asset of the world today. Don't you agree, Miss——?"

"Heald," muttered Rosemary, colouring with vexation. If there was anything she hated it was these awful stale platitudes about youth, from people who'd forgotten they'd ever been young.

"I'm Councillor Foster Ormerod. I'm going to the meeting; come along with me. To the right here."

He led the way into a lighted room where a lot of old people were sitting round a long table with a green cloth. Rosemary hung back diffidently, holding her head down; she was so confused and daunted that room and people swam before her eyes. A very old man, tall and thin, with stubby grey hair, so stooped that his coat hung off in front, rose from the top of the table and smiled at her; his eyes were kind.

"The Youth representative?"

"Miss Heald from the Youth Groups," explained Councillor Foster in a loud overbearing tone. "This is our Chairman, Miss Heald; Mr. Armitage."

Mr. Armitage stretched out his hand and the dazed Rosemary took it in her own. It felt cold and dry against her own warm soft palm; her spine prickled, but she repressed her shudder because he spoke and smiled so kindly.

"Won't you sit here by me?"

Rosemary glanced round wildly in search of some obscure back seat, but there was none; willy nilly she fell into the chair on Mr. Armitage's right, as if into a disaster. Councillor Foster, clearing his throat, hung up his coat and closed the door. She was shut in with them now, there was no escape. Oh if only she had gone to the Speedway!

A man on the opposite side of the table stood up and began to read from a large book. Everyone was silent, listening, and Rosemary's head began to clear. Without moving her head, she glanced round at the Committee. There was a woman sitting next to her. Oh, a most beautiful woman, thought Rosemary, suddenly interested. Dark and sophisticated. Her hair most beautifully groomed. Her nails and lips a lovely dark shade, a kind of cyclamen colour, very elegant and exclusive. A silver bracelet on her slender wrist. A black costume and something cyclamen underneath. Oh; I wish I looked·like that, thought Rosemary ardently, instead of having such pink cheeks and such plump legs and such huge hands and feet. (Her extremities seemed positively to swell as she looked at her neighbour; her hands felt enormous, lumps of stiff red flesh.) She looked as if she knew all about men. Fancy somebody really beautiful, like her, having to sit next to an old bore like Councillor Foster Ormerod. Beyond him, at the bottom of the table, sat a sandy-haired man; his eyes were odd, somehow; perhaps they had a cast or something in them. His arms were folded, he sat up very straight, for some reason or other he seemed to be seething with rage. Next to him was a dark smooth-looking man, who looked at Rosemary as if she were something the cat had brought in. (Dear old Tinker, thought Rosemary; I wish I were at home with him now.) Then there was an empty chair, then the man reading aloud, who was probably the Secretary. He was rather good-looking; fierce but jolly, like Harry when he made a good smash at Badminton; Lilian would say he had what it takes, Father would call him a bit of a lad, she shouldn't wonder. But he looked married. . . . Now the door behind her opened; Rosemary turned her head sharply, hoping that in some way it might mean release for her—the real Youth delegate might turn up after all, or something. But no; the newcomer was an oldish person; she wore a nice bright blue costume to match her eyes, and a bright blue hat which sat lopsidedly on her thick fair plaits. My word, I shouldn't like to perm all that hair, thought Rosemary shrewdly—well, of course, you couldn't; it's too long. She looks quite nice and kind, though, and more cheerful than the rest of them. She came round the table to the empty place, and stumbled over the smooth cross man's chair as she did so. He hitched it in with a scowl. Well you should have done that earlier, thought Rosemary rebukingly, then she wouldn't have stumbled.

Now that she had taken a good look at all the members, she felt less nervous. No doubt they were all very important people in their way—V.I.P.'s, as the picture papers called such folk—but they didn't *look* anything much. Not really. Except the Beauty. It was an honour to be sitting next to her, of course. If she would look at me, or smile, or speak, or something, it would be interesting. But just to sit and listen to all this stuff being read out is so dull, it's so tedious, it's such a *bore*. Oh, if only I were at the Speedway! It's after seven o'clock now; the machines will all be roaring and the loud-speaker playing, and Tony will walk out of the changing-hut into the paddock without his helmet and the track lights will go on—oh I *do* wish, thought Rosemary wistfully, I do *wish* I was at the Speedway now. However, I'm not; I'm here; I'm representing the Youth Clubs; I suppose I ought to listen to what's going on. . . .

With a sigh she wrenched her mind away from the Speedway and crossly, reluctantly, critically, opened her ears to the voice of the Secretary.

Part Three

BUSINESS TRANSACTED

I

MINUTES

THE SECRETARY READ:

"Minutes of the first meeting of the Ashworth Textile Pageant Committee held at 7 p.m. on Tuesday September 6th, 1949, at the Mechanics' Institute, Ashworth.

"*Present:* Mr. Thomas Armitage, J.P., in the Chair; Sir Charles Considine, Mrs. Deborah Sykes, Miss Elizabeth Marrison, Councillor Foster Ormerod, Mr. Gamaliel Greenwood and the Secretary.

"*Terms of Reference:* The Committee's terms of reference, as laid down by the Ashworth 1951 Festival Council, were read by the Chairman for the information of members, and it was confirmed by him that the duty of the Committee was to investigate in full detail the possibility of presenting in Ashworth in 1951 a Pageant of the history of the textile trade, as part of Ashworth's contribution to the Festival of Britain in that year, and to report on the same to the Ashworth Festival Council. Recommendations could of course be made from this Pageant Committee to the Festival Council, but the work required was chiefly of an exploratory nature, to enable the Council to survey the whole field of possible contributions.

"*Secretary:* Proposed by Councillor Ormerod and seconded by Mrs. Deborah Sykes that the temporary Hon. Secretary, Roderick Bairstow, be confirmed in the post of Honorary Secretary and empowered to send out notices and purchase a Minute Book. *Carried unanimously.*

"The question of the Pageant was then thrown open for discussion.

"Councillor Ormerod suggested that the first thing to do was to decide whether to have a Pageant at all. Until that was decided they were wasting their time. The Chairman pointed out that while sympathising with Councillor Ormerod, he must insist that such a decision would be outside their terms of reference. The Committee might recommend that no Pageant be held, for some specific reason, for example that the cost would be great, the historical material inadequate, the personnel required unavailable, and so on, but it was their duty to present a full report on all these matters so that the Festival Council could make its own decision.

"*Sub-Committees:* Mrs. Deborah Sykes then said that perhaps the best way to deal with a large matter of this kind would be to analyse it at once into its component parts. Information could then be sought from experts in the several fields and if necessary sub-committees could be appointed. The Chairman remarked that this principle had already been observed, in some measure, in the composition of the Committee, whose members represented several important spheres of Ashworth life, and it could be carried still further by a process of co-opting, for which the Committee had been given the necessary powers. Mrs. Sykes said she had made some rough notes as a basis for discussion, of the kind of divisions she had in mind. They were as follows: One: the contents of the proposed Pageant. In this she included the episodes to be chosen, the writing of the text and so on. Two: Where was the Pageant to be held. Three: Who was to perform it. Four: Presentation of the Pageant, dress, scenery and so on. These were mere suggestions to start the ball rolling.

"*Finance:* Sir Charles Considine proposed that Finance should be added to the list of sub-committees. Seconded by Councillor Ormerod. *Carried nem. con., Mr. Greenwood abstaining.*

"*Scenery, Costume, Music Sub-Committees:* Mrs. Sykes proposed that Music should be added to the list. Miss Marrison seconded. The Secretary proposed as amendment, and Sir Charles Considine seconded, that music should be allotted to the Presentation Sub-Committee. Miss Marrison strongly dissented, and said that when Mrs. Sykes spoke she had been about to propose that Costume and Scenery should be dealt with by separate Sub-Committees. There was an enormous amount of work to be done in each sphere. The Chairman pointed out the necessity for co-operation in the three spheres of dress, scene and sound. Miss Marrison

252

agreed but thought this could be achieved by joint meetings of the three committees. Mrs. Sykes thereupon modified her original proposition, substituting that there should be Sub-Committees for Costume, Scenery and Music, Miss Marrison seconded, and the Secretary withdrew his amendment. Sir Charles Considine proposed as amendment that there should be a Presentation Committee with three sub-divisions for the subjects named. There being no seconder for this amendment, the proposition was put. *Carried 5-1.* Mrs. Sykes promised to enquire into methods of providing music followed by other pageants, and to prepare a list of local personalities and groups suitable for the Music Committee. Miss Marrison promised to do the same for Costume. With regard to scenery, it was difficult to know how to proceed until one knew whether the Pageant was to take place inside or out.

"*Site:* Councillor Ormerod thought that until this decision about outside or inside was taken the Committee was wasting its time. Mr. Greenwood thought the Town Council would surely allow them to use the Park. Councillor Ormerod felt that the Council could not do this unless the Pageant became a Town enterprise, which at present was not the case. Sir Charles thought that, as the idea of a a Pageant had been broached at the public meeting when the Festival Committee was formed, the Pageant was emphatically an Ashworth Town enterprise, deserving the financial support of the Council. Councillor Ormerod said that speaking unofficially and without committing himself, he believed the Town Council viewed the Pageant idea favourably and might make a financial grant; but he was sure they would not undertake either the financing or the organising of the whole enterprise. The Chairman recalling the meeting to a consideration of sites for the Pageant, it was proposed by Councillor Ormerod, seconded by the Secretary, to write to the following halls and enquire their terms: Mechanics' Institute, Town Hall, Albert Theatre, Technical College, Victoria Assembly Rooms. *Carried unanimously.*

"*Outdoor sites:* Outdoor sites were then considered.

Mr. Greenwood again proposed investigating the possibility of the Park, Mrs. Sykes seconded. *Carried nem. con., Councillor Ormerod abstaining.* Mrs. Sykes suggested the open space beyond the Aske Bridge, near Bolland Foot Mill, as centrally situated. Councillor Ormerod said the field in question was named Miryroyd, which gave a good clue to its nature; it did not belong to the Mill, as he happened to know for he worked there, but to Lord Intake. Miss Marrison thought the site odiously unromantic, with nothing whatever in its favour, unless indeed the surrounding mill chimneys would possibly obviate the need for scenery. Sir Charles Considine mentioned a sloping field at Mount Hey which might be available. The Secretary said that Miryroyd had the great advantage of being near both the main bus station and the railway station; visitors from out of town would thus find it easy of access, and it was not more than two or three minutes' walk from the centre of Ashworth. He proposed that an enquiry be addressed to Lord Intake. Mrs. Sykes seconded. *Carried 4-2.*

"*Date and Duration:* Mrs. Sykes brought up the matter of the date and duration of the Pageant. If school-children or teachers were to be involved, dates of holidays and examinations must be given careful consideration. It was agreed that speaking generally a week in June or July would be desirable, and Mrs. Sykes promised to bring a list of the relevant dates as soon as they were available. Sir Charles Considine hoped the decision as to date would be given high priority by the Festival Council, for a campaign of advance publicity must be carefully planned and put into effect, and for this time was essential.

"*Publicity Committee:* This brought to his mind the idea of a Publicity Committee, and he would like to propose that such a Committee be added to the list. Miss Marrison seconded. *Carried unanimously.*

"*Episodes:* Mr. Greenwood said that he had been waiting impatiently for the main business of the evening to be dealt with, namely the contents of the Pageant. Were the episodes to be presented such as the Unions could approve? Would they show the struggles of the Workers and the development of capitalism, in line with the Marxist view of history? The Chairman stated that the aim of the Pageant was not propaganda of any kind, but truthful presentation of historic episodes. Mrs. Sykes enquired whether the Pageant was to be confined to local, i.e. Ashworth, textile history, or whether the whole of West Riding textile history was to be drawn upon. Councillor Ormerod thought the Town Council would not be interested unless the material were limited to Ashworth. Mrs. Sykes said the Pageant would be much more exciting and also more balanced, if the whole of West Riding textile history were available. A long discussion followed.

"Sir Charles Considine thought the Pageant finances would be benefited if the whole West Riding felt themselves concerned. Miss Marrison's view was that the whole West Riding could scarcely provide enough material for a fairly interesting Pageant, much less Ashworth alone. Mr. Greenwood said that whichever scheme showed the Workers in revolt most clearly was the one he favoured. Mrs. Sykes pointed out that the most interesting episodes of social textile history, concerned with the revolts of Luddites, Chartists, Plug-drawers etc., had mostly taken place in other West Riding towns, though Ashworth had, of course, its own notable figures and incidents. The Chairman said that when he listened to Mrs. Sykes he realised his own ignorance of textile history other than technical; he thought experts must be called in. There was surely in Ashworth some local historical society which could assist them. Mrs. Sykes agreed, and thought the A.T.P.C. insufficiently equipped on the literary side. Who was to write the script? Would it not be well to invite the Borough Librarian to join the Committee so that his advice might be available? She proposed this; Miss Marrison seconded. *Lost 2-4.*

"Mrs. Sykes then proposed that the Ashworth Historical Society be invited to prepare a list of Ashworth textile episodes; possibly the Ashworth Textile Society might be invited as well. Councillor Ormerod said that if there was one body in Ashworth ignorant of textile social history it was the Ashworth Textile Society. The Chairman thought this a little hard, but agreed that the Society mentioned concerned itself chiefly with technical processes. Mrs. Sykes then limited her proposition to the Historical Society, who should be asked to prepare two lists of suitable historical textile episodes, one concerning Ashworth only and one the whole West Riding. The Secretary seconded. *Carried nem. con.* Mr. Greenwood abstained, saying that he knew nothing of the Historical Society's political outlook.

"*Script:* Mrs. Sykes then proposed that the Borough Librarian should be consulted as to a possible writer for the script. There were one or two authors in Ashworth, and several in the West Riding, who might be capable of writing a good Pageant. Sir Charles Considine thought it would be better to pay a high fee to a London author. Miss Marrison agreed, but feared a London author would not undertake the task. Mr. Greenwood expressed the wish that the late Mr. Milnes were still alive to write the script. Councillor Ormerod thought the thing should be kept to local talent, but possibly pulled together at the end by some London man. Mrs. Sykes thought this unacceptable, and repeated her proposition. The Chairman seconded, saying that as a first approach to the problem the proposition seemed sound; it did not commit them to accept the Librarian's suggestions but would give them an idea of the available Yorkshire authors, whose work, standing, views etc. could then be investigated. The proposition did not preclude other approaches, official or unofficial. If Sir Charles or Miss Marrison had literary friends in London who could give unofficial advice, the Committee would be grateful for it. Miss Marrison promised to make enquiries. The motion was *carried unanimously*.

"*Personnel:* The Chairman said they had now set on foot, he thought very satisfactorily, investigations into the what, when, where and how of the Pageant; there now remained the Who, for discussion. Who was to act in the Pageant? Adults? School-children? Were any performers to be professional, i.e. paid? Had the Unions any strong views? What did Mrs. Sykes think of the attitude of children and school-teachers? In Hudley there had recently been a most successful Pageant acted entirely by school-children. Certainly the participation of children was very desirable from the educational point of view. How would the Town Council, the educational authority, regard the participation of teachers and children in a Pageant dealing with one industry? Councillor Ormerod promised to make enquiries on this point. Mr. Greenwood said that the Workers would wish to be strongly represented in the Pageant. The Secretary thought children had always a wide appeal. Mrs. Sykes promised to enquire unofficially from the teachers; she thought that a mixture of children and adults would be best. Councillor Ormerod mentioned the Youth Groups, for whom such activity would be educational; he proposed that a representative of the Youth Groups of Ashworth be co-opted on to the Committee. Mrs. Sykes seconded. *Carried unanimously.*

"*Date and time of the next meeting:* It was agreed to meet regularly on Tuesday evenings at 7 p.m. until further notice.

"The proceedings then terminated."

"I'm afraid the Minutes are rather long and informal, sir," apologised Roddie.

"I was about to observe that it is customary to include in Minutes only formal resolutions and amendments," said Considine, looking down his nose.

"Yes, of course—it's just that there were so many valuable suggestions made, I hardly liked to leave them out," agreed Roddie hastily.

"I'm sure we shall find them very useful," said Thomas kindly. "But perhaps in future we need not be quite so detailed. Will someone propose that these Minutes be accepted as a correct record?"

"I propose," said Gamaliel, who was pleased by the record—it showed he had struck some shrewd blows for the Party.

"Second," said Elizabeth.

"Any amendment as to their correctness?"

257

"Just one little matter, Mr. Chairman," said Foster, leaning forward. "If you don't mind, I like to be called Councillor *Foster* Ormerod, not just Ormerod. There's so many Ormerods, you see."

"Not on this Committee," muttered Considine.

"After all, Sir Charles," began Foster loudly, colouring: "You wouldn't like it if we just called you——"

"Certainly, Councillor," interposed Thomas. "You'll make that addition, Captain Bairstow?" Seeing the dismay on Roddie's face he went on without a pause: "The Secretary will make the necessary insertions after the Meeting, so as not to hold us up now, if that's agreeable to you, Councillor Foster?"

"Oh, by all means."

"Then: those in favour of the Minutes with that slight amendment? Thank you," said Thomas.

As he spoke he felt an access of strength. These familiar, well-tried formulæ of the committee process, in which he believed with all his heart, seemed to support and steady him. As honourable chairmanship required, he firmly laid aside his private affairs so as to conduct the proceedings with complete impartiality; his worries rolled from his shoulders like a loosed burden, he raised his head and no longer felt afraid of Considine.

II

FINANCE

"Now: ARISING OUT OF the Minutes," continued Thomas in a brisk cheerful tone, drawing the loose-leaf quarto volume which held the Minutes towards him.

"Pretty well everything seems to arise out of the Minutes, sir."

"Yes. *Terms of reference.* As a new member, did those seem quite clear to you, Miss Heald?"

"Yes, thank you, Mr. Armitage," whispered Rosemary.

"*Secretary.* Nothing there, I think. *Sub-Committees*—they

come up more formally later. *Finance*. Have you had time, Sir Charles, to sketch out the plan for our investigation, as you promised?"

Considine put his hand into his breast pocket and drew out a folded paper. At once every nerve in Roddie's body leaped in agony, for the action was the same as that of the process-server that morning, drawing out the summons. His troubles, forgotten for the moment in the interest of reading the Minutes, rushed back upon him in a fiery flood: Good God, that forty pounds! Considine! Armitage! The Building Society!

"The problem as I see it is one of balancing receipts and expenditure," said Considine rapidly in his cold smooth tones. "In pre-war days a certain Midland city, for example, spent twelve thousand pounds on its Pageant."

"The Town Council won't 'ave anything to do with a scheme of that size!" exclaimed Foster crimsoning.

"If you would allow me to finish, Mr. Councillor. The receipts in that case were sixteen thousand pounds."

"They must 'ave 'ad a heck of a lot of performances."

"Exactly. The Pageant was continued for three months."

"That's out of the question for the children," observed Deborah.

"And for the Workers," said Gamaliel. "Unless they were paid, of course."

"If I might be allowed to complete my statement without interruption, Mr. Chairman, I believe it would be to the general advantage."

"Of course. Order, please, ladies and gentlemen."

"I approached this problem from the point of view of what receipts could be expected. From these, with the addition of possible grants from the Town Council and the Employers' Federations and Trade Unions concerned, we could form an estimate of the amount we could legitimately spend."

"A thoroughly business-like point of view," murmured Deborah with an ironic inflexion.

"Really, Mr. Chairman!"

"I beg your pardon," said Deborah.

"I understood it to be the wish of the Committee that the

259

price of the seats should be low, indeed in the case of school-children almost nominal. For an indoor Pageant therefore I calculated as follows: With six performances the maximum audience would be twelve thousand."

"That's only if us gets the Albert Theatre—the other halls don't hold nothing like two thousand."

"*And* only if each performance were *full*," said Elizabeth: "Which seems to *me*, considering the limited appeal of the subject, *very* unlikely."

"I said *maximum*," said Considine in a scornful tone. "I thought that expression would be understood. Then with five thousand seats at a shilling for school-children, two hundred and fifty pounds; five thousand seats at half a crown for the general public, six hundred and twenty-five pounds; and one thousand at five shillings and one thousand at ten shillings for the higher income brackets, seven hundred and fifty pounds, we reach a total of sixteen hundred and twenty-five pounds. For an outdoor Pageant the possible attendances would be larger, as fields"—he looked contemptuously at Rosemary, making this point clear to her limited intelligence—"fields are larger than theatres. But as vagaries of weather have to be taken into account, we shall probably be wise to put our maximum for six performances as low as fifteen thousand. In this case we had probably better allow ten thousand entrances at a shilling, five hundred pounds; I say entrances because we could not provide seats for them all, they would need to sit on the grass only; then the total receipts, using the same figures as before, would be eighteen hundred and twenty-five pounds."

He took off his spectacles and looked expectantly at the Chairman.

"Rather a disappointing total," said Thomas.

"Yes. That's why I have stressed that side of the matter first." He replaced his spectacles. "Now as to the possible allocation of expenditure."

"Wait a minute, Sir Charles!" exclaimed Foster. "Could we have them figures again?" He took out his stubby pencil, found an envelope and prepared to write them down. "You went a bit too quick for me."

"Yes, we can't keep up with your financial jugglery," said Elizabeth.

Considine started. "There's no jugglery about it!" he exclaimed sharply—the last thing he wanted was that either Armitage or Bairstow should suspect him of jugglery in finance, or his scheme for securing Highshaw would fall through. "Just plain straightforward arithmetic, I assure you." He hesitated, then since the matter was so important decided to add: "I really must ask you to withdraw that word, Miss Marrison."

He protests too much, thought Deborah, and all round the table, in their several mental languages, the committee members thought the same. Oh, yeah? jeered Rosemary; dirty Capitalist finance, thought Gamaliel with contempt; Foster, writing down seat-prices laboriously, remembered Considine's tricks with his Labour force; Roddie, startled, had a sudden misgiving as to whether Considine's advice about the debt was sound. "I'd rather borrow from Mr. Armitage if I could," he thought. Considine's a thorough-paced rogue—he'll end up a millionaire—or in gaol, thought Elizabeth; why didn't I see it before? She felt a sudden deep movement of sympathy towards him because he was at war with respectable society; he could twist all these boring worthy numskulls round his little finger, she thought admiringly. She turned on him the full gaze of her beautiful eyes, and spoke with less emphasis and more sincerity than was her custom.

"I'm sorry, Sir Charles—I really intended to be flattering. Please accept my apologies."

Her quiet tone deepened the effect of the incident by treating it as serious. Considine felt the increase of tension round the table and decided to relax it by a joking tone.

"I'm sure the Chairman agrees that the word *jugglery* should never be used in connection with any financial operation."

If this man is a rogue my problem is solved, thought Thomas; and immediately his scrupulous integrity, strengthened by many long years of unremitting practice, unremitting faithfulness to his ideal, rose up and commanded him: "On that account you must now be especially fair." His practised skill in chairmanship warned him, too, even as Elizabeth and Considine were speaking: If you allow this to go any further it will create definite prejudice against Considine. Accordingly, passing over their remarks completely, he said at once:

"I've been wondering whether we could all have copies of your estimates, Sir Charles? We shall probably wish often to refer to them."

A quick murmur of agreement showed the wish of all the members to extricate themselves from the jugglery question.

"I can type copies for next time," offered Roddie.

"I have copies here," said Considine coldly, handing them to Roddie to distribute.

"Good. I suggest we all study them before the next meeting," said Thomas, examining the figures through his eyeglass. "One cardinal fact which has already emerged will be very useful at our present stage, namely that our receipts will not be on a very large scale if the period of one week is adhered to." He laid down the sheet of paper carefully to one side, and began: "Now the next item." Seeing a frown of perplexity on Rosemary's young forehead, however, he felt obliged from compassion to ask: "Do you wish any explanation, Miss Heald?"

"Well, there's just one thing," hesitated Rosemary, blushing. "Surely no field could hold fifteen thousand people, could it?"

"Fifteen thousand is the total for *six performances*," said Considine contemptuously.

"Oh, I see. Thank you," said Rosemary. She blushed deeper and hung her head. Do be quiet, she told herself urgently; you'll make a fool of yourself every time you open your mouth. All the same, she thought as Mr. Armitage passed on to the Music Sub-Committee and Mrs. Sykes began to read out a list of local people whom she thought suitable to serve on it, all the same I hate that Considine. Why should he always snub me and try to humiliate me! Dorothy's nothing to him!

"Would anyone care to propose this list of names for the Music Sub-Committee, then?"

"Beg to move," said Foster—there was no harm in leaving matters of art to the middle class.

"Second," said Elizabeth. There's more in the old girl than meets the eye, she thought; her list's a good one.

"I propose the list be amended by the addition of Mrs. Sykes' own name," suggested Gamaliel. He thought this a good first move towards winning Mrs. Sykes' confidence and approaching the E.V.W.'s, and was pleased to see Mrs. Sykes look pleased.

"Oh well I'm quite content to have Mrs. Sykes' name included in the proposition I seconded," said Elizabeth. "What do you feel, Councillor Foster?"

"Content."

"Very well. All those in favour of the list including Mrs. Sykes. Thank you."

"There's just a point, Mr. Chairman," said Considine in his silkiest tone. (I must say something to get back into favour, he thought; something democratic.) "Miss Heald here—I believe she said she was not the Youth Groups delegate, but merely taking his place. In that case, has she voting power?"

Foster and Gamaliel turned on him angrily.

"Of course!" boomed Foster from his years of experience.

"It's customary committee practice," barked Gamaliel, who had learned it all up in a manual.

"I await your ruling, Mr. Chairman," said Considine.

"Miss Heald is representing the Youth Groups and has every right to vote," said Thomas. He spoke coldly, for he felt that even as a Chairman he was beginning to have the right to dislike Considine. The child, one could see, was almost in tears; she hung her head so that her fair curls drooped over her face, and fidgeted nervously with the sheet of figures which lay before her.

"The Youth Organiser asked them this afternoon to get somebody from the Worth Lane district and they got me," said Rosemary. It was an agony to speak through her tear-filled throat, and her voice trembled, but Mr. Armitage seemed so good and kind she felt she must be very particularly honest about everything.

"It was very good of you to come at such short notice,' said the Chairman.

"Hear, hear! Hear, hear!" came from all round the table, and Deborah and Elizabeth carefully looked away from, while Foster and Gamaliel looked askance at, Considine.

III

ANALYSIS OF PROJECT

"Now about the Costume Sub-Committee."

"You haven't dealt with scenery yet," said Foster.

"It seems difficult to consider scenery until we know whether it's for inside or out," said Roddie.

"It's very much the same with costume," drawled Elizabeth fretfully.

"I don't see why," said Gamaliel.

"I told you before, ladies and gentlemen, we're wasting our time till the site's decided," said Foster impatiently.

"To me it becomes increasingly clear," said Deborah in a slow thoughtful tone: "That the nature of an outdoor entertainment differs so markedly from the nature of an indoor entertainment that their problems cannot usefully be considered together. Their respective spheres should be delimited. We should therefore, I think, present two schemes to the Festival Council: one for an Indoor Pageant and one for an Outdoor Pageant."

"Now that's talking sense," said Foster approvingly.

"It certainly clarifies my problem," said Elizabeth.

"At least we shall know where we are and not keep dithering," said Roddie.

"Yes, that seems an illuminating suggestion. Is it the general sense of the meeting that it should be followed? Then shall we have a proposition?"

"Beg to move."

"I'd like to second," said Deborah.

"It's proposed by Councillor Foster Ormerod and seconded

264

by Mrs. Sykes that two reports be presented to the Festival Council, one concerning an Indoor and the other concerning an Outdoor Pageant. Those in favour? That's unanimous."

"That's a big step forward," said Foster, nodding approvingly across the table at Deborah, who smiled with pleasure.

IV

SITE

"SINCE THE QUESTION of site seems so important, could we perhaps take it next?" murmured Considine, looking down.

"It's slightly out of order with regard to the last Minutes, but only very slightly, and perhaps we should be wise to establish the priority of the site for our future Minutes and final report. Shall we therefore take the site next?"

"Beg to move."

"I hardly think we need a formal proposition. Is it agreed?"

"Agreed. Agreed."

"I have some correspondence on this subject," said Roddie nervously, shuffling his papers. "Which will you take first, Indoor or Outdoor?" He gazed appealingly at the Chairman, and was relieved when old Thos said firmly:

"Indoor."

Even a moment's postponement of the awkwardness to come was a relief to Roddie, and his voice brightened as he read the replies to his enquiries from the various possible local halls. The Education Committee stated that the Technical College Hall could not be used for other than Town or National purposes, the Town Clerk said the same of the Town Hall. The Victoria Assembly Rooms asked a hundred pounds, the Mechanics' Institute two hundred, the Albert Theatre three hundred for a week's hire.

The older members of the Committee laughed a little at this symmetrical progression of cost, but Rosemary listened with awe. Three hundred pounds! Why, her father did not earn much more than that in a year! For one week at a hall! This was high finance indeed! So high that it was frightening. The Secretary, she felt, was upset about it too. (At any rate, he was upset about something.) She looked at Mr. Armitage to see if he too was shocked, but he appeared quite calm. A trifle reassured but still nervous about her own presence at such high consultations, Rosemary looked timidly round at the other members. Deborah caught her eye and gave her a warm and friendly smile. Such a pretty child, thought Deborah, so young and so bewildered. Damn Sir Charles Considine for making a young thing unhappy. On an impulse, still smiling warmly, she suddenly winked one of her large blue eyes at Rosemary. The child was astounded, but slowly over her perplexed and unhappy face there stole a timid questioning smile. Had Mrs. Sykes really *winked* at her? Deborah nodded, smiling. And suddenly Rosemary began to enjoy herself. It was rather exciting to be mixed up in such great affairs, after all. She, Rosemary Heald, whom Mum and Dad and Dorothy regarded as such a child, was actually voting about a huge Pageant which would concern thousands of people and perhaps cost thousands of pounds. What happened about the Pageant depended, really, upon how she voted. Yes, it was really ever so exciting: when you came to think, it was almost as exciting as the Speedway. In a different way, of course. What a lot she would have to tell them all when she got home! And Mrs. Sykes winking at her!

"The Albert's much the most suitable, think on."

"It's the most suitable Indoor, but I don't care for the idea of an Indoor Pageant at all."

"I agree with you, Mr. Greenwood."

"I'm surprised to find you in agreement with me on that, Sir Charles. *I* don't want an Indoor Pageant because I think it will be a small, acted affair, like. *I* want a great mass of Workers to participate."

"But think of the *weather*, Mr. Greenwood. Even if it's fine, think of the awful Ashworth winds."

Why is Miss Marrison always so horrid about Ashworth? wondered Rosemary, vexed. It's no worse than anywhere else. I think she'd be a very tiresome peevish client; although it's so lovely I shouldn't like to do her hair.

"The colours and costumes will all run in the rain, and everyone will look blue and get pneumonia, and we shan't hear a word they say."

"My dear Miss Marrison, we shall have a loud-speaker system."

"Oh, Sir Charles, how can you! You know what loud-speakers are like out of doors! All crackles and distortion except when they go off altogether, which is most of the time."

"That depends on how good they are."

"On a point of order," said Thomas mildly: "We have committed ourselves to present reports on both Indoor and Outdoor schemes, so this argument is not very relevant."

"Still I suppose we may express a preference between the two, in our final report, may we not, Mr. Chairman?" suggested Deborah.

"We may if we can agree on a preference, but at present that seems unlikely. Sir Charles and Mr. Greenwood are strongly for the great Outdoors, Miss Marrison for the cosy Indoors."

"I'm against the outdoor idea and think we're wasting us time discussing it."

"But, Councillor Foster, you voted for the resolution calling for a report on both schemes."

"Aye, and I still think we should report on both, to satisfy the Council like. But there's one very serious fact against Outdoors. Seating. How can we possibly put up seats for two or three thousand folk, under present restrictions?"

"Mr. Chairman, may we please return to the subject under discussion, which is Indoor halls?" said Considine irritably. "I shall oppose the Indoor scheme when the proper time comes, but meanwhile I suggest that the Albert Theatre is the only possible hall for a Pageant because of its seating capacity, as my finance statement showed. We should therefore confine our scheme to the Albert."

"That excellent local Pageant by school-children a couple of years ago in Hudley was held in a theatre," said Deborah.

"The rent of the Albert's disgracefully high," said Gamaliel. "Exploitation, I call it."

"But the seating capacity repays that," argued Considine. "Surely my figures, although so fleetingly considered, showed you that you must have a seating capacity of ten thousand per week, at least, if we're to pay our way at all."

"Beg to move Albert only suitable Indoor site."

"I second that," said Deborah. "I and some of my colleagues saw the Hudley Pageant, and from their comments I think a properly equipped theatre is the only suitable place, from considerations of staging, lighting and so on as well as seating."

"We need a theatrical expert of some kind on this committee," said Elizabeth.

"Hear, hear."

"Mr. Chairman, may we please return to the subject under discussion?"

"Yes. But I don't want to be too severe on members who stray from it at this stage, Sir Charles; our discussions are still very preliminary and exploratory. We have a proposition before us: that this Committee recommends the Albert Theatre as the only suitable Indoor site. Those in favour?"

"Does voting for this imply voting for an Indoor site?"

"*No*, Mr. Greenwood, it does *not*," Considine told him with biting contempt—he could hardly restrain his impatience to pass to the next item.

"Will members address the Chair, please," said Thomas mildly. "Now are we ready to vote? Those in favour? You're not voting, Mr. Greenwood?"

"I'd rather not. It might be misunderstood."

Considine gave a slight laugh.

"Or misinterpreted by interested parties," said Gamaliel, gazing at him with flashing eyes.

"What are you two quarrelling about? You're on the same side," said Foster with a guffaw.

"Order, order! That was passed *nem. con.*, then," said Thomas. "Now for the Outdoor site."

"I have received two letters on this subject," said Roddie. "Shall I read them now or take them under Correspondence?"

268

"I think now please."

Roddie cleared his throat. "Letter from Lord Intake—you remember you asked me to write to him about Miryroyd." He took up a folded sheet of excellent rough writing-paper, upon the four sides of which a few words were scrawled in such schoolboyishly large handwriting that they could be seen across the table by all the committee members. "*Dear Sir, Glad to let you have Miryroyd for as long as you need for the purpose of a cloth pageant, free of charge. Fear however the surface is in bad condition and cannot put it in repair, but if it's any use in its present state to your Committee you are welcome. My regards to Mr. Armitage. Yours, Intake.*"

"Very kind of him," said Thomas mildly.

"I'd rather we paid rent. If we were obligated to him he might insist on introducing some reactionary element into the Pageant."

"Nonsense," said Considine. He was furious that Intake had got in before him with a generous offer, but couldn't allow Intake's generosity to be questioned, lest his own should experience a similar fate. "Really, Mr. Greenwood, such wild accusations should not be made against respectable citizens. But the surface of Miryroyd is really bad. Since our meeting last week I've visited the field, and really it is very rough. Much débris has been dumped there."

"I should be very glad to 'ave the Pageant in my ward, of course," said Foster thoughtfully. "But I can't honestly say I think Miryroyd is suitable."

"Its surroundings are hideous, but of course very typical of Ashworth," drawled Elizabeth.

"It's very central," said Deborah.

"Aye, that's so. But Sir Charles here is right about the dumping. It's full of old tins in one corner."

"Only a day's work to clear it, and such clearance a boon to the town, perhaps?"

"Maybe."

"Councillor Foster Ormerod's opinion on this point would naturally carry very great weight with the Committee, because of his long familiarity with the locality," observed Thomas.

"Aye, but I don't just know what to say, d'you see," said Foster. "I'm in a difficult position. What will Bolland folk think if it come out I've kept Pageant away from t'ward? Then again, though Miryroyd isn't very good, it might be best of a bad lot."

"We can't risk having the Pageant on a bad site just to please Bolland Ward."

"That's just what I'm saying, Sir Charles, if you'd let me finish. At the same time, it's an awkward position for me."

"You'd prefer to consider other sites before giving a decisive opinion?" suggested Thomas.

"Aye! That's about the long and short of it," said Foster with relief.

"Shall we hear the next letter, then?"

"Letter from Sir Charles Considine," said Roddie, drawing out a very well typed sheet with a business heading. In spite of himself he coloured and held his head somewhat down, and all the members except Foster and Gamaliel noticed his embarrassment. "*Dear Mr. Bairstow: SITE FOR ASHWORTH TEXTILE PAGEANT: As I mentioned at the meeting last night, there is a field across the road from my house, High Hey in the Mount Hey Road, which forms part of my property. I should be delighted to lend this free of charge for the Pageant. (This of course would include time for the necessary rehearsals.) The field is salubriously situated, with a fine view of Ashworth, and the slope and small plateau of which it consists are well adapted to stage an audience. I shall be obliged if you will bring up this matter at the next meeting of the A.T.P. Committee. Yours faithfully, Charles Considine.*"

So that's why he rang me up and made mysterious insinuations about Lord Intake's field, thought Elizabeth. Well, well, well! She was amused and even a little pleased, and found herself again moved to sympathy with Considine. He was a sophisticated and skilful intriguer, a man of the world, born to rule, to move amongst large affairs; he would twist these provincial mugs round his little finger, she thought again with admiration.

"If the town wants a Pageant, it should requisition a field for one and not be dependent on the so-called generosity of private capitalists."

"Aw, turn it up, Gamaliel. Beg to move our best thanks be given to Sir Charles Considine, but field not regarded as suitable."

"Why not?" snapped Considine.

"It's too far out."

"Imagine trailing all the actors and properties up there," drawled Elizabeth. It would be fun to provoke Considine, to see what he would say. At the same time she gave him a humorous sidelong glance as if to encourage him to the fight.

"Imagine trailing all the *audience* up there."

"People will go anywhere if they like it enough," suggested Rosemary doubtfully.

"Mr. Chairman, we're wasting us time even to discuss this field," said Foster. "The slope of it makes the whole thing absurd."

There was an assenting murmur, and Considine perceived that his scheme was in danger of being voted down. He exerted himself to change the current of feeling.

"Would the Committee prefer that I should retire during this discussion?" he said in a mild reasonable tone, half rising. "I shall of course be happy to do so."

This shrewd and decorous offer produced, as he meant it should, murmured disclaimers from some of the members. "Nay, there's no need—oh, don't do that—you're the only one who can inform us about the field."

"I hardly think that will be necessary, Sir Charles," ruled Thomas. "We know you will not resent frank expressions of opinion."

"Thank you, sir. May I then make a point or two in favour of Mount Hey?"

"By all means."

"I had thought its slope might prove one of its recommendations," said Considine in a good-humoured deprecating tone. "I remember seeing a Pageant as a boy, held in Kirklees Park I think, and the natural slope of the ground was utilised by the audience."

"What did they sit on?"

"The ground."

"Pooh!" Foster tossed his head. "Times have changed,

Sir Charles. You won't catch thousands of people sitting on the ground to watch a Pageant nowadays."

"Especially in the West Riding climate," cooed Elizabeth. She gave Considine a smiling glance again to soften her opposition. In return she received a look of such vicious anger that a slight delicious tremor of fear ran along her nerves. "What a pleasure to find a man who isn't afraid of me!" she thought cynically: "Really a rare treat!" Landsberger and his plea for compassion crossed her memory and stimulated still further her appreciation of Considine's uncompromising hostility. On an impulse she said suddenly: "Still I think there's no harm in keeping both fields on the list. I should like to propose that, Mr. Chairman—that we keep Miryroyd and Mount Hey on the list and investigate both."

"There's already my proposition before the meeting," growled Foster.

"But it hadn't a seconder, I think."

"I'll second it," said Gamaliel, thinking: "We'll make a demonstration of working-class solidarity."

"Then I'll put forward mine as an amendment," said Elizabeth.

"Does anyone wish to second that?"

"I feel we have really no option at present but to keep both fields on the list," said Deborah slowly: "Since no others have been suggested. Though I am not at all happy about Mount Hey. But do we really know enough about these fields to reject them? The evidence at our disposal seems to me quite inadequate for a decision, and accordingly I should have preferred not to take a vote on this matter yet." She looked at Considine and Foster but received no encouragement. "If the matter *is* to be voted upon now, I shall second Miss Marrison's amendment, though I must make it clear that I hope eventually to reject both fields in favour of a better one as yet undiscovered."

"Is there any support for the suggestion of deferring the matter?" enquired Thomas.

"Not from me, anyway," said Foster stoutly. "If we defer it the result will be the same as if we passed the amendment, and we haven't passed it, so that isn't fair."

"True," conceded Deborah.

"We shall never get anything done if we defer everything," said Gamaliel in his aggressive scornful tones.

"Any other views before I put the amendment?"

Considine made a quick calculation. The two women will vote for the amendment since they proposed it, he thought, and Bairstow of course is on my side. Three for me. Ormerod and Greenwood are against me, and the girl's doubtful. If I can vote myself it will be carried for certain. I'll try.

"I find myself in rather an awkward position, Mr. Chairman," he said quietly. "I agree with Mrs. Sykes that we should keep both fields, indeed all suggested sites, on our list at the moment—it is too early, and we know too little, to come to any definite decision. But I cannot very well vote for a proposition concerning my own field."

"No," said Thomas decidedly. "Of course not."

Considine cast down his thick white eyelids to conceal his chagrin.

"It would be better to take the fields separately," said Thomas. "Indeed I'm not quite sure whether your amendment including Miryroyd to a proposition on the Mount Hey field, is in order, Miss Marrison. It will be preferable to vote for or against Mount Hey and then have a separate proposition for Miryroyd. I think I must give a ruling in that sense. I will therefore put Councillor Foster's motion, that our best thanks be conveyed to Sir Charles Considine for his generous offer together with our regret that the Mount Hey field is considered unsuitable. Those in favour?"

The hands of Foster and Gamaliel shot up energetically. Rosemary hesitated.

"I don't really know the field so I don't know how to vote," she said unhappily.

"It is perfectly in order for you to vote on the evidence you have heard, or to abstain from voting if you wish," Thomas told her.

Rosemary sighed with relief. "I'll abstain," she said.

Considine slightly smiled, for his triumph now seemed secure. The two women were committed to voting against the exclusion of his field, and young Bairstow on account of favours to come would vote against it too. "Perhaps it will be well just to show him that I take this seriously and count on him," thought Considine. He leaned forward a little, apparently to pick up a copy of his financial statement which had floated away to the table's centre, and glanced towards Roddie. His look was full of meaning, and Roddie who was trying to consider the proposition impartially suddenly fully understood.

"My God he expects me to vote on his side because he's lending me money," he thought with horror. The blood rushed to his face. "All right. He can keep his filthy money," thought Roddie, and with the same reckless and impetuous courage as he had displayed on the road to Rome he threw up his hand.

Considine turned very white, and his hands trembled with rage. "You'll wish you hadn't done that, my lad, before I've finished with you," he thought, slightly pursing his pale thick lips.

"Those against?" said Thomas.

Deborah and Elizabeth quietly raised their hands.

"The motion is carried by three to two," said Thomas. His tone was dry; he felt that there were undercurrents in the meeting concerning this Mount Hey field, and as a responsible chairman he did not like undercurrents, for the proper working of a Committee depended on the candid avowal of honest opinion. But he was thankful that he had not been obliged to give a casting vote, for the decision would have been difficult. On general principles he agreed with Mrs. Sykes that their knowledge of sites did not yet warrant a decision, but his dislike and distrust of Considine was growing so rapidly that the thought of holding the Pageant in Considine's field was odious to him. Good heavens! The fellow had actually tried to bluff Thomas into allowing him to vote about his own field! Intolerable! How abominably obstructive he would have proved as owner of the site! "So, Mr. Secretary," said Thomas formally: "You will write to Sir Charles with our thanks and regrets, according to the resolution."

"Yes, sir."

"I move that Miryroyd remain on our list of possible sites," said Deborah.

274

She looked at Elizabeth, expecting her to second the resolution, but Elizabeth avoided her eye and was silent. Elizabeth guessed that it would annoy Considine to have Miryroyd retained, after his own field had been excluded, and she felt a strange reluctance to annoy Considine any further.

"Beg to second," said Foster.

"Bolland Ward's interests are in good hands," sneered Considine.

"I'm only voting for it to be investigated," said Foster stoutly.

"Any amendment? Those in favour?"

Deborah and Foster raised their hands, and Considine felt obliged to do the same, having committed himself to this course by his previous remarks.

"I may as well be hung for a sheep as a lamb," thought Roddie cheerfully, and he voted for the resolution.

"I'm not voting," said Gamaliel.

Rosemary also shook her head.

"Those against?"

"Well, I seem to be in a minority of one," drawled Elizabeth, putting up a finger. Her bracelet jingled, her hand with the cyclamen finger nails was graceful; she felt with secret pleasure that Considine approved her action. "But I think either both fields should be retained, or neither."

"That sounds logical but it isn't really," thought Deborah.

"The motion is carried," said Thomas.

"What exactly shall I say to Lord Intake, Mr. Chairman?" enquired Roddie.

"Our grateful thanks for his generous offer; we note what he says about the surface of the field and are keeping it on our list of possible sites; the final decision of course does not rest in our hands. Something like that."

"Thank you."

"Is it too late to suggest another site?" suddenly piped up Rosemary.

"By no means. Have you one in mind?"

"Well, yes. Why couldn't we have it at the Speedway?"

"The Speedway?"

"It's the football ground in winter, sir," explained Roddie.

"Oh, I see."

"It's got seats already built," said Rosemary, nervous but determined. "And lots of them are under cover. It holds thousands—I think," she added honestly.

"It strikes me as an excellent idea," said Deborah with warm approval. She smiled happily at Rosemary, delighted that the child had made such a sensible contribution to the meeting. "The field is very central, too."

"It's a right down good idea," said Foster heartily. "See what the Youth Groups do for us!"

"It has pay-boxes at the entrance, and a pavilion to dress in, and everything," said Rosemary, trembling with joyous excitement.

"The syndicate who run it will probably charge a heavy rent," objected Considine.

"You can be sure of that," agreed Gamaliel.

"They might give it us free if we asked," contended Rosemary. "Or at any rate, free except for one night, when it's a Speedway."

"Do I understand that it is only used as a Speedway one night a week in the summer months?" enquired Thomas.

"That's right."

"I propose we put the Speedway ground on our list for investigation as a possible site," said Deborah, beaming.

"Beg to second."

"I must say I think it's the best suggestion we've had so far," said Gamaliel. He began this remark grudgingly, but halfway through bethought himself of his plan to influence Rosemary into Communism, and ended on quite a friendly note.

"Those in favour? Ah, that's unanimous. You'll write an exploratory letter, then, Captain Bairstow."

V

ART WORK

"THE NEXT ITEM," continued Thomas: "Is the date and duration, about which Mrs. Sykes promised to enquire."

Deborah reported that she had been in touch with the Ashworth Education Officer; it seemed that the school holiday dates for the coming year would not be announced until December, and those for 1951 presumably not till the December following. He suggested, however, certain suitable weeks in June. Deborah handed Mr. Armitage a list of the dates.

"Forgive me, Mr. Chairman," said Considine with his supercilious air: "But if my memory serve me we have omitted one or two items in the Minutes. The Costume committee, for instance."

His tone suggested—as it was meant to do for Considine was still bitterly angry at his defeat about the field—that Thomas was a wandering old dodderer who was not fit to occupy the Chair, and Thomas felt this. "He'd have me out of Highshaw and into a nursing home inside six months," he thought. Outwardly he replied with some dignity:

"You are right, Sir Charles; we diverged from the order of the Minutes to give precedence to the question of site, on which all the other departments seemed to depend, and we ought now to return to the Minutes and deal with scenery and costume. The divergence was at your request, I believe."

"Good old Thos," thought Roddie with affection. "You won't catch Mr. Armitage out on a question of procedure, Sir canting Charles," thought Foster brutally: "He's the best Chairman in this part of the country." Deborah, looking carefully at the wall so as to catch no one's eye, tried to analyse the quality which made her left-hand neighbour odious. The line *the slave of falsehood, pride and pain* flashed into her mind. "Yes," she thought: "But there's more than that; he's actively malevolent." Gamaliel half-laughed, and Rosemary thought with triumph: "That's one for you." Only Elizabeth took no pleasure in Thomas's neat turning

277

of the tables. What a bore he is with his highfalutin principles and formal speech, she thought; what a narrow stilted provincial bore. If the best came to the best with Bernard and he divorced his wife and we married, should I have to keep running round looking after this old man? What a bore! Accordingly her tone was fretful when in response to the Chairman's request for a report on costume she drawled:

"I should like to repeat what I said at the last meeting, that I know *nothing* about costume."

"You can hardly expect us to believe that, Miss Marrison," joked Foster heartily. "We can use our eyes, you know."

"I mean, nothing about theatrical or pageant costumes. The only useful thing I know about historical costume is that you can knit very good suits of armour for knights, from grey wool."

"But that's not useful at all in the present case," said Considine in a suave tone which made the insult more biting. (Never show a wound, he was telling himself; but by God I'll make Armitage pay for this; I'll make them all pay for this.) "We're dealing with the textile industry; not with knights in armour."

"Oh, but that depends how far back we go, surely!" exclaimed Deborah. "The Monks from Ashworth Priory used to sell the clip of their sheep to Italy in the thirteenth century; if we have such a scene in the Pageant we can certainly throw in a knight or two."

An uproar of protest came at once from Foster and Gamaliel.

"We don't want that sort of stuff in a textile Pageant."

"We want the story of the struggle of the Workers."

"Personally," said Considine: "I thought we should tell of the evolution of textile processes and close with an exhibition of fine cloths of today."

"Gentlemen, please!" said Thomas mildly. "We are discussing costume at the moment, not episodes."

"But the costume depends so entirely on the episodes," said Elizabeth crossly. "Here's Mrs. Sykes wanting armoured knights; Councillor Ormerod—I beg your pardon, Councillor Foster Ormerod—and Mr. Greenwood wanting Workers

278

and Sir Charles wanting machines and bales of cloth. We can't do anything about costume really until we've settled the episodes to be presented. Again, for an indoor pageant you need two or three hundred players, I suppose, but for an outdoor pageant two or three thousand. On the other hand, dress has to be much more carefully made for indoor affairs than for outdoor. All these considerations have been very inhibiting."

"In a word," said Considine icily: "You have nothing to report."

He enjoyed saying this, and believed himself to be enjoying the venting of his spleen against the Committee, but Elizabeth took a different view. When a man scolds a woman, it is really a sex manifestation—she had heard that from the painter in London who had given her the picture which hung over her mantelpiece, and had found it often to be true. So now, when Considine thus scolded her, she felt with delight the first faint stirring in herself of physical response. "Sex rears its ugly head," she thought voluptuously. She turned towards him, smiled and gave him an archly appealing glance from her lovely violet eyes.

"It isn't *quite* as bad as that, Sir Charles," she said in her sweetest tone.

Considine perceived her intention and was amused. If I weren't so busy with this Highshaw affair, I'd take her on, he thought. She's certainly a beauty. Elegant too. And agreeably cynical. Knows all the answers. He was through with Lily Binns and had no other woman in view. But I can't take on a new affair at the same time as Highshaw, he chided himself. Or can I? A sudden rush of belief in himself warmed and stimulated him, and all at once he felt happy and confident. I'm playing this wrong, he thought; I must conciliate old Armitage and young Bairstow too—I must conciliate them all—plenty of time afterwards to get my own back. Accordingly he smiled—looking like a cat over a saucer of milk, thought Rosemary irreverently; Tinker has just that smug conceited grin—and said pleasantly:

"I was joking, Miss Marrison. What you have said has already greatly clarified the problem."

"Exactly," said Deborah with approval.

"Well, I *have* devoted a good deal of thought to it," said Elizabeth, pleased in spite of herself. "And I've been in touch by telephone with the secretaries of two pre-war pageants. It seems what they usually do about dress is to buy several thousand yards of plain cheap material, cotton or jute, and have it dyed in a few harmonising bright colours. Then that is used for all but the main costumes. Local artists or the local art school are asked to design the costumes, and then volunteers—teachers, schools, youth groups, women's societies —make them up."

"Thank you, Miss Marrison. That report certainly opens new vistas," said Thomas thoughtfully.

"But we can't have a Wool Pageant dressed in cotton!" shouted Foster.

"I was about to say the same thing, Councillor Foster," cooed Considine.

"We couldn't afford to dress it in wool," said Elizabeth, delighted to wound.

"What do we want bright colours for? The exploited Workers of the past wore shabby old clothes," said Gamaliel sternly.

"But we must have some colour and beauty in the Pageant, Mr. Greenwood," contended Deborah.

"Yes—or people won't come to it," said Rosemary.

"I thought truth was our aim."

"There is colourful truth about the West Riding textile industry as well as sombre truth," said Deborah.

"If this Pageant is going to be dolled-up Capitalist propaganda my Union won't have anything to do with it."

Oh dear, thought Deborah, here he goes again. The moment our Gamaliel speaks, we are no longer a group of people trying to make something fine together for the common good; we are divided at once by politics, thoughts of the prestige of our class and party and profession and so on; we fall apart. He is a political catalyst, he crystallises the political ideas in the minds of all to whom he speaks. Sure enough, Considine was saying:

"And if it is to be dolled-up Communist propaganda my Federation won't support it, Mr. Greenwood."

"Gentlemen, the story of the West Riding textile trade is a matter of historical fact," said Thomas. "We shall present episodes of historical fact, not propaganda of any kind."

"Aye, but it depends which episodes you choose, doesn't it?" boomed Foster shrewdly.

"The presence on the Committee of people of all shades of political opinion is intended as a guarantee of impartial selection. Have you any report from the—er—Historical Society and the Borough Librarian, Mrs. Sykes?"

"The Librarian is on holiday but I've had a card from him saying that he is thinking about suitable Yorkshire authors and will write to me immediately after his return to Ashworth. The Ashworth Historical Society seem quite excited by the prospect of preparing material for the Pageant, and they're setting to work on it at once. They offer to provide, not only a list of episodes but also references to the historical documents where the events listed can be read in full."

"Really, ladies and gentlemen!" exclaimed Thomas in a tone of pleasure: "I think we may congratulate ourselves on the amount of work we have done in a mere week. Already the projected Pageant begins to take shape."

The Committee preened itself and felt united.

"There's just a point, Mr. Chairman," drawled Elizabeth: "Have we decided yet whether the Pageant is to concern the whole West Riding, or Ashworth alone?"

"Oh, I forgot that point, I'm sorry," said Deborah. "Naturally the Historical Society incline to an Ashworth-only Pageant, but they will prepare lists for both."

"What do we mean to call the Pageant? That will have great importance from the Publicity angle."

"That's an important point, Sir Charles."

"I thought just: Ashworth Pageant."

"Why Ashworth? They'll know they're in Ashworth all right, heaven help them. No need to tell them."

"Still, Miss Marrison," protested Rosemary indignantly: "The Ashworth buses have Ashworth painted on them. So I don't see why——"

Several members laughed, but kindly, for they were all

rather tired of Elizabeth's constant derision of their native town. Considine however gave Elizabeth a look of secret understanding, of superior knowledge; I hate and despise the place, his glance said, as much as you do. Pleased by this evidence of intimacy, Elizabeth spoke good-humouredly.

"Well, my dear," she said: "I dare say you're right. In dealing with the public, one can't stress the obvious too often."

"We can't discuss the title very usefully as yet, I think," said Thomas: "Until we have the proposed episodes before us. But perhaps members will give the matter some thought before next week. The only remaining item in the Minutes is Personnel."

"Aren't we through the Minutes yet?" muttered Gamaliel.

"I think we shall find there is very little other business when the Minutes items are concluded," Thomas encouraged him.

VI

PERSONNEL

"Now, Personnel. We have the Youth Group delegate here with us this week, and I am sure she will be very helpful."

"Hear, hear."

"Well, now, I've been talking to the Chairman of the Education Committee, unofficially like, about the children taking part," said Foster: "And he's a bit doubtful. It all depends on the attitude, I might almost say the relation, of the Town Council to the Festival Council."

"In Hudley the children took part," said Deborah.

"Aye, but that were a Town Pageant, celebrating the centenary of the town's incorporation as a Borough. This is an industrial pageant, d'you see. It's a bit awkward like—the Council seem to think they can't decide what they should do about the Pageant till they know more about it, and we can't decide much till we know what resources we can draw on."

282

"In other words, as in all spheres of life in this country today, we're going round in circles."

"You can't expect me to agree to that, Sir Charles," said Foster loudly, turning crimson as Gamaliel gave a short bark of laughter.

"We can draft alternative reports including and excluding the children," suggested Roddie.

"My dear Captain Bairstow," said Considine pleasantly: "Our report is going to be as complicated as an Income Tax return if we're not careful."

At this mode of address Roddie perceptibly started. Captain, indeed! "So Considine's trying to smooth me down now, is he?" he thought, and at once he was on his guard. For why should Considine try to conciliate him? What did he seek from Roddie? As far as Roddie knew the boot was on the other foot. Look out, my lad, said Roddie to himself, doodling hard in the corner of his notebook.

"We must remember that it is our report which will form the basis of the Town Council's decision," said Thomas. "Our work has therefore a very special importance."

"Not but what members of the Council individually seem very favourably disposed towards the Pageant," concluded Foster in a half mollified, half grumbling tone.

"What about the Unions, Mr. Greenwood?"

"The Unions will only wish to take part in episodes which specially concern them," said Gamaliel quickly.

Foster looked at him with suspicion. "Is that a formal decision? I haven't heard owt about it."

"I'm just expressing my opinion as my Union's delegate," said Gamaliel, slightly colouring.

Foster grunted.

"Perhaps the different episodes can be performed by different groups," suggested Elizabeth. "School-children for some, adults for some, Youth Groups for others, and so on."

"But we shall want children in as many scenes as possible, to make them attractive," objected Roddie.

"Don't tell me you *like* seeing children act, Captain Bairstow," drawled Elizabeth.

She's captaining me now—takes her cue from Considine.

"As a father of three I adore it," said Roddie lightly.

"Well, well, well!"

"We shall need children in the Industrial Revolution scenes," said Deborah: "And besides, I'm hoping that one episode will show Councillor Foster Ormerod meeting my great-grandfather in Bolland Wood."

Foster crimsoned. "Nay—I make no claim to belong to West Riding history," he said.

"But of course you do!"

"Such an episode will, I am sure, be very interesting," said Considine, courteously inclining his head towards Foster—he hadn't the least idea what the alleged episode was about but in view of his next remark thought a little flattery necessary: "But as to those sordid episodes of children working in mills, I think we should omit them."

Gamaliel cried sharply: "If we do I leave this Committee," and Foster growled: "You'll omit them over my dead body."

"We are discussing Personnel, gentlemen, not Episodes," interposed Thomas. "What do you feel about the Youth Groups, Miss Heald? Do you think they will wish to participate as such?"

"Well, I don't know. We should have to ask them. Some would. Others only join for the games and dancing," said Rosemary honestly.

"How soon do you think you could get in touch with them and obtain a decision?"

"I really don't know. I shall have to report to them about this Meeting. I shall have to ask the Youth Organiser. I'm sorry I don't know more about how to do it. But I'll do my best," promised Rosemary: "I will really. I'll be as quick as ever I can."

A friendly murmur greeted this declaration. Considine however observed impatiently:

"Wouldn't it be simpler to contact the Chairman of the Youth Council direct? After all, if the Education authority decided that the Youth Groups shall participate in ꞏthe Pageant, they will have to do so, willy nilly," said Considine.

"That would put it on a clearer footing," began Gamaliel, but his voice was drowned in a storm of protest.

"Surely we should not introduce the element of compulsion, Mr. Chairman!" exclaimed Deborah, realising as soon as she had spoken that she had quoted her great-grandfather.

"The whole point of the Youth Groups is that they manage themselves," boomed Foster.

"I don't think they'd like that—being told what to do, I mean," said Rosemary warmly. (Because that was why she rebelled against Dorothy who was always telling Rosemary what to do, and liked Dad, who didn't.)

"But you're compelling the school-children to take part, Mrs. Sykes."

"Only if the work is to be undertaken during school hours. The Youth Groups meet in their own leisure."

"Still, the fact is as I have stated; the Groups are under the Town's authority."

"I think we must allow all our fellow-citizens to take their own decisions about the Pageant, Sir Charles," said Thomas. "Of course we have the right to lay our views persuasively before others, but we must not take their decisions for them."

But that's just what I'm doing to Kate and my father, thought Roddie in a flash. I'm deciding for them that my father can't come to live at Upper Head Cottage. They ought to have a say in it, after all. If I ever get out of this Building Society mess, thought Roddie, I'll tell them both about it and let them help me to decide.

"Each of us," Thomas was concluding in a quiet reflective tone: "Each of us has the right to make his own decision."

"I bow to your ruling, Mr. Chairman, but of course it will cause delay if every participant has to give in a separate and voluntary adherence."

"If they're not paid of course they're voluntary."

"We've just fought a war to show we prefer democracy, even with delay, to dictatorship," muttered Roddie.

"True," agreed Considine, pretending to be convinced.

It wasn't true for you, my man, thought Foster, so you needn't pretend it. A warm office and a title was the nearest you got to the war. But fancy that Gamaliel agreeing with

285

Considine! Aye, they're both of them dictators at bottom, thought Foster; you can't trust either of them an inch.

"Is it agreed then that Miss Heald should take whatever steps she finds necessary, in conjunction with the Youth Organiser, to consult the Youth Groups about participation in the Textile Pageant?"

"Agreed. Agreed."

"They may want to participate not only as actors," suggested Elizabeth. "There'll be sewing and knitting and carpentering to do."

"An excellent suggestion, Miss Marrison. No doubt Miss Heald will bear that in mind."

"Oh, I will," said Rosemary.

"Well, now at last we've worked our way through the Minutes," said Thomas with satisfaction. "What else is there on the Agenda, Captain Bairstow?"

"There's the question of the Pageant Master, if any. It belongs in a way to the subject of personnel."

"Ah, yes. Shall we recommend a paid Pageant Master, or not?"

"What exactly is a Pageant Master, Mr. Chairman?"

"He rehearses the actors, produces the whole thing," said Elizabeth impatiently.

"Hudley had a volunteer from the local amateur dramatic society."

"Leeds had a paid one."

"How much do they charge?"

"Must be quite a bit, because it'll take several months, I imagine."

"Beg to move Secretary makes enquiries about paid Pageant Masters: who they are, how much, how long and so on."

"I second that," said Considine.

"Those in favour? To the contrary? Carried unanimously."

"I propose that we also consult the Hudley producer," said Deborah.

"Beg to second."

"What do you mean by 'consult,' Mrs. Sykes? A letter or an interview?"

286

"Well, Sir Charles, I hadn't really considered that question; but clearly an interview would be rewarding."

"An interview with who?" said Gamaliel sharply. "We ought all to be in on it."

"Aye—you're right. Why not invite him to attend one of our meetings? Beg to move that, Mr. Chairman."

"I'll second," drawled Elizabeth, pleased at the thought of another man.

"Those in favour? Unanimous. Captain Bairstow, in writing to him you might mention that if transport is a difficulty I can easily send over a car."

Someone always gets a good deed in a step ahead of me, confound him, thought Considine with annoyance, and he said:

"Or I could easily drive over and fetch him, Mr. Chairman."

"I don't think that will be necessary, thank you, Sir Charles," said Thomas formally. "Now is there anything else?"

There was a pause.

"I believe we have covered the ground pretty thoroughly," said Thomas, running over their proceedings in his mind.

"There's just one point, Mr. Chairman," said Elizabeth. "I mentioned it but it got sidetracked somehow. Other Pageants have had their costumes designed, and working drawings executed, by the staffs of the local museums and the art departments of their technical colleges. Should I get in touch with ours in Ashworth?"

"And invite their comments and suggestions? It seems a good idea."

"Then again," said Considine with his habitual slight sneer: "If the Town Council instructs these employees to execute designs for the Pageant, they will do so, and if not, not."

"Not necessarily," said Deborah staunchly. "They might do it as private individuals, you know. Several of my teaching colleagues have already expressed to me their wish to co-operate, either as teachers or as persons."

"Of course it'll be better to get the Town's co-operation if we can," said Foster cautiously.

"Yes, of course. Agreed."

"The whole thing seems a muddle to me," said Considine impatiently. "This mixture of voluntary co-operation and Town officialdom strikes me as a contradiction in terms."

Yes, it's capitalism in decay, thought Gamaliel, but he did not wish to agree openly with Considine again, so he was silent.

"Very characteristic of this country, though," said Roddie.

"And I think you will find that it will work, Sir Charles," said Thomas.

Considine shrugged and exchanged a glance of derision with Elizabeth, but said no more.

VII

SECRETARIAL

"Anything further? No? Next Tuesday at the same place and time? Have you booked the room for us, Captain Bairstow?"

"Yes, sir."

"Then that concludes—oh no; one other point. I think the Secretary should have a float for his expenses."

Roddie started.

"Beg to move."

"But we have no funds yet, Mr. Armitage," objected Considine.

"I shall be glad to advance the necessary funds," said Thomas mildly. "Perhaps you as our"—he almost said *treasurer* but changed the word because he had determined not to have Considine as treasurer if it could be avoided—"perhaps you as our financial expert will keep an account of sums spent, Sir Charles?"

"Oh, certainly."

"How much is the float to be?" asked Gamaliel suspiciously.

"How much does this room cost, Mr. Chairman?"

"Captain Bairstow?"

"Ten shillings a night, sir."

"It's too dear," boomed Foster.

"It's well heated and very central."

"Well—shall us say five pounds?"

"Are you including that sum in your proposition, Councillor Foster?"

"Aye."

"I propose ten pounds as an amendment," said Deborah.

"That's a lot for petty cash, Mrs. Sykes."

"I can see a great many small expenses ahead of us, and the room will soon eat up a couple of pounds."

"Oh, is the Secretary paying for the room?"

"Presumably."

"I could undertake that duty, if it were felt desirable," offered Considine.

There was a pause. I mustn't speak, of course, thought Roddie in an agony, but I hope they make it only five. I hope they don't pass it at all. An expense cheque for ten pounds is too great a temptation for me till tomorrow's difficulty is past.

"I have two propositions put forward, neither of them seconded," said Thomas.

"Well—I'll make the sum ten pound, and then the Secretary can pay for the room," said Foster. "Will it suit you to second, Mrs. Sykes?"

"Yes, certainly."

"Of course it must be entered in the Minutes that the Chairman has advanced the funds."

"Naturally."

"Well, those in favour? Against? Carried *nem. con.*," said Thomas. He had difficulty in keeping the surprise out of his voice, for really it was too marked on Considine's part to abstain. What it marked he did not know, but he observed that Roddie flushed and kept his eyes down.

That's torn it, Roddie was thinking. I shall be obliged to speak to old Thos now. I'll put off taking the cheque till next week. I can't muck anything up in old Thos's committee. Yes, I shall be obliged to speak to the old man about it, now.

VIII

CONCLUSION

"Anything further anyone wishes to bring up?" enquired Thomas. "No? Then, that concludes the business of the meeting."

Chairs scraped on the linoleum as the members rose.

"I'm in the car park across the street, if you want a lift, Bairstow," said Considine, and slipped out.

"Thanks," said Roddie drily.

Elizabeth felt as if Considine had struck her across the face when he left her thus without a word. That's twice in one day I've been given the air, she thought; I must be slipping. Oh, well! I suppose it'll have to be Bernard after all, but he's such a bore.

"Do you think you'll like Committee work, love?" said Foster in a fatherly tone to Rosemary, as he took down his coat from the peg behind her chair.

"I dare say," hesitated Rosemary. She pulled the belt of her coat very tight, then without knowing why, slightly loosened it again.

"There's nothing like it, nothing. I've been at it nigh on forty years, so I should know, you know. And you've made a good beginning tonight. Now I'm telling you," said Foster, giving her an encouraging nudge: "You've done well. It's a pleasure to me to see young people do well like you. Well, I must be off to catch my bus. Goodnight, all."

Councillor Foster and Rosemary went out of the room together. Gamaliel followed with Deborah Sykes.

"I'll just make out a cheque for your float," said Thomas to Roddie, drawing out his cheque-book and fountain pen.

"Could I have a private word with you about that, sir?" said Roddie in a low tone.

"Of course," said Thomas, inclining his ear. As Roddie remained silent, Thomas looked up and saw that Elizabeth Marrison was the only Committee member left in the room. A look of deep unhappiness on her beautiful face, she was slowly drawing on a pair of violet suede gloves.

"Miss Marrison, I wonder if you would be so very kind as to do an old man a great favour?" said Thomas, standing to speak to her.

"I shall be delighted to do something for *you*, Mr. Armitage," said Elizabeth with a charming smile (for it would have to be Bernard, after all): "But I decline to regard you as an *old* man."

Thomas thanked her with a courtly little bow. "It's just my chauffeur, Fred by name," he said. "I'm delayed here with Captain Bairstow on Committee work for a few moments, and Fred will be waiting outside and wondering what has happened to me. If you would be so very kind as just to reassure him as to my whereabouts?" He described his car.

"I shall be delighted, of course."

"And I shall be most grateful," said Thomas with another little bow.

Elizabeth, smiling a farewell, caught Roddie's eyes fixed on her in a look of anguished impatience. They're longing for me to go, she thought; I must say it's not very complimentary. All the miseries of the day—her foster-mother's letter, Landsberger, Leni—rushed back into her memory, drawing with them in a writhing train all the miseries of her life. A savage despair clawed her heart.

"Goodnight," she said abruptly, going out.

"Goodnight."

Part Four

THE COMMITTEE PARTS

I

MISS ROSEMARY HEALD

"Oh, Harry, I *am* so glad you've come," cried Rosemary, slipping her hand through the crook of his arm. "Is it as late as that? Have you finished your class at the Tech? How did your demonstration go? Aren't we getting grown-up and important, attending Pageant Committee meetings and demonstrations? I'd no idea it was as late as that. Have you been waiting long? The time's just flown! There was so much to decide, you know. Do you think we should have an Indoor Pageant or an Outdoor Pageant, Harry?"

"Well, I hadn't given it much thought, really," said Harry, taking her warm little paw in his own large hand and marching her off across the road towards the bus stop.

"That's what Mrs. Sykes said; we don't know enough about it to decide yet, she said, we must find out some more. It makes such a lot of difference to everything, you see, Harry; scenery and costume and personnel, and oh everything. And what do you think?" prattled Rosemary happily: "They'd never thought of holding the Pageant in the Speedway till I suggested it. *I* suggested it, Harry! Because it has seating already there, you know. And they put it on the list of sites. I felt quite proud, really. Yes, I felt ever so proud. And it was so exciting," she cried with a happy laugh: "There was quite a battle with—*him*," she said, dropping her voice suddenly as they passed Considine's elegant coupé, where he sat stiffly behind the wheel. "And we won. Yes, we did. Every time. It was ever so exciting."

"Seems to have been almost as exciting as the Speedway," said Harry, gently teasing.

Rosemary paused. How was she to explain that it was exciting in a different way? A more grown-up way. It made the Speedway seem somehow—well, childish. Would she ever go to the Speedway again? Well, yes, perhaps; why not? It was fun and she enjoyed it. But she wouldn't go with Lilian. And all that idolising of Tony and Ken and Ron, that hanging over the paddock and begging for autographs and shouting—she didn't think she'd do that again. She'd outgrown it. After a Committee Meeting where you saw people like Mr. Armitage and Mrs. Sykes discussing and deciding—and even Councillor Foster Ormerod wasn't too bad—after that, somehow all that hero-worship for motor-cyclists seemed rather exaggerated. Undignified. What her father called silly work. And also, really, rather boring. In a word, childish. But it was difficult to explain all that without sounding affected. She hesitated.

"It was different," she said.

"I know what you mean," said Harry soberly. "More responsible, sort-of."

"Yes."

"And did you really suggest a site and they put it on the list?"

"Yes."

"Well, I *am* proud of you, Rosemary," said Harry, squeezing her hand. "I knew you'd do it well if you could once take an interest in it. But to suggest a site! I really am proud of you."

Suddenly Rosemary felt so happy that tears stood in her eyes.

"You know, Harry," she said, giving his hand just a very tiny, very modest, very shy, responsive pressure: "I know I can't go on attending the A.T.P. Committee because I'm not the real Youth Group delegate—I wish I could but I can't, I know; but——"

"Perhaps you'll be able to do, who knows? We'll see," said Harry staunchly.

"But in any case, if there's a Youth Committee formed for the Pageant, I should like *very much* to be on it. After all, we do want Ashworth to have a *good* pageant, don't we? Oh, Harry, there's the Worth Lane bus!"

The driver was just settling himself in his seat, but they ran in big strides together and reached the bus just as it was moving off. They could easily have leaped on to the step, but the conductor put up his hand against them. "Full up, love!" he said. "You'll have to walk." With his other hand up to the bell he looked down at them as they stood there hand in hand, and added in joking sarcasm: "And aren't you sorry?"

They laughed, Rosemary a little bashfully but not ill pleased. The bus moved away and Harry drew Rosemary's hand through his arm again and they walked off together happily.

II

GAMALIEL GREENWOOD

Deborah found herself walking along the main street of Ashworth beside Gamaliel Greenwood. She was tired and hungry, and it struck her that she had probably been silent for too long a period to be polite. She forced herself to listen to what her companion was saying, and found him in the middle of a long harangue about the beauties of the Government of Soviet Russia. They were not alone on the pavement, for the cinemas had just released their last-show audiences and many members of these took hurried flight towards the bus station. Gamaliel was obliged to dodge from time to time round some of these citizens, but he always resumed his place at her side and in his speech.

"I'm sure we don't want to get into a political argument, Mr. Greenwood," said Deborah mildly.

"Why not?"

"Well, why not indeed after all," said Deborah, thinking: I detest this man's political views, but I respect the way he's always on the job. "Let me say then that I used to belong to the Society for Cultural Relations with Russia, but gave up membership because of the recent purges in music and science."

"I know a man who met Shostakovich in Moscow, and he was very surprised that in England he was supposed to have been purged."

"Really?"

"Yes, and one of Shostakovich's musical works was being performed at each of the five concerts in the Tchaikovsky Hall."

"I'm delighted to hear it," said Deborah heartily. "But in general I don't feel that the U.S.S.R. allows freedom of thought to its citizens, you know."

"I suppose you're referring to the Lysenko controversy?"

"That and other things. You see, Mr. Greenwood," said Deborah seriously, rallying her forces: "As a scientist, the light of truth is what I serve. Freedom of thought, so that the light of truth has freedom to penetrate every mind; that is what I believe in."

"And you think Soviet Russia forbids the light of truth?"

"All truth but its own."

"But you're judging Soviet Russia from what you read in British newspapers, Mrs. Sykes," said Gamaliel earnestly. "I appeal to your knowledge of social history in England in the last century. Would you expect to find the truth about Chartists and so on in the influential newspapers of those days?"

"That's a very good point, Mr. Greenwood," said Deborah, laughing: "Provided you apply it also to the newspapers of Soviet Russia."

Gamaliel was silent. Unused to argument by analogy, he did not follow her line of thought. Of course Soviet newspapers tell Soviet truth, he thought angrily; what a fool the woman is, after all. Deborah guessed from his silence that she had not made herself clear, and added presently:

"If we accept the possibility that all popular newspapers tend to be harsh to all minorities, in all countries and all ages, we shall probably be on safe ground."

But Gamaliel had already concluded the matter to his own satisfaction, and did not wish to return to it. Instead he said:

"I really wanted to have a word with you about the E.V.W.'s in Ashworth."

"Yes," said Deborah, sighing.

"You teach them English, don't you?"

"Some of them," said Deborah.

At his words the class of the afternoon rose before her eyes: Stephanie cross and sallow, Maria fat and jocular; the spruce engineer, the pretty housemaid, the bright-jerseyed pompadoured Austrians; the kind stupid Anna, the freckled Leni. Leni! "I must do something about that poor young

Leni," thought Deborah with decision: "She sounded heart-broken, and Stephanie wasn't at all sympathetic, I shouldn't like to cry on Stephanie's shoulder. I ought to try to comfort her, to urge her to cheer up. Have I the right to intrude, to interfere? Well, we all have the right to lay our views persuasively before others, as old Mr. Armitage said." After all, with those boys in the park, had she not done just that? And had the results been bad? Those boys, or some or one of them, might just possibly remember the principle of examining evidence, all their lives. Whether they did so or not, at least she had given them the opportunity—she had called their attention to the principle; they could judge its value for themselves. Surely with Leni too, one could not just pass by on the other side. A stranger in a strange land. "I'll go to see her. It's rather too late tonight. I'll go round tomorrow morning before school—no, she'll be at work—she doesn't come back to Fairfax House at noon, she lunches in the canteen—that means it will be tomorrow evening before I can see her. That's a long time away," mused Deborah; "Perhaps I ought to go tonight." She sighed, reluctant, for having had neither supper nor tea and only a congealed and therefore unappetising lunch, she felt really famished. "But if this young man beside me had some Marxist duty to perform, he'd do it now," reflected Deborah: "I'm not above learning from my enemies." She swerved aside and joined a queue.

"I'll take this bus. I've remembered I must go to Fairfax Place," she said.

Gamaliel stood awkwardly beside her.

"Please don't trouble to wait."

"I thought I should like to volunteer to help teach the E.V.W.'s," blurted Gamaliel.

"Why not? May I suggest you write to the Principal of the Technical College?"

"That seems rather a long way round."

"It will be shortest in the end. Tell him your qualifications, and so on. Do you know any East European languages?"

"No."

"I'm afraid you might find it difficult, then."

Gamaliel's disgust at this unexpected barrier to his scheme was so obvious that Deborah felt sorry for him, and to cover his discomfiture began to talk brightly on the first subject that came into her head.

"We had a good meeting tonight, hadn't we. Old Mr. Armitage is so good in the Chair."

"I don't see what's so specially good about him."

"He sees that we all get free expression for our views, without straying too far or quarrelling too much."

"I don't set much store by that false democracy," said Gamaliel.

"Why do you call it false? I always think Committee meetings are such a fascinating study. The delays, the arguments, the compromises, the criss-cross of votes and personalities, finally the synthesis, built up for good or ill from each member's contribution."

"It always seems to take a long time to get anything done in Ashworth committees," said Gamaliel in a critical tone: "But of course that's due to reactionary elements."

Deborah sighed again. He was hopeless; blinded by pride; incapable of mental growth because impervious to any argument. The bus drew in and the queue moved forward.

"Goodnight, Mr. Greenwood," said Deborah, mounting the step.

Gamaliel jerked his head at her gravely and marched off, encased in the armour of his own self-righteousness. It had been a poor evening's work, he thought as he considered all its incidents; but that was hardly his fault, was it. All these counter-revolutionary elements. . . .

III

COUNCILLOR FOSTER ORMEROD

"Well, Foster."

"Well, Nathan."

"There's room 'ere."

"Thanks."

"Had a good evening?"

"Aye. Have you?"

"Aye, not bad, not bad at all. Pageant's beginning to take shape. Three-ha'penny, please, love. Of course there's some on Committee as wants things all their own way."

"Ah!" said Nathan, shaking his head.

"That Gamaliel Greenwood," said Foster, lowering his voice. "But I'll wait till bus starts before I start on our Gamaliel."

When the bus was toiling up Bolland Bank and the sound of the engine was at its maximum, Nathan said:

"Well?"

"Well, we shall have to get him out. Gamaliel, I mean. He's so pig-headed. He isn't open to reason at all. No moderation. No common sense. All on one line. Can't see owt but his own ideas."

"And them not very clear," suggested Nathan.

"That's right. Of course he's honest enough—which is more nor you can say for some."

"Ah!"

"That Sir Charles Considine!"

"I've allus heard he's a tricky piece of work."

"Tricky's the word! But he were a bit too tricky tonight. Got tied up in his own knots. Old Thos Armitage were well up to him. Sir Charles weren't half mad."

"Likes his own way, does he?"

"He does that. Wanted to approach a certain matter in a certain way, so as the Youth Groups would have to join in the Pageant willy nilly. Willy nilly—those were his words."

"Whether they want it or not."

"Aye!" began Foster. But he broke off and looked at his brother-in-law suspiciously, for it came into his mind that when they had disputed about the Steel Nationalisation Bill on the way down into Ashworth that evening, he himself had committed the Labour Party to that measure in precisely those terms. He coloured and muttered; Nathan, sucking in his pipe, was looking straight ahead in an innocent non-committal sort of way. Did his lean cheek wear a faint smile? Salty, was Nathan. All Lizzie's family were salty in their speech, Lizzie herself the saltiest of the lot when she had a mind. Lizzie and Nathan, Sir Charles Considine and Deborah Sykes and old Thos Armitage all united suddenly to draw him back into the past, to Bolland Wood and old Jonathan Bamforth and Lizzie's shawl, his own rebellion against going to the mill and his father's shouted reply. Tha'll go whether tha wants or not. Willy nilly.

"Tell thee what, Nathan," he said with his cheerful grin: "It makes a lot o' difference which side of that sentence you're standing."

Nathan looked interrogative.

"Whether you're telling or being told," explained Foster.

"Ah!" agreed Nathan, shaking his head.

IV

MRS. DEBORAH SYKES, M.Sc.

DEBORAH HURRIED UP the steps and rang the bell at Fairfax House. After a longish wait a light appeared, a latch was clicked, the door swung open and Stephanie stood before her. She was still dressed, and with Stephanie's hair it was not very easy to tell whether it was up or down. She looked severe.

"Mrs. Sykes! You are very late. We have all retired."

"Yes, I'm sorry. But I felt I must ask after Leni. How was she after the class?"

"I have not seen her. She went to her room and came not down."

"Not for supper?"

"We have no supper."

"Tea, then."

"She came not to tea."

"Have you really not seen her since she ran out of my class?"

"That was the last time I have seen Leni."

"Then I must come in."

"It is against the rule at this time for a stranger to enter," said Stephanie. "Leni surely sleeps."

"Please fetch the housekeeper—she will give me permission, I am sure," insisted Deborah.

"*Nu*," said Stephanie uneasily, drawing back to allow Deborah to enter: "The housekeeper is out. I do not know what is right to do. It is right you come in, perhaps. I will go up with you. You will explain to the housekeeper afterwards, *nicht wahr?*"

After knocking gently at Leni's door and receiving no response, Deborah tried the handle. The door did not open.

"It is locked," said Deborah, relieved in spite of herself at being excused a tearful scene. "She must be asleep, as you say."

"No, no!" cried Stephanie. "We have no locks here."

"Help me to push."

The handle turned and the latch drew back, but the door would not move.

"We go through the next room—there is a balcony."

Stephanie hurriedly threw open the next door, switched on the light and ran to the window, which was closed. The startled occupant of the room sat up in bed and demanded in exclamatory Polish to know whether there was a fire. Stephanie and Deborah seized each a handle of the large old-fashioned window and heaved with all their might. The pane flew up, Stephanie stooped, and Deborah followed her on to a rusty and rickety iron balcony. They edged along this towards the windows of Leni's room.

"Her window is open!" exclaimed Deborah with relief, for her mind had begun to run upon gas.

"But the curtains are not drawn," said Stephanie, shaking her head.

"She went to sleep while it was still light," whispered Deborah.

"It is possible," agreed Stephanie doubtfully.

"In any case I think we should go in, just to make sure."

"You go in," said Stephanie, shrinking.

"I don't know where the light is, but if you'll go first, I'll follow right behind, I'll hold your hand."

The light glared. Not knowing in which direction to look for the bed, Deborah saw first that the dressing-table had been moved against the door. Stephanie screamed.

"Look, look! *Sie ist tot!* She is dead, she is dead!"

In the bed, resting quietly, in a white silk nightdress embroidered in the fashion of her country, lay Leni, marble-white herself. Her lips, almost blue, seemed to smile peacefully; her freckles showed like brown blotches against her skin; her dark tumbled hair took on a statuesque dignity now that it lay motionless. Her hands lay clasped above the shabby green coverlet. Everything was very still; there seemed no movement anywhere. On the table beside the bed, a glass half full of water and an empty bottle labelled *Aspirin* told their sad tale.

"She is dead!" wailed Stephanie. "Come away!"

"Nonsense! She's not dead, she can't be dead, she hasn't had time to die!" exclaimed Deborah angrily. (Oh, if only I had followed her out of the class! How wicked, how wrong of me to let her go!) She knelt beside the bed, chafed the girl's hands, felt for her pulse, laid her head on Leni's quiet breast and listened for the beat of her heart. It seemed to her that she caught just a faint, dim, far-off, tiny sound, but she could not be sure.

"Help me to move this dressing-table. Chafe her hands. *Reiben*. Not that way—towards the heart. *Nach sein Herz.* Where's the telephone?"

"*Kein Telephon hier.*"

"Where's the nearest?"

"I show," said the Pole, who had followed them in. Seizing Deborah's hand, she ran swiftly down the stairs, out of the house, along the Place and round several complicated street turnings, bringing her out eventually in triumph at a kiosk.

Deborah fumbled for coppers and dialled the Ashworth hospital. "I mustn't shout at the night porter," she told herself sternly: "It's not his fault, it's mine." Aloud she said in a quiet but urgent tone: "This is Mrs. Deborah Sykes, on the staff of the Ashworth Girls' High School. There has been an accident at Fairfax House, Fairfax Place. An overdose

of aspirin has been taken by mistake. A doctor and an
ambulance are wanted there immediately."

"They'll be with you in four minutes, madam."

Sure enough as Deborah and the Pole returned along
Fairfax Place the ambulance, clanging its bell, overtook
them.

"I must run or they won't understand a word!" cried
Deborah.

In the hall the young house-doctor, the nurse and the two
stretcher-bearers stood perplexed, while bewildered E.V.W.'s,
woken by the commotion, poured down the stairs, calling
out their natural alarm in several languages. Stephanie
appeared on the landing, in her distress and excitement
shouting in her own tongue.

Deborah explained, the doctor was led to the proper room,
Leni was quickly placed on the stretcher and loaded into
the ambulance.

"Is she alive, doctor?" asked Deborah as the young man
prepared to climb in after his patient.

"Yes, yes, of course. We shall pull her through. Good
thing you found her when you did—if she'd been left till
morning it mightn't have been so easy. She owes her life
to you."

"She owes her life to the Committee meeting," reflected
Deborah thankfully. "If there be any further evil, O Life,"
she prayed as she trailed slowly homewards: "If there be
any further evil, spare this young creature Leni, let her be
happy, let the evil descend on me."

V

SIR CHARLES CONSIDINE

As Elizabeth stepped away from her colloquy with
Fred, who had been pacing the pavement impatiently, she
was hailed by name from the car standing next to Mr.
Armitage's. She approached, and in her body which had felt

withered and dry and stiff with pain the blood seemed to move again in warm life-giving currents, for it was Considine who had spoken. He was leaning across from the driving-seat to put his head out of the window.

"Are you going to offer me a lift?" drawled Elizabeth, fixing her eyes on him meaningly.

Considine hesitated.

"I'd promised to take young Bairstow."

"Oh you'll have a long time to wait if you wait for *him*. He's having a heart-to-heart with old Thos Armitage. Judging from our Roddie's expression, I should say he was trying to borrow money."

Considine exclaimed in fury. The insurance scheme was lost to him, then. Well, perhaps it was for the best. The scheme was perhaps over-risky. A trifle far-fetched. But where the devil was he to find that twenty-five thousand pounds for the Highshaw purchase from, then? Oh well, he'd think of something. He ran his eyes cynically over Elizabeth's beautiful body, which in the light from the Institute's door-lamps, showed its seductive moulding very clearly. A spot of sex always stimulated his planning ability, reflected Considine. As he looked, Elizabeth slightly but unmistakably changed her pose; it was the lascivious preening, beneath male admiration, of a female animal. Considine gave a coarse laugh. If she wants it she shall have it, he thought savagely. He threw back the car door.

"Get in," he said.

Elizabeth obeyed. She felt as she did so that she was indeed obeying him, that he had already a mastery over her no other man had ever achieved. A voluptuous pleasure thrilled along her nerves; her skin grew warm; her rich lips pouted, her great eyes glowed. She turned to him.

"It's *most* kind of you to give me a lift, Sir Charles," she cooed, pronouncing his name with a delicate precision which gave her a real sensuous enjoyment.

"I was thinking of offering you something more than a lift," said Considine in his silkiest tones.

"Oh? And what might that be?"

"Supper at the Hey Dean Inn," said Considine, driving

306

off. "The food's good. The licensee knows her way about."

"I couldn't say no to *supper*," drawled Elizabeth.

"You won't say no to anything by the time I've finished with you," thought Considine, turning into the Mount Hey road. Aloud he remarked urbanely: "Silly meeting we had tonight, don't you agree, Elizabeth? By the way, I may call you Elizabeth, may I not?"

VI

CAPTAIN RODERICK BAIRSTOW, D.S.O.

"I DON'T KNOW WHAT the Building Society is thinking of, to press so hardly on an ex-officer for such a small sum," said Thomas severely, carefully inserting below his signature the two dots which he always placed there in cheques. "I shall have something to say about it next time I chance to see their Chairman of Directors—that is, if you've no objection."

"None, sir. I'm afraid I may have been rather tiresome with the Building Society, though. I can't tell you how grateful I am."

"Don't try, my boy. Have you told your wife about all this? Tell her."

"Yes, I will, Mr. Armitage. I was thinking about that when you were speaking of the individual's right to take his own decisions, sir. It's too long a story to tell, but I've been trying to take my wife's and my father's decisions for them."

"Ah, well," said Thomas. "That's never right. Would you mind giving me a hand with my coat?"

"It's an honour," said Roddie fervently, putting Thomas very carefully and gently into his sleeves. "I should just like to say, Mr. Armitage," he went on: "I should just like to say thank you, not only for the loan, which has saved me—yes, saved me—but for the way you've conducted the meeting tonight. It's a pleasure and a privilege to watch you in the Chair."

"Well, well, well!" said Thomas, surprised but greatly

pleased. "Very nice of you to say so, I'm sure. I'm afraid Sir Charles Considine might not agree."

"Oh, he's a crook," threw out Roddie.

"You mustn't say that sort of thing even in jest, my boy," said Thomas gravely.

"But he is! He half offered to lend me the—money—this morning," explained Roddie: "And on that account he expected me to vote with him on the field question tonight."

"Surely not," said Thomas. Not taking the young man seriously, he moved off towards the door.

"He gave me a very dirty look at that point, anyway," said Roddie.

"No!" Thomas wheeled to face him, and the two men regarded each other for a long moment. "Well! I must go and I expect you have a bus to catch," said Thomas at length. "Or perhaps your last bus has gone?"

"It has but it's of no consequence, I can easily walk," said Roddie, turning out the light.

"Your wife will be worrying. I'll run you home."

"You're very kind, sir," said Roddie from his heart.

Accordingly—for Fred seemed cross and drove very fast—it was only a few minutes later that he was sprinting up the cobbled lane towards Upper Head Cottage. He couldn't run fast enough; he could hardly have run faster, thought Roddie, pressing firmly on the sore spot in salutary self-reminder, if a process-server had been running after him. The wind was blowing pretty hard, as usual, and carrying the beginnings of rain in its burly breath, but on the other side of the sky the moon, riding behind clouds, cast a grey diffused light over the rugged Ashworth landscape. Roddie thought he had never in his life seen anything he loved so well as those massive and firmly interwoven hills, with his own home nestling into the fold beneath Mount Hey brow. The windows all darkly reflected the moonlight except one, which shed a dim yellow light. The children of course were all in bed, and Kate was sitting waiting for him in the room below. Kate! It seemed centuries since he had seen Kate. He turned off the cobbled lane into the farm entrance, ran at top speed along the muddy path, reached his own doorstep and began to fumble for his key; before he could find it the door swung vigorously open. Kate in her blue woollen dressing-gown, rather shabby, with her two long dark plaits lying over her shoulders, stood before him in the little hall. Her eyes were wide with fear. One of his socks, with a darning-needle stuck across it, masked her left hand.

"I heard you running, Roddie. Is anything wrong?"

"No. Not now. Oh Kate I've been so miserable. I've been in trouble and keeping it from you. Debt. But it's all right now. Do you think you could bear to have my father living with us here?"

Kate broke into sudden tears.

"Oh yes, *yes!*" she cried. "I've been so miserable, Roddie, because you wouldn't trust him to me."

"Oh Kate!"

They fell into each other's arms. The darning-needle pricked Roddie's ear but he accepted it in manful silence.

VII

THOMAS ARMITAGE, J.P.

FRED TURNED THE car and drove away.

"I noticed a telephone kiosk in the village, Fred," said Thomas. "Stop there, please, and telephone Shaw Thorn. I have to see Mr. Bernard tonight. If he's there, tell him I'm coming along now. If he's not there, find out where he is and tell me."

Fred followed these instructions and putting his head into the car reported that Bernard was at Shaw Thorn.

"Good. Take me there," said Thomas.

"It's very late, Mr. Armitage," said Fred in a grumbling tone.

"I know. I can't help being late tonight, I have important business. You must take extra time off some other day."

"I wasn't thinking of that," said Fred virtuously. "You won't have much petrol left for the rest of the month if you go on like this, Mr. Armitage, that's what I've been thinking."

"Then I shall take taxis."

Fred said nothing, though every line of his coat expressed disapproval, until he had reseated himself behind the wheel, when he remarked with assumed innocence:

"Your Committee Meeting seems to have done you good, Mr. Armitage."

"It has."

Fred slammed the door sharply and drove off. As they passed a steep wooded turning on the left, Thomas observed that the man glanced in that direction with an appearance of special interest. Feeling that he had been a little short in his manner just now to Fred, and wishing to resume friendly relations, he observed pleasantly:

"Where does that turning go, Fred? I noticed you spoke about it to Captain Bairstow as we came along."

Fred chuckled. "It goes down to Hey Dean Inn."

"Oh," said Thomas, uninterested.

"The Captain was telling me it's like a roadhouse, now."

"Oh."

"Not a very good reputation."

"Very well, very well," said Thomas impatiently, wishing to drop the subject and resume his thought about what he meant to say to Bernard.

"Funny Sir Charles Considine turned down there."

"Now, Fred, there has been no car near us since we left Ashworth, and you couldn't possibly have recognised Sir Charles's car at a distance in this dim light."

"Oh yes, I could," said Fred, aggrieved, and went off into a mass of technical details about the make, shape, colour, gadgets and price of Considine's unique and well-known car.

"Well, never mind; I'm not interested."

"He had that young woman with him, though."

"Fred, I am *not* interested."

"The one you sent out to me with a message."

Thomas was taken aback. Miss Marrison, he thought. Poor girl! I'm sorry for any woman who has anything to do with Considine. A tiger would be less ruthless.

"Well, it's not our concern, Fred," he said in a different tone.

"I just mentioned it like seeing it was Sir Charles Considine," said Fred, excusing himself.

"Sir Charles Considine has nothing to do with us, Fred," said Thomas with decision. "Nothing at all."

Fred was silent.

Bernard met his uncle at the door and ushered him into the drawing-room where their momentous interview had taken place earlier in the day. Bernard, still in his bird's-eye suit, looked pale and harassed, and Thomas's shrewd eye noted a whisky decanter and a glass on a small occasional table by the side of a chair on the hearth. A crumpled cushion, and a detective novel open face downwards on the arm, proved fairly conclusively that the chair was the one previously occupied by Bernard. It's not good for young men to live alone, thought Thomas soberly, sitting down on the other side of the hearth. The fire was low; after a glance at his uncle's face Bernard stooped and threw on a log.

"Well, what's all this in aid of, Uncle? Bit late for you to be out, isn't it?" he said then, throwing himself into his chair.

"I've been thinking over the matter we were discussing here at noon, Bernard, and I want to have it out with you now. No use waiting."

A look of weary distaste crossed Bernard's small aquiline features, and the frown in his forehead deepened.

"What's the use of going over it all again? Nothing has changed in the situation since this morning."

"Yes, it has. I've made up my mind."

"I hope you don't mean you intend to ruin my life by vetoing the transfer of shares."

"Listen, Bernard. We have a right to take our own decisions, to manage our own lives."

"Exactly; and I intend to manage mine."

"Let us analyse this situation into its component parts, and discover and delimit our several spheres of responsibility."

"Well, put it in words of one syllable for me, Uncle."

"You want to get divorced and marry this girl, whoever she is, and you're prepared to pay high for it."

"Yes."

"I hope you *are* sure of her, Bernard."

"I intend to make sure tomorrow night."

"Good. But that's by the way. Now there are two ways in which you can do this. One: you can sell some of your Highshaw shares to settle a sum on Olive, marry and continue to live in the West Riding and work at Highshaw."

"But——"

"Two: you can sell out of Highshaw altogether, settle a sum on Olive, marry and go out to South Africa. Now as your mother's brother, your only surviving competent relative, I feel I have a right to indicate to you what I think of those two courses of action."

"Go ahead," said Bernard grimly: "That is, if you think it worth while. I shan't change my mind."

"Very well. To me the second course appears foolish and cowardly: to desert England and throw away your textile skill seems silly work to me. Failing in your duty to the community, too. You're needed here, in textiles."

"Uncle——"

"But it's your life and your money, and you must do as you like."

"Thank you, Uncle. It's damned decent of you."

"I've laid my view before you and I shan't mention it again. You must choose for yourself which you do. But when it comes to *how* you're going to do it, that impinges on my life and I have a right to take my own decisions."

"And does that mean you intend to veto the share transfers?"

"Yes."

"My God!" exclaimed Bernard, springing up and pacing the room. "And you call yourself a progressive, liberal-minded man."

"Being liberal-minded doesn't mean you have to countenance evil. Listen, Bernard. Whichever way you choose, I'll help. I'll buy out a proportion of your Highshaw shares if you choose the first way, and the whole lot if you choose the second."

"That means mortgaging one half of Highshaw to pay for the other."

"Yes."

"In effect it means running Highshaw with just half the capital there is in it now."

"Yes."

"It's madness, Uncle!"

"That's my affair."

"But why do it? Why?"

"Because I won't have Considine in the place. There's a third alternative, by the way; that you sell out to some thoroughly reputable person or combine, whom I know and approve."

"But the delay, the delay! Besides, I've put out feelers before—nobody seemed interested in the proposition but Considine."

"In that case, as I said before, I'll buy you out myself."

"You leave me no choice, Uncle. You make it so that if I do what I want I ruin you."

"Not at all. You take your decision and I take mine. I won't have Considine in Highshaw."

"You could retire, Uncle, in a year or two. He'd probably be glad to buy you out."

"And leave him in charge of Highshaw? No, thank you."

"The workpeople wouldn't care, if that's what you're thinking," said Bernard bitterly.

"I have a responsibility to them all the same."

"But what have you got against Considine? What's set you so dead against him since lunch-time?"

"I've sat on a Committee with him," said Thomas drily.

Bernard stood still and ceased to jingle the keys in his pocket.

"But what has he done?" he said in a different tone.

"Oh, just a series of small things," said Thomas reflectively. "It's difficult to lay a finger on them. But a Committee's a wonderful revealer of character, you know, Bernard. Considine was somehow always on the wrong side. And then, he wanted to vote on a matter concerning his own property."

"Did he, by Jove!"

313

"This mustn't go further than our two selves, Bernard, but during the meeting one woman spoke of his financial jugglery. Of course she didn't mean it seriously, but these involuntary phrases are very revealing. And a young man after the meeting told me straight out that Considine was a crook—had tried to influence his vote. I merely mention these remarks, Bernard, not to expect you to believe the accusations they contain, but to show you that I'm not alone in my opinion of Considine. Of course this is in the deepest confidence."

"Who was it spoke of his financial jugglery?"

"You can hardly expect me to tell you that, my boy," said Thomas stiffly.

"No, I suppose not."

"And then to go off with her to that Hey Dean Inn," mused Thomas.

"What?" shouted Bernard.

"Of course his private life is no concern of mine," said Thomas hastily. "But I can't help disliking the incident. He shouldn't take a young unmarried woman to such a place."

"No," said Bernard: "He certainly should not."

"Especially at this late hour."

"No."

"Though perhaps Fred exaggerated its disrepute."

"I don't think so," said Bernard drily.

"Then how does it manage to retain its licence?"

"It won't for long."

"However this is all by the way and I apologise for intruding it. But I believe, Bernard—and I say this very seriously—I believe every member of the A.T.P. Committee felt as I did about Considine tonight."

"It's not easy to judge what people are feeling."

"It's reflected in their votes."

"But I've gone so far with the sale, I can't withdraw!" exclaimed Bernard uncomfortably.

"You'll have to, because I shan't initial the transfer. There'll be a forfeit to pay, perhaps. I'll pay it."

"Well, Uncle," said Bernard, yielding—not altogether

reluctantly, Thomas was pleased to believe—"I suppose I shall have to agree."

"Have I your word, Bernard, not to introduce Considine or any other buyer without my consent?"

"Yes, yes! You're a terrible old fellow, Uncle Thos, you really are."

Thomas smiled.

"Now think it over, Bernard, as between South Africa and Highshaw," he said. "Think it over *well*, and let me know. Whichever you decide, we'll start on it at once with accountants and solicitors. I don't want to keep you from your happiness. But we shall be ready before the divorce is through, I should imagine."

"I shouldn't be surprised," said Bernard drily. He seemed preoccupied, stood jingling his keys again and invited his uncle to have a drink in a very perfunctory fashion. As soon as Thomas refused, he bundled him off rapidly into the car, and before Fred had started the engine he could be heard dialling the telephone.

Now that the excitement of the interview with Bernard was over, Thomas felt exceedingly tired. Yes, tired. Drained. Chilly. He lay back in the car and was thankful for the fur rug which Fred had tucked around him. Well, fatigue was natural at his age and he must learn to take it with dignity. But fatigue was not incompatible with happiness, and Thomas was deeply happy. The A.T.P.C. meeting had gone well under his Chairmanship, and he had settled this terrible business with Bernard. He was not useless; he still had much to contribute, even to this changing modern world. If one could not throw up mountains, as that poet fellow said, in one's old age, one could at least build roads up them as starting points for the young. And that reminded him: he must compose a speech for that prize-giving tomorrow. He laid back his head, closed his eyes and concentrated his thoughts.

"I'll expound the beliefs I've lived by to those young things," he thought energetically: "If it's the last thing I do . . ."

VIII

MISS ELIZABETH MARRISON

IN ELIZABETH'S FLAT the telephone rang. It received no answer, and continued to ring at quarter-hour intervals until some time after one o'clock. Then Elizabeth, who had just come in, snatched it to her ear.

"Who's that?" she said, assuming a drowsy tone.

"Bernard here. Where have you been, my dear? I've been ringing you for hours."

"In bed," lied Elizabeth. "Where did you think?"

"You wouldn't have been supping at the Hey Dean Inn with Sir Charles Considine, by any chance?"

Somebody saw us, Elizabeth calculated swiftly.

"Yes; why not? Until I came in and went to bed."

Bernard was silent.

"Don't you believe me, my poppet?" drawled Elizabeth.

"Not altogether."

"That's very rude, Bernard."

"Well—you're dining with me tomorrow?"

"Am I dining with you tomorrow?" Elizabeth repeated aloud for the benefit of Considine, who stood at her side. She looked up at him for guidance; slightly but decisively— he'd get back at that Highshaw crowd one way if he couldn't another—Considine shook his head. "No, Bernard dear, I'm sorry I can't. Since you rang up this afternoon I find I can't. Business, you know."

"*I* know," said Bernard sardonically.

"Goodnight, Bernard."

"Goodbye, Elizabeth!" said Bernard, and rang off.

Part Five

TRIBUTE TO A RETIRING MEMBER

TRIBUTE TO A RETIRING MEMBER

Extract from the *Ashworth Evening Times* of Wednesday, September 14th, 1949:

SUDDEN DEATH OF MR. THOMAS ARMITAGE

COLLAPSE AT SCHOOL SPEECH DAY

Many Tributes to Mr. Armitage's Long Record of Public Service

Mr. Thomas Armitage, J.P., died with tragic suddenness this afternoon, while attending the prize-giving of the Denbridge Grammar School (Boys and Girls) where he was distributing the yearly awards.

Mr. Armitage had made a most moving speech to the school on the ideals of freedom and public service which are the heritage of our race. He spoke with such deep feeling and ardent eloquence that all who heard him were very much moved. The pupils in particular listened to him spellbound and showed their appreciation by prolonged and thunderous applause. In response to a gesture from the headmaster Mr. Armitage rose to acknowledge this applause, when it broke out again with great enthusiasm. The headmaster seeing that Mr. Armitage was very much affected gave the signal to the master at the piano to begin the National Anthem in order to conclude the proceedings. This was sung, but it was barely concluded when Mr. Armitage sank down heavily in his chair. While the audience dispersed the headmaster, the Mayor of Denbridge and the Chairman of the Denbridge Education Committee helped Mr. Armitage to the ante-room behind the platform. A doctor, father of one of the prize-winning pupils, who chanced to be in the audience, had perceived Mr. Armitage's distress and made his way to the ante-room, and he administered restoratives, but it was seen that Mr. Armitage was lapsing into unconsciousness. Further medical aid was summoned and Mr. Bernard Clough (nephew) was sent for, but before either could arrive there came the distressing announcement that Mr. Armitage had passed away.

Mr. Armitage was Chairman of Directors of Highshaw

Mills, taking over the management of the concern on the death of his father in 1899. He leaves a married daughter (in Kenya) and a nephew, Mr. Bernard Clough.

The death of Mr. Armitage is felt as a great loss throughout the West Riding, and at the time of going to press tributes to him are pouring into this office from all sections of the community.

In a special interview the Mayor of Ashworth said: Mr. Thomas Armitage won the respect of all who knew him. His passing is a real loss to the town. On the Bench he always dealt sympathetically and fairly with every case which came before him. He was a man of wide experience and fine character, and for fifty years has given splendid service to all the social welfare activities of Ashworth. Last night he was presiding at a meeting of the Ashworth Textile Pageant Committee, this afternoon he attended a school prize-giving, and this is typical of his unobtrusive but steady public service. His sense of public duty was so strong that he had not in any way slackened off in his public work recently or allowed himself the relaxation due to his advancing years, and this has no doubt hastened his demise. He died in harness, as he would wish. He was a good man, whose life was an inspiration to all.

The President of the Federation of Worsted Spinners stated that Mr. Armitage's schemes for the welfare of his workers were among the earliest of their kind, and did credit no less to his heart than to his head. At this crisis in the country's affairs we could ill afford to lose men of the administrative ability, tolerance and vision, of Mr. Armitage. He was a highly valued member of the Federation.

Since the first edition of this paper has appeared and conveyed the sad news to the inhabitants of Ashworth, many other tributes have also reached this office. Among those of special interest are several from members of the Textile Pageant Committee, who met under Mr. Armitage's chairmanship last night, as stated above. Captain Roderick Bairstow, D.S.O., mentioned that Mr. Armitage was ever willing to give a helping hand to all who needed it. Councillor Foster Ormerod said that Mr. Armitage was a staunch adherent of his own political faith, but he kept an open mind and had the welfare of the whole community at heart. The Ashworth Youth Groups sent a message through their delegate to express their true sorrow at the loss of Mr. Armitage, who was so kind and helpful to young people entering public life. Mrs. Deborah Sykes, M.Sc. (Ashworth High School) said that it was a privilege to attend a meeting presided over by Mr. Armitage. The principles on which he conducted such meetings, said Mrs. Sykes, namely scrupulous respect for the individual personality and belief in free co-operation by free persons, freely given, for the sake of the general good, would never be out of date. . . .

THE END

PORTWAY JUNIOR REPRINTS

PORTWAY REPRINTS

NON-FICTION

Armstrong, Martin	LADY HESTER STANHOPE
Arnothy, Christine	IT'S NOT SO EASY TO LIVE
Barke, James	THE GREEN HILLS FAR AWAY
Bentley, Phyllis	THE PENNINE WEAVER
Bishop, W.A.	WINGED WARFARE
Blain, William	HOME IS THE SAILOR
Buchan, John	THE CLEARING HOUSE
Cardus, Neville	DAYS IN THE SUN
Cobbett, William	COTTAGE ECONOMY
Day, J. Wentworth	GHOSTS AND WITCHES
Dunnett, Alastair M.	IT'S TOO LATE IN THE YEAR
	originally published as *QUEST BY CANOE GLASGOW TO SKYE*
Edmonds, Charles	A SUBALTERN'S WAR
Evans, A.J.	THE ESCAPING CLUB
Falk, Bernard	OLD Q's DAUGHTER
Fields, Gracie	SING AS WE GO
Gandy, Ida	A WILTSHIRE CHILDHOOD
Gibbons, Floyd	RED KNIGHT OF GERMANY
Gibbs, Philip	REALITIES OF WAR
Gough, General Sir Hubert	THE FIFTH ARMY
Hart, B.H. Liddell	THE OTHER SIDE OF THE HILL
,, ,, ,,	A HISTORY OF THE WORLD WAR 1914-18
Jobson, Allan	SUFFOLK YESTERDAYS
Jones, Ira	KING OF AIR FIGHTERS
Jones, Jack	GIVE ME BACK MY HEART
Jones, Jack	UNFINISHED JOURNEY
Jones, Jack	ME AND MINE
Kennedy, John F.	WHY ENGLAND SLEPT
Kennedy Shaw, W.B.	LONG RANGE DESERT GROUP
Keyhoe, Donald	THE FLYING SAUCERS ARE REAL
Lawrence, W.J.	No. 5 BOMBER GROUP
Lethbridge, Mabel	FORTUNE GRASS

Lethbridge, Mabel	AGAINST THE TIDE
Lowe, George	BECAUSE IT IS THERE
Masefield, John	THE BATTLE OF THE SOMME
Neumann, Major Georg Paul	THE GERMAN AIR-FORCE IN THE GREAT WAR (translated by J.E. Gurdon)
Price, Harry	THE MOST HAUNTED HOUSE IN ENGLAND
Price, Harry	THE END OF BORLEY RECTORY
Raymond, Ernest	IN THE STEPS OF ST. FRANCIS
Stamper, Joseph	LESS THAN THE DUST
Stoker, Bram	FAMOUS IMPOSTERS
Stokes, Sewell	ISADORA DUNCAN
Tangye, Derek	TIME WAS MINE
Torre, Lillian de la	ELIZABETH IS MISSING
Vigilant	RICHTHOFEN – RED KNIGHT OF THE AIR
Vigilant	GERMAN WAR BIRDS
Villiers, Alan	SONS OF SINDBAD
von Richthofen	THE RED AIR FIGHTER
Whipple, Dorothy	THE OTHER DAY

FICTION

Aldington, Richard	DEATH OF A HERO
Aldington, Richard	ALL MEN ARE ENEMIES
Anand, Mulk Raj	SEVEN SUMMERS
Anderson, Verily	SPAM TOMORROW
Anthony, Evelyn	IMPERIAL HIGHNESS
Anthony, Evelyn	VICTORIA
Arlen, Michael	MEN DISLIKE WOMEN
Arnim, Von	ELIZABETH AND HER GERMAN GARDEN
Ashton, Helen	DOCTOR SEROCOLD
Ashton, Helen	THE HALF-CROWN HOUSE
Ashton, Helen	LETTY LANDON
Ashton, Helen	FOOTMAN IN POWDER
Ashton, Helen	SWAN OF USK
Ashton, Helen	FAMILY CRUISE

Barke, James	MAJOR OPERATION
Barke, James	THE LAND OF THE LEAL
Barke, James	THE SONG OF THE GREEN THORN TREE
Barke, James	THE WELL OF THE SILENT HARP
Barke, James	BONNIE JEAN
Benson, R.H.	LORD OF THE WORLD
Benson, R.H.	COME RACK COME ROPE
Bentley, Phyllis ✓	TRIO
Bentley, Phyllis	LOVE AND MONEY
Bentley, Phyllis	THE PARTNERSHIP
Bentley, Phyllis	TAKE COURAGE
Bentley, Phyllis	A MODERN TRAGEDY
Besant, Walter	DOROTHY FORSTER
Birmingham, George A.	THE INVIOLABLE SANCTUARY
Birmingham, George A.	GENERAL JOHN REGAN
Blackmore, R.D.	MARY ANERLEY
Blaker, Richard	MEDAL WITHOUT BAR
Blaker, Richard	THE NEEDLE WATCHER
Blain, William	WITCH'S BLOOD
Bottome, Phyllis	MURDER IN THE BUD
Bromfield, Louis ✓	THE RAINS CAME
Brophy, John	ROCKY ROAD
Brophy, John	GENTLEMAN OF STRATFORD
Brophy, John	WATERFRONT
Broster, D.K.	A FIRE OF DRIFTWOOD
Broster, D.K.	SHIPS IN THE BAY
Broster, D.K.	SEA WITHOUT A HAVEN
Broster, D.K.	CHILD ROYAL
Broster, D.K. & Taylor, G.W.	CHANTEMERLE
Broster, D.K. & Forester, G.	WORLD UNDER SNOW
Buchan, John ✓	GREY WEATHER
Buchan, John	WITCH WOOD
Buck, Pearl S. *(Trans.)* ✓	ALL MEN ARE BROTHERS (2 vols)
Buck, Pearl S.	FIGHTING ANGEL
Buck, Pearl S.	A HOUSE DIVIDED
Burney, Fanny	CAMILLA (in five volumes) (the set
Caldwell, Taylor	THE TURNBULLS

Caldwell, Taylor	THE STRONG CITY
Caldwell, Taylor	THE BEAUTIFUL IS VANISHED
Caldwell, Taylor	EARTH IS THE LORD'S
Caldwell, Taylor	LET LOVE COME LAST
Callow, Philip	COMMON PEOPLE
Chandos, Dane	ABBIE
Chapman, Hester, W.	SHE SAW THEM GO BY
Chapman, Hester, W.	TO BE A KING
Collins, Wilkie	ARMADALE
Collins, Wilkie	POOR MISS FINCH
Collins, Wilkie	THE DEAD SECRET
Collins, Wilkie	THE HAUNTED HOTEL
Comyns, Barbara	OUR SPOONS CAME FROM WOOLWORTHS
Cookson, Catherine	FIFTEEN STREETS
Cookson, Catherine	MAGGIE ROWAN
Cookson, Catherine	ROONEY
Cooper, Lettice	THE NEW HOUSE
Cooper, Lettice	PRIVATE ENTERPRISE
Cooper, Lettice	WE HAVE COME TO A COUNTRY
Cordell, Alexander	THE HOSTS OF REBECCA
Cordell, Alexander	RACE OF THE TIGER
Corke, Helen	NEUTRAL GROUND
Craik, Mrs.	AGATHA'S HUSBAND
Crockett, S.R.	THE GREY MAN
Crockett, S.R.	THE BLACK DOUGLAS
Crockett, S.R.	THE RAIDERS
Cusack, Dymphna & James, F.	COME IN SPINNER
Dane, Clemence	THE FLOWER GIRLS
Dane, Clemence	THE MOON IS FEMININE
Darlington, W.A.	ALF'S BUTTON
Davenport, Marcia	EAST SIDE, WEST SIDE
Davies, Rhys	RINGS ON HER FINGERS
Davies, Rhys	THE TRIP TO LONDON
Davies, Rhys	HONEY AND BREAD
Davies, Rhys	THE RED HILLS
Davies, Rhys	THE BLACK VENUS
Davies, Rhys	JUBILEE BLUES

Raymond, Ernest	DAPHNE BRUNO
Raymond, Ernest	THE FULFILMENT OF DAPHNE BRUNO
Raymond, Ernest	THE FIVE SONS OF LE FABER
Raymond, Ernest	FOR THEM THAT TRESPASS
Renault, Mary	THE FRIENDLY YOUNG LADIES
Riley, William	JERRY AND BEN
Riley, William	LAYCOCK OF LONEDALE
Roberts, Kenneth	OLIVER WISWELL
Roche, Mazo de la	DELIGHT
Roche, Mazo de la	GROWTH OF A MAN
Saunders, Margaret Baillie	QUALITY FAIR
Seton, Anya	THE MISTLETOE AND SWORD
Shellabarger, Samuel	CAPTAIN FROM CASTILE
Sherriff, R.C.	THE HOPKINS MANUSCRIPT
Shiel, M.P.	PRINCE ZALESKI
Shiel, M.P.	HOW THE OLD WOMAN GOT HOME
Sienkiewicz, Henryk	THE DELUGE (2 vols)
Sienkiewicz, Henryk	WITH FIRE AND SWORD
Sinclair, Upton	WORLD'S END
Sinclair, Upton	BETWEEN TWO WORLDS
Sinclair, Upton	DRAGON'S TEETH
Sinclair, Upton	WIDE IS THE GATE
Sinclair, Upton	PRESIDENTIAL AGENT
Sinclair, Upton	DRAGON HARVEST
Sinclair, Upton	A WORLD TO WIN
Sinclair, Upton	PRESIDENTIAL MISSION
Sinclair, Upton	ONE CLEAR CALL
Sinclair, Upton	O SHEPHERDS SPEAK
Sinclair, Upton	THE RETURN OF LANNY BUDD
Smith, Betty	A TREE GROWS IN BROOKLYN
Soubiran, Andre	THE DOCTORS
Sutcliffe, Halliwell	WILLOWDENE WILL
Sutcliffe, Halliwell	PEDLAR'S QUEST
Sutcliffe, Halliwell	A MAN OF THE MOORS
Sutton, Graham	NORTH STAR
Sutton, Graham	THE ROWAN TREE
Sutton, Graham	FLEMING OF HONISTER

Thane, Elswyth	YOUNG MR. DISRAELI
Thane, Elswyth	TRYST
Thomas, Gwyn	A FROST ON MY FROLIC
Thomas, Gwyn	NOW LEAD US HOME
Thomas, Gwyn	THE WORLD CANNOT HEAR YOU
Thompson, Morton	NOT AS A STRANGER
Tibber, Robert	LOVE ON MY LIST
Tilsley, Frank	CHAMPION ROAD
Trollope, Frances	THE LIFE AND ADVENTURES OF MICHAEL ARMSTRONG
Trouncer, Margaret	ORIFLAMME
Tunstall, Beatrice	THE DARK LADY
Turnbull, Agnes Sligh	THE ROLLING YEARS
Turnbull, Patrick	RED WALLS
Turner, Sheila	OVER THE COUNTER
Urquhart, Fred	TIME WILL KNIT
Vaughan, Hilda	HARVEST HOME
Viereck, G.S. & Eldridge, P.	MY FIRST TWO THOUSAND YEARS
Walpole, Hugh	FORTITUDE
Walpole, Hugh	KATHERINE CHRISTIAN
Warren, R.P.	AT HEAVEN'S GATE
Watson, Winifred E.	FELL TOP
Watson, Winifred E.	ODD SHOES
Weidman, Jerome	I CAN GET IT FOR YOU WHOLESALE
Wells, H.G.	MR. BLETTSWORTHY ON RAMPOLE ISLAND
Werfel, Franz	EMBEZZLED HEAVEN
Whipple, Dorothy	SOMEONE AT A DISTANCE
Wilkins, Vaughan	FANFARE FOR A WITCH
Wilkins, Vaughan	LADY OF PARIS
Wilkins, Vaughan	SEVEN TEMPEST
Wilkins, Vaughan	A KING RELUCTANT
Wilkins, Vaughan	A CITY OF FROZEN FIRE
Wilkins, Vaughan	AND SO – VICTORIA
Wilkins, Vaughan	HUSBAND FOR VICTORIA
Zweig, Arnold	THE CASE OF SERGEANT GRISCHA

PORTWAY EDUCATIONAL REPRINTS

ACADEMIC REPRINTS

Abbott, W.C.	COLONEL THOMAS BLOOD
Andrews, Kevin	THE FLIGHT OF IKAROS
Balzac, Honoré de	THE CURE DE TOURS
Braithwaite, William J.	LLOYD GEORGE'S AMBULANCE WAGON
Broke-Smith, P.W.L.	THE HISTORY OF EARLY BRITISH MILITARY AERONAUTICS
Cameron, A.	CHEMISTRY IN RELATION TO FIRE RISK AND EXTINCTION
Crozier, F.P.	A BRASS HAT IN NO MAN'S LAND
Crozier, Brig.-General F.P.	THE MEN I KILLED
Dewey, John	INTEREST AND EFFORT IN EDUCATION
Fearnsides, W.G. & Bulman, O.M.B.	GEOLOGY IN THE SERVICE OF MAN
Ferrier, Susan	DESTINY (2 vols)
	This is the last and best of the three books written by the Scots novelist.
Galt, John	THE PROVOST
	This comprises a series of short Baconian styl essays on everyday events in which the Provos was engaged during his magisterial life.
Gates, H.L.	THE AUCTION OF SOULS
	The story of Aurora Mardiganian, the Christia girl who survived the Great Massacres of th Armenians.
Gilbert, Edmund W.	BRIGHTON OLD OCEAN'S BAUBLE
Glass, David V.	THE TOWN – AND A CHANGING CIVILISATION
Gronlund, Norman	SOCIOMETRY IN THE CLASSROOM
H.M.S.O.	REPORT ON THE CONSULTATIVE COMMITTEE ON INFANT AND NURSERY SCHOOLS
H.M.S.O.	THE GEOLOGY OF MANCHESTER AND THE SOUTH EAST LANCASHIRE COALFIELD
Harrison, G.B.	THE LIFE & DEATH OF ROBERT DEVEREUX, EARL OF ESSEX